Praise for In Flight

In Flight offers a healthy dose of self-reflection and romance that everyone who has ever loved and lost will enjoy. Between the romance and suspense of murder, readers will have something to turn the page for from the get-go, all the way to the end

~ Writer's Digest Book Awards

…a brilliantly written, compelling, and fast-paced story with the sheer ability to completely captivate your mind and draw a real connection with the character. Each page of the novel is filled with drama and adrenaline racing action with characters that are truly believable and a plot that feels real. A perfect fusion between the dark and light sides of the plot to create a novel with a flawlessly balanced reading thrill that feels like riding on a roller coaster in a perfect breeze, but at twice the normal speed.

~ Readers' Favorite

Also by Tamara Ferguson

TALES OF THE DRAGONFLY

In Flight

In Tandem

Emergence
Coming Soon

TWO HEARTS WOUNDED WARRIOR

Two Hearts Surrendered

Two Hearts Unspoken

Two Hearts Undone

KISSED BY FATE

That Unforgettable Kiss

In Flight

A TALES OF THE DRAGONFLY NOVEL

by **TAMARA FERGUSON**

Windswept

Livonia, Michigan

Cover design, interior book design,
and eBook design by Blue Harvest Creative
www.blueharvestcreative.com

Published by
Windswept
an imprint of BHC Press

Library of Congress Control Number:
2016954822

ISBN-13: 978-1-946006-14-1
ISBN-10: 1-946006-14-9

Visit the author at:
www.sbpra.com/tamaraferguson
www.bhcauthors.com

Also available in softcover and eBook

Dedicated

to all of those parents out there with
'special kids,' who recognize that life
can be rewarding with hope,
acceptance and unconditional love.

Works Cited

(1)Dragonfly. (n.d.).
Retrieved from http://en.wikepedia.org/wiki/Dragonflies

(2)Lyons, R. (n.d.). Damsels and Dragons-the Insect Order Odonata.
Retrieved from http://uci.net/~pondhawk/odonata/ips_odonata.html

 *It is said some Native Americans believe dragonflies are a symbol of renewal after a time of great hardship. (1)*

Dragonfly Order Odonata

The dragonfly is an impressive insect, a master of the air, daring enough in some cases to hover almost within arm's reach in front of human invaders in its territory. (2)

In Flight

Friday, June 3, 1988

ext stop...Madison..." The barely audible voice blasted from the train's worn speakers, echoing throughout the long line of mostly vacant passenger cars. Somewhat aged, the railway car slowed and shook on its approach to the station, its grinding wheels squealing rebelliously along the tracks.

Sean Murphy eyed the misplaced, beautiful woman who'd boarded the train with him back in Chicago. With her eyes fixed on one of the speakers, she strained to hear the crackling voice muffled by the scrape of metal.

"How much longer before we reach Éclair?" Her exotic dark eyes focused on Murphy while her thick southern accent oozed like molasses.

With what appeared to be lazy indifference, he studied the woman as she glanced at her watch. "Do you mean *Eau* Claire?

"Oh, whatever," she answered, rather haughtily.

"Should be at least another hour." Presenting her with, what he hoped, was his most charismatic smile, Murphy folded his newspaper in half and dropped it into his lap. His concentration had been mightily challenged since this curvaceous young woman in a skirt had settled into a seat across from him, crossing her shapely long legs.

Although she wasn't quite as young as she'd first appeared—heavy makeup couldn't disguise the shadowy circles under her eyes. She had to be in her late thirties; possibly even forty.

Digging through her patent leather clutch, she hesitated, carefully schooling her features to reflect calm indifference. "Sorry. It's been about three hours since I've had a cigarette, and it's making me irritable."

Murphy greatly doubted the sincerity of her apology.

"Here, take one of mine." He pulled his pack from the pocket of his T-shirt. When she leaned forward, the cigarette cinched between her lips, he met the tip of her cigarette with the flame of his lighter.

She inhaled and coughed.

And Murphy held back a grin. Narrowing his eyes, he silently questioned *what was she up to?* His twenty years as a Chicago prosecutor had definitely made Murphy overly suspicious.

But, regrettably, he'd always seemed to have a weak spot for women.

"Look. Someone stole my cash." She leaned forward, and laid her hand over his. Batting her lashes, she pleaded with, what must've been, her most seductive southern drawl. "Could I borrow a few dollars? If you leave me your address, I'll pay you back later. I promise."

Although Murphy was rather surprised by her lack of subtlety, he suspected she was usually quite proficient at procuring what she sought from the opposite sex. Obviously, she'd been aware of his admiration of her shapely long legs when she'd boarded the train, so she'd chosen him as her target.

He *could* call her bluff and offer to bring in the law. But, as usual, curiosity got the best of him. How far would she take this? When she maneuvered the upper half of her body even closer, intentionally displaying an enticing view of her lovely breasts, Murphy struggled to hold back a smile.

But suddenly envisioning his wife, Meg, and the elbow she would've undoubtedly jabbed into his ribs, he frowned ruefully. "Sorry—I'm not carrying a whole lot of cash on me."

"Oh." She sighed resignedly. Easing back into her seat and closing her eyes, she suddenly appeared wearily defeated. With a porcelain complexion accentuating her almost too-perfect features, she had the face of a Botticelli angel. Silky-straight hair, inky-black, was brushed back from a widow's peak into a sophisticated chignon, emphasizing the beauty of her profile.

Opening up his paper, Murphy continued to discreetly observe her somewhat puzzling behavior. She seemed to have already forgotten his presence. Staring through the window, she continued to drag short puffs from her cigarette before she quickly rubbed it out in the nearby ashtray, only halfway spent.

Pretending to study his paper, he examined her more closely. Her clothing definitely wasn't inexpensive. Accessorized with patent-leather heels and a matching purse, although rumpled, the black skirt and blazer she wore over a creamy silk blouse was elegantly tailored.

Hardly ordinary travel-wear for a jaunt through northwest Wisconsin.

She had lovely hands with meticulously manicured nails. Lithe fingers were layered with an assortment of rings hosting a multitude of sparkling stones. The entire ensemble was accompanied by a dazzling set of earrings and a bracelet.

Were those stones *real*?

Probably.

Undeniably, she was someone accustomed to wealth. Murphy wondered if she was married? But after studying each of the rings on her fingers, he found it was too difficult to tell.

Another twenty minutes flew by. Laying aside his paper, he reclined in his worn leather seat attempting to relax. With less than an hour remaining before reaching Eau Claire, he tried to turn his thoughts elsewhere.

This would be the fifth year Murphy had traveled by train for his yearly fishing expedition. When he'd considered cancelling this trip because of his heavy workload, Meg had balked. "You *need* this break." Jabbing her finger into his ribs, she'd gone on to berate him. "And just be sure to clear the next couple of weekends too, Mr. Prosecutor, so you can make it to a few of your boys' baseball games." Meg could be pretty damned pushy, Murphy had to admit, grinning wryly. But *that* was why he loved her.

Murphy would be on his own for the next couple of days. His cousin wouldn't be able to meet him in Hayward until Sunday. Evidently, there was a huge wedding in Mike Callahan's hometown tomorrow, and his daughter Lucy was the maid-of-honor.

Murphy grimaced. Apparently, the entire Callahan family was seriously concerned about Lucy—she seemed to be sinking into an even deeper depression. Hopefully, the excitement of the wedding would help lift her spirits. *Only nineteen-years old.* Murphy frowned at the thought. She was so damned fortunate to be alive after her abduction and assault.

Murphy heaved a sigh, shifting restlessly in his seat. Anne hadn't been quite so lucky. It'd been almost twenty-three *years*—so why did he keep on dwelling on the past? Since marrying Meg, he had everything he'd ever wanted. And look at those boys of his. Murphy couldn't have been any prouder than he was of Mike, Kyle, and Ethan.

With the wheels of the passenger car grinding rhythmically along the tracks, Murphy began to doze off.

With a start, he awoke, feeling disoriented. Peeking at his watch, he realized that at least another forty-five minutes had flown by. Apparently aware of his discomfort, his fellow passenger seemed to have set aside her troubles and was studying him with undisguised curiosity. Ignoring her and focusing his gaze through the window, Murphy remained unconsciously unaware of his surroundings as the landscape passed by in a blur.

His damned nightmares were returning. With a shaking hand, he reached for the handkerchief stashed in the back pocket of his jeans. Yanking it out, he wiped the sweat from his brow. Memories he'd suppressed, of the honeymoon he'd shared with his first wife, Anne, haunted him each time he traveled through this part of Wisconsin. And now, since Lucy Callahan's kidnapping nearly nine months before, Murphy's usual control was slipping,

It seemed that those memories haunted him around the clock.

Excepting that her eyes were the color of a clear blue sky, while Anne's had been chocolate brown, Lucy was the spitting image of Anne.

He was troubled that Anne's murder still remained unsolved. But there'd been rapid advancements in technology over the last few years.

He'd been considering reopening her case—they might just get a hit on the DNA.

But he was worried about how Meg would react to his dredging up of the past. Not to mention the fact that his sons knew nothing about his first marriage.

And Anne had been pregnant with his child.

Admittedly, he'd been reluctant to reopen the case for purely selfish reasons. What other disturbing issues from the past might be brought to light, by initiating a new investigation? He wasn't worried about his reputation professionally, as much as he was personally. He'd sure hate to disappoint his sons.

But it was time, he suddenly realized, releasing a ragged sigh. *He needed the truth.* The guilt throughout the years had been tremendous. If he'd been with Anne, like he should've been that night—if they hadn't argued—maybe she'd be alive today. Her murder had been brutal and senseless.

Squaring off his shoulders, he came to a decision. He owed it to Anne to discover her killer.

Struggling for self-control, Murphy refocused his attention on the magnificent view through the window. The scenic backdrop was transforming, with the train travelling deeper into the majestic northwest, and, as the landscape became more densely populated with birch and pines, lakes and waterways encompassed what remained. Afternoon gradually dimmed into dusk as the sun, spitting out shades of amber, gloriously descended.

In his sudden moment of weakness, Murphy returned his attention to the woman sitting nearby. Digging through her purse, she concentrated on gathering change from the bottom, counting it as she found it. Despite her seemingly calm exterior, her hands were shaking.

Signaling their approach, the familiar muffled voice echoed through the loudspeaker, "*Next stop...Eau Claire...*"

"Ah, what the heck," Murphy muttered. Sitting up from his seat, he reached into his back pocket for his wallet. Fingering a twenty, after shrugging his shoulders, Murphy pulled out a fifty instead. Hopefully, this would allow for the cost of a motel and transport to wherever she needed to go. "Here," Murphy spoke gruffly. "This should help you out."

With a quirky smile on her beautiful face, she accepted the fifty. "Thanks."

Although her thank you wasn't quite as sincere as Murphy would've wished, he still acknowledged her response with a smile.

She hesitated for a moment before attempting to escape. "Your address?"

Having already kissed his fifty goodbye, he was a little surprised by the question. He slipped one of his cards from his wallet and handed it over.

Frowning, she definitely became nervous as she studied the card. "You're a D.A.?" She slid the card into a pocket of her purse. Seeming even more anxious to distance herself, she turned and began making her way down the aisle.

"In Chicago. But I'm on vacation this week. Just send the fifty to my work address. Don't worry—it's okay if it takes a while.

"Thanks." Almost at the exit of the passenger car, she lifted her hand in a careless wave, before stepping out and down onto the station platform.

Murphy had his nose back in his paper when he suddenly became aware of another presence, rising up from the very rear of the deserted passenger car. Odd, Murphy frowned, with a confused shake of his head. He was slipping—he could've sworn he was the only one left in the car. Of medium height, the individual held his head down as he quietly shuffled by. Murphy struggled to get a glimpse of his face and features. But bundled up tightly behind a navy-blue, hooded sweatshirt, not recognizable as male or female, the stranger kept his hood tied securely in place; seeming purposely to conceal himself.

Peering through the window and scoping out the dimly lit platform of the station, Murphy caught a glimpse of his former traveling companion, intently studying the wide range of newspapers displayed. As her gaze traveled from headline to headline, she suddenly halted, dropping her purse and bag inadvertently to the ground. After a moment of seemingly stunned concentration, scooping up her purse, she began digging frantically through it for change. Finally inserting a few coins, she pulled out a paper from the farthest rack. Folding and slipping the paper into her purse, she picked up her bag before continuing on her way.

"Funny," mumbled Murphy, with a snort. "Seems too self-absorbed to give a damn about the news." Glancing down at the front page of his Tribune, nothing unusual caught his eye.

Suddenly, a calculated movement from further down the station platform snapped Murphy's eyes back through the window. Hovering only a few yards behind the woman, the stranger in the hooded sweatshirt stole out stealthily from the shadows of the dimly lit stationhouse.

What the...?

Impulsively attempting to draw the woman's attention, Murphy knocked on the window of the train. Apparently aware of the knocking, seeming to tauntingly challenge Murphy, the stranger in the sweatshirt met his gaze through the window with a shattering, bleak hollow stare. Murphy watched helplessly, when the woman entered the stationhouse, with the shadowy figure in the sweatshirt following closely behind.

Abruptly, the wheels of the passenger car began squealing in protest, when the train jerked treacherously into motion. As the train began sluggishly continuing on its way, Murphy continued to stare through the window at the station platform, oddly troubled. With a deep sense of foreboding, he realized he'd never even asked the woman's name.

Saturday, June 4, 1988

*T*he golden orb of the descending sun spun out radiant iridescent beams of light, firing the sky ablaze atop the tranquil sparkling waters of Crystal Rock Lake.

Sam Danielson and Penny Wentworth strolled leisurely under the very arbor where Jake Loughlin and Danielle Reardon had been married earlier that day. Framed by the backdrop of the picturesque Dragonfly Pointe Inn, they both stood mesmerized as they gazed at the glorious sunset from their perch above the steep rocky shore.

Under the dense shade of the towering white pines, the waterfall spilling wistfully into the lake nearby sounded peaceful and comforting, and added to the enchantment of their surroundings. Providing ambiance for wedding festivities, sparkling miniature lights shimmered overhead and around the inviting wrapped porch of the inn. With glowing radiance fading into dusk, at that moment, the atmosphere surrounding the inn exuded a mysteriously magical quality.

Still somewhat nervous, pulling her sunglasses from her purse and quickly sliding them over her eyes, Penny snuck a peek at the chiseled profile of the handsome man standing beside her. Once finished with his task of ushering guests in and out of their seats, before and after the wedding, Sam had escorted Penny through the reception line to congratulate Jake and Danielle, the new owners of the Dragonfly Pointe Inn. Despite nine months of chaos and construction at Dragonfly Pointe, they'd managed to pull off an impressive wedding ceremony and celebration.

Although Sam had remained by her side throughout the entire day, this was actually the first chance they'd had to be alone.

Penny sighed. Regrettably, she was pretty sure that'd been Danielle's idea for Sam to keep her company today.

"Beautiful, isn't it?" Turning away from the glorious sunset with his mouth tipped up into an appreciative smile, Sam was obviously focusing his eyes on *her.*

She nodded her agreement rather numbly.

Unreal. To be here with *Sam.*

The obsession of every single one of her teenage fantasies.

Amazingly, up until she'd met Sam, Penny's heart had remained relatively intact. With her family transplanted from state to state because of her father's calling as a minister, she'd been especially depressed when she'd been forced to relocate from Minnesota to Crystal Rock, only a few months shy of her eighth grade graduation.

"Remember the first time we met?"

His voice sent shivers down her spine. Startled to realize that Sam's thoughts must've been echoing hers, she laughed softly. "You almost ran me down."

While babysitting for a young couple the summer she'd arrived in town, Penny had been maneuvering the little girl's stroller along the sidewalk. Sam had been driving his turquoise-blue Comet rather recklessly down the usually deserted, dead-end street. Fortunately, he'd been able to pull his car to a screeching halt before turning into his driveway.

Sam grimaced. "I loved driving that car. Every time I had a chance to crank up the speed, I would. But I was damned lucky that I was able to stop just in time that day. I could've killed the two of you."

Sam had rushed from his car to apologize, most definitely stunned by his own negligence. Suddenly, his voice had cut off into a stammer when he'd glanced up from the baby at *her.* After a long quiet moment, Sam had finally smiled, gazing deeply into her eyes.

And time had stood still.

Along with the beat of her heart.

Just like that, she'd fallen for Sam.

Sure, he was great-looking. At eighteen, Sam was tall and beautifully built with broad shoulders and narrow hips. His job as head lifeguard at the Dragonfly Pointe Beach had left his handsome face deeply tanned; accentuating the crinkles at the corners of his eyes when he'd smiled.

And she'd melted, gazing into those eyes, the color of creamy dark chocolate.

Penny had spent the entire summer babysitting newborn, Sophia Barelli, whose home just happened to be immediately across the street from the Danielson's.

So it was pretty hard *not* to be aware of Sam.

While other kids his age were either enjoying summer on the lake or cruising around the countryside, barely escaping trouble, Sam was handling the maintenance and upkeep of their home for his mother. Apparently, around five years earlier, Sam's father had tragically passed away.

After hanging out that summer with a few new friends at the Dragonfly Pointe Beach, Penny had instantly recognized that Sam was not only well-liked, but tremendously respected. As the head lifeguard, he'd been wholly attentive to his job.

She'd had *such* a crush on him.

And then, that August, tragedy had struck Crystal Rock. A six-year old girl was brutally assaulted and murdered at Dragonfly Pointe. An ongoing investigation was initiated, and business at the Dragonfly Inn began to decline. It'd only been three short months since Penny and her family had arrived in town.

Penny cleared her throat. "That ended up being an *awful* summer."

Sam frowned, and slanted her a side glance. "That's for sure—in more ways than one. The Dragonfly Inn fell into a decline, and Crystal Rock practically turned into a ghost town after that little girl's murder."

Despite the upheaval in the community, one week later, school had still begun. Penny hadn't been sure what to expect when she'd entered Crystal Rock High that fall as a freshman. Although, as a senior, Sam had been much older than her, building up foolish hopes, Penny had obviously misinterpreted his interest in her over the summer.

She'd been *so sure* he'd been hitting on her.

And in one single day, she'd suddenly realized her romantic expectations had been totally misguided. Penny had been heartbroken when she'd noticed Diane Malloy, a popular senior and cheerleader, all over Sam.

But, surprisingly, even though he'd remained slightly distant during that first week of school, Sam had continued to single Penny out. So it'd been difficult setting aside her fantasies.

Until the following weekend, that is, Sunday night at dusk. Penny and her mother were cleaning out the cabins from the previous week's summer camp activities, at the deserted Crystal Rock Campgrounds. With a large trash bag in hand, Penny had been circling the picnic area and scoping out the beach, searching for missed debris.

They hadn't noticed her. Obviously unaware of the vehicles belonging to the clean-up crew, parked in the recreational center parking lot, Sam and Diane were half-naked on the tiny isolated beach, a longstanding make-out place for local teenagers.

Stupidly, the discovery of Sam's extra-curricular activities hadn't completely discouraged her, though. After all, Penny had found out that Sam had no steady girlfriend.

It'd taken another glimpse of Sam, in action again, with a different female at the same beach only a few weeks later.

Almost twenty-three years ago, berating herself at her own stupidity, she'd finally accepted the obvious. With every girl at school throwing herself at *him*, why would Sam have been interested in *her*, a short, skinny freshman?

Apparently more mature than his peers, in public, Sam had appeared polite, yet remained isolated.

He'd definitely hidden a dark side.

What was it about Sam that'd made her forget her strict and proper upbringing? As a teenager, she should've been shocked when she'd found him, twice, on the verge of having sex with two different women. But, instead, she'd been *jealous*.

As well as confused. Had she only just *imagined* Sam's interest? It'd been an enormous effort attempting to subdue her disappointment and heartache.

And who had she been fooling? Even if Sam had been the type of guy her father had approved of, her father, being obsessively overprotective, would never have actually let her go out with him. Even at eighteen, when she'd eventually acquired a steady boyfriend, she'd snuck around with Jason rather than risk her father's disapproval.

Penny shook her head, snapping back to the present. *What was wrong with her?* How stupid *was* she—to keep on dwelling on the past? How could Sam's obvious rejection of her as a teenager still hurt so much *now*? She sighed, resignedly. After all, over these past several years, she'd learned the hard way that there was no such thing as happily ever after.

With these still startlingly sensitive thoughts in her mind, turning away from Sam, Penny attempted to blink back her tears. "You've got a lot of friends here. You don't have to stay with me for the rest of the night, you know."

Glancing at her face and quickly gathering her mood, Sam frowned, as his cheerfulness abruptly vanished. "I'm sorry. I didn't realize…"

Studying Sam, she was somewhat surprised to observe a pained, fleeting glimpse of dejection cross over his face. Turning away stiffly, he determinedly strode back toward the inn.

Like a hurt little boy.

Suddenly panicking, Penny quickly reigned in her self-control. "Sam," she called out. "I only meant that you don't need to stay with me, just because Danny asked you to."

Sam turned back, and his eyes met hers. *"Asked me to?"* With a brow raised, he studied her face, somehow reassured. Unhurriedly, he strolled back, confronting her face to face. "Didn't Danny say *anything*?"

"About what?"

"That *I wanted to be with you.* That's why she sat us together for dinner. You acted like you didn't mind me tagging along all day, so I thought you knew." Noticing the subtle trace of tears covering her cheeks, reaching over, Sam gently raised the sunglasses covering her eyes to the top of her head. Hypnotically, his fingers soothed her brow while his hands framed her face. "What's wrong, Penny?" he questioned softly.

"Oh. I think I'm just a little tired and I've had a lot more champagne than I'm accustomed to. The flowers were a lot of work. And this is the first time I've been away from my son, for more than a night, since...I don't remember when," Penny responded, dazedly.

He'd *asked* to be with her? As his gentle fingertips brushed the tears from her eyes, Penny gazed numbly into his reassuring brown eyes.

She couldn't help but wonder—what kind of a man *had* Sam become? Now divorced, he'd been married nearly fifteen years. Although he no longer appeared to be a womanizer, he'd always easily attracted the eyes of the opposite sex. Even though there'd been quite a few women today who'd, most obviously, attempted to draw his attention, after several opportunities for escape, he'd never left her side.

Thoughtfully, she realized she'd let the information slip out about her son. Sam hadn't seemed surprised. How much had Danielle revealed? Was Sam aware of Penny's never-ending difficulties, as a single mother of a sixteen-year old special needs son?

"You did a great job with the flowers," Sam reassured her. "I don't know much about these things myself, but you wouldn't believe how many people I heard today—talking about how beautiful your flowers were."

Reluctantly acknowledging that Sam's awkward compliment meant even more to her than praise from her peers, she gazed at him with a grateful smile. "Thank you, Sam." Owner as well as lead designer of Sander's Floral Innovations in New York, Penny had won awards for her specialty wedding bouquets. After flying in from New York on Thursday to supervise her meticulously detailed plans for flowers and décor, she'd worked straight up until the moment of the wedding.

But right at that moment, all Penny could think about was how much she'd like to strangle Danielle for not mentioning *anything* about setting her up with Sam. Danielle's recent manipulations were finally beginning to make sense. When she'd insisted Penny accompany her for her final fitting of her wedding gown last month in New York, she'd persuaded Penny to purchase the lovely, but revealing, teal gown she'd worn today. Penny was decidedly uncomfortable wearing a gown she normally wouldn't have had the courage to wear otherwise.

But Penny had been thrilled at the warmth in Sam's gaze before the wedding. And when Sam had suddenly whispered she was beautiful, she'd almost crushed the boutonniere she'd been pinning to his lapel.

A couple months ago, Penny had been visiting Crystal Rock to finalize the details for the wedding when she'd accidentally run into Sam. Even though she hadn't seen him in over twenty years, that day, when Sam had looked into her eyes, all the turmoil she'd experienced as a teenager had come rushing back to haunt her.

"So." Sam's fingers cradled her chin, as he steadily held her gaze. "Are you okay—with me being with you?"

Captivated by his gaze, unable to utter a response, Penny bobbed her head up and down.

"Good," Sam replied, in a voice, low and husky. Only hesitating for a moment, he bent down, and gently touched his lips to hers.

And what was meant to be light and reassuring turned into something much, much more. As Sam's mouth lingered over hers, while his tongue gently invaded, Penny discovered she was helpless to resist, and her mouth responded eagerly to each of his subtle searching strokes.

Somewhat dazed and disoriented, she sighed and gradually began pulling away. While Penny eyed Sam in stunned confusion, Sam smiled with obvious satisfaction, releasing her gently.

He peeked at his watch. "It's almost six. Are we ready to go inside?" Not even bothering to await an answer, Sam tucked his arm within hers. Although she was hindered by her five-inch heels and full-length gown, Sam matched her steps patiently as he escorted her through the deserted courtyard.

Pausing at the base of the staircase leading up into the entrance of the inn, Penny removed her sunglasses, folding and slipping them back into her purse. As she anxiously studied Sam, he suddenly winked. With a quick bemused shake of her head, she smiled resignedly, and traveled up the steps with her arm, once again, hooked within his.

They paused on the threshold before moving inside.

Sam blinked as he gazed around him. "Wow. It's like stepping into a fairy tale, Penny."

Penny couldn't help but be pleased by the results of the inn's transformation for the wedding. The lobby and ballroom appeared absolutely enchanting—now that the entire lower level of the Dragonfly Pointe Inn was alit with lights and adorned with greens and topiary.

Penny smiled at Sam. "You wouldn't believe how many miniature lights we had to use, since we decided to dis the overhead lighting—it was just too harsh."

Penny had been astonished at the beauty of the restoration, when she'd first laid eyes on the inn again this past spring. Although the expansion had been extensive, clever renovations had kept the atmosphere of the inn both warm and inviting. Just stopping short of encompassing the entire shoreline of the lake along Dragonfly Pointe, with its graceful columns and fresh white siding, the exterior of the inn was barely recognizable. There'd been two additional stories integrated above the original two, while elevators had been installed to provide convenient access to the luxurious upper quarters. Elegantly appointed balconies had been extended outdoors, from the most exclusive hotel rooms and lakefront suites.

Although the entire ground floor of the inn, apart from the lobby and the artisan's gift shop, had been set up solely for dining, it'd all been utilized for the wedding today. Partitions and walls, equipped to break up the individual dining rooms, had been folded back and stored into pockets, designed specifically for that purpose. Having been kept open as an alternative location for Jake's and Danielle's nuptials—just in case problems had arisen due to inclement weather—the solarium was also intended for dining, but tonight, for the reception, had been set up for dancing.

From the corner of her eye, Penny was aware of Danielle's conspiratorial smile at Sam as he and Penny crossed quickly by the head table.

Sam escorted Penny directly to their table, where his mother, Shirley Edmonds, was already seated alongside her husband, Craig. Shirley was smiling brightly—clearly pleased to see Sam with Penny. After seating Penny at the table next to his mother, Sam settled in next to Penny.

"Oh, Mrs. Danielsss—I mean *Mrs. Edmonds*. It's so good to see you again! How *are* you?" Friends since Penny's family had resided in Crystal Rock, Penny's mother and Shirley had kept in touch through the years. But even though she'd been frequently informed about Shirley's progress in her fight with lung cancer, Penny had struggled to control her shock when she'd first seen Sam's mom. Despite the vibrant cap of gray hair, that'd obviously grown back since discontinuing her chemotherapy, she appeared to be exceptionally fragile. Shorter than Penny, who only topped five feet by three inches, Shirley had always been thin with delicate features.

But now a slight breeze would probably carry her away.

"Penny, it's *so* good to see you again. I think we can skip the Mrs. Edmonds stuff." She lifted a brow and grinned. "You're probably about the same age that I was when I met *you*—although, I'm afraid, I'm *definitely* feeling my years these days."

Sam was staring at his mother, obviously startled. "I never realized that you and Penny knew each other back then."

"Besides the fact that her mother, Monica, is still writing me regularly Sam, Penny used to come by to help me clean house years ago when you went away to college. Craig always pretended he never asked her to check up on me."

"I knew that you were lonesome after Sam left. *And* I was worried that you weren't taking care of yourself." Craig tenderly patted his wife's hand. "Before you finally married *me*."

Smiling wryly, Penny turned to Craig. "You must've realized that I was feeling a little lost too, Craig, after moving here away from my friends. It didn't help that my father was beginning to behave strangely then. He wanted to know where I was every minute of the day. He trusted me more with adults in the community, than he would with kids my own age." Once a highly respected minister, Penny's father had suddenly become seriously ill, the summer after Penny had graduated from Crystal Rock High. His health had eventually deteriorated so much, their family had been forced to move back to New York, so that they could live with her paternal grandparents. Penny had attempted to put aside the most agonizing memories from those last few years of her father's life.

Aware of Sam's questioning gaze, Penny continued, "My dad had an inoperable brain tumor. Of course we never knew for several months. He went through a total personality change, before my mother and I even considered it could be some medical problem that was changing him." Tears shimmered in Penny's eyes. She felt surprisingly comforted when Sam wrapped an arm around her shoulders and gave her a reassuring squeeze.

Just then, Danielle Loughlin's longtime business partner, Brian Johnson, appeared, pulling out a seat at their table. Eyeing Sam, he grinned. "Get your hands off of her. I know about that reputation of yours."

Nine months before, Sam had returned to Crystal Rock, Wisconsin to become the town's police chief.

"Better than that playboy reputation of *yours*, I'd say," Dawn Wellman added dryly, seating herself next to Brian. A jeweler with training as an artist, Dawn had been hired to create artwork for the inn and, in turn, both her artwork and jewelry would be sold by the inn on consignment.

Brian snorted. "Playboy? *Me?*" Flashing Dawn an indulgent grin, he'd apparently decided to play along. Just shy of six-feet tall, with naturally sun-streaked, dark-blonde hair, Brian had a muscular build that was slim and wiry. Yet to get serious with any woman, it was difficult to recall the names or faces of the women he'd dated.

There'd been many.

Penny turned to Dawn with a rueful grin. "Yeah, I'd have to agree with you, Dawn."

"Not you too, Penny?"

Brian groaned, scowling at Penny.

Mischievously eyeing Brian, who was squirming uncomfortably, Penny nodded a definite acknowledgement at Dawn.

Dawn turned to Brian, playfully whacking a thick linen napkin over his head. "First Danielle, and now I find out you put the moves on Penny, *too*? How can you expect me to take you seriously, whenever you ask *me* out?"

"I can't seem to help it," Brian reasoned, cautiously. "I'm a sucker for a pretty face?"

As Dawn shook her head with exaggerated frustration, her eyes turned fiery blue. "Yeah, but does it have to be *every* pretty face?" The expression of utter exasperation, on Dawn's lovely animated face, set everyone seated around the table off into explosive laughter.

To Brian's relief, a rhythmic and melodic chime began echoing from crystal. Guests throughout the room joined in and tapped spoons on their water glasses. When most of the members of the wedding party began smiling and chanting, the newlyweds finally kissed, and were rewarded with thunderous applause.

Arriving at their table and seating his wife, Olivia, along with his two boys, Jarrod and Rodney, Sam's deputy, Nat Benet, finally sat down on the remaining chair. After meeting the family earlier that day, Penny had discovered The Benet's had relocated to Crystal Rock only seven months ago. Nat had left his job with the police in New Orleans to enable his family to escape the escalating violence in their community. But as only one of a few African American families that were residing in the Crystal Rock area, Sam had told Penny he was worried that Nat and Olivia would still have their share of problems to contend with in the future.

"The boys are getting restless." Nat grinned. "It's been a pretty long day."

Olivia sighed, struggling with a weary smile. "We'll probably head home after we eat." Once the boys seemed settled, Olivia finally picked up her napkin. But when Jarrod and Rodney began to wrestle, she slammed it back down on the table.

"Hey, guys," Sam reprimanded, sharply. "Don't forget—you both promised me you'd be good today. You won't be sleeping over at the cabin next week if you're not."

"Okay, Sam." Turning his startling sea-green gaze on Sam, nine-year old Jarrod was obviously attempting to flaunt his best behavior. He nudged his brother in the ribs with his elbow. "Rodney, remember—no camping or fishing at the cabin next week—unless we're good."

Seemingly angelic, Rodney zeroed in on Sam with his dark-chocolate eyes. At almost seven-years old, Rodney was a slighter, mirror image of his older brother.

Olivia was apparently aware of Penny's consternation as Sam took charge of the boys. With mischief in her eyes, she winked at Sam. "Sam's been keeping an eye on the boys for us. He's Rodney's godfather, you know. Sam and Nat have been friends for years. Sam would make a great father himself someday."

Sam's eyes held Penny's intently, obviously gauging her reaction to what Olivia had to say.

Somewhat flustered, Penny was suddenly aware that, curiously contradictory of the typical unattached male, Sam appeared to be unusually at ease around kids.

"Olivia, you're scaring Penny. This is only our first date."

Date? Although she was startled when she noticed Sam's mischievous grin, Penny realized that all the barriers she'd purposely erected to safeguard her heart were gradually tumbling down. What did the past really matter anyway?

Longingly, her eyes swept over Sam's face. Unbelievably, after all these years, he was even *more* handsome. His sandy-blonde hair, slightly graying at the temples, was neatly trimmed into layers to frame his slightly weathered face. Drawing attention to the perfectly proportioned features of his face, boyish dimples dented his mouth's curves. When he gave her warm smile, there was a definite twinkle in his brown eyes.

She'd only been involved in a few casual relationships since her husband had been declared missing in Vietnam. With her whole life revolving around her son, Alex, Penny hadn't actually been out on a date in several months. Long ago, she'd discovered that it was difficult enough for most men to handle a relationship with a woman who already had a son; let alone a son with mental and developmental disabilities. Later, when Alex's problems had worsened and he'd developed diabetes, she'd completely put aside the notion of a long-term relationship with anyone.

Although there'd been one man who'd been overwhelmingly persistent at pursuing her. Even without any encouragement, Todd Shelton had been ready to marry her.

But what she'd never really been able to figure out was *why* Todd had become so fixated on her. Apprehensive when he'd gradually become more obsessive and controlling, she'd intentionally avoided a sexual relationship with him. After about a year of casual dating, Todd, not wanting the distraction of children, was ready to take over Penny's role as a parent and was insisting on depositing Alex into a full-care mental facility.

But Alex was *her* son. She'd brought him into this world. She'd do everything she could for him for as long as she was able. It'd been pleasant to have someone to lean on for a while, but she hadn't been in love with Todd. She'd already been married to a control freak once, and the last thing she needed was someone else to take over her life and strip away her identity, as well as her freedom of choice.

The night she'd refused to marry Todd Shelton, she'd discovered he'd had the same propensity for violence that David Wentworth had had.

And their relationship hadn't ended pleasantly.

Although, even now, Todd refused to believe it was over. Penny shivered, momentarily reliving their last sordid encounter. It'd been a perfect time to leave New York. Hopefully, she'd be able to continue to avoid Todd once she returned home.

Penny had enjoyed these last few days in Crystal Rock *so much*. Her whole life, now, revolved around the needs of her son. Her mother had Alex under control—or, so, she'd said—when she'd continuously reassured Penny over the phone these last couple of days.

It'd been over ten years since she'd had a break from the everyday burden of Alex. Turning her eyes back to Sam, Penny considered following her mother's advice for the first holiday she'd allowed herself in over ten years—*just have a good time.*

Soup and salad, the first of many courses arrived at their table. Melding with the low hum of contented chatter and conversation, the melodic ring of silver on china echoed throughout the spacious grandeur of the inn. The dishes were systematically cleared from the table after each course.

"My prime rib was delicious," Sam muttered as Nat and Brian immediately agreed.

"So was my salmon." Penny grimaced, patting her stomach. "I'm stuffed."

Sam grinned.

Even the kids' meals had been thoughtfully planned. Jarrod had chosen ravioli, while Rodney had decided on fish sticks, and each, of course, upon seeing the other's plate, had wanted what the other had.

Several times throughout the course of their meal, Sam had been forced to remind the boys of their promise to behave. Penny discovered that the boys loved to hang out with him at his cabin. Amazingly, Sam thought little of giving up his own time off on the weekends. Nat occasionally joined Sam and the boys, and Olivia appreciated the break.

Nat and Olivia had ended up residing in the Edmonds' home on the lake, Penny discovered, because Craig required additional help with Shirley's care. The Edmonds had moved into the smaller, remodeled guest cottage located nearby. While Nat was remodeling the Edmonds' home in his spare time, Olivia, having once been employed as a LPN, was assisting Shirley when needed.

Craig was obviously grateful to both Nat and Olivia. "The house is looking better than it's looked in years. Nat moved in and immediately knew which updates were the most important. I can't believe how much he and Olivia have accomplished in only six months."

"It's so nice having Olivia around when I need her." Shirley sighed. "Some days it's an effort for me to accomplish anything."

With a trace of tears in her eyes, Olivia was smiling when she reached over to squeeze Shirley's hand.

"It's great to have Sam home again, too." Shirley turned to Penny. "I hope you're coming with Sam for dinner tomorrow night, Penny. Olivia and Nat are cooking out."

Ruefully, Sam admitted, "I haven't had a chance to ask her yet, Mom." With a smile, he turned to Penny. "When do you have to return home?"

"I'll supervise the outdoor cleanup tomorrow. But Danny insisted I needed some extra time, while I was here, to enjoy myself." Penny's eyes met Sam's. "My flight back to New York isn't until Monday morning, so I'd love to come to dinner."

Appearing to be pleased, Sam suddenly smiled.

And exactly like she had all those years before, when she'd first laid eyes on Sam, she found herself falling.

All over again.

Penny's smile suddenly faltered. This couldn't be happening *again?*

But who was she fooling? It was time to face facts—she was *still* attracted to Sam. Had she *ever* really quit thinking about him? How many times had she come up with an excuse to question her mom about him throughout the years, aware that her mom had kept in touch with Sam's mom, Shirley? And how many times had she pumped Danielle about Sam—after discovering that both she and Jake had become close to him over these last several months?

And even though she'd loved her first boyfriend, Jason, more dearly than any other man she'd ever met, she'd never felt the deep physical attraction for him that she'd felt for Sam.

Attempting to battle her chaotic thoughts, Penny was relieved when, for the next twenty minutes, everyone's attention was focused on the head table. Once the sumptuous five-tiered wedding cake was rolled out for display, the newlyweds were filmed and photographed after finishing up with their toasts. The newlyweds would depart for their honeymoon at noon tomorrow, and return before the scheduled reopening of the Dragonfly Pointe Inn. After flying out privately for a stay at Jake's Bridgeport Bay Hotel in San Francisco first, Jake and Danielle would travel up the Pacific coast and escape to their northern California hideaway.

There was a lull in activity after the cake was sliced and served. A crew of servers scoured the reception area, quickly scooping up the remaining dishes and utensils. Within twenty minutes every table in the entire ballroom had been cleaned and rearranged in preparation for the final band to entertain onstage.

All the tables had been shifted to skirt the edges of the massive ballroom, opening up the entire area for dancing. While Jake escorted his new bride out onto the dance floor, Brian and Dawn ventured over to the head table to converse with the remaining members of the wedding party.

"How about some champagne? Mom—Craig?" Setting up the flutes on their table, Sam poured for his mother and Craig first, and then filled flutes for him and Penny. Still remaining seated while attempting to control the boys, both Nat and Olivia decided to forego the champagne.

Soft music began drifting through the room. Lighting up the lush greenery in the solarium, where the remains of the radiant amber sunset cast a faint warm glow, sparkling miniature lights draped the exterior windows.

Penny studied the magnificent stone fireplace, centered between the lobby and reception area. Majestically crowning the soaring vaulted ceiling, the chimney stretched upward through every floor. Concrete castings of dragonflies, sprinkled with iridescent sand, had been randomly inset throughout the mortar bracing the stones of the fireplace when it'd been built. With the roaring fire crackling, there was an intermittent flickering of iridescence that set the entire structure aglow. Penny was startled to observe as the lights were dimmed, clusters of luminescent dragonflies appeared to be, magically, in flight.

Pairing gracefully to a sentimental romantic ballad, the bride and groom were reintroduced with applause as they swept across the dance floor.

"Mom—did you remember to bring along my camera?"

With a smile, Shirley reached into her carry-all, promptly pulling out the case housing Sam's thirty-five millimeter.

"Penny, would you mind taking a few pictures?" When Sam smoothly pulled her into his arms, to quickly run through the basic operation of the camera, Penny found it was extremely difficult to concentrate. Leaning back, she suddenly become aware of his shaky indrawn breath. *What a relief*, she thought—Sam appeared to be just as affected by her as she was by him.

Sam's smile was unsteady when he gently twisted her around, gazing intently into her eyes. "We'll dance later. Okay?"

With a shaky smile, Penny nodded.

Reluctantly pulling away, Sam glanced over at his mother. "May I have this dance?" he requested, with obvious tenderness.

Shirley answered with a radiant smile.

Gently raising her from her seat and silently offering her his arm, he carefully escorted her out onto the dance floor. For several minutes they drifted along slowly and gracefully, in perfect time to the music.

Shirley was aglow with happiness when Sam finally returned her to the table. After settling back in her seat, she gazed at her son curiously. "Where *in the world* did you learn how to dance like that Sam?"

He smiled, wryly. "Vanessa made me take lessons."

"Humph. Probably about the one and *only* good thing that woman did for you." Shirley's tone of voice was uncharacteristically vehement.

Sam barked out a laugh, appearing astonished by her candor. "Mother—you're talking about the woman I married. But that's alright," he reassured her, turning his eyes back to Penny.

Appearing uncomfortably indecisive, Penny was aware of her stomach fluttering nervously as Sam continued holding her gaze. She quickly returned her attention to the camera. After snapping several pictures of Sam with his mother, Penny switched her angle and added a few quick shots of Shirley with Craig. With his dark auburn hair only touched by a hint of gray, Craig was the picture of health for a man his age. The contrast between them was evident as Craig cradled Shirley tenderly in his arms, and the pose brought tears to Penny's eyes.

Apparently recognizing the disparity of Penny's thoughts, Sam quickly stood up from the table, in an obvious attempt to distract her. "I'm, most definitely, willing to admit, that I made a *huge* mistake when I married Vanessa." Meeting her gaze, he held it reassuringly. "Maybe the biggest mistake of my life," he whispered into her ear, as he carefully pulled the camera strap from around her neck and laid the camera on the table.

Craig turned to Shirley, somewhat reluctantly. "Well, sweetheart. I'd say we've probably had enough excitement for one day. I'm tired."

"Me, too," Shirley admitted. "It's been a beautiful day for Jake and Danielle—hasn't it? I can't wait to see all of their pictures."

After running through a succession of farewells to everyone who was seated nearby, Craig tugged at Shirley's chair while gently easing her to her feet.

Penny smiled reassuringly. "I'll see you tomorrow, then." After a shake and a squeeze to Craig's outstretched hand, Penny wrapped her arms around Shirley and pressed a quick kiss to her cheek.

While Craig hovered behind Shirley, Sam wrapped a steadying arm around his mother as they moved slowly through the crowd, and began their escape to the lobby.

Penny dropped back into her seat at the table. Reaching for assurance, she was sipping on her second glass of champagne when Brian and Dawn returned.

"Penny. *You'll* dance with me, won't you?" Engaged in another friendly argument with Dawn, Brian was obviously suffering her rejection. Reaching over to grab Penny's champagne from her hand, he rested the flute on the table.

Suddenly, a disapproving voice cut in, "Hands off, Brian. She's gonna dance with *me*."

Two

What was going on? When Penny reluctantly glanced over her shoulder, discovering the *last* person she'd expected to see, the sense of contentment she'd experienced for most of the day immediately vanished. "*Todd!* What are *you* doing here?" Earlier, Danielle had assured her that Todd *hadn't* been invited. Suddenly aware that she was trembling, Penny reached for her champagne and gulped down what was left.

"I was invited, of course. I've provided a lot of business to Danielle and Brian, after all," he replied, haughtily. Todd Shelton, owner of several exercise facilities in and around New York, had a contract with Danielle and Brian's company, *A New Leaf,* for landscaping and maintenance services.

Avoiding his eyes, Penny struggled to maintain a steady voice. "Oh. I didn't expect to see you here." *Now what?* Immediately, she felt suffocated by Todd's obsessive attention. *Did he have any remorse, at all, for the way he'd treated her?* How could he *still* assume they were a couple? Although he'd left several messages at the shop over the last few weeks, she hadn't returned a single one. It didn't seem to occur to him that she'd be with someone else.

But she really wasn't, was she? Sam was only escorting her for the day, after all.

She drew in an unsteady breath as Todd's words slipped out, clipped and cool. "I didn't arrive until this afternoon. I had an emergency come up and couldn't get away until this morning."

Resignedly, Penny sighed. "Alright, I'll dance with you." Catching Brian's sympathetic eye, she arose unsteadily.

Studying them both curiously, Dawn peered back and forth from Penny to Todd.

"By the way Todd, this is Dawn."

Without a word, Todd nodded his head stiffly at Dawn before escorting Penny out onto the dance floor. For the first few minutes, Penny remained silent. But when Todd suddenly attempted to fold her into his body, she stiffened. With the cloying scent of his heavy cologne immediately evoking a disturbing mental image of their last unpleasant confrontation, she realized it was time for her to take control. "You weren't very nice to my friends," she observed impatiently, bracing a palm against his chest.

"Why didn't you let me know your flight arrangements before the wedding?" Todd demanded, pointedly ignoring her words.

Disturbed by the unusual intensity in his glittering dark eyes, Penny frowned. "Todd. It's *over* between us. You just don't seem to get that." It was strange how Todd reminded her *so* much of her husband, David. Although about the same height and build, Todd was a golden, bleached-blonde, while David's coloring had been dark, the color of his hair nearly raven-black. Todd was much more handsome than David, after all, with his almost too-perfectly sculpted nose and high cheekbones. But it was just so eerily familiar, this controlling manner. Much like David's cool gray eyes had terrified her during his abusive fits of temper when they'd been married, there was something equally frightening about the darkness lurking in Todd's eyes as well.

All of a sudden, Penny began to shiver. She just had to escape. *Why* had she let Todd get away with nearly assaulting her when she'd rejected his proposal? Had she only been fooling herself—believing she'd grown stronger since living through those tormenting years of marriage to David?

"Penny? I've been looking all over for you. You promised *me* the next dance." Standing in the middle of the dance floor with an inquisitive brow raised at Todd, Sam had somehow managed to weave through the dancing couples. Not awaiting an introduction, he casually plucked Penny from Todd's arms. Expertly steering her through the crowded dance floor, he remained quiet until they ended up almost hidden on the other side.

"I'm sorry, Penny. Usually, I'm not quite so rude. But the man looked like he was terrorizing you. You should've seen the look on your face."

"It's hard to believe he actually expected me to marry him, isn't it?"

"*You mean you've been dating him?*" Scowling, Sam dragged Penny off of the dance floor. Pulling away from her, he impatiently awaited her response.

Aware of Sam's disapproval, she admitted, reluctantly, "We dated for about a year and a half, off and on. I met him through Danielle."

Momentarily, his frown became deeper as his stare across the room turned intense. Dropping his arms, Sam stepped back deliberately as his eyes met hers. "So, you're still seeing him?"

"No. *Of course not.* He just doesn't seem to give up, though." She stumbled through her words uncomfortably. "I—I'm not really sure why, Sam. I've never given him *that* kind of encouragement."

Sam studied her face. She knew he suspected there was more to the story but, much to her relief, he dropped his inquisition.

Seemingly reassured by her denial, Sam suddenly relaxed, pulling Penny back into his arms. "Well—we'll just have to make sure he finally understands that you're *not* going to see him again. Alright?"

As if on cue, the music turned mellow. While notes of a love song trickled softly into play, a cohesive symphony of lights dimmed gradually, and somewhat dramatically, throughout the room.

Perceptibly heightening her senses, Sam lightly slid his fingers down from her bare shoulders and rested them at her waist. She became increasingly aware of the enticing scent of his soap and cologne, when he determinedly pulled her back into his arms. Once Sam swept Penny gracefully back onto the dance floor, all awareness of Todd's unwelcome presence immediately fled her mind.

Effortlessly following Sam's skilled maneuvers, Penny melted deeper into his arms. She was definitely feeling her champagne, when she stretched up and confessed in his ear, "I don't think I've ever danced with anyone who dances as well as you." Pulling back and studying him intently, she added, "I loved old movie musicals when I was a kid. I used to dream about how romantic it'd be to dance with someone who actually *knew* how to dance.

He eased back, as he studied her face. "Then those stupid lessons were well worth it—just so I could dance with *you*," he whispered softly. As he gave her a tender smile, Sam pulled her body back against his in perfect sync with the music. With a gentle nudge, he launched her into a smooth spin, before wrapping an arm around her again. He grinned, as he held her hand and acted like he was going to let her drop. Penny smiled as she finally caught on, and trusted him to hold tight when she fell back over his arm. On point with the music's beat, he tugged lightly, landing her upright and into his waiting arms. When his lips nuzzled delicately along her brow, she drew in a steadying breath.

She was so in trouble.

Absorbed in awareness, they both failed to notice when the music began fading away. As the band members prepared for their break, Penny realized that they were the last remaining couple on the dance floor. Hearing a startling spatter of applause, suddenly embarrassed, Penny nervously attempted to ease away. But with a lazy grin, Sam reached for her hand while he bowed to their audience. Sam must've realized she was still uncomfortable, because he squeezed her hand with reassurance, before they began making their way through their crowd of admirers.

Penny gazed anxiously at the faces of the guests when she and Sam finally began to mingle.

Sam was definitely aware of Penny's disquiet, because he lengthily studied the ballroom until he finally found Todd. "Danielle's got him under control on the other side of the dance floor."

Penny stared at Todd uneasily from across the room. With a frown on her face, Danielle, alongside Jake, appeared to be bruising Todd's ears with a roaring lecture.

Pulling out a chair, Sam seated Penny back at their table. With his body tense and his eyes cold and fierce, he was appearing increasingly irritated. For the first time ever, Penny got a glimpse of the rigid and controlling, forceful side of Sam; apparently his underlying strength in enforcing the law. "Forget about him, Penny," he muttered. Dragging out another chair from under the table, he dropped into it impatiently.

"I'm just trying to figure out *why* he's even here. Danny already made a point of telling me that she *didn't* invite him," Penny confessed to Sam, with reassurance.

Suddenly at ease, Sam's expression softened as he crossed his arms and studied Penny thoughtfully. "Seems odd with all the security in place for the wedding, doesn't it?"

Due to the previous year's discovery of a hidden human trafficking ring, operating for several years at the long-deserted point, countless security measures had been put in place at Dragonfly Pointe. What was particularly worrisome was the fact that none of the perpetrators had yet been captured.

Penny nodded her agreement. "He's been pumping me for months, now, about the names of the wedding guests."

Sam raised a brow.

"He's opening an exclusive health spa and resort, just outside of New York. He needs to attract wealthy clientele."

"Well, there *are* a lot of celebrities here. You don't seem to be particularly flustered around anyone."

Relaxing, Penny laughed quietly, slowly surveying the multitude of guests. "Danielle's been directing business our way ever since she learned I managed Sander's Floral. I can't believe all the well-known people I've mingled with over the last few years." Besides many recognizable musicians and actors, a half-dozen reporters and photographers had been hand-selected by Danielle for their reputations as professionals.

Finally, with the clamor of activity on stage, Penny and Sam refocused their attention. Returning to actively participate in the festivities, Jake and Danielle each took a seat alongside the band. Even though Jake still wore his formal black tux, sometime during the last few minutes, Danielle had swapped out her stunning mermaid-style wedding gown for an elegantly simple, but shimmering, floor-length gown of white.

Jake grinned as he began tuning his guitar. "The things we do for love," he observed aloud. He watched Danielle adjust her microphone. "I promised Danny—when we got engaged—that I'd sing at our wedding. So she's been rehearsing me." Although Danielle had partnered with Brian Johnson to run a flourishing landscape business in New York now, at one time she'd experienced enormous success as a vocalist as well as a model.

As Jake strummed his guitar, Sam and Penny stared at each other in astonishment. Although it was obvious Jake was head over heels in love with Danielle, it was totally against his nature to be demonstrative in public.

Raising a brow, Sam murmured, "He's not too bad, is he?"

Penny nodded her agreement as Danielle's beautiful voice soon echoed throughout the room. In a lazy, meaningful rendition of a popular rock ballad, Jake's pleasant baritone melded flawlessly with Danielle's soprano.

"They're *both* really good together, aren't they?" Penny's eyes met Sam's before scoping for reactions throughout the room. Absentmindedly laying a hand over her heart, Jake's mother, Jocelyn, appeared to be the most affected, as her eyes shimmered with tears.

When the final few notes of their ballad trickled softly to a finish, there was a moment of silence.

But, before long, the applause became rampant. Still seated, Danielle and Jake both appeared to be unusually flustered. Danielle shook her head, looking dazed, while Jake rolled his eyes. After sharing a brief smile and a kiss, they stood up, waving to their audience, and Jake hung a possessive arm loosely around Danielle's shoulders as they exited the stage.

Within a few short minutes, the music resumed with a series of requests. As the evening wore on, the mood of the reception turned extraordinarily festive. Most of the guests who remained had rooms reserved at the inn.

Penny realized her earlier tension had finally vanished—probably because Todd hadn't approached her again the entire evening. Sticking to her like glue, Sam had even refused to switch partners while dancing. She should've been exhausted.

But, instead, she felt recharged.

"Penny. How about we get out of here for a while? Maybe go for a drive around the lake? After we each take a turn dancing with Jake and Danielle, that is. Unless you have any unfinished work to do, here at the reception?" Sam must've belatedly recalled Penny might have additional responsibilities, as the primary wedding designer.

Penny eyed Todd uncomfortably as his dark eyes glittered from across the room. Standing near the bar, he appeared to be barely controlling his temper as he became increasingly belligerent. Staring her down, he deliberately chugged down a shot.

"No. Jake's hired caterers to do all the cleanup. I don't actually have anything to do until tomorrow. And, even then, all I have to do is pull down the lights and outside decorations. I wouldn't mind getting out of here for a while, either."

Unconsciously, Sam glared at Todd with a warning of his own before he turned back to her with a lazy grin. "It's been kind of a long day. I didn't even see Nat and Olivia sneak out with the boys. C'mon." Reaching for her hand, he pulled her to her feet. A few other guests had gathered around the head table waiting for the opportunity to speak with Jake and Danielle. When the band struck up into an unusually frenzied, upbeat song, Sam and Penny finally had their chance to converse with the newly-married couple.

Sam slapped Jake companionably on the back. "You *are* multi-talented, aren't you?"

"I'm just glad that it's over. I was nervous as hell," Jake grumbled, shaking his head with relief.

"Well, you sure didn't look it," Penny reassured him. "I can't believe how *good* you two were."

Jake grinned. "Why, thank you."

"He had me believing he was out of practice, and hadn't picked up a guitar—or sang—in years." With a weary smile, Danielle admitted wryly, "I should've known better. I'm beginning to realize just what a perfectionist this guy really is. And he hides it well. It makes me wonder what other secrets he still has hidden away."

Jake appeared sheepish when he wrapped an arm over Danielle's shoulders.

Sam's eyes met Jake's as he held Penny's hand. "I think we're gonna get out of here for a while—if you two don't mind?"

"*Oh, no.* Not at all." Danielle grinned smugly at Penny.

Penny squirmed uncomfortably, as she rolled her eyes upward.

Jake yanked impatiently at his neatly-knotted black and gray tie. "I can't wait to get this stupid tuxedo off, myself."

"But you look *so* handsome." Danielle snuggled up closer to Jake.

"And you look absolutely beautiful in that dress, but that doesn't mean I still can't wait to get you out of it." Jake's comment set off spurts of laughter from a few of the guests lingering nearby.

Danielle was unusually flustered as she muttered under her breath. "I don't know what it is that you do to me, but you *still* make me feel like a teenager when you tease me like that.

Jake gazed adoringly at his breathtakingly beautiful new wife. Ignoring their surroundings, they melted into each other's arms.

Shaking her head with resignation, Penny turned to Sam. When Sam grinned, rolling his eyes, she let out a soft snort of laughter.

Once Jake and Danielle had a sufficient amount of time to recover from their heated embrace, Sam swept Danielle out onto the dance floor, while Jake stepped out with Penny.

With an engaging smile, Jake studied Penny as he spun her slowly around the room. "Are you having a good time?"

"It's been great, I'll have to admit—even though I'm a little worn out. It's been so nice just getting away from home." She admitted hesitantly, "Except for Todd Shelton showing up here, that it."

"Yeah. Danny's gonna look into that, Penny. She thought she made it pretty clear to Karen exactly *who* needed to be cut from our guest list. Brian insists Karen is usually pretty efficient. When we get back from California, Danny's gonna go back to New York to handle a few things at the office. She'll talk to Karen, too. We're worried about security. We specifically held back several invitations when some of our background checks came up questionable, and Todd Shelton wasn't the only one we cut from our list that showed up here today. I hope he isn't bothering you too much."

"I think that's why Sam wants to take off for a while."

"Oh, that's not the *only* reason, I'm sure." Jake's green eyes twinkled.

Penny avoided his eyes. She was actually *blushing*.

Unexpectedly, Jake turned his conversation to a more serious note. "Are you still having a lot of trouble with Alex?"

With the shift in conversation, she suddenly felt disheartened. "Yeah—unfortunately. He's been so much worse. I don't know what we're gonna do about school next year. His behavior's been *so* out of control—I'm not sure that they'll let him come back."

"Penny. Danny and I came up with a plan—and it's been in place since last fall. It could possibly solve all your long-term problems. A few more details need to be worked out yet, though. Danny won't have any time to talk to you about it tomorrow. But I think she'll be coming by to see you in New York. Just try to stay positive. Okay?"

Even though she was confused by Jake's reassurances, Penny agreed, "Alright."

"You know Sam likes you? I mean *really* likes you. He'd probably kill me for telling you, but he came by the inn after work—that day you were here back in April—just hoping you hadn't left town yet. He let it slip that he was really attracted to you back in high school."

What? Penny's eyes widened. "I just figured that he was only being nice to me because I was the new kid in town." Recalling her uncharacteristic lapse into melancholia earlier that day, she cleared her throat nervously. "Plus I knew he was...uh, dating other girls."

"He was getting a lot of slack from the other guys, because you were so much younger than him, I guess. His priorities changed a lot too, after the murder of that little girl, here on Dragonfly Pointe. He was one of the search party who discovered her body, you know."

Penny was taken aback. "No, actually, I didn't. That must've been awful! From what I've heard, the crime scene was gruesome." Penny shuddered, vaguely recalling that early morning in August of 1965. Almost every adult from town had driven out to Dragonfly Pointe to search for Anna Ivers. The crime scene at the base of Crystal Rock had been a bloodbath. As the only minister in town, Penny's father had performed a eulogy for the Ivers family at Dragonfly Pointe several weeks after the murder.

With the lights beginning to brighten overhead, the band leader announced they were taking their next break. Sam and Danielle were waiting when Jake escorted Penny back to the head table.

"Are we ready?" After somewhat impatiently glancing at his watch, Sam grinned.

Penny turned to Sam with a huge smile. Her confidence had been given a big boost by Jake's reassurance of Sam's sincerity. "Maybe we could leave a number at the front desk—just in case my mother has any trouble with my son."

"We'll probably see you in the morning, Penny. We're not taking off until noon." Danielle smiled reassuringly.

Jake winked at Sam. "Have fun, you two."

Reaching for Penny's hand, Sam tugged her gently away. Stopping occasionally to chat, they slowly made their way back to their table.

Stunning in a slinky gossamer-blue gown, reflecting the beautiful color of her eyes, Dawn was seated by herself and gazing broodingly out across the dance floor.

She smiled, when she noticed Sam and Penny.

"Brian was a little buzzed and getting on my nerves, so I walked around the room and took a whole bunch of pictures for you, Sam. And I also held on to your purse for you, Penny—since everyone else left." Standing up and tugging the camera strap from around her neck, Dawn handed the camera over to Sam. "He's really annoying when he drinks too much. He wouldn't keep his hands off of me!"

Sam grinned. "If it's any consolation, I can't blame him."

Dawn blinked. "Wow. Flattery from Sam. You *must* be enjoying yourself!"

"Thanks for taking the pictures for me, Dawn. I wasn't exactly motivated today. I don't remember the last time I actually had a date."

He was openly flirting now, and Penny could feel herself blushing again. "Sam and I are going for a drive. We'll probably be back in a few hours."

"Okay. Have fun." When Dawn teased Penny with, yet another, deliberate wink, Penny rolled her eyes.

Dawn peered out again across the dance floor. "Oops. I see that Brian's making a nuisance of himself again. I'll see you two later, then." Dawn began making her way through the crowd on the dance floor.

Sam loaded his camera back into its case, and Penny scooped up her purse as they prepared to depart.

Three

esting an arm gently over her shoulders, Sam steered Penny through the crowd and out into the lobby. Making a detour at the reservation desk, he listed the digits of his phone number for the receptionist, who promptly entered the number under Penny's contact information.

They finally escaped from the inn. Deciding on a circuitous route to avoid the crowd, Sam kept an arm wrapped around Penny's shoulders as they followed a staircase down from the length of the extended porch, and strolled along a scenic lighted pathway. Fanciful wind chimes and ornaments hung from the trees while, lining the cobblestone pathway, groupings of whimsical dragonfly planters charmingly spilled over with impatiens, lobelia, and ivy. Aside from the colorful beds of annuals planted to soften the hardscape bordering the walkways, additional raised beds, clustered with circular plantings of blue-green hostas and vibrant burgundy impatiens, had been wrapped around each of the distinctive wrought-iron lamp posts, scattered throughout the brightly-lit parking lot.

"I thought we'd drive out to my cabin, since it's just on the other side of the lake. Then I can have you back here in a few hours."

Sam's eyes met hers and she smiled. "It'd be nice to be able to relax for a little while."

As they approached Sam's truck, he unlocked the doors with the remote on his key ring. After pulling open the passenger door, Sam startled Penny by wrapping his hands around her waist and lifting her effortlessly into the seat.

Before she had a chance to protest, he'd already sped around the truck and hopped into the driver's seat. Pulling on his seat belt and slipping the key into the ignition, he met her discomfited gaze with an easy smile. After studying the crowded parking lot, he carefully backed out into the exit lane. "Seat belt," he gently reminded.

With a start, she tugged at the belt and quickly latched it. The champagne had *definitely* left her buzzed, she realized, with a rueful shake of her head.

Or was it just because she was here with Sam?

After exiting the congested parking lot, heading east, he skillfully wound the truck around the access road of the bay. Approaching the extended crossing, and then traveling over the Crystal Rock River on a newly-constructed bridge, he drove north onto a recently-widened road. Finally pulling off from the main road, he maneuvered his truck along narrow curves, following the northeastern shoreline of Crystal Rock Lake.

Sam suddenly veered off from the main road. After grinding and spitting out loose rock, the tires of his truck held steady as he made his way along the worn graveled driveway that led to the isolated cabin. Although the positioning of several posts topped with reflectors allowed Sam to maneuver the twisting path, overhead lighting made the road more visible as they followed the narrow drive, that was shrouded with cover from the towering pines.

A detached two-story, three-car garage suddenly appeared, nestled along the drive. When the cabin finally came into view, Penny was smiling with delight when she eagerly stretched up from her seat to study the tranquil setting. "Oh, it's beautiful here, Sam!"

Sam seemed pleased by her reaction. He quickly parked along the drive and slipped out from his truck. Pulling open her door, he reached for Penny's hand and carefully guided her down from her seat.

As a light cool breeze swept in from across the lake, Penny appreciatively lifted her face upward. "I probably should've grabbed a jacket before we left."

She was shivering on their approach to the lakefront, and Sam tugged her closer for warmth. Momentarily they stilled, staring into each other's eyes. Moving soothingly down the length of her spine, before settling over the turn of her waist, Sam's fingers gently glided over bare skin.

Penny stumbled, in reaction to his searing touch. She let out a ragged breath, as desire, such as she'd never known, slammed intensely through her senses.

Sam must've assumed Penny's loss of step was due to her high heels sinking into the soft surface of the rutted ground—the deck and porch had only been recently built. Scooping her up into his arms and traveling up a short row of steps, Sam planted Penny on the porch. With her arms resting loosely over his shoulders, Sam kept her wrapped securely within his arms.

As, all the while, his warm brown eyes gazed intently into hers.

"You've got the most beautiful blue eyes I've ever seen," Sam whispered, hoarsely.

Penny anxiously held her breath.

As his hands skimmed up from her waist along the curve of her spine, and then moved to lightly cover her bared shoulders, Sam used his skillful fingers to gently stroke where he touched.

Strongly aware of each of his subtle soothing strokes, her eyes closed helplessly in response. With a breathless sigh, Penny clung to Sam.

And then, he kissed her.

Drowning out the beauty from the sliver of the moon overhead and the brightness of the stars, there was only this mesmerizing magical moment. Beneath them, the secreted creatures hovering in the depths of the shadowed lake stirred an occasional ripple.

But to Penny and Sam, both spellbound, the splendor of nature dimmed.

Penny's unexpected passionate response seemed to throw Sam completely off balance. While Penny's lips eagerly responded to the deepening of his kiss, Sam gently kneaded under her arms, before moving his hands to cup the fullness of her breasts.

Aware of Sam's rigid state of arousal, she fought to keep her legs from collapsing out from under her. Sigh for contented sigh, and kiss for lingering kiss, Penny returned Sam's increasing passion heatedly.

Hungrily.

With lips and tongues battling and hands exploring, what'd started out gentle became tumultuous.

Until increasingly becoming aware of the brisk cool breeze drifting in from across the lake, they finally, reluctantly, pulled apart. Staring lengthily into each other's eyes, Sam and Penny were both, most obviously, struck with stunned disbelief.

"*Wow!*" Sam mouthed, fervently.

Penny blinked, inhaling a shaky breath.

Suddenly, they were both smiling.

"Come on." Shaking his head somewhat dazedly, Sam drew in a deep steadying breath before reaching for her hand. "Let's go inside and I'll get a fire going. Jake sent along a bottle of champagne. Let me go get it."

Unlocking the door of the cabin for Penny and guiding her through, Sam flipped on the switch for a nearby lamp. Launching himself back through the door, he ran out to the truck to retrieve the champagne.

Dim lighting highlighted the velvety mahogany finishes layering the interior of the cabin. The chimney of the original stone fireplace towered upward through the open-beamed ceiling. Sleekly refinished, a wide wooden staircase, with an intricately carved railing, ran up alongside the fireplace, and led to a spacious balcony extending on either side. Constructed over a deck and porch that was nestled beside the lakefront, a roomy loft, supported by pine trees stripped of their bark, had been built on the opposite side of the upper chimney. Peering through a door at the rear of the living room, Penny discovered the enormous dining room and kitchen were both still works in progress.

Returning with the champagne and two Styrofoam cups, Sam set them down on a rustic coffee table. Moving over to a small stacked pile of wood, he laid a few logs on top of the pair of rusty old andirons, resting inside the fireplace. Crumpling up newspapers, he stuffed them under the logs. After striking up a large matchstick from a box on the mantle, he soon had a roaring fire blazing.

Sam turned to Penny with a rueful smile. "It should warm up in here pretty quickly. Hopefully, I'll have the entire addition finished up by the fall, so that I can finally have a furnace installed."

Pulling off the jacket for his tux, he hung it over a hook near the door. Sliding the tie from his loosened collar, he stuffed it into one of the jacket pockets.

After rolling up his sleeves, Sam reached for Penny's hand. "C'mon. I'll show you around." Leading her through the doorway into the dining room, moving out into the kitchen, he flipped on the switch for a dim, outdated overhead light.

Sam pointed to an empty space where cabinets had once stood. "We're ripping out the entire exterior wall to pour concrete underneath the structure for a sturdier foundation. That's why the walls are stripped down to two by fours." Along with a slightly updated stovetop and oven combination, an outdated refrigerator remained stationed along the inner wall. "I'm pulling out the wooden floors—and I'll reinstall them and refinish them once I've found more flooring to match. After I've enlarged the kitchen, that is. Or I might use tile and a new radiant heat system I can sink into the concrete. I'll have to decide if it's worth the expense, though."

Grasping the enormous amount of effort entailed in Sam's remodel, with widened eyes, Penny studied the space thoughtfully. "With all the work you have to do, why not just tear down the cabin and start from scratch?" Becoming increasingly aware of Sam, Penny kept on sipping her champagne. But all of a sudden, her nerves began tingling, and she became unsteady. After noticing a large sheet of plywood lying flat over two sawhorses, she attempted to balance inconspicuously on a stool resting near the makeshift table.

"Well—two reasons actually." Sam hooked his thumbs over his front pants pockets. "Because of the updated zoning laws, if I tear down the original structure, I wouldn't be able to rebuild directly on the lake. If my original structure remains standing, I can get away with adding onto it. The same goes for the boathouse. But since it's been neglected for so long, I've been trying to replace all the rotting lumber. Brian's even made up plans for me. That's why they're taking so long to remodel Danielle's lakehouse. Brian's trying to cover all the technicalities—so that they can build a huge addition off from the original cottage. Plus, they want the addition to blend in."

Penny raised a brow. "What's the second reason?"

"Purely sentimental." Sam's mouth twisted into a bittersweet smile. "My dad and Craig were best friends. I spent a lot of time here as a kid. When Craig handed over the keys to me this past Christmas, I nearly lost it. Dad and I used to spend almost every weekend here fishing on the lake. Pretty much any friend of Craig's had an open invitation, as long as he brought beer. At night, we'd always have a campfire." He motioned to a large clearing visible through the window. "Or, on the cooler nights, we'd use that fireplace in the living room."

For several minutes, they were silent while Sam remained distracted, deep in thought.

With a quick shake of his head, he returned his attention to Penny. "As you can see, we're still not set up for dining. We've been using paper plates and plastic silverware. I can't make up my mind about this kitchen." He switched on a brighter light over the still-remaining, farmhouse-style sink. "I don't know much about colors—or what's popular with cabinetry and countertops. I've never been much of a cook."

With curiosity, Penny studied the cabinetry and countertop samples spread out before her on the makeshift table. "I've always loved to cook," she mumbled, absentmindedly.

With her head bent down studying samples, Penny failed to notice Sam's quick tender gaze as he slipped an arm over her shoulders. "What would you pick out?"

She pointed to a sample of stone that was labeled mottled nutmeg. "Darker is probably better. I remember we used to have problems with ants when we lived near the Crystal Rock Campgrounds. We had countertops that were made from shiny white Formica. Even after my mom scrubbed every surface of that kitchen, every morning, there'd be lines of ants marching along the countertops—especially during the summer. It used to drive her *crazy*. These new stone surfaces are scratch resistant and easy to clean. Or, so, I've heard. But they're expensive, aren't they?"

"Well, I'd rather spend more money on something permanent, that won't become outdated." A bit hesitant, he added, "I was thinking about moving out here year-round when I'm done. Brian's still finishing the plans though, so I'm not sure how long it'll take to make the place move-in ready."

"Brian's been working with Danny for so long in their landscape business, I almost forgot that he actually started out as an architect."

"From what Jake's told me, Brian's pretty good at it, too."

After Penny answered a few more questions about her recommendations for remodeling the kitchen, Sam eventually led her back into the much warmer living room.

Continuing to detail his plans for the cabin, Sam motioned to a passageway on the opposite end of the living room. "I'm even installing a darkroom."

"Wow—you're *that* much into photography?"

"Yeah, off and on." He grinned, wryly. "During the summer, when I was a kid, my mom and I used to drive back and forth to my grandfather's resort in Michigan after my grandmother passed away. My mom would help out with cleaning and updating the cabins. Anyway, my grandfather was a war photographer during World War II, and I used to enjoy messing around with his camera. When he noticed my interest didn't ease up after a year or two, he bought me my first camera and taught me all the basics." Staring unseeing into the fire, with a sigh, he continued, "But after my grandfather died—and then my dad—I kind of put my interest aside when I had to get a job and help out my mom. I still took a few fill-in courses at college that included photography. So I learned a lot of technical information about cameras—including how to develop my own pictures. Jake and Danny insisted on giving me that top-of-the-line, thirty-five millimeter last Christmas, and I've been back into photography ever since."

Penny suddenly noticed a pile of photos laid out on an extended sofa table, that was backed up against the wall. "Are those all yours?"

Sam answered sheepishly, "Uh-huh." With a rueful grin, he casually dropped an arm over her shoulders, as she began thumbing through the photos. "I find I'm more interested in the beauty of the sunset, along with the trees, birds, deer—stuff you see on postcards."

She smiled appreciatively. "Well—these are beautiful—and pretty enough for a postcard." Unnervingly aware of Sam's arm resting over her shoulders, she spent an unusually long period of time gazing down at a striking scene of an ice-coated Crystal Rock Lake. Sam had snapped a glorious amber sunset from the very top of Crystal Rock.

For a moment their lighthearted moods became decidedly grim.

Crystal Rock. Where the broken mutilated body of six-year old Anna Ivers had been discovered over twenty-two years ago.

While his gaze, strangely and reflectively, focused on the snapshot, Penny snuck a side glance at Sam.

"Amazing how something so evil can happen somewhere so beautiful."

Penny shivered at his words. After a brief reassuring squeeze of her shoulders, he dropped his arm. Crossing his arms and settling back, he openly studied her reaction as she thumbed through the remaining photos. She examined several pictures lengthily, with obvious delight. Once she'd carefully returned the stacks of pictures to the table, Penny was steered back near the warmth of the fireplace.

Seating Penny on the striped brown and cream cushions of a wood-framed couch, that'd, most obviously, seen better days, Sam grinned as the worn out springs began to squeak. "As you can see, I *really* need furniture. I decided that it'd be better to wait until most of the construction's done."

Popping the cork of the champagne, Sam refilled their cups. For a second, he had his eyes on a worn leather recliner positioned near the fireplace. But after handing Penny her champagne, he dropped down beside her on the couch.

For the next few hours, with anticipation thrumming, Penny focused her attention on Sam. It was amazing how easily their conversation flowed. Sam stoop up several more times to stoke the fire and refill their champagne.

Suddenly aware that the bottle was nearly empty, Penny realized that she'd consumed much more champagne than Sam. For the last few minutes, he'd been staring into the fire, remaining oddly silent. "Will you be okay to drive me back over to the inn?"

"I should be in a few minutes."

Disgruntled, she felt oddly disappointed. This wasn't exactly the romantic response she'd been hoping for. When Sam kept staring into the fire, she finally asked, "What about the fire?"

"Oh. I'll probably just come back here to sleep tonight."

Penny was puzzled as she studied the living room. Surely, he didn't mean to sleep on this uncomfortable wooden couch?

Noticing Penny's confusion, Sam nodded at the stairway leading up into the loft. "I didn't give you the complete tour. The bedroom's up there. I finally got it set up last week after I refinished the floors. The bedroom's nice and toasty since the stone from the fireplace runs through the room. The chimney used to be the primary source of heat for these cabins, you know." Sam pointed out the solid wall of the original exterior. "We'll eventually cut doorframes through those walls to the addition, once the drywall and finish work have been completed over there."

Appearing oddly anxious, Sam rambled on. "Craig and Mom used to spend every weekend here. I had Danielle and Dawn stop out here a few months ago to give me suggestions on furniture and bedding—so Mom can be comfortable when she visits. Anyway, it's nice to finally have a king-sized bed to sleep in."

Suddenly feeling the effects of her champagne, Penny stared at Sam in confusion when she unexpectedly felt tears brimming in her eyes. She didn't want to return to the inn where she'd have to sleep alone. She wanted to stay *here*.

With Sam.

How had he kissed her—the *way* that he'd kissed her—when they'd arrived two hours ago—and not even made one single attempt to do it again? God, the champagne *must* be catching up with her. She'd never been much of a drinker.

Obviously noticing the tears beginning to spill down her cheeks, Sam seemed instantly concerned. Quickly he slid over, instinctively wrapping a comforting arm around her. "Penny, what's wrong?"

She buried her face against his shoulder. "I don't want to go back to the inn tonight."

He groaned with apparent relief. "I don't want you to go, either." Lightly nuzzling her cheek, he laughed softly. "But you've had an awful lot to drink," he whispered.

But it wasn't just the champagne talking, she realized. Penny had *always* wanted this man. He was probably the only man capable of making her forget her everyday burden of responsibilities.

And she really *wanted* to forget.

Just this one night.

Locked in Sam's embrace, falling deeper into his arms, she covered his lips eagerly with hers.

Tense only moments before, Sam released a ragged sigh, finally surrendering to the inevitable. The tentative caressing strokes of Penny's tongue seemed to urge him into a feverish response.

Stroking...exploring...discovering.

It was several breathless minutes later before Sam finally summoned the strength to pull away from her. "Danny told me to take it easy with you. She'd probably never believe that *I'm* the one who needs protecting!"

Studying him, Penny numbly shook her head in confusion. When she finally realized he was teasing, narrowing her eyes, she protested unsteadily, *"Stop!"*

He returned her rueful grin.

She couldn't believe the way she was behaving. *No* man had ever made her lose control before.

To respond like this.

In Sam's arms, somehow, for the first time in her life, she felt safe. Secure.

Penny sighed contentedly as Sam cradled her gently within his arms.

Yes—*this* was what she needed.

But how had she ended up in his lap?

Penny shivered when Sam's fingers slid down lightly over her bared skin, his thumbs gently arousing the nipples of her breast.

Sam's shirt was unbuttoned.

Had she done that?

Curious fingers explored, running through the silky soft hair covering his chest while, dazedly confused, Penny buried her face against his shoulder.

Suddenly standing and lifting her into his arms, Sam turned, and rested her on top of the couch.

She immediately missed his warmth. Penny bit back a protest when she opened her eyes.

With his mouth only inches away, he leaned over and whispered hoarsely, "I wasn't quite prepared for this. I'd probably better run out to my truck for something we might need."

Realizing this precaution might not be necessary, Penny stilled, as a shadow cast through her mind. But she wasn't quite ready to reveal all of her secrets to Sam.

He tweaked her nose with a thumb and a finger before gentling her lips with his sweetest kiss. Obviously reluctant, he pulled away from her, moving to the door. "I'll be right back." His smile was tender when he stepped outside.

When the door closed behind him, Penny turned lazily to enjoy the blazing fire. What an incredible night. She couldn't remember the last time she'd been this happy.

Minutes later, she realized the fire was turning hypnotic. It'd been almost fifteen minutes since Sam had stepped outside. "He'll wake me," she mumbled. It was a struggle holding open her eyes, and, with a weighted sigh, Penny drifted off reluctantly into an exhausted slumber.

Four

Twelve hours earlier.

*I*nstantly recognizing, from pictures, the tidy white-sided exterior of the ranch-style house on Pine Street, Vanessa Gerard Danielson was relieved to realize she'd finally reached her destination.

It'd been a long forty-eight hours. Since Thursday morning she'd traveled through the south, up through the Midwest, switching trains in Chicago. Exiting the train last evening in Eau Claire, Wisconsin, she'd slept fitfully at an inexpensive motel located across the street from the bus station.

Now that it was close to noon on Saturday, she was grudgingly aware that it was still forty-eight hours before she'd originally been scheduled to arrive in Crystal Rock. After a moment of deliberation, Vanessa sighed resignedly. Where else *could* she go? Picking up her suitcase and making her way up the drive, she followed the short sidewalk leading up to Sam's front door.

She impatiently awaited a response from the doorbell. Hmm—no one appeared to be home. When she finally decided to try the knob, she was astonished to discover that the door was actually *locked*. Didn't everyone in small towns supposedly leave their doors *unlocked*?

"Now what?" Just for the hell of it, she decided to peek under the doormat.

Relieved, she snorted, after pulling out a key from under the mat. She studied the deserted street with a swift furtive glance before quickly slipping the key into the lock. Twisting the knob, she pushed open the door and slid in her luggage. When she was finally inside, she leaned back against the door and heaved a sigh of relief once the deadbolt was locked behind her.

She eyed the key in her hand. Shrugging indecisively, she slid it into a side pocket of her purse. Until she was contacted, there was a possibility she might need that key again.

Her eyes slowly traveled over the stained wooden floor of the entry, before moving over the bare walls and ceiling, muddily reflecting their rather drab tones of pink and beige. "So this is it," she muttered aloud. "It's isn't much, is it?" Well, at least there was a bright side. Obviously, Sam had never discovered the truth about his *actual* financial circumstances.

Picking up her bag, she moved straight ahead through the tiny entryway. On the left was an empty living room, apparently undergoing a major makeover. Half of a shaggy green carpet had been removed to expose a stained wooden floor, while assorted tools were piled atop a tool chest in the corner of the room. The carpeting had already been completely removed from the dining room, attached to the living room, that extended to the rear of the house.

The startling results of the makeover were in evidence on the right. The walls of the hallway leading to, what appeared to be the bedrooms, had been brightened to a buttery cream, while the floors had been stained and buffed to a sheen resembling the shell of an acorn.

Traveling down the hallway and peeking into the first room to the left, she studied the beautifully remodeled bathroom. Taupe porcelain tile lined the floor and the walls, while a simple inserted cream and tan mosaic twisted around the vanity mirror, and above the tub and shower. Refinished and stained the color of nutmeg, an antique dresser with curves and carved medallions had been fashioned into a vanity with an inset porcelain sink. Since supplies and towels were nowhere visible, and its linen closet was bare, Vanessa figured the room must've just been completed.

The next door at the end of the hallway led into, what had to be, Sam's sanctuary. Tasteful, of course, the furniture was dark, elegant, and antique. This was where she and Sam had clashed in their tastes. While Sam had preferred a more traditional style, Vanessa had embraced all things contemporary. Once she and Sam had moved into their own home, she'd wanted no reminders of the richly-decorated, grandiose mansion in which she'd grown up.

The home where her father's collection of pricey antiquities had always been more important to him than his own daughter.

Where her father had only valued *her* as one of his possessions.

A possession he'd used for barter and trade.

After Sam and Vanessa had married, although insisting on his own comfortable furnishings in his den and bedroom suite, Sam had eventually given in to her decorating preferences.

And this room was very similar to the room he'd once occupied in Cypress Manor. Its decadent headboard covered almost an entire wall, and a queen-sized bed set boasted two matching dressers. Bearing a scrolled, wood-framed mirror, one bureau slung low against the longest wall, while a tall graceful highboy adorned the wall across the room. With the aged caramel and chocolate patina nearly blending into the newly buffed flooring, simple curves and elegant carvings bespoke the quality of the oak furnishings.

The master bedroom was much larger than she'd expected and Vanessa suddenly realized there'd been an addition attached to the house. The walls of the bedroom were painted the same buttery cream as the hallway, while drapes, area rugs, and a comforter, all in shades of sage and cream, stopped the wood tones from becoming heavy and monotonous. With a leather-clad wing chair situated near a window, and its marble-topped side table lined with a neat row of books, even to Vanessa, the room appeared to be a warm and peaceful retreat.

"So *where* is Sam, anyway?"

Dropping her purse and suitcase onto the floor in the hallway, she crept into Sam's room. Covering the entire wall on her left was a deep, spacious walk-in closet. Pulling open the doors and quickly surveying the interior, she studied the neatly folded sweatshirts occupying a portion of the top shelf, along with the orderly row of shoes lined up in pairs on the floor. Men's clothing hung precisely along the horizontal pole. The half-full closet only seemed to contain Sam's clothing, she was relieved to discover. She slid the closet doors back into place. The reports seemed to be accurate—Sam didn't appear to be involved with another woman.

This should make her mission a little easier.

She approached the door beyond the closet, peering inside. Similarly decorated to the other bathroom, this roomy luxurious space boasted a more opulent vanity as well as a jetted tub large enough for two. After years of playing high school and college football, Sam must've still been suffering from a myriad of aches and pains.

As comfortable as this bedroom was, there was no use instigating trouble with Sam by unpacking her belongings in here. She had yet to devise her strategy.

Returning to the hallway, she picked up her suitcase and purse and began to inspect the other two bedrooms. The spacious empty corner room appeared to be intended for guests. Immediately across the hall from the bathroom was a smaller room fitted with shelves. This would probably serve as Sam's office. An oversized chair with a side table and dresser were the only furnishings in the room. She carted her suitcase inside and laid it on the wide seat of the chair.

Soon, she had her scant collection of clothing unpacked. Luckily, she'd had a variety of clothing and accessories stashed in the bedroom of her childhood home. Not bothering to change out of her suit of black linen, Vanessa had hurriedly packed the most appropriate of her available clothing for her trek to the upper north.

Hanging her suit carefully into the closet, after pulling on slim-fitting navy slacks, she paired them with a white and navy tunic.

"I'll definitely need to find some shoes," she grumbled, making her way barefoot into the hallway and out into the living room. The black heels that she'd traveled in were all that she had.

Arriving early this past Thursday morning for a scheduled meeting with her father at her family home, she'd been greeted by the most gruesome sight she'd ever seen. After the horror of discovering her father's lifeless mutilated body, by noon, Vanessa had escaped New Orleans on a train traveling north.

Most likely, she'd be a murder suspect.

But, then again, she *might* be the next target.

Considering the designer wardrobe and jewelry she'd been forced to leave behind, she suddenly realized, once her father's murderer was discovered, not only would she be able to recover her personal property and possessions, she might actually be in the position to gain *control* over her family's business empire.

That is, unless the situation became complicated, and the murderer was revealed to be one of her father's associates. Each, individually, had an investment in her family's business.

The frown on her face softened. *Rye Carlton*. She wished she'd had the time to reassure him before rushing from town.

Momentarily, she reflected grimly on the gruesome crime scene and the excessive amount of blood at the site of her father's murder.

This didn't seem the typical retribution of her father's disreputable associates.

As her body suddenly began trembling and her eyes filled with tears, for a moment, she allowed herself to feel the pain. But she would *not* allow herself to dwell on her father's murder.

He'd been a cold-hearted bastard.

With only thoughts of escape as she travelled further and further from New Orleans, her hysteria had eventually diminished. Her only option, she realized, was to follow through with their original plans.

Plus she *knew* that they'd find her. What other choice did she have?

Determinedly squaring off her shoulders, she moved through the living room, approaching a doorway on the opposite end of the dining room.

When sharp pain suddenly pierced through the bottom of her foot, she released an anguished cry. Her gaze jerked downward. Although the tack didn't appear to have entered her foot deeply, another anguished cry of pain erupted at the sight of blood.

Suddenly, she broke down, dropping onto the floor. How long she sobbed, she couldn't say. It was as if all the pain and deceit of the last thirty-nine years of her life had finally caught up with her. She finally allowed herself to see her father as she'd seen him last; the blood, his positioning on the floor, and his body as it twisted unnaturally.

While his head hung nearly decapitated from his body.

Lying limp, she finally began sucking in deep cleansing breaths as she gradually regained control. From her prone position on the floor, she studied objectively the hundreds of carpet tacks still embedded in the wooden floor. Noticing a pair of pliers nearby, she realized Sam must've recently begun to rip out the carpet and was in the process of removing tacks and nails from the floorboards before the refinishing process.

When she eventually rose to her feet, she was careful now to avoid the sharp tacks protruding from the floorboards as she hobbled into the bathroom. She found some Band-Aid's in the slim cabinet behind the mirror. Wetting down toilet paper with warm soap and water, she dabbed at the hole in her foot.

When had she actually had her last tetanus shot? Ah, well, she reassured herself with a humorless smile; she'd had an eerie premonition, and tetanus would probably be the *last* thing that'd kill her.

Although the puncture seemed to take forever to quit bleeding, she was finally able to top it off with a couple Band-Aid's. Slipping back into Sam's room, she studied the selection of shoes in his closet. Noticing several pairs of flip-flops, she pulled out the smallest pair she could find. Sam had always begun his day with a swim when they'd been married, so Vanessa wasn't surprised to discover that he still owned a large assortment of comfortable, casual shoes.

With her composure seemingly restored, she returned to exploring the house. When she pushed through a hinged door from the dining room, she was astonished to discover a recently remodeled kitchen in the style of French country. Lined with a six-burner stove, a huge side-by-side refrigerator, and even a dishwasher, the kitchen boasted brand new, coming-back-into-style, stainless steel appliances. Grudgingly, she admired the granite countertop surfaces complementing the traditional crème-colored cabinetry.

And then, ruefully, she frowned. Maybe Sam *had* found out about his inheritance.

The attached family room was lovely. Rustic beams supported the soaring cathedral ceiling, while vaulted windows allowed the room to remain light and airy. Positioned on the rear wall between the windows, the French doors slid open onto a spacious wooden deck. The opposite inner wall boasted a large entertainment center featuring a huge television and a deluxe stereo system. An enormous fireplace fashioned from creamy river rock was centered on the furthest wall. With its mantel framed by the same rustic beams of the ceiling, the fireplace was surrounded by shelves from floor to ceiling.

Even the furnishings were inviting. Backed up to a sofa table, the chocolate-brown leather couch was positioned for an optimum view of the fireplace, while two club chairs, upholstered in a patterned buttery caramel, stood at an angle, facing the big-screen television.

Moving through the room, Vanessa peeked behind a door centered on the shared wall of the family room and kitchen. The combination closet and breezeway held three different doors. Opening the door on the right, she discovered three steps leading down into the attached garage. The two-car garage was neat and clean, and contained the bedroom and office furniture missing from the empty bedrooms at the other end of the house.

Behind the second door, she found an understated half-bath.

Opening the third door, immediately to the left, she realized that the stairs led down into a newly-created basement under the addition. Heading down the stairway, she took a brief look around. A quarter of the new space was occupied by a finished laundry room, enclosing the furnace and water heater. While the remainder of the basement was large and still unfinished, another area next to the laundry appeared to be fitted for an additional bath. Since two long vertical windows allowed in large amounts of daylight, the space didn't have the feel of a typical basement. With her curiosity satisfied, Vanessa returned upstairs.

Moving into the kitchen, Vanessa studied the contents of the refrigerator. Besides the usual side shelves stocked with condiments, a half loaf of bread, a small package of deli meat, and a six pack of beer appeared to be all that Sam had stocked.

Pulling a ripe banana from a hook on top of the refrigerator, she began peeling it back. Chewing down small bites of banana, she began absentmindedly opening and closing doors, checking out the inventory in the kitchen cabinets. "Definitely the kitchen of a single man," Vanessa observed, thoughtfully.

But wait until Sam discovered the truth.

That he actually *wasn't* a single man.

Vanessa grimaced. She'd have to handle this situation delicately.

Sam wasn't going to be pleased.

And *that* was definitely an understatement.

Pulling out the deli meat from the fridge, she sniffed at the package to ascertain its freshness. All of a sudden, she rolled her eyes. *What was she thinking?* Of course it was fresh. This was Sam, after all. He'd always been strangely neurotic, as well as a neat freak. Knowing Sam, he'd dump out the contents of his *entire fridge* before he'd actually allow something to go bad.

Grabbing the bread and mayo, and digging through the drawers for a knife, she put together a sandwich. When had she eaten last? It must've been last night. No wonder why she was starved. She had an entire two dollars and forty-seven cents left from the fifty she'd borrowed from the D.A. on the train.

Although, she'd never have hit him up for the cash if she'd known he *was* a D.A.

But even though he'd been suspicious, he hadn't asked questions. And, without that fifty, she would've had to sleep on a bench at the train station last night. Who knows how long it would've taken her to get here? Without knowing if she was in danger, *or* if the police would attempt to arrest her for her father's murder, she'd been hesitant to use charge cards. Vanessa had left home with barely enough cash to cover her train fare. She'd traveled overnight on the train from New Orleans to Chicago on Thursday, until her transfer in Chicago. After staying in an inexpensive hotel last night, she'd hopped on the greyhound in Eau Claire this morning. The bus had dropped her in downtown Crystal Rock.

But Crystal Rock was curiously like a ghost town, with very few cars cruising along the streets. Vanessa couldn't understand why all the businesses appeared to be shut down on a Saturday afternoon. While she was walking along Main Street, she'd discovered an old-fashioned pay phone situated in the parking lot of, what appeared to be, a long-established gas station. Amazingly, Sam's name and address had been easily accessible in the small phone book chained inside the telephone booth. Pine Street was a simple two block walk from the gas station.

Seated at the large kitchen island, munching on her sandwich, Vanessa eased back into a surprisingly comfortable swivel back stool.

She'd also discovered a bag of corn chips on top of the fridge, so she snacked on those, sipping on the milk that she'd poured.

Eyeing the unusually healthy meal before her, she sighed. Sam had always been somewhat of a health nut too. Years ago, she'd developed a palate for more unusual and exotic foods, but now, most foods no longer agreed with her.

There hadn't been much of anything that she and Sam had had in common. The chore of staying on his good side, pretending to be happy, had become increasingly difficult the longer they were married. So they'd come up with an alternate plan when Sam had insisted on a divorce.

A legal separation, with papers to sign, issued by the family lawyer.

It was hard to believe it'd been almost twenty years since she'd first heard the name, Sam Danielson. How stupid she'd been to think that she'd be free from her father's rule once she'd turned eighteen.

Not if she wanted to continue living the lifestyle she'd become accustomed to.

And not if she wanted to insure the integrity of her inheritance.

Although her father had operated the majority of seafood packaging plants along Louisiana's ocean coast—as well as in several neighboring states—even as a child, Vanessa had recognized the unsavory element fueling his prosperity.

Having just turned eight-years old, after her mother had died, Vanessa had been forced to accept the weakness in Peter Gerard's character.

But it wasn't until she'd turned twelve-years old, that Vanessa had discovered just how truly perverted and diabolically ruthless her father actually was. Frank Carlton, an associate of her father's, had arrived on the scene as a partner in their family business. Owning a large fleet of transport barges and vessels, that'd operated throughout the country on the ocean and river waterways, Frank Carlton had assumed the title of business manager. But Vanessa had instantly realized, though her father was still the front man, he was taking orders from Frank. And Frank Carlton, Vanessa eventually found out, answered only to Vincente DeMarcus.

Vincente DeMarcus.

Closing her eyes, Vanessa shuddered with revulsion. Slipping off of the kitchen stool, she strolled over to the sliding French doors in the family room. Seeking to escape the sudden unbearable chill encompassing her body, she moved outside onto the sunny deck.

Lies and promises, promises and lies; the premise of the relationship between herself and her father. The whole of her life had been spent being manipulated by Peter Gerard.

Along with the person manipulating *him*.

After escaping high school, she'd finally been allowed to fully develop the only interest she'd ever been passionate about: fashion. The promise of her own business had kept Vanessa focused through design school, and had led her into an apprenticeship with Celeste Devoux, a successful designer based in New Orleans.

And that focus had kept Vanessa from dwelling on Peter Gerard's *other* exploitations.

Despite her proven dedication to her studies, Vanessa's plans, yet again, were put on hold by her father, when the promised funding for her business was delayed. In the beginning, Vanessa hadn't had a clue as to why she'd been ordered to seduce Sam. Before departing for New York, she'd spent months studying everything there was to know about him. Frank Carlton had produced a lengthy report and history regarding Sam's past and time in college. A private investigator had followed him, compiling and regularly updating his activities from the moment he'd entered the police academy in New York, up until the present.

Several months of study had made her an expert on the subject of Sam Danielson.

Once Vanessa reached New York, she'd immediately entered a prestigious design school where her enrollment had been prearranged. It hadn't taken much, of course, to breeze through her studies because of her previous experience. If necessary, a job in New York was even awaiting her upon graduation.

Having been informed of Sam's whereabouts beforehand, she'd simply appeared at the deli he'd frequented daily. At age twenty-four, with slim hips and broad muscular shoulders, Sam was even more handsome in person than he'd been in his pictures.

Especially wearing his uniform.

With a late start out of college, he'd entered the police academy and set out as a rookie in New York. He'd noticed Vanessa immediately. But, back then, what man hadn't? As had her mother's, and her mother's before her, her beauty had simply overshadowed other women's. She'd never been vain; it was merely a fact. With long dark hair, flawless skin, and eyes the color of rich chocolate, Vanessa had been the envy of every woman she'd ever known.

But, to herself, her beauty had been a curse. Without her beauty, she suspected, she'd have never been used as a tool of manipulation by her father.

Or as a release for his cruel, sadistic sexual perversions.

With her eyes closed and her face tipped up into the sun, Vanessa found that its warmth filled her with longing. Strangely, the scent of honeysuckle drifted through the air. It'd been her mother's favorite scent. Opening her eyes, she noticed the tangle of flowering vines, covering a trellis attached to the garage.

What would her life have been like if her mother had lived? Fleeting recollections of trips to a sunny beach, as a child, intermingled with memories of a sparkling beautiful presence. For a short while, at least, Vanessa's life had been filled with joy and laughter.

Just like in her dreams.

After a moment, Vanessa sighed, reluctantly returning her thoughts to the present. Frank Carlton and his associates would probably turn up soon.

Most likely, today or tomorrow.

Would one of them slink in through the back of the property, or just pull up into the driveway? Of course, she reasoned cynically, they would've already come up an alternate plan because of her father's death.

She studied Sam's enormous backyard that was backed up to a wooded conservation area. Located on a dead-end street, his ranch was angled on the corner while another home, a two-story of a different design and age, stood in a more traditional pose across the street. A shed, the size of a single-car garage, had been built at the rear of Sam's property, near a dead-end barricade. With sawdust under the railings and dusting its edges, the empty deck that she was standing on appeared to have just been completed.

Yawning, Vanessa left the sliding glass door open when she headed back inside. She was exhausted. Who knows how long it'd be before Sam would come home?

Or would Frank show up first?

All she could do was wait.

Vanessa picked up the remote and clicked on the television. Peeking under a sofa cushion, she realized the sofa was a sleeper. "No use going to that much trouble," she mumbled. She pulled out a light-weight quilt and a pillow from the trunk that served as a coffee table. "God, I'm tired."

Yawning again, she spread the quilt over the soft leather cushions of the couch. Propping the pillow against the armrest, as she dropped on top of the couch, her eyes were closed before her head hit the pillow. Within seconds she was sound asleep.

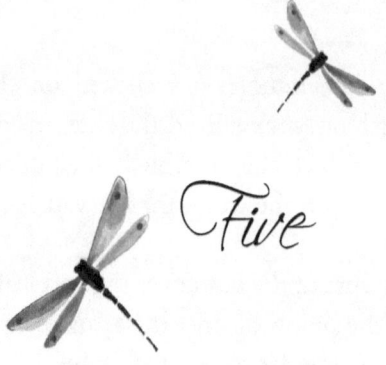

Five

$\mathcal{R}$eluctantly heeding Danielle's earlier warning about not coming on too strong with Penny, with great effort, Sam had *almost* been able to keep his hands to himself. Throughout the day, Penny's emotions had scurried up and down on a rollercoaster, with Sam traveling along for the ride.

He'd give anything to know *what* she'd been thinking about.

And earlier today—when it'd suddenly crossed his mind that Penny might not have been interested in *him*...well...he'd been totally devastated.

Since running into her again, back in April, he hadn't been able to go a single day without thinking of her. As a teenager, Penny had been lovely.

But now, she was beautiful.

And there was no doubt in his mind, that even when she reached the age of seventy, to Sam, she'd still be beautiful.

He knew now—it had to have been love at first sight. If he'd only acted on his desire for her all those years ago, maybe his life today would be as he'd pictured it, and not a lonely life without a wife or kids.

But whatever stupid logical reasoning that'd turned him into an idiot as a teenager definitely had nothing to do with what was happening tonight.

A beautiful woman wanted to have sex with him.

And what was *wrong* with that?

He'd sworn off meaningless sex, that's what.

With Penny unaware of the Loughlin's plans for relocating her to Crystal Rock, meaningless sex must be all that Penny wanted from *him.* Wryly, Sam realized, not without guilt, he couldn't recall *ever* being on the receiving line for sex with no strings. And he wasn't too thrilled about it, to say the least.

With his search finally successful, hoisting his holster over a shoulder, Sam locked up his truck. Hoping that he and Penny might be settled in for the evening, he'd removed his weapon from the lock box. Recalling a colleague's particularly rough learning experience down in New Orleans, having had his weapon stolen from his vehicle and eventually used in a homicide, even though his truck was equipped with a quality alarm system and lockbox, Sam rarely left his weapon unattended.

Distractedly, he gazed down at the package in his hand. The condoms he'd purchased months ago were an all-too-familiar reminder of another life. After his divorce from his wife, Vanessa, and then his move from New Orleans, he'd ended up as the police chief in the small town of Crofton, Arkansas. A few months later, he'd struck up a relationship with lovely, thirty-five year old Geraldine Branyon, a nurse who was employed at the local clinic. Their relationship—if it could even be called *that*—had lasted almost two years.

Sam still felt guilty about how he'd ended it. He hadn't intentionally led her on.

At least, that's what he'd told himself.

Sam had *never* made any promises when they'd begun dating. But more and more, as time went on, their relationship had turned totally physical. When she'd learned he was moving to Crystal Rock, Gerry had been stunned to realize Sam was apparently moving on without her. Sam had the impression that she'd actually expected him to *marry* her.

He hadn't felt good about himself.

For almost fifteen years, the only lengthy relationship he'd had was with his wife, Vanessa. Before that, he'd been purposely single, never in a relationship that had lasted over six months.

Until he'd recognized the similarities between himself and his father, and had begun hating himself.

Marriage had been his solution.

And despite Vanessa's deception about desiring a family, and *her* lapse in fidelity, unlike his father, Sam had been faithful to his wife.

And look how well that'd turned out.

He'd told himself, when he'd moved here to Crystal Rock, because of his status and proximity to family, he wouldn't entangle himself in another casual relationship just to satisfy his sexual needs.

The truth was he'd never been satisfied, anyway.

So except for a single lapse while visiting Madison in January, with a recently divorced friend who he'd dated years ago in college, he'd stuck with abstinence.

Not that he'd actually expected *that* to last. But after one failed marriage, he'd sincerely doubted his ability to risk commitment again.

Then, this past spring, Penny had unexpectedly returned to Crystal Rock. After his last pitiful attempt to contact her in New York over seventeen years ago, he hadn't once allowed his thoughts to drift back on her. Stunned to discover she'd been married at only nineteen-years old, Sam had just assumed she'd been *happily* married. It was amazing how, with just one look into Penny's beautiful sapphire-blue eyes, the connection that'd turned into an obsession for him at eighteen-years old had returned with a vengeance.

To leave him totally off-balance.

Not once, with *any* other woman, had he come close to feeling what he was feeling both then and now for Penny.

They hadn't had a serious conversation all day. And even after Todd Shelton had been castigated by the Loughlins, Penny hadn't really explained her disturbing reaction to the guy.

Sucking in a deep, unsteady breath, Sam attempted to shake off his disquieting thoughts. What would it take for her to open up and really *talk* to him about her life?

Finally, he strode up the steps of the porch, entering the door. Except for the intermittent crackling from the roaring fire, the room remained warm and peaceful. Quietly, Sam hooked his holster over the arm of a sturdy bench resting near the door.

With her gaze fixed at the fire, Penny remained unresponsive as Sam stepped softly through the room. Shimmering like a silken, strawberry-blonde shower, her loosened hair spilled sleekly over the arm of the couch. *God, she was so beautiful.* And also, he realized as he quietly approached her, very sound asleep.

Suddenly realizing that she might be out of his life again on Monday, he was overcome with an overpowering sense of urgency. "Penny?" he whispered softly. Her exhaustion must've finally kicked in after consuming so much champagne. When she didn't stir, he shook her gently. With still no sign of a response, he finally gave up—feeling incredibly disappointed.

Closing his eyes and groaning with frustration, all of a sudden, he began laughing out loud. Sinking down into the recliner, he acknowledged wryly that this moment wasn't quite what he'd envisioned only minutes ago. "It figures," he mumbled, still laughing softly. But, as much as he hated to admit it, it might be for the best. Penny hadn't been the only one rolling up and down on an emotional rollercoaster all day. He didn't want Penny to want him only because *she* was buzzed and *he* was convenient.

Sam sighed resignedly. It was getting late, and he'd have to return Penny to the inn in the morning. He'd carry her upstairs and tuck her into bed. Maybe he'd try to get some sleep himself.

Maybe she'd wake up—eventually.

Yeah, right. What an idiot he was. If he hadn't spent so much time outside, regretting his fate, he wouldn't be in this position right now. Time was slipping away from him. He had only a little over twenty-four hours to convince Penny that they had something special together, and her return to New York didn't have to end it.

He finally stood up. After straightening up the area, he dropped a few more logs into the fire. Grabbing his Styrofoam cup that was still filled with champagne, he slipped through the screened-in porch, moving out onto the deck.

Sipping his champagne, he restlessly roamed the edge of the deck near the water. "I think I've had enough of that," he murmured aloud, dumping the rest of the champagne into the water. Crushing his Styrofoam cup, he stuffed it deep into his pocket. Resting his elbows back on the railing of the deck, he gazed up at the slivered silver moon, peeking out from above the cabin.

Damn, what a frustrating night. And the night had started out perfectly. What could've been more romantic than ending up here at the cabin?

For several long minutes, he remained preoccupied.

But eventually peering out across the water and then back at the shore, he became vaguely uneasy as he studied his surroundings.

Something was wrong. What was it?

His sixth sense kicked in.

That's it. It's too quiet.

Ordinarily reassured by the comforting sounds of the night, he scoped out the shoreline. Typically, his thoughts were drowned out by the tree frogs, with their scratchy musical drone echoing through-out the inlet and across the lake. Thoughtfully, he turned his gaze on the clusters of birch and pine trees surrounding the cabin and lining the edge of the water. Lifting an ear, he became abruptly aware of the absence of rustling wildlife.

It remained eerily silent.

Strolling along the pier toward the boathouse, Sam tested the lock on the door. Beginning back in March, there'd been a string of robberies in the summer homes around the lake. Typically, boats along with skiing equipment were left behind, and usually only fishing equipment went missing. Sam, Nat, and Terry suspected that the per-petrators were most likely local kids. Recently, Sam had become more concerned when a few of the homes and cabins had also been ran-sacked. The perpetrators were probably searching for cash.

Suddenly becoming aware of the nearby snap of branches, Sam stepped into action as someone, or something, quickly made their way through the tangled brush.

Scrambling back across the pier, Sam rushed into the cabin and pulled his revolver from its holster. Releasing its safety, he aimed downward, making his way silently through the living room into the kitchen. Stepping up to the back door, after carefully unlocking it, he reached up into the closet for his flashlight.

Slipping stealthily out onto the back step, he promptly flipped on the switch for the overhead outdoor flood, drenching the entire exterior of the cabin with light.

There. Cloaked in dark clothing, the intruder turned hastily, blending easily into the nearby cover of greenery.

"Stop!" Switching on his flashlight, Sam chased the prowler as he raced through the woods. He could barely make him out as he skidded along. Relying more on instinct, Sam attempted to follow the grown-over path leading down toward the abandoned boat landing.

"Don't make me shoot!" *Yeah, right. Like he was really gonna shoot. What if the intruder was just a kid?*

All of a sudden, hearing a shuffling, grinding and scraping, followed by a loud splash, Sam realized that a grounded boat was apparently being dragged along the shallow pebbled landing. With a canoe or lightweight fishing boat, most likely, left easily accessible for his escape, the trespasser must've jumped into the boat. Sam was only halfway down the path when his flashlight highlighted the prowler slamming an oar frantically, hurrying to dip it over the edge of the boat. Digging his oar into sand and pebbles, the intruder quickly shoved the boat away from the shore.

With his flashlight revealing only portions of the landing, Sam strained for visibility. There was just too much brush along the shore. Sure enough, Sam could see that whoever was maneuvering the oars was gliding along stealthily near the edge of the water.

What the hell could he do? His old dilapidated fishing boat was locked up tight inside the boathouse. Even if he somehow managed to launch its motor, Sam realized it'd be practically impossible to shine a flashlight out on the water, while attempting to steer the boat manually.

He sighed, turning away. Pushing his way through the tangled brush, he examined the area, searching for other obvious signs of disturbance. He'd wait until tomorrow to investigate the path and landing for any clues as to the intruder's identity, he decided, switching off the flashlight. It was pretty isolated out here. Maybe some teens were hanging out here when Sam wasn't around during the week. He'd hate to see any property damage affecting his construction deadlines, since he'd scheduled ahead for plumbing and electrical work.

Returning to the porch, he flipped off the floodlight. Locking up the door, he switched off all but the night light in the kitchen. It was sometimes difficult reaching the cabin's only bathroom in the dark. It might be another month before he'd finally have functional plumbing upstairs in the new master bath.

After returning to the living room, he immediately tested the lock on the sliding doors. Flipping the safety back into place, he holstered his revolver. Eyeing Penny, he realized he'd come trampling through the cabin—twice—and she hadn't budged an inch. After another small attempt and failure to awaken her, he gently slid his arms underneath her prone figure, lifting her off of the couch.

Gazing tenderly at her face, he carried her up the wide staircase and into the loft. It was amazing how this tiny slip of a woman had always seemed to have so much power over him, he reflected rather dazedly, resting her gently on top of the bed. As her long dark lashes feathered delicately against her creamy complexion, Sam studied the faint shadows of fatigue darkening her eyes. Yep—she must've been exhausted.

Slipping off her shoes, he dropped them onto the floor. Deliberating on what to do about her clothing, he was aware of the wrinkles already creasing the silky fabric of her gown. He'd make sure she was wearing something underneath, he supposed, before attempting to remove her gown. She shouldn't mind, after all, since she'd been prepared to have him remove it earlier, he reasoned. With a rueful shake of his head, he snorted, grumbling aloud, *"You're an idiot, Sam.*

He finally discovered a hidden zipper beneath her arm, along the side of her gown. Gentle fingers slipped over the nape of her neck, unhooking the halter bodice. After sliding down the zipper, tugging the dress gently, he pulled it down from her waist and over her hips. Carefully twisting the flimsy straps of the gown over a wooden hanger from his closet, he hooked the hanger over the top of the closet door.

He turned back to Penny. Even while she slept, his body was responding shamefully to her beautiful full breasts and shapely long legs. With her curvaceous body covered only by a lacy camisole and half-slip, she was so damned tempting. With a long loud groan, he quickly dragged a blanket over her scantily clad body.

Sam stepped out of his shoes. Once he'd pulled off his shirt and slipped out of the pleated slacks of his tux, he laid his clothes neatly atop the chaise positioned near the window. Momentarily, he hesitated, before sliding under the blanket next to Penny. Since the bed was huge, he shouldn't have any trouble distancing himself. Reaching over to the lamp on top of his nightstand, he switched it off.

The open French doors of the balcony allowed a fresh cool breeze to sweep through the room. Restlessly, Sam turned, gazing at Penny's lovely face. Although her delicate features were enhanced by the light streaming in through the French doors, the moonlight also emphasized the subtle dark shadows under her eyes.

Sam's thoughts drifted back to their conversation from earlier that day. Penny had mentioned she'd had very little sleep over the last few nights. And not just because of the enormous amount of work involved with preparing for the wedding. Detailed arrangements had needed to be set up beforehand to enable her to leave her son.

Her son, Alex—whose behavior was becoming increasingly violent.

Sam frowned. What *exactly* did that mean? Although Danielle had answered as many of Sam's questions about Penny as she felt comfortable answering, she hadn't relayed much information about Alex.

Penny rarely spoke of him.

Although, so far, they hadn't let Sam in on the details, the Loughlins had supposedly devised a plan that could potentially alleviate Penny's difficulties with Alex.

Would Penny be offended by their manipulations on her behalf? Sam suspected that the effectiveness of the Loughlin's plan relied on some pretty important problems needing to be solved first, though. How would Penny earn her living? Where would Alex go to school? And, of course, Penny would have to *agree* to relocate to Crystal Rock, once Jake and Danielle revealed the particulars.

Propping his head up on the palm of his hand, Sam gazed at Penny, willing her to awaken.

But her breath feathered gently into the pillow.

Punching his pillow, he sighed, dropping his head back down. "How the hell am I gonna get to sleep?" Sam grumbled aloud.

For the next few hours, he tossed and turned until he finally slept.

Fitfully.

Six

Thrashing, Vanessa bolted upright, as she awakened abruptly. With a hand over her heart, she sucked in an uneven breath awaiting the beat of her heart to become steady. Having thought she'd outgrown the terrifying nightmares she'd had as a child, Vanessa reluctantly admitted to herself that along with her lack of sleep, the stress of these last few days had greatly affected her usually rigid self-control.

She'd alternately slept and watched television throughout the afternoon and evening, eventually feasting on the chicken noodle soup and microwave popcorn she'd discovered after another itemized search of Sam's kitchen.

Hastily, she froze. *Something* had awoken her. *Was that the sound of someone coming through the front door?* As her eyes adjusted to the darkness, she peered at the wall clock. It was half past midnight. Out in the living room, light steps clicked steadily across the surface of the wooden floor, echoing hollowly throughout the empty rooms. The rhythm and echo of the steps gradually faded away as whoever they belonged to must've begun walking down the hallway that led toward the bedrooms.

Well—apparently it was time to face Sam.

With a grimace, Vanessa smoothed out the creases of her silky nightshirt as she sat up on the couch. Slipping on her flip-flops, she stood up unsteadily from the couch, quickly straightening up her pillow and quilt.

Silently slinking through the kitchen, she sucked in a steadying breath before shoving open the swinging door of the dining room, mutedly lit by moonlight. But instead of the rustle of activity she'd expected to overhear from Sam's room, Vanessa was startled when the overhead light was suddenly switched on, in the bedroom where she'd stashed her own belongings.

Traveling quietly down the hallway and peering silently into the bedroom, Vanessa was surprised to discover the interloper was a woman, tall and slim. Although the woman in the room appeared to be somewhat attractive, her hair was frizzed into the tightest and most unflattering perm Vanessa had ever seen.

Could *this* be someone Sam was dating? She seemed a bit young.

Vanessa peeked back into the room. *Wow.* This woman might be having a gruesome hair day, but Vanessa couldn't find a single fault with her gown. With a lovely jeweled clasp offset at its waist, the sleeveless wrap dress of pale-yellow chiffon had a deep V-neck. The delicate ruffle edging the neckline layered stylishly down from the waist into a sophisticated fabrication of frothy delight. Borrowing a phrase from her quirky friend and business associate, Celeste Devoux—*it was a couturier's confection of perfection.*

Vanessa just *had* to get a closer look at that gown. Crossing her arms and propping her shoulder against the doorway, she waited patiently.

Unaware of Vanessa's presence, the woman stepped away from the closet with Vanessa's sundress in hand. Staring into the mirror attached inside the inner closet door, she held up the shimmering silver and lavender concoction, admiring herself from angle to angle.

"Honey," Vanessa drawled, southern style. "The color's great for your skin tone. But I'd have to advise you to keep your fingers out of the electrical sockets—if you actually decide to hook up that sterling silver collar around your neck, that is. I don't think your hair could stand another jolt."

Squeaking, the girl dropped the gown onto the ground. Wide-eyed, she stared at Vanessa in confusion. "*Who* are you?"

"Why, honey, I'm Vanessa—the owner of *that*." With a casual wave of her hand, Vanessa motioned at the sundress heaped in a bundle on the floor. "Who are *you*?"

"Oh, I'm Sophie," she responded, with a tipsy giggle. "We live across the street. Mom and I saw lights on earlier, and we usually keep an eye on the house for Sam." Reaching down onto the floor, she scooped up the hanger and began shaking out the gown. After lightly brushing it with her hand, she carefully hung the gown back into the closet.

"If that's the case, what are you doing in *here*?"

Sophie cleared her throat. "Well, we saw Sam earlier tonight, and he was with a pretty blonde. He usually spends his weekends at his cabin." Vanessa's earlier observation must've finally registered, because Sophie turned and studied her hair in the mirror. God, you're *right*. My hair *does* look awful," she moaned.

Vanessa stepped into the room. Although slightly intoxicated, the girl was actually rather lovely. Excepting for her eyes, practically turquoise in color, Sophie had a height and build relatively similar to her own. Reaching out, Vanessa pinched a few strands of Sophie's hair. "I think if you use a whole lot of conditioner and cut it shorter, it'd still look cute while it grows out." Vanessa cleared her throat before continuing, "So. No professional would've left your hair looking like that. Did a *friend* give you that perm?"

"I *thought* she was my friend, anyway," Sophie grumbled. "Come to think of it, Connie was always bad-mouthing me back in high school. I thought she was being a little *too* nice when I moved back home."

"Well, honey," Vanessa mumbled, distractedly, as her attention became focused on the details of Sophie's lovely gown, "when a girl's as pretty as you, some women are just naturally jealous." Raising a brow, Vanessa lifted her gaze and stared into Sophie's eyes. "And I'll bet you've never had a mean word for this *supposed* friend—right?

Missing the whole of Vanessa's question, Sophie appeared startled. "Me—pretty?"

"Why, sure, honey. Now, can I see how this fastens?" Back to studying the intricate details of the gown, Vanessa unhooked the jeweled clasp at Sophie's waist. With reverence, her fingers traveled delicately over the finish work of the hem and seams. The positioning of the darts was perfect, and the fit of the gown was flawless on Sophie. "Honey. *Where* did you get this gown?"

Appearing somewhat bemused, Sophie answered, "Why, I made it myself. I wanted something special to wear to the wedding today."

"*Wow*. I don't employ a single seamstress who sews as beautifully as you do," Vanessa observed, carefully reattaching the clasp.

"Thanks," Sophie replied, obviously puzzled. Attempting to close the closet door, she took a misstep with her heels and began to stumble.

When Vanessa moved in quickly to steady her, she noticed Sophie's stylish sandals. "Even those sandals work. *How* did you coordinate the colors?"

"Oh, I bought the shoes first—one of my big time splurges when I was living and working in Chicago. And then I found *just* the right fabric. I've had the sandals and fabric tucked away for almost a couple of years now, since back when I was still married."

Vanessa studied Sophie more closely. Married and apparently divorced? She seemed too young. "What about a bag?" Vanessa inquired.

"Oh—it's at home. But it's a woven clutch—I dyed it, to kind of a deep shade of aqua, and had the clasp made similar to the one that's on this dress."

"You *made* that too?"

"Well, *yeahhh*. It had to look *right* with the dress."

Vanessa turned her gaze on Sophie's stylish bracelet, and then on her earrings. Intricately cut stones in jeweled tones not only echoed the lemony color of her gown, but coordinated with the teal blues and purples featured in the clasp at her waist. "Honey, you're a natural at this. You *have* to be a stylist. *Who* do you work for?"

Sophie blinked. "Ah, the Crystal Rock Police Department? I'm their dispatcher and computer programmer—and kind of a secretary, too."

This time Vanessa blinked. "You've *got* to be kidding me."

But Sophie's alcohol induced buzz was most likely beginning to wear off, and she suddenly appeared worn and wobbly.

"Come on." Vanessa began to coax. "Why don't you come out into the kitchen with me? You can pull off those shoes for a while." Flipping off the lights in the bedroom, Vanessa steadied Sophie as she hobbled over the staple-ridden, wooden floor.

After reaching the kitchen, Sophie plunked down a large set of keys on the counter, before slipping off her shoes and settling back into her seat.

"How about some iced tea?" Vanessa asked. After discovering a large jar of instant that afternoon, she'd mixed up a pitcher.

"Doesn't Sam have some beer in the fridge?"

"Sure. But haven't you had enough to drink?"

"It's not like I'm driving. I usually don't drink this much, though."

"Yeah, honey. You don't appear to be a seasoned drinker. I don't drink much myself—mainly because of my weight."

"I'd sure love to look like *you*. I don't think I've ever met anyone as beautiful as you are."

Vanessa stilled, oddly moved by Sophie's comment. Women generally *did not* pay her compliments. She finally pulled a bottle of beer from the fridge. "You must not look at yourself in the mirror too often then, honey. You look enough like me to be my little sister," she observed. Pulling an opener from the drawer, she removed the cap from the bottle before handing over the beer to Sophie.

Sophie hesitated, appearing startled by Vanessa's observation. Finally, she snatched up the beer and took an uneasy swallow.

"Why drink that beer if you don't really like it?"

"Oh—I guess I just wanted to get a little drunk tonight."

"So," Vanessa proceeded, somewhat cautiously. "How long have you had the hots for Sam?"

Sophie groaned, suddenly looking embarrassed. "How'd ja figure?"

"I guess I just put two and two together. You mentioned that Sam was with some blonde today at the wedding you went to. Right? Then you said that you don't usually drink. So *seeing* him with the blonde must've set *that* off. Right again? Then, as soon as you got home, you came here."

Sophie chugged down another swallow of her beer before resting the bottle down with a distasteful grimace.

Vanessa continued, "So you assumed that the clothes, that were hanging in the closet, belonged to the woman that Sam was with tonight. You thought that you were checking out *her* stuff?"

"Yeah," Sophie answered, rather sheepishly. "They left together from the wedding, and I could tell Sam wasn't coming back here tonight. He usually leaves a few lights on."

"I presume that this blonde is closer in age to him than you are?" When Sophie nodded, Vanessa continued, "Oddly enough, Sam's rather traditional. It would've never worked out between you two. And not *just* because of the age difference," Vanessa suggested, gently.

Now slightly churlish, Sophie asked, "How do you know that?"

"Why, *because*, honey, as it just so happens, *I'm* still his wife."

Sophie's half-empty beer bottle slipped from her hand, and crashed into pieces on top of the counter.

Seven

Located on the northeast corner of Crystal Rock Lake, Sam's cabin was situated along the shoreline of an isolated inlet, so he had a glorious view of the sunrise. After knocking out one wall to open up the two small bedrooms of his loft, to create a spacious master suite, he'd added French doors leading out onto a balcony overlooking the lake, and a large floor to ceiling window.

Once he finished up with work on Fridays, he'd head out here immediately to the cabin. Although Sam had always been an early riser before acquiring the property, now he was lured awake by the beauty of the magnificent sunrise rising at daybreak. He'd spent most of this spring pounding out framing for the new addition. With the exterior framing and roofing nearly completed, he'd finally begun taking more time to relax. Sam spent many mornings sipping coffee outside on the deck, with a fishing line in the water.

So even after a few hours' sleep, his body was conditioned to awaken early.

No surprise there.

But something was different this morning.

The enticing fragrance of roses and lavender tickled his nose.

When was the last time he'd actually spent the entire night with a woman? Even Vanessa had refused to sleep in the same bed with him after their first year of marriage, complaining about *her* lack of sleep due to his erratic hours as a detective back in New Orleans.

Contentment invaded his senses. The French doors he'd cracked open last night continued to invite in a cool breeze. Obviously, sometime during the night Sam's body had gravitated toward the warmth, and he found himself wrapped around Penny.

With his hand covering her breast.

Her full, firm and, undoubtedly, lovely breast.

Also, a very *naked* breast.

And Sam was aroused.

Painfully aroused.

Carefully muffling a groan, Sam opened his eyes to the soft rosy glow of sunrise bathing the room. Totally aware of the rigid state of his arousal, nudging up, somewhat insistently, against Penny's bottom, he pulled his hand from her breast and eased away cautiously.

And then she stirred, turning slightly. Lovely, with her cheeks rosy and her hair tousled, she gazed at him with a hesitant smile. "I can't believe I slept so soundly," she whispered, scanning her surroundings. "How did I get *here*?"

With a rueful smile, Sam sat up. "You must've really been exhausted. I had to carry you upstairs."

Balancing on her arm, Penny scooted up to face him. Aware that Penny's eyes followed his when the comforter slithered down and suddenly exposed the luscious upper contours of her breasts, Sam swallowed. With several hooks undone, her strapless, flesh-colored bra gaped open. Even half asleep, Sam realized his hands had been *very* busy.

It took a conscious effort for him to focus his eyes upward. "I'm sorry, Penny. I guess I got a little carried away."

A delectable blush crept up over her cheeks as she steadily held his gaze. "Don't be sorry. I didn't exactly try to stop you. Did I?"

Laying a hand gently on either side of her face, Sam tangled his fingers through the silky lengths of her strawberry-blonde hair. With his lips merely a whisper from hers, Sam moved in closer. "I was afraid I might be taking advantage of you."

She nodded her dissent distractedly. Reaching out hesitantly, she ran the tips of her fingers through the hair on his chest, gently grazing his nipples.

With a contented sigh, he brushed his lips over hers. Needing to savor, Sam ran his tongue lightly down the length of her lovely bared collarbone, making her shiver when he reached the deep soft hollow of her throat. Gently, he pulled away, staring deeply into Penny's eyes. Filled with passion, the most exquisite blue eyes he'd ever known darkened into an even deeper blue.

With a groan, he covered her lips with his. Achingly aware of the softness of her skin and the fullness of her breasts, as her tightened nipples rubbed enticingly against his bare skin, he became lost in sensation.

When her lips parted helplessly with a shudder of anticipation, he deepened his kiss. His tongue gently explored the softness of her mouth and the silkiness of her tongue, as it swirled to tease his.

Had he ever been as aroused as he was right now?

Until, reluctantly disassembling, he became gradually aware of pounding footsteps enthusiastically rushing up the staircase from the living room below.

"Sam. Where are you?" A child's voice called out.

Somewhat dazed, Sam eyed the alarm clock on his nightstand. "How did I forget that it's Sunday?"

Most obviously confused, Penny quirked her brows.

Sam sighed resignedly. "Nat and the boys usually have breakfast with me on Sundays. It gives Olivia a chance to sleep in." Sam yanked up the comforter, tucking it under Penny's chin.

Sliding out from under the covers, Sam gazed down grimacing, painfully aware of his rigid state of arousal. Picking up one of the decorative pillows, swept off from the bed the night before, he casually held it before him as he approached the door.

Although Sam was able to stop Jarrod and Rodney in the hallway, both boys got a glimpse of Penny. "Wait out there a minute, guys. Will ya?"

Throwing the pillow back onto the floor, Sam stalked through the room until he stood before an antique bureau. Pulling out a pair of loose-fitting sweats from one of the drawers, he quickly slipped them on.

"If you had a sleepover, why didn't *we* get to come over?" Rodney demanded from outside the doorway.

Ignoring the question, as well as Penny's muffled snort of laughter, Sam returned to the hallway. Splitting them apart, Sam wrapped an arm over each boy's shoulders while subtly steering them back to the staircase.

In a loud hoarse whisper, Nat called out from the base of the staircase, "Sam—if we're in the way, we can go into town for breakfast."

Sam snorted, rolling his eyes. "Nah. Of course not. It's Sunday. I'll be down in a sec."

Releasing the boys, he gave them each a gentle shove. "Have your dad get the coffee started. We'll be down in a minute. Okay?"

"Alright," Jarrod answered agreeably, nudging a reluctant Rodney quietly down the staircase.

"I knew there was a reason I should've hauled the door back up here last week, after I finally refinished it," Sam muttered, eyeing the hinges remaining on the doorframe.

Penny's shoulders heaved under the comforter, while her face remained buried in her hands.

What in the hell was wrong? Was she *crying*? "Penny?" When she looked up with her hand covering her mouth, in an obvious effort to contain her laughter, Sam grinned, instantly relieved.

"You must have some really *great* sleepovers. But it looks like I might never get the chance to find out. First, I fall asleep, and then, at *exactly* the wrong time, we get company."

Sam snorted. Moving near the bed, he braced both arms against the headboard, to effectively hem her in. "Don't give up on me yet. We still have tonight. Don't we?" When Sam's eyes held hers, with a riveting unspoken promise of what was to come, Penny's laughter suddenly silenced.

Sighing resignedly, Sam dropped his knees onto the bed. "Let me help you." With his fingers sliding sensually over the delicate lace edging of her bra, he turned her gently. Fastening the closure from top to bottom, he was unable to help himself, and his fingers lingered deliberately on each hook, as they skimmed the silky-softness of her skin.

But when he came across the widened scar, slightly offset from the base of her spine, Sam's hand stilled. Several lines and stitch marks slashed through the mottled upraised layers of lumpy skin, covering the thickened scar with an x.

Penny tensed, not saying a word.

And then Sam knew.

Why Jake and Danielle, and yes, even Brian, were all so protective of Penny.

Tightly maintaining his self-control, he struggled to contain his sudden rage. *Who in the hell had done this to her?* With gentle fingers, he turned her face back to his. When her eyes refused to meet his, Sam reached for Penny's hand and squeezed it consolingly. For a long quiet moment, he rested his forehead against hers.

Slowly, Sam drew in a steadying breath before clearing his throat and waving a hand at the bureau. "You'll find some extra shorts, sweats, and a T-shirt in that dresser there. Mom dumped off all my stuff from high school here, when they rented out the house on Pine Street. Anyway, I'll go down and have coffee with Nat while you get dressed. If you're not comfortable, you don't have to join us. I'll give you about fifteen minutes and start breakfast if you don't come down. Alright?" Sam sighed, before slowly standing up from the bed.

Although Penny nodded her agreement, her eyes still refused to meet his.

Crossing the room, he opened another dresser drawer, and, after pulling out a T-shirt, he quietly left the room.

When Sam reached the bottom of the staircase, he attempted to plaster a smile on his face. Observing Nat had already set up coffee on the screened-in porch, strolling outside, he dropped down resignedly into a seat at the table.

Nat flashed Sam a sheepish grin. "Bad timing?"

"Nah." Picking up the coffee carafe, Sam reached for a mug.

Hesitantly, Nat continued, "Thought you didn't go in for one night stands anymore?"

"That's not what this is about." Calmly, Sam filled his mug with coffee.

"But she lives in New York—doesn't she?"

Finally turning to Nat, Sam stared him straight in the eyes. "Yeah, but there's a pretty good chance she might be moving here to Crystal Rock."

"What about her kid?"

Sam continued to hold Nat's gaze. "Him, too."

"But that's not what I meant, Sam." Nat cleared his throat before continuing, "I've heard her kid is mentally impaired. Are you sure that *you're* prepared to take on the challenge? You're not just dating the mom in a situation like this, you know."

"To tell you the truth Nat, we haven't really talked about *us* yet. I know you're just trying to help, but you don't have to worry about me. I've finally realized exactly what I want. Listen. Don't mention anything to Penny about moving here. Alright? It's not a sure thing yet. Jake and Danielle are making plans. I think they're trying to locate a school for Alex to attend, and there's some kind of business deal involved for Penny. But they're not cluing me in as to what they're up to."

"It just seems like she's got an awful lot of problems for you to take on if you're just planning on dating her. Doesn't it?" Nat frowned into his coffee mug, shaking his head.

Swallowing the remains of his coffee, Sam reached for the carafe. "Sam?"

Sliding Nat a side glance, Sam remained silent.

"I never understood why you married Vanessa. I mean, I know she was beautiful, but you two never had anything in common. She was just so damned cold and self-centered. But this woman—Penny—you've been talking about her constantly over these last few months. Why *her* all of a sudden?"

Nat continued to frown into his coffee.

Until, suddenly enlightened, he grinned, turning back to Sam. "*She's the one.* Isn't she? The one you talked about, that one night, after you and Vanessa began having problems?"

Startled, Sam nearly dropped his coffee as his eyes met Nat's. Before he could reply, the boys ran into the screened-in porch.

Rodney whined, "*Sam.* We were gonna get out the fishing poles but the boathouse is *locked!*"

"Hold on, guys. Jarrod, you know where the key is—on the hook in the kitchen?"

"Yeah. I'll get it, Sam. Just stay here for a minute, Rodney." Sliding open the screen door that led into the living room, Jarrod flew back and forth through the cabin, returning quickly with the key. Gently shoving Rodney outside onto the dock, Jarrod held open the screen door for Sam as he followed along after the boys. Jarrod unlocked the door for the boathouse before handing the key back to Sam.

Slipping inside the boathouse, Jarrod carefully reached up and pulled down two cane poles from their racks.

"Just remember to watch out for those hooks," Sam reminded both boys gently.

"I'll get the worms, Jarrod." Returning to the screened-in porch, Rodney pulled out a carton of night crawlers from the compact refrigerator, that'd been installed under the counter of the outdoor kitchen.

While Jarrod carefully twisted each pole to unwind its line, before adjusting hooks and bobbers, Rodney dug out two worms from the container. Once Jarrod picked up one of the squirming night crawlers and began to slowly thread it on his hook, it took all of Sam's patience to hold back and not attempt to assist. But, at nine-years old, Jarrod was old enough to be trusted. And it was important for Jarrod's self-esteem. With the move from New Orleans, Jarrod was having more of a problem adjusting and making friends, as opposed to his younger brother Rodney, who was much more outgoing.

Plus, Sam suspected the race issue was a much larger problem than Jarrod, or even Nat, let on. After all, Sam had grown up in Crystal Rock. There was a reason so few African-Americans had attempted to settle in this town.

Once he'd thrown both fishing lines into the water, Jarrod turned to Sam. "Can I help with breakfast?"

"Sure. Why don't you go pull out the fry pan, and maybe bring the paper plates and silverware out here to the table. I'll be back there in just a minute."

Taking control of Jarrod's pole, Sam calmly surveyed his surroundings. Sunlight teased the ripples on the lake. Sipping his coffee, Sam concentrated on the tall slim bobber, jerking gently up and down. Perching precariously on the very tip of the bobber, laced in a vibrant teal blue, a delicate dragonfly fluttered in protest.

Sam sighed contentedly. At that moment, there was no place else on earth he'd rather be. Wryly, he admitted that his surroundings alone weren't responsible for his sudden contentment. He suspected that Penny had always been the piece of the puzzle that'd been missing from his life.

After ten minutes without a bite on his line, Sam decided it was time for breakfast. "Can you handle both poles, Rod?"

"Sure, Sam." Balancing his body loosely on the edge of the bench, built alongside the railing, Rodney flashed Sam a toothy grin as he settled his pole into two inverted hooks, screwed into the top of the deck's railing. With an affectionate smile, Sam surrendered his pole to Rodney.

Distractedly, Nat glanced up from his paper when Sam stepped back inside. Sam smiled wryly, obviously disappointed. "I was hoping Penny would join us." He helped himself to another cup of coffee. "By the way, I had a visitor last night."

Nat waggled his brows suggestively. "Yeah. I think I kind of realized that already, Sam."

With a snort, Sam rolled his eyes. "An *uninvited* visitor—slinking around outside. I chased him away before I could get a good look at him. He had a canoe or rowboat pulled in at the landing."

Nat's comic expression suddenly turned serious. "Suppose it has something to do with our robberies?"

Sam answered thoughtfully, "I don't know. Maybe, maybe not. This person was alone. I don't know that these guys are sophisticated enough to send out a front man to scout the layout."

"Yeah. I agree. These robberies seem random. Although I think that whoever's behind them already knows what they're after before they strike. Possibly because they're already been an *invited* guest at each targeted property? I'd guess someone local, almost definitely, since the robberies began in March. I still think we're dealing with teenagers. Certainly has to be more than one involved, though."

"I agree. Think we might be able to find a teen who'd be willing to snitch? And maybe keep us informed about any kids making trouble at school, or living in the area?"

"What about the Callahan kid?"

"You mean Dan Callahan? Yeah—he's about the right age. Plus, he's a good student and plays baseball, too. Probably has a lot of friends—so he socializes a lot. He'd be a good choice. I'll talk to his parents first though, before I approach him."

"So," Nat continued. "Who was *here*?"

"I couldn't see much last night. What've I got *here* that anyone would want, except for construction materials? I need to study the landing in daylight, and check out my locks on the outbuildings." Chugging down the last of his coffee, Sam stood up. "Guess I'll go see what Jarrod's up to and then get breakfast started."

As he slowly approached the kitchen, Sam became aware of a low thread of conversation.

"So—what do *you* think, Jarrod?" Penny was questioning.

"I don't know," he sighed. "I sure wish they'd let me be friends."

Deliberately, Sam halted in the dining room, keeping out of sight. Nat strolled unhurriedly into the dining room behind him, carrying the empty coffee carafe. Purposely holding him back, Sam lifted a finger up to his lips and motioned at the kitchen, rolling his eyes.

Aware of a mixture of enticing aromas wafting through the air, Nat was smiling.

Until he suddenly became aware of the depth of conversation drifting from the kitchen. His smile disappeared as his concentration turned intense.

Penny was gently admonishing. "I don't know, Jarrod." Bluntly, she continued, "Answer this for me—do you really want to be friends with kids that call you names because of the color of your skin?"

Jarrod sighed, answering bleakly in a hollow voice, "No, I guess not. It's just that I had lots of friends back home. Cal hasn't even written me once—even though I've written *him* three times!"

"I've heard that boys are usually worse at writing letters than girls are."

"Yeah, I guess. School's out too, so Cal has John and Red and Richie to hang out with now. It's just that Dad said our family would be *happier* here."

"What, exactly, did these boys from school do, besides calling you names?"

"Well—first someone squirted ketchup in my locker at school and ruined *all* my homework. Then my boots went missing. And then someone rubbed *something* all over my new winter coat."

Sam peeked into the kitchen. With Penny's attention focused between the stovetop and Jarrod, Jarrod's face was fully visible to Sam.

Jarrod refused to meet Penny's eyes, so she asked gently, "*What* do you think that it was?

"It smelled like dog poop." Determinedly, Jarrod swiped away his tears. "I hid the coat from my mom, and then I washed it in the washing machine the next day, when she was over helping Mrs. Edmonds."

Penny turned to Jarrod and blinked. "You know how to use the washing machine?"

"I used to watch my mom when she used it, and sometimes, back home in New Orleans, Rodney had accidents. He didn't want my mom to know because she used to get upset a lot."

"Upset with Rodney?"

"Oh, no. With my aunt, and then with my grandpa. He had a disease that made him forget everything. He used to just walk out of the house. Mom and Dad would take us in the car to go looking for him. My mom used to cry a *lot*."

Penny answered Jarrod reassuringly. "You know—I think that if I had all of that to worry about Jarrod, I'd cry a lot too. It was so nice of you to try to help your mom and make it easier for her. But if you're having trouble with these kids, I really think your mom and dad would want to know. If I were your mom, *I'd* want to know."

"I tried to tell my teacher, but he didn't believe me."

"Hmm." Penny frowned. "What was your teacher's name?

"Mr. Williams."

"Well, just wait. I bet by the end of this summer, you'll have at least one real friend."

"I hope so." Rodney sighed. "If Alex were here, would *he* be my friend?"

"Well—even though Alex is sixteen, he'd love to have a real friend. Most kids are kind of scared of him, though."

"Why?"

"Well—it's kind of hard to explain. He has a bad temper and, sometimes, he gets pretty mad. But he can't really help himself."

"Why?"

Letting loose an obvious sigh of relief, Penny grinned when Sam entered the kitchen with the coffee carafe in his hand. "Jarrod was just helping me out with breakfast."

Four burners were lit on the stove. Bacon and sausage fried in one pan while hash brown potatoes sizzled in another. Penny busily cracked eggs into a bowl as onions, peppers, and mushrooms sautéed in another fry pan.

Sam hid a smile as he glared at Jarrod. "I see you talked Penny into cleaning out the fridge."

Jarrod snickered guiltlessly. "She just asked me what we usually ate for breakfast."

"I was surprised to see you had so much food in the fridge," Penny said, adjusting one of the burners on the stove.

"Like I said last night, Mom and Craig come out here occasionally. And I always cook for myself when I'm working here on the weekends." Laying down the coffee carafe, Sam proceeded to make another pot of coffee after noticing the pot was empty.

"I thought I'd divide the eggs into scrambled with cheese, and then make a large omelet, too." After scooping the onions, peppers and mushrooms from the pan, she carefully poured half of the whipped eggs into a sizzling pan, and the rest into another. With quiet efficiency, Penny laid a cover over one of the pans while gently stirring the eggs in another. She added a large cup of shredded cheddar to the eggs, once they were nearly hardened. After lightly stirring the eggs when the cheese was melted, she tipped the contents of the pan into an empty bowl.

"How can the food coming out of *those* pans look *so* good?" Bemused, Sam studied an ancient cast-iron fry pan she'd been using, as well as an assortment of rusted pans and utensils. They'd been occupying the cabin's kitchen for almost as long as he could remember.

"Sam's eggs always taste like rubber," Jarrod observed.

"Gee, thanks kid," Sam grumbled.

With a silvery laugh, Penny continued to work. Fascinated, Sam watched Penny uncover the other fry pan and flip the large omelet. Lightly covering half of the omelet with the peppers, onions, and mushrooms she'd sautéed earlier, she sprinkled out shredded cheese before replacing the lid and removing it from the burner. Switching off the heat for another burner, she forked bacon and sausage onto a large porcelain platter covered with paper towels. Lifting the lid from the fry pan she'd set aside, she carefully loosened the unadorned half of the omelet from the pan, neatly flipping it over.

Penny turned to Jarrod. "We moved an awful lot when I was a kid. Since we were always provided with a place to live cause my dad was a minister, the parishioners furnished most of our supplies. Sometimes we had brand new pots and pans and dishes, but a lot of the time our supplies were donated. It would hurt their feelings if we didn't use what the parishioners provided—especially since the standard of living was really poor in some of the places where we lived. I think I began helping out at soup kitchens and church buffets when I was only about six-years old."

Quite a different upbringing from his own, Sam mused, somewhat startled. And then, all of a sudden, he abruptly became aware of the cling of his twenty-year old athletic shorts on the curves of Penny's bottom. Unable to help himself, he moved up behind her, sliding his arms around her waist. His voice was hoarse when he asked, "What can I do?"

With her cheeks already rosy from the heat of the stove, her blush became deeper. "Maybe you could carry out the orange juice and coffee to the porch? You kind of distract me," she muttered.

When Sam gently nipped on her ear, Penny shivered.

Unable to hide his fascination, Jarrod stared at Penny and Sam. "Sam, are you gonna *marry* Penny?"

In the process of flipping the potatoes, Penny jerked her hand unconsciously, sending the spatula flopping onto the floor.

Sam grinned. *God, she was jumpy.* But Penny was definitely as much aware of him as he was of her. "Oh, you just never know, Jarrod."

Jarrod giggled. Instead of waiting for Sam, he grabbed the juice and a bunch of paper plates and headed toward the porch.

As Penny eyed Sam with stunned confusion, he reluctantly pulled away. Smiling widely, Sam reached down to pick up the spatula from the floor, and rinsed it under running water before handing it back over to Penny. Gathering up a basket filled with plastic silverware, napkins, and condiments, he snatched up the bowl of scrambled eggs, and began whistling as he passed by Jarrod, who'd returned to retrieve more food.

Soon, Jarrod followed Sam outside, onto the porch, clutching a long tray with sausage and bacon in one hand, and a neatly sectioned omelet in the other. Carrying a bowl of hash brown potatoes and a fresh carafe of coffee, still appearing to be rather dazed, Penny trailed closely behind them.

"Wow. This is a regular feast." Nat beamed. "Even Livie doesn't go this crazy over breakfast."

Just as everyone began seating themselves around the table, the silence of the inlet was interrupted by the steady drone of a small boat motor.

Glancing across the pier at the water, Sam stepped out from the porch. Shading his eyes from the sun, he made his way toward the narrow pier on the opposite side of the boathouse, quietly strolling past Rodney.

Jeff Thompson called out from his fishing boat. "Hey. Am I too late for breakfast?"

Sam called back. "Just in time." When Jeff tossed out a rope, Sam quickly looped it around one of the hooks screwed into the pier. "Surprised you're out this early, after all the activity yesterday."

"Couldn't sleep." For a moment, Jeff lost his smile as his expression turned grim. No longer the easygoing, and rather reckless, young friend Sam had grown up with, Jeff *still* struggled with nightmares, even though more than thirteen years had passed since his return from Vietnam. War had changed him. And that was an understatement.

"C'mon." Giving Jeff a hand as he stepped out from his boat, Sam gently nudged him along the pier. "There's lots to eat today.

"Hey, ya, Rod. How's the fishing?" Bending down, Jeff rubbed the top of Rodney's head affectionately.

Rodney sighed. "Not so good."

"Well, you don't wanna miss breakfast. Need any help with the poles?"

"That's okay. I'll get 'em." Once Rodney had carefully inserted his pole into a second set of hooks screwed into the top of the railing, he followed Sam and Jeff up onto the porch.

Surprised to see a woman seated at the table, Jeff halted and grinned, somewhat wickedly. "Introduce me, Sam."

Penny was definitely startled as she struggled with a smile.

Sam rolled his eyes. Jeff's thick dark hair was laced with gray, and buzzed into a military cut. Although leaner and slightly shorter than Sam, Jeff was muscular and fit. Even at forty, Jeff had always been an obvious flirt—he had an easygoing personality appealing to women. But Jeff was much different now than he'd been as a teenager—the realities of war had significantly altered his slightly irresponsible attitude toward life.

Settling back against the doorframe with his legs and arms crossed, Sam was suddenly irritated when he realized he was *jealous.* "Penny. I don't know if you remember Jeff from high school? He wasn't at the wedding yesterday."

Standing up, she grinned, holding out her hand. "Sure. I remember."

"*High school?* I don't think I'd ever forget a face like yours." Jeff's words belied his meaning as his eyes roamed appreciatively over her.

"Well, I was a little younger than you two." Penny responded frankly. "I also hadn't developed quite as-uh-memorably as most of the other girls my age had by thirteen or fourteen."

"Wait a second." Jeff blew out a long, low whistle. "You're not *that* Penny?"

"*Jeff,*" Sam reprimanded gruffly. "You'd better help yourself to the food before it's all gone.

When Jeff finally noticed that Nat and the boys each had their paper plates loaded with food, his eyes widened in astonishment as he gazed at the feast spread out upon the table. "Geez, Sam. Not your usual fare. Everything actually looks *edible.*"

Sam snorted, and everyone laughed. With a gentle nudge, Sam shoved Jeff into a chair, before he dropped back down into his.

Sam was still frowning when Jarrod grinned, sneaking a side glance at Penny. "Told ya."

Penny's eyes met Sam's, and she grinned.

Sam finally admitted, smiling wryly, "Penny did all the cooking."

"No kidding," Nat added dryly, obviously enjoying a perfectly crisped slice of bacon.

The conversation halted while everyone went to work on the food.

Appreciatively, Jeff eyed Penny, several minutes later. "Wow. If you ever need a job, you know where to find me." Crumbling up his napkin, he dropped it onto his plate.

Presenting a cheerful smile to Jeff, she was sure to include Sam. She'd obviously noticed Sam's irritation. "I love to cook, but I don't think I'd enjoy it as much, if I actually had to do it for a living."

Dragging a lined plastic trash can next to the table, Nat began scooping up the dirtied paper plates. "I noticed that you guys were really busy last night, when we drove by the Tap after the wedding," Nat said to Jeff.

Jeff had taken over the family business, the Crystal Rock Tap, almost fifteen years ago. Struggling at the time under his father's management, the business had been turned around by Jeff's simple, yet effective, reorganization efforts of modernizing, changing the menu, and adding entertainment. Of course, Sam had to admit grudgingly that Jeff's easygoing personality had a lot to do with its success. He'd made a point to interact and get to know his customers. Plus, he rarely took time off.

"We were packed. I sure didn't expect it—with that wedding going on at Dragonfly Pointe," Jeff answered.

"You must've got the carryover from town. Most of the locals were only invited for the wedding and afternoon reception, while the out of town guests received invitations for the evening too." Sam added. He snatched up the last slice of bacon from the platter.

Penny stood up and began clearing the serving platters from the table, while Sam and Nat swept the remaining disposables into the trash. After Nat and the boys wiped down the table, Sam, Penny, and Jeff each settled back in their chairs to enjoy a final cup of coffee.

"Come on boys." Nat began to head indoors. "Time for us to clean up the kitchen." Without a complaint, the boys followed their father into the cabin.

"Nat always insists," Sam said, in response to Penny's inquisitive stare.

"They're such good kids," Penny acknowledged.

"Yeah, they are. I think they might be having more trouble fitting in here than I thought, though. Rodney's made a few friends, but Jarrod seems to be having a lot more problems than Nat and Olivia realized."

"Well—at least they'll be aware of it now."

Sam reached out and laid his hand over Penny's. "I think that Nat was impressed by your advice to Jarrod."

"Was Nat listening, too? That's good. I know how hard it can be to fit in. I spent most of my childhood moving from town to town. Even for me, it was really difficult making new friends."

"It's tough for Sam and me to envision that, being born and raised here," Jeff admitted.

For a few more minutes they sipped their coffee in companionable silence.

"Well, I guess I'd better get a move on." Jeff sighed, slugging down the rest of his coffee. "I still haven't figured out if it's good—or bad—that I decided to open up the Tap for weekend breakfasts."

Sam asked, "Has the breakfast business been good, then?"

"We started out slow, but it sure has picked up since spring. Not enough for me to risk opening up for breakfast on weekdays, though. Lunch and supper is enough for me to handle. Seems like I'm always at that bar."

"You need to hire an assistant."

"Ah, I wish. Julie's college expenses are getting up there, and *now* she's talking about going out of state. A school in Illinois. She wants to go into Special Education."

Penny appeared startled. "Well, that's an interesting coincidence. I have a son who *is* in Special Ed," she observed.

Jeff raised a brow. "Rough?"

"It can be," Penny acknowledged, with a tight nod of her head. But she wasn't willing to open up in front of a stranger, Sam finally realized, when Penny continued to remain silent.

"Well, Penny, it was good to see you again." Standing up from his chair and reaching for Penny's hand, Jeff squeezed it reassuringly. "Thanks for a great breakfast. I don't think I'll ever be able to choke down Sam's food again, without thinking about how *good* your food was."

"Ha, ha," Sam retorted, mockingly.

Penny's silvery laughter echoed through the inlet, as Sam trailed behind Jeff on their way to the dock.

Jeff hopped into his boat. "You always knew, didn't you?"

Bending down, Sam unhooked the rope that was securing Jeff's boat to the dock. "What?" Distracted, Sam wound up the rope, and attached it to the fishing boat's bow.

"That she'd grow into a beauty." Jeff threw Sam a teasing grin. "I always knew that you had it *bad* for her. Is she divorced?"

"Nah, widowed. Husband MIA seventy-four or five."

"Wow, seems like she and me got a lot in common."

"Well, that's too damned bad—she's *mine*," Sam growled.

Jeff appeared highly entertained. "It's about time you did something about it, then. I could never figure out why you were running around with all those other women in high school when it was obvious Penny was the only one you really wanted. Remember how we used to follow her all over town after Stu Arends began stalking her?"

Sam appeared sheepish. "The guy was a pervert. I used to watch him suck up to Penny's mom and dad. But *I* knew what he was *really* up to. His whole damn family was strange."

Jeff raised a brow. "Always wondered—how'd he end up with that black eye?"

"I caught him peeping into windows. Remember all the complaints from women in town?"

"That was *him*?"

"Yep. Followed him enough, I caught him in the act—more than once. But it was my word against his, until I set up a trap with one of Jim Callahan's deputies. The family moved away not too long after that."

Jeff shook his head good-naturedly, bobbing a nod toward Penny. "How bad's her son?"

"She hasn't told me about him herself, but Danielle says he's mentally impaired as well as autistic. And, as if that wasn't bad enough, he's an insulin dependent diabetic, too." Sam asked hesitantly, "You're not gonna to try to discourage me from seeing her? Nat did."

Jeff answered dryly, "I think that you're old enough to make your own decisions."

"Thanks, man."

"I do have one observation."

Sam groaned.

But then Jeff held up a staying hand. "I think that it takes a person with a lot of courage to raise a kid with so many problems. A lot of parents give up on these kinds of kids and just drop them into institutions. Although some of these places, I guess, aren't as bad as they used to be. But I think it says a lot about Penny's character, given that she's a single parent, since I know what it's been like for *me,* bringing up Julie all on *my* own." Jeff shook his head, obviously considering. "*What kind of a life does Penny really have?* She must really love that kid. Because that's probably all he'll *ever* really be Sam, just a kid."

After, what had to be, Jeff's longest speech on record, Sam's eyes misted up suspiciously.

Clearing his throat awkwardly, Jeff finally grinned. "Not what you expected, huh?" With a quick tug of its handle, the motor roared to life. Waving lazily with his hand, Jeff shoved off, and began cranking up the engine's speed.

By the time Sam returned to the porch, Nat and the boys were relaying their goodbyes to Penny.

Nat was squeezing Penny's hand. "We'll see you tonight then." With a side glance at the boys, Nat seemed reassured that they were out of hearing range. "Thanks for your help with Jarrod, earlier. I had no idea he was keeping so much from Livie and me."

"I just hope that what *I* said was what *you* would've."

"Definitely."

Sam thumped Nat on the back reassuringly. "We'll catch you later."

After an emotional nod of his head at Penny, Nat slipped through the door.

"Well." Sam cleared his throat, standing in the doorway. "Finally alone."

Penny smiled. "And it's almost time for me to get back to the inn."

"It figures." Sam grinned. "Why don't you go ahead and get your stuff together, while I put away the fishing poles and lock up?"

"Alright. You don't think I'll attract too much attention, if I return to the inn dressed like this—do you?"

Studying her curves in his ancient, form-fitting T-shirt—that claimed she was cool to be in school—Sam's gaze grew heated. "Nah. I think you look adorable."

She grinned wryly, pausing from straightening the chairs around the table.

With a sigh of resignation, Sam made his way outside, onto the deck. Pulling up both poles, he pinched the night crawlers from their hooks and dropped them into the water. Neatly twisting the line of each pole, he carried them back into the boathouse and returned them up onto their racks.

He'd lock up the boathouse again, he decided. There wasn't anything of much value inside, but why invite a theft? He'd better study the landing and double-check the locks on the garage, too, before he forgot.

Sam carefully made his way down the well-worn path, approaching the landing. He definitely needed to make an effort to clear the brush soon. There'd been more rain than usual this past spring, and with his spare time taken up by construction, Sam had neglected the surrounding property.

Despite the heavy earlier spring rains, at present, the ground was dry, Sam discovered. It'd been nearly three weeks since it'd rained. Although there were a few large holes in the softer ground near the water's edge, there appeared to be no visible footprints. The gouges had most likely been dug by the oars from the intruder's boat, as he shoved away from shore. Grimacing, Sam continued to study the trampled area.

And then suddenly, a shiny flash of silver caught his eye. Since the silver and cellophane wrappers that were scattered near the base of a maple sapling appeared to be fresh, he'd better collect them properly, he decided, returning to the path. Long ago, he'd learned that even one small clue could make a difference sometimes in breaking a case.

Glancing upward from the deck, Sam called out. "Penny?"

Penny quickly strode out on the balcony above.

"Are you in a big hurry?"

"Nah," she answered. "I'll just need a quick shower and a change of clothes, when I get back."

"Will another half an hour be okay?"

"Sure. What's up?"

"I'll fill you in later."

"Okay. Take your time."

Distractedly, Sam entered the cabin, retrieving the keys for his truck.

A few minutes later, Sam was heading back down the path, on his way toward the landing, with a box of assorted evidence collection materials in hand. As Crofton's chief of police, this same kit had traveled with him in his squad car.

Carefully resting the box on the ground, he grabbed a disposable camera from inside and eyed its expiration date. Reassured, he prepared the camera for use.

First, he snapped a few quick pictures from various angles. Pulling out forceps and two evidence bags from the box, he carefully dropped the foil wrapper into one bag and the cellophane into another. Sam searched his mind, oddly troubled. Something about that faint scent of butterscotch prodded his memory.

After repacking his supplies, he headed back up the path. The evidence bags would have to go to the state forensic lab for prints. Although Sam, Terry and Nat had attempted to collect evidence from the robbery sites, because most of the burglaries had occurred at vacation homes, it was difficult to rule out prints from guests and home-owners. The best they could hope for were duplicate prints from multiple properties.

And it could be weeks before they had results from the lab.

Of course, Sam wouldn't be surprised to discover the perpetrators had been intelligent enough to wear gloves, anyway.

When Sam unloaded the box into his truck, he discovered Penny's teal-blue gown hanging inside.

Making a quick trip down the driveway to inspect the garage, Sam slipped completely around the structure and examined the locks on the windows and doors.

The garage appeared to be secure.

When he entered the cabin, Penny was fumbling around in the kitchen, attempting to neatly stack the pans and utensils that Nat and the boys had washed up.

"I'll be ready in about five minutes," he responded, to her inquiring smile.

In the living room, Sam made a cursory study of windows and doors. Slipping out onto the patio, he locked the screen door leading out onto the deck. Returning indoors, he made sure that both the patio and entry were secured before running upstairs to slip into a pair of jeans.

Double-checking the latch on the French doors, and tugging at each window, Sam was relieved when the locks held securely in place. Scooping up shoes and the pieces from his tux, he slipped into a pair of worn leather sandals, before hooking his holster loosely over his shoulder.

Once he returned downstairs, he found Penny awaiting him on the landing of the back steps. Obviously enjoying the antics of a squirrel, she laughed softly as the squirrel kept peeking out at her from behind the tree.

She looked *so damned cute* wearing his shabby old shorts and his T-shirt.

All of a sudden, he'd give *anything* to be able to go back upstairs. Why had he wasted these last few minutes, when he could've been spending more time with Penny?

Because, he admitted, thirty minutes wouldn't have been *nearly* enough time with her. Abandoning the pile of clothes that he was carrying onto the steps, he reached over and pulled her into his arms. She was obviously startled, but her body was warm and welcoming. When his mouth covered hers, she responded with an enthusiasm that was deliciously arousing. But way too conscious of the approach of mid-morning, Sam sighed, reluctantly pulling away. Bemused, as well as delightfully disheveled, Penny asked "What was that for?"

"Just something to think about," Sam growled, his voice uneven.

Her smile was a little shaky. "I have a feeling I'll be thinking about *that* for the rest of the day," she mumbled unsteadily.

Sam blinked, barking out a laugh. Quickly scooping up his clothes before reaching for her hand, he walked her down the stairs and over to the truck.

They both remained amazingly quiet on their short trek back to the inn.

Sam finally snuck a side glance at Penny when he turned into the parking lot. "How about I pick you up at five? We'll probably eat around six or six-thirty."

"That'll be fine. We should be finished with the cleanup by then," Penny answered, almost shyly. "So what was going on earlier, when you were following the path through the woods?"

Frowning, Sam switched on his two-way radio. "This past spring, several of the more exclusive homes located near the lake were robbed. For some reason, last night, someone had a boat pulled into my landing."

Sam would've said more, but just as he was attempting to secure a parking place, loud static emitted from the two-way radio. Penny was obviously startled. She straightened up attentively in her seat when Deputy Terry Lutz's voice jumped out from the station's radio dispatch. "Sam. Are you available?"

Sam punched a button before lifting and cradling the small radio handset. "I'm here, Terry. Give me a minute."

"You can just drop me here." Penny reached for the gown, hanging in the back seat. "It'll be easier for you to get back on the road, if you don't have to park."

Since the parking lot was relatively congested, Sam was forced to pull up a rather lengthy distance from the entrance. Before Sam could even utter goodbye, Penny had slipped out from inside the truck. She rushed down the long pathway leading up onto the wraparound porch.

What the heck? Sam struggled for a glimpse of her.

Another vehicle pulled up behind him, and the driver began impatiently honking his horn. Still puzzling on Penny's hurry to escape, Sam pulled forward reluctantly and spun around in the parking lot.

Turning onto the main road and making a sharp left, he skidded into the driveway of the Loughlin's lakehouse. Sam radioed back with his truck still in motion. "I'm here, Terry."

"We've had another robbery, Sam. The old Peterson place—across from the campgrounds, on the Stone Lake access."

"How bout I meet you out there in about forty-five minutes?"

"Gotcha. Over and out."

Eight

Once Sophie had returned home with her hurt feelings soothed, Vanessa had spent the remainder of the night tossing and turning on the couch.

By six in the morning, after finally giving up on sleep, she was up sipping coffee with Sam's newspaper in hand. But this local edition wasn't current on national news. After a detailed study of the paper, she headed back into the bedroom to retrieve the clothing she'd worn yesterday. Unfortunately, she'd been limited on her selection of casual wear, when she'd been scrambling to gather clothing before escaping New Orleans.

After enjoying a lengthy soak in Sam's jetted tub, she dressed before arranging her hair and applying her makeup. Fortunately, her battered set of luggage had still been loaded with personal items packed from a previous buying trip.

Having decided she'd most likely be contacted sometime today, Vanessa was prepared.

Or as prepared as she could be, that is.

After her father's death, *what* would they expect from her now? The longer she waited, the more apprehensive she was becoming.

What would happen to Gerard International? And her boutiques? She'd *have* to inherit everything. Wouldn't she?

But what if the terms of Peter Gerard's will left Vanessa's inheritance guided solely by the dictates of his business partners? And what if *they* were behind her father's death?

Still—there might be something she'd be able to do, to gain a modicum of control over the situation. After all, she had a legitimate fear for her own mortality.

And not only because there was a killer running around loose. After receiving the fateful results of the blood tests she'd finally, reluctantly, submitted to, whatever happened, there wasn't much chance that the future would be kind to her anyway. Was there?

"Hello. I'm back." Sophie's lilting voice carried through the living room into the kitchen. "I have breakfast." Plowing in through the swinging door, Sophie entered the kitchen with her arms loaded up with an assortment of baked goods.

"What'd you do, honey—rob a bakery?" Vanessa asked dryly.

Sophie laughed. "Since my parents actually *own* a bakery...I didn't have to." Resting the boxes on the counter, she slipped out a pair of sandals from the shopping bag that was hanging over her arm. "I even remembered your shoes," she said, handing them over to Vanessa.

"Cute." Dropping them onto the floor, Vanessa stepped into the stylish white sandals. "We even wear the same size. How coincidental is that?

"I counted my shoes when I moved back home. Would you believe I own more than fifty pairs?"

Vanessa grinned. "Honey, that's *nothing. I own over a hundred.* I'm starved. What've you got in those boxes? Sam doesn't have a whole lot of anything."

"My mom's famous cinnamon rolls, some breakfast crepes, and even a fresh baked loaf of bread." After opening up the boxes, Sophie untwisted a tie on the bread. "I'll cook. My mom even sent us some eggs and orange juice. I told her that you were a friend of Sam's, who showed up a few days early, and you haven't had a chance to talk to him because of the wedding."

It was surprising to Vanessa that law enforcement hadn't actually caught up with her by now. Of course, they might've already contacted

Sam before she'd even arrived. "I'm glad that *you* can cook—cause *I* sure don't know how."

Sophie appeared startled as she readied a pan on the stove. "I don't think I've ever known anyone who doesn't know how to cook."

"Well, honey, you sure do now," Vanessa answered, good-naturedly. Amazingly, even someone as jaded as herself couldn't help but *like* Sophie.

Slipping into easy conversation, Vanessa helped herself to a couple of cinnamon rolls as Sophie scrambled the eggs and set the toaster in motion.

"That was really good, honey," Vanessa drawled, several minutes later. "Usually I watch my fat and cholesterol."

Sophie appeared to be doubtful as she studied Vanessa. "I don't know if you really need to. You might be a little *too* thin."

Vanessa sighed. "Yeah, life hasn't been treating me too well lately."

Gathering dishes and silver along with the dirty fry pan, Sophie loaded and engaged the dishwasher. After quickly wiping off the counter, Sophie poured herself the last cup of coffee, and settled into the stool next to Vanessa's.

"So," Vanessa began. "Tell me a little about this wedding. Why was it such a big deal?"

"It was the first wedding to take place at the new Dragonfly Pointe Inn. The inn's finally reopening after being completely renovated. Jake Loughlin—he grew up here—married Danielle Reardon."

"Danielle Reardon. Hmm. Why does that name sound so familiar?"

"Danny used to be a model. And then she was a vocalist, in a band that was kind of famous—back when I was still in high school."

Vanessa stilled, staring at Sophie. "*The* Danielle Reardon? No wonder why the entire town was deserted yesterday. I've even read about the details of their wedding down in Louisiana."

"Yeah, it was huge. Our whole family was invited," Sophie observed.

"Where does Sam fit into the picture?"

"He's a friend of Jake's—so he was an usher."

Astonished, Vanessa shook her head. "What does this Jake *do*?"

"Well, Jake owns the Dragonfly Pointe Inn—and a bunch of other hotels too, I guess. But the kicker is, he used to work for the FBI."

"So how did Sam hook up with Jake?"

"I'm not really sure, because I didn't move back to Crystal Rock until last November, but I think that they worked together on a case last summer and ended up becoming friends."

"Well." Vanessa appeared thoughtful. "Come to think of it, Sam might've worked with a *John Loughlin*, from the FBI, several years ago in Louisiana. After we were married, he couldn't really talk about his work. But he used to tell me a little about some of the people he worked *with*." Then reluctantly recalling her purpose here in Crystal Rock, Vanessa continued guardedly, "So, *who's* the blonde that Sam was with at the wedding?"

"I really couldn't tell you," Sophie replied, obviously unhappy. "I could swear he wasn't seeing anyone. I mean, I work with him every day. If anyone would know, it'd be me. Wouldn't it?"

"Okay. I have a proposition for you, honey." Meeting her eyes, Vanessa knew she had Sophie's complete attention. "You know my clothes that you were admiring—in Sam's closet back there?"

Sophie nodded her head up and down.

"You get me some information about this blonde—her name, where she's from, or anything else that seems to be important—and those clothes will all be *yours*."

"You mean that designer suit, and even *that sundress?*"

"Sure. That suit is brand new. Everything else is a few seasons old, but they're *all* designer. Even my handbags. Have you ever heard of Celeste Devoux? She designed that sundress just for me."

"Really?" Sophie shoved out her hand, and eagerly shook Vanessa's. "It's a deal. I suppose, I'd better get home. Our entire family gets together every Sunday for dinner, and a few of our cousins are visiting. Do you want some company later tonight? I can rent some movies. Maybe I'll know something about the blonde by then. My mom and dad both spoke with her and Sam at the wedding." Sophie appeared sheepish. "But when I saw her with Sam, I was a little too bent out of shape to go over and meet her."

"Sure, honey. I know you're disappointed. You probably designed that gown of yours just to snag Sam's attention—didn't you? When you come back later, we can do something about that frizzy hair of yours, too. That should cheer you up."

Sophie smiled agreeably. Slipping from her stool and preparing to depart, she hesitated as she stared at the shopping bag still laying on the counter. "I almost forgot. I brought along my sketchbook."

"You actually have a sketchbook? Let me see." Vanessa reached for the album Sophie pulled out from inside the bag. Laying it down on the counter and sifting through the pages eagerly, she examined each sketch systematically. Thoughtfully, she tapped a finger on a detailed drawing of Sophie's shorter-length, simplified wrap dress that was sleek and fitted. "This could be your signature." The following pages displayed stylish combinations using the same basic design. Paired with slacks as well as Capri's, and also offering a varied selection of sleeves, the gown had been transformed by adjusting its length. "You've designed clothing for virtually *every* body type. I've always felt that the plus size market's been neglected. *All* women should have stylish options available." The last few pages of the sketchbook hosted an array of evening wear of courtier quality.

"Honey, you *have* to work for me! You're *wasting* yourself as a *receptionist*," Vanessa spit out, emphatically. "You even *sketch* beautifully. I was considered talented when I interned with Celeste, but I don't think I was half as talented as you are.

"Work for *you?*"

"I own a string of boutiques. Maybe you've heard of them—Le Chic?"

"*Le Chic?*" Sophie appeared bemused. "*Your* fashions are carried at some of the largest retailers in Chicago."

Vanessa shrugged. "We're in every major city. Every year I search out new designers. We usually have a big fashion event at least four times a year." And maybe this would give Vanessa something to look forward to, taking on the role of Sophie's mentor. It'd been a long time since she'd shown a personal interest in one of her designers. She'd quit putting her all into the business when she'd realized that, not only had her father been taking advantage of her label's profits, but he'd most likely never meant to hand over the business.

Vanessa tapped on the cover of the sketchbook. "Leave this here for me this afternoon. Will you?"

Still appearing somewhat dazed, Sophie replied, "Sure. Would you like to see that purse?" Pulling out a delicate clutch of vibrant aqua, she lightly fingered the clasp before handing the purse over to Vanessa.

"This is so inventive." After studying the gemstones lining the opening, Vanessa popped open the clasp. "What about the jewels? This clasp is amazing. What's it supposed to be—*a bug?*"

Sophie grinned. "It's a dragonfly, of course. You know—for the Dragonfly Pointe Inn?"

"Oh, I see." Vanessa studied the detail. "It's quite well done, isn't it?"

"Dawn Wellman custom soldered the clasp for my gown as well as the clasp for that purse. She's a jewelry designer. Jake sells her work on consignment at the inn's gift shop. The stones she used for that bag were relatively inexpensive. Mostly quartz, I think. She usually works with quality gems."

"I've got some news for you, honey—all of these stones are definitely quality—turquoise and quartz along with amethysts. Even moonstones. And all nicely cut."

Sophie seemed suddenly frustrated. "But why would she do that? I told her *not* to use anything costly."

"Well, maybe she sees your potential. Just think about the possibilities, if the two of you worked together."

"She did ask if I'd consider designing a gown for her."

"Well, there ya go," Vanessa replied, thoughtfully. "You should really think about consulting with her. Possibly draw up another series of designs. I'm totally serious, you know, about recruiting you."

"Well—I'm committed to the department for another six months. But I've sketched at least half of those designs in that book since I returned to Crystal Rock."

"Just keep up with the creativity. We'll put a plan together sometime soon." Vanessa handed over Sophie's clutch. "The construction and detail of that bag is absolutely faultless too, Sophie."

Sophie blinked.

"What?" Vanessa stilled, observing Sophie's owlish stare.

"It's just that you actually called me by my *name.*"

In her thick southern drawl, Vanessa began with emphasis, "*Hunnee,*" and grinned. "Before you go, do you happen to know if Sam might have a typewriter around here somewhere?"

"I can do one better." Sophie scrambled into the family room, and pulled open two cabinet doors. Complete with a computer, a compact office space had been built within the bookshelves.

Vanessa followed Sophie into the family room. "A computer! *Sam—with a computer?*"

"You got that right." Sophie snorted. "He's finally getting the hang of it. He purchased this one for himself, just so he could practice. There's a new federal database being set up. The state is requiring all of their departments to have computers for interstate access. That's why they hired me. I can answer the phones, dispatch, and use the rest of the time to enter data and set up the new system. Anyway, here's the printer." Sophie pointed out another shelf underneath the screen and keyboard. "If you have any trouble using it, just let me know later," she said, taking a seat on the stool that'd been tucked in under the bookshelves.

"I should be alright," Vanessa answered. "I use computers to keep track of inventory at Le Chic."

Switching on the modem and fiddling around with the computer, Sophie printed out a test page. "I'll just load up some extra paper in the printer for you." She reloaded the printer efficiently. After typing out a few miscellaneous words, she demonstrated its operation for Vanessa.

"Got it." Vanessa nodded.

"Okay. Gotta run." With a wave of her hand, Sophie snatched up her shopping bag from the counter and sped through the kitchen.

"See ya later, honey." Lifting her hand lazily in farewell, Vanessa eyed the computer. "Hmm," she murmured aloud. "I need to think about this." Wandering around the kitchen, she set the room to order before brewing another pot of coffee.

Moving into the family room, Vanessa stuffed her quilt and pillow back into the large battered trunk that functioned as a coffee table. Wandering over to the stereo and redirecting the dial from numerous broadcasts of Sunday morning services, she sighed contentedly when dreamy classical music floated through the room.

Deciding that the first of four letters should go to Sam, she poured herself more coffee before settling into to stare at the computer's screen.

For the next twenty minutes she typed and deleted, finally composing a draft that would adequately, yet subtly, inform Sam of the situation.

As well as warn him of the danger.

Several thoughtful minutes later, still sipping on her coffee, she began her letter to Rye.

A sudden tap on the patio door had her jumping so high, she nearly dropped from her seat onto the floor. Panicked, with a touch to save, she executed a quick move to reduce the document on the computer's screen. Standing up, she drew in a steadying breath.

Vanessa froze, stunned to observe the familiar face at the door. What was one of DeMarcus's goons doing *here*? As she slid open the door reluctantly, she plastered an inquiring smile on her face. "John?"

With only a brief nod of acknowledgement, he said, "He wants to see you."

"He's *here*?" Vanessa was shaken.

Obviously aware of her unease, John turned and studied the backyard. "I'll be waiting out front. Ten minutes. Okay?" When his eyes met hers, she was suddenly taken aback. Was that *sympathy* she read in his eyes?

"Alright. Let me go get my purse."

Sliding the door closed, she flipped over the lock. Deciding to leave the computer on standby, she silenced the stereo and passed through the kitchen to switch off the coffeemaker. Hurrying through the house into the guestroom, she scooped up her handbag, and made a quick visual sweep of its contents.

She'd forgotten about the journal.

Removing everything from her purse but sunglasses, identification, and her key to Sam's house, she spun around the room with the journal in her hand. Spotting a thick liner covering the shelf in the closet, she slipped the journal under the liner and slid it back into the furthest corner.

Drawing in a steadying breath, she sped through the hallway to the front door. After opening the door and peeking back and forth, at first, she couldn't find John.

"Here," he said, quietly appearing from alongside the house.

She locked the door hastily and began following him across the lawn. Somewhat confused, she finally realized that, just past the barrier of the dead-end street, a limo sat hidden discreetly in the picnic area beyond Sam's backyard. The limo would've, most definitely, stood out if it'd been parked on Pine Street.

By the time they'd hiked across the uneven meadow of the field into the parking lot, Vanessa was grateful for the low heels of the sandals she'd borrowed from Sophie.

An unfamiliar driver dressed in chinos and a sport shirt swept open the door for Vanessa and John. Sliding into the seat reluctantly, she scooted over while John stepped in closely behind her. Soon, they were on their way.

Shielding them from the driver, darkly tinted privacy glass rose slowly into place. She immediately felt trapped. Running her hand over the creamy leather upholstery, Vanessa began studying the luxurious interior of the car objectively, as she reclined in her seat. A custom cabinet located above the bar displayed a compact stereo and television.

And also, most likely, hid some kind of camera or recording device; enabling DeMarcus to listen in and observe their movements.

"What—no blindfold this time?" Vanessa observed, caustically.

John shrugged. "The tint of the windows is dark enough."

He was right, she realized. Vanessa couldn't see a thing through the windows.

"Better settle in. It'll be a while." Crossing his arms and stretching out his legs, John rested his head back and closed his eyes.

Settle in? Right.

Attempting to calm her anxiety, Vanessa pulled out an abandoned newspaper wedged between the seats. "Oh, jeez," she muttered, studying the headlines. As if the story in the paper she'd discovered yesterday at the train station hadn't been bad enough, a quarter page picture of her father, along with a smaller picture of herself, front and center, was plastered across the front page.

John opened his eyes just long enough to peer over her shoulder. "Yeah," he agreed, soberly. Once again, he settled back and closed his eyes.

Nine

*I*t was mid-morning when Sam finally pulled his truck into the garage. But when he strolled through the breezeway into the kitchen, something appeared to be off. Puzzled, he halted, as his eyes searched the family room and kitchen.

And then the scent of cinnamon tickled his nose. Suddenly observing Maria Barelli's freshly-made cinnamon rolls laid out on the counter, somewhat relieved, he shrugged. They'd have to wait until tomorrow, he decided. After gorging on Penny's breakfast, he didn't have room for one more thing.

And he really needed to get moving. Scooping up the cinnamon rolls and opening the fridge, he hesitated momentarily, before sliding them onto a shelf. Baffled once again, he eyed the odd assortment of groceries and bakery items loaded inside. "Must've had some extra eggs, too," he muttered aloud.

Sam made a quick dash into his bedroom. After snatching up a pressed pair of khaki's, along with a navy-blue T-shirt, Sam headed into the shower.

Minutes later, standing at the sink with his razor in hand, he paused, studying the bathroom through the reflection in the mirror.

The towel that was hanging on a hook near the tub appeared to be rumpled and damp.

Drawing his razor down for a final sweep over his chin, he shrugged. He was aware that Sophie sometimes dropped by here, on the weekends, searching for space and time alone. Her parents' home *was* a hub of activity and, since her divorce, she was still rather fragile. It wasn't like her to invade the bedrooms, though. But it was obvious *someone* had used the tub.

Slipping the towel from his waist, Sam pulled on briefs and khakis before dropping his T-shirt over his head. He ran a comb quickly through his hair. Returning to the bedroom, he studied the shoes in his closet. He'd better go with boots, he decided, pulling out his spares. The Stone Lake terrain was rather steep and rocky.

"Shoot. I'll need some extra clothes," he mumbled, checking the time on his watch while strapping it back onto his wrist.

Moving back over to the closet, he grabbed an overnight bag from the shelf. Hurrying through the room, he packed the bag with a pair of sandals along with a T-shirt and jeans. After driving Penny to the airport tomorrow, he'd pull on his uniform once he returned to his office.

With I.D. and wallet secure in his pocket, Sam snatched up his holster and strapped it on over his shoulder.

Grabbing his bag, he rushed through the house and returned to the kitchen. He only had another fifteen minutes before he was supposed to meet Terry. With a last puzzled glance around the kitchen, he sighed. He'd have to figure out what was going on around here later, he decided, hurrying out into the garage.

Exactly fifteen minutes later, Sam sighted the mailbox belonging to the Peterson property. Located on the first access road, immediately past the overhead bridge separating Crystal Rock Lake from Stone Lake, the Peterson cabin had been completely demolished and rebuilt less than ten years before. Having once been a seasonal cabin, lacking even insulation, the home had been completely redesigned for comfort.

When remodeling his cabin, Sam had recycled some of the Peterson's siding and flooring before the old cabin's demolition. Jake

Loughlin and his construction manager, Mike Callahan, who also happened to be one of Sam's best friends, had offered him leftovers after completing the restoration of the Dragonfly Pointe Inn.

Apparently, Terry had just pulled up into the driveway too. Rolling down the window of his squad car, he grinned. "I stopped by the reception last night, but you were already gone."

"Why? Did something come up at work?"

"Nah." Terry laughed. "Your dancing was the talk of the reception, though. Some of the ladies were irritated that you'd left before they had a chance to dance with you—specifically Diane. She made a point of whining to *me* that you'd hooked up with some blonde."

Sam snorted. "Diane knows better. For some stupid reason, she's been after *me* since we were kids." He shook his head in frustration. "I never had any intention of becoming husband number one—let alone number three. With her, it *never* seems to sink in." Sam rolled his eyes. "Any *other* problems over the weekend?"

Due to the additional traffic anticipated from the reopening of the Dragonfly Pointe Inn, the three-man force of the Crystal Rock Police Department had recently added a late shift. Sam, Nat and Terry took turns working weekends, so each man subsequently acquired two days off during the week while remaining on call. The department had even acquired funds for a secretary, and hiring Sophia Barelli Ruston as a combination secretary, dispatcher, and computer programmer had been a brilliant move. At Terry's suggestion, Sam had contacted several other departments in the state to offer Sophie's computer programming services; thus converting her position from part-time to full. The state was requiring all departments begin entering files in the new nationwide criminal database, but there were surprisingly few qualified programmers available.

"Ahh. So I guess you're not gonna reveal the identity of your mysterious blonde? Nah—no other problems. I was worried about drunk drivers, but everything was pretty quiet around town. Except for *these* guys striking again, that is," he added sheepishly.

"You couldn't be everywhere at once. They probably couldn't resist the opportunity to strike again *because* of all the activity at Dragonfly Pointe."

After popping open his trunk, Terry scrambled from the squad car. While Terry retrieved his supplies from the trunk, Sam made his way to the Peterson's door.

Before Sam could knock, Jerry Peterson stepped out onto the porch, and, with a grim smile on his face, greeted Sam with a shake of his hand. "Glad to see that you made it here so quickly, Sam," Jerry acknowledged. He immediately led Sam and Terry over to a staircase leading down into the boathouse. "I kind of wanted to get out on the lake this afternoon, but I was afraid to touch anything, once I realized a lot of my skiing equipment and fishing supplies were missing."

Both in their mid-sixties, Jerry Peterson and his wife Mary were still a few years away from retirement. But, with their kids and grandchildren visiting several times during the year, they spent much of their summer in Crystal Rock. They owned a chain of fast food restaurants, and had no problem delegating responsibility.

"I noticed that the door to the boathouse was unlocked," Jerry admitted, raking a hand through his coarse gray hair. "Mary and I left Friday evening for a golfing weekend in Fondulac with friends. We just got back a few hours ago. I remember specifically checking this lock before we left because I'd heard about the robberies. Looks like I might've been better off installing a security system."

"Probably still not a bad idea," Sam acknowledged, gruffly, pulling on a pair of latex gloves. "So far they haven't hit the same place twice, though." Sam studied some chiseled markings near the latch in the doorframe. "Looks like someone probably pried open the door with a screwdriver."

Terry pulled out a notebook. "Why don't you walk around with me, Jerry? I'll need to make a list of what all you think is missing."

Combing the interior of the boathouse with Jerry for the next twenty minutes, Terry compiled an extensive list of stolen items, while Sam went to work writing down observations in his report.

"We'll need yours and Mary's prints, and the rest of your family's as well," Sam said, once Terry had finished with the interview.

"Both of my sons and their families are coming up this weekend. We can drop by the station Friday or Saturday. If that's okay?"

"That'll be fine. The lab isn't exactly speedy at getting our results to us, anyway. I presume you have insurance for most of this?"

"Yeah. We should be covered."

"They haven't stolen this much before."

"Great." Jerry sighed. Stepping out from inside the boathouse, he suddenly paused on the landing. "Damn," he cursed loudly, smacking a palm against his forehead.

Preparing to begin the tedious process of searching for prints, Sam peeked out from inside the boathouse. "What's wrong, Jerry?"

"I forgot to check my shed. My son Tom dropped off his Jet Ski a few weeks ago."

Sam nodded his head at Terry.

"I'll come up and check inside the shed with you, Jerry." Terry turned back to Sam. "I'm gonna drop off this paperwork in my car first."

"Grab the other evidence kit from my truck if you need it, Terry. If that Jet Ski's missing, this whole situation's just become a lot more serious."

Sure enough, the Jet Ski had been stolen. Nearly ninety minutes later, Sam and Terry were both lounging in the Peterson's kitchen with coffee in hand, posing a few final questions.

Eventually, Sam and Terry were standing near their vehicles and preparing to depart, while they discussed their next move. Since Tom Peterson still had the title and registration for the Jet Ski, it should prove slightly more difficult for the thieves to unload it. Sam filled Terry in on his and Nat's idea of recruiting a local teenager. Since the Peterson's had mentioned their twin grandchildren had just turned seventeen, and had hosted a party here two weeks earlier, it seemed even more urgent now to move on with their plan. Coincidentally, the party had taken place the same weekend their son had brought along his Jet Ski.

Sam reminded Terry he wouldn't be in the office until the following afternoon. Deciding they'd develop their strategy immediately upon Sam's return, they parted.

Trailing behind Terry in his truck, Sam prepared to follow his turn off from the Peterson property.

But *why* was he returning to the cabin? Even though Penny had arrived on Thursday, he hadn't been able to spend any time with her until yesterday, because of the wedding. And in less than twenty-four hours, she'd be back in New York.

Ten

Making a quick U-turn on the road near the campgrounds, Sam finally caught up with Terry, who was on his way back into town. Raising a hand of farewell at Terry, as he pulled into the parking lot of the police station, Sam continued down along Main Street, eventually cruising by the Crystal Rock Tap. Traveling south along the access road, easing out and around the bay, a short time later, he was approaching Dragonfly Pointe.

It was amazing how many wedding guests had chosen to take advantage of their invitation to stay through the middle of the week, Sam observed, reaching the inn's still congested parking lot. He finally discovered a parking place in the furthest corner of the lot. After securing his weapon in its lock box, he made his way through the parking lot along the pathway.

Finally strolling into the lobby, Sam did a quick double-take. All signs of the previous day's wedding reception had completely disappeared. With partitions back in place, the lobby and dining room were now elegantly transformed for function.

Studying the receptionist's desk in the lobby, observing the brightly lit addition beyond, Sam found himself drawn along the spacious hallway encased in glass. With less than a week remaining before the grand opening of the Dragonfly Pointe Inn, the gift shop was finally open for business.

"Hi, Dawn." Relieved find her there, he strode into the shop.

"Hi, Sam," she answered, cheerfully. Lovely in a blue sundress and sandals, she was busy rearranging souvenirs in a creative fashion. Jewelry was temptingly displayed in cases surrounding the register, while an interesting assortment of antiques, ceramics, and artwork stood on exhibit, and lined rows of glass shelving, suspended alongside the exterior walls.

He cleared his throat. "I need your help. I know that Penny is only here for the weekend. But I'd like to continue seeing her—even if it has to be a long-distance relationship."

As if on cue, Danielle was cheerfully mocking when she swept into the gift shop, wearing a huge smile on her face. "What'd you do to Penny, Sam? When you dropped her off this morning, she looked like she'd been on a camping trip."

Becoming sheepish, Sam defended himself. "Actually, we had a pretty interesting night."

Dawn snickered when Danielle snorted. "I'll bet."

Normally, he wasn't in the position of being embarrassed, but sharing their laughter with a rueful shake his head, Sam decided he was better off remaining silent.

"Sam needs a gift for Penny."

Grinning at Dawn, Sam cocked a brow. "I do?"

Danielle patted Sam on his shoulder. "She'd probably love that, Sam. I think she might be worried about getting too involved with you."

"Must be why she practically ran from the truck, when I brought her back here this morning."

"Maybe. I sure wish I could let her in on our plans for her future."

"I wish you'd just let *me* in on your plans for her future," he grumbled.

"Next week. I promise. Everything's almost in place. Jake and I are just waiting for a confirmation on our final step."

"Oh. And what would *that* be?" Sam asked, somewhat irritably.

"The closing on a purchase of property in downtown Crystal Rock."

Sam was becoming increasingly curious. "For Penny?"

Danielle wrinkled her nose. "Hopefully for Penny, Dawn, and the Dragonfly, too."

"I guess that's all you're gonna tell me?"

"Yeah. Penny needs to know the details first," Danielle answered, firmly.

"She doesn't know it yet, but I'm driving her to the airport tomorrow," Sam informed them.

Danielle smiled. "Jake and I already figured on that."

"Yeah, they did. I was standing at the reservation desk this morning, when they cancelled Penny's ride to the airport tomorrow," Dawn added, grinning.

As well as providing transportation to the airport in Eau Claire, the inn scheduled charter service to the much smaller Crystal Rock Airport, located west of town.

"Women." Shaking his head with pretended frustration, Sam gazed around the gift shop. "So. What do you ladies suggest?"

With a mischievous grin, Danielle began fingering the lovely dragonfly pendant hanging from around her neck. "Why not jewelry? Then she'll have *something* to remember you by." She began studying the display cases.

Sam snorted, rolling his eyes. But thoughtfully indecisive, he gazed at a colorful display of gemstones encased near the register. "How about something that matches her eyes? They're a really beautiful deep shade of blue."

Dawn held up a chart highlighting gemstone and birthstone samples. "Like one of these?"

"Exactly," Sam responded, pointing at a dark blue sapphire.

"I have the perfect pendant," Dawn muttered excitedly. As both an artist and jeweler, Dawn had created a new line of jewelry for the inn, as well as designing Jake and Danielle's engagement and wedding rings. Sifting impatiently through several boxes stacked underneath the display counter, she finally smiled triumphantly when she pulled out a dainty pendant from a box. Fashioned with wisps of shiny sterling silver, a delicate dragonfly graced each of the two upper curves of a heart, shaped from a vibrant blue sapphire.

Although Sam grimaced when he observed the price, he nodded his approval with a rueful smile.

"Quality, Sam, quality," Danielle reassured him, patting him on the shoulder. "Besides, you know we'll give you a great discount. She'll love it, Sam."

"I hope so. I'm not exactly sure where I stand with her."

"Let me wrap it up for you." Sliding over a sheet of precut silvery paper from a stack beside the register, Dawn laid the box on top.

"I'm probably not gonna give it to her until tomorrow. Can I come back for it later, when I'm ready to return to town?"

"Sure, Sam. I'll be here until five." A customer suddenly strolled in and drew Dawn's attention.

Hooking her arm within Sam's, Danielle accompanied him back into the lobby. "I think Penny's working out near the lakefront. I guess I'd better go up to the suite and make sure I've got everything packed. Jake and I aren't taking off for a few hours yet. Our pilot got held up by weather on a charter, so he won't be in Crystal Rock until three or four."

After a reassuring squeeze of Sam's hand, Danielle made her way into the elevator.

Well—it was time to find Penny. Sam exited through the doors he'd entered earlier. Stepping down from the porch and making his way around the exterior of the gift shop, Sam decided to take a short cut towards the lakefront. The path that wound north around the bar had been transformed into a nature walk. Fashioned from glass, artisan-designed hummingbird feeders had been hung outside the windows of the bar, to make them easily visible to patrons seated inside. Planted against a backdrop of tall white pines, groupings of shade-loving ferns, along with an assortment of perennials, lined the walkway. Bird feeders and squirrel feeders were well-stocked, Sam observed, while a few wrought iron benches had been placed advantageously along the pathway, to allow a peaceful respite for guests.

Sam hesitated. Would Penny be annoyed that he'd shown up early? Strolling determinedly along the final curves of the pathway, Sam attempted to pass quietly by the waterfall. But obviously he hadn't been quiet enough, as flocks of finches and sparrows, clustered around the tray of a huge copper feeder, began to scatter frantically. Still perched on the feeder and flapping his wings frenziedly, a solitary blue jay was obviously enraged, and emitted a piercing caw.

Suddenly at ease, Sam began laughing at the blue jay while staring him down.

Searching the busy lakefront, he finally located Penny at the top of a ladder. For several long moments he studied her as, quickly and efficiently, she removed and disentangled miniature lights from the arbor. Sam felt an unusual aching rush of emotion. With her shimmering strawberry-blonde hair loose over her shoulders, dressed in a pair of jeans and a lavender T-shirt, she looked incredibly lovely.

Despite their audience, he began to approach her anyway. "Penny?"

For a moment, she seemed to let down her guard. "Sam!"

Her reaction nearly knocked him from his feet. If Sam wasn't mistaken, her face actually lit up with pleasure.

When she began to step down, Sam moved over to the ladder and quickly steadied her in his arms. "I hope you don't mind. I didn't have anything else to do today. I thought I could help," he whispered unevenly. It was pretty amazing that this woman didn't have a clue as to how much power she held over him.

Reluctantly, he let her loose from his arms. Taking in the scene, he observed that the members of Penny's crew were unusually busy removing lights and wedding decorations from the restaurant windows, and were obviously pretending to ignore him and Penny, while a few individuals stared over at them and smiled.

In an uneven voice, Penny observed, "Just in time—I still haven't had my lunch, yet." She studied the lakefront approvingly. "Everyone's due for a break now, anyway."

"I haven't eaten either." Realizing it was close to one o'clock, Sam laughed softly. "I must *really* have it bad for you." Pleased when a delicate blush colored her cheeks, he observed dryly, "Usually, I'm never distracted enough to *ever* miss a meal."

Penny waved a dismissive hand at the crew members. "Take an hour for lunch, everyone," she called out. "Let's meet back out here at two."

Penny's crew had been offered the incentive of free meals with room and board during their five day stay as part-time employees. Mostly made up from men and women supplementing other income, after reference checks, thirty individuals had been hired directly by Jake Loughlin through two Wisconsin caterers. Some of the employees had found the atmosphere of the inn so welcoming, they'd inquired about permanent job openings.

"Our second *date*," Sam teased, moments later, seated in a booth near a window in the restaurant. Sitting across from one another, they each studied a menu.

"You're just trying to get lucky," she mocked dryly, hiding behind her menu.

Startled, Sam laughed as his head shot up from the menu. "Damn right." Sam growled, smiling wolfishly.

Wearing a rueful smile, Penny peeked around the menu.

After her efforts to keep him at a distance yesterday, Sam was pleased that Penny finally seemed to be more comfortable with him.

Operations seemed to be running smoothly in the restaurant. Despite the fact that Jake would be away on his honeymoon, his hotel manager from San Francisco had flown in especially for the week to open up the restaurant. Greg Garner would make sure all the final preparations were made for the Dragonfly Pointe Inn's first guests, due to arrive on Friday. Along with the valued employees from the Loughlin hotel chain, who'd chosen to transfer for pay raises and promotions, many local residents had acquired jobs at the inn.

The menu of the Dragonfly Pointe Inn was quite unexpected. Offering refined variations of the usual long-time local favorites such as fish and shrimp on Fridays, the inn's menu would also present a widely diverse range and style of foods. Experimentally including everything from appetizing pastas with fresh shrimp, scallops, and lobster, to selections from Mexican and Chinese cuisine, their nightly specials would vary until the management decided on a permanent menu.

"I can never make up my mind." Penny studied her choices enthusiastically. "Everything I tried on Thursday and Friday was delicious." She finally decided on a tasty pasta dish while Sam just opted for a hamburger. "I hope you don't mind sharing your fries—they're the best I've ever had.

Sam was surprised, but delighted, when he and Penny found a great deal to talk about. Obtaining her bachelor's degree in agribusiness and plant science while training in horticulture, despite her disconnection from her grandfather and his flower shop as a child, Penny had discovered she was extraordinarily talented at arranging flowers. After becoming manager of Sander's Floral, not only had she remodeled and modernized the shop to encourage walk-in customers, she'd brought in more business by specializing in wedding flowers. Reassured by her success, her grandfather had been grateful, so he'd eventually turned over the reins of the family business to Penny.

The only shadow over their conversation fell when Penny spoke of her son, Alex. She seemed reluctant to touch on the severity of his behavior problems.

Tucked in next to the solarium, the dining room had a spectacular view of the lakefront. Gazing through the window absentmindedly, Sam immediately sat up in his seat. Dressed for fishing, a middle-aged man was approaching the steep row of steps leading down onto the dock.

No—it couldn't be! Was it really Frank Carlton?

Sam was baffled. What would the partner and business manager of his former father-in-law, Peter Gerard, be doing here in Crystal Rock?

Penny must've noticed Sam was distracted, because she smiled curiously.

"Oh, it's nothing," he explained. "I could've sworn I just saw someone I used to know. I thought I saw him yesterday at the wedding, too."

Just at that moment, well-rested and cheerfully anticipating their honeymoon, Jake and Danielle appeared to join them.

"We've been looking all over for you two." Danielle smiled. "Jake finally decided to check the security surveillance."

"We're getting ready to take off soon, and we wanted to make sure we said goodbye. We've already said our farewells to my mom." Jake grinned. "And we've just been over at the lakehouse, visiting Brian and Ralph."

The Loughlins planned to reside in Crystal Rock permanently. While supervising the renovations of the Loughlin's lakehouse, Brian would care for Ralph, their infamous Black Lab. Taking a break from his job as a landscape architect, Brian, a former architect, had drawn up plans to transform the cottage into an updated and modernized residence.

"I think Ralph was offended when he wasn't invited to the wedding," Danielle announced, drawing everyone's laughter.

"I can only imagine what kind of trouble he'd have gotten into," Sam added, dryly. With Jake and Danielle needing to finalize their plans for the wedding the previous month, Sam had volunteered to take care of Ralph. Ralph had joined Sam, Jarrod, and Rodney for a weekend at the cabin.

Since it'd been extremely difficult to stop Ralph from jumping into the lake, Sam had finally just given up. Once Ralph had tired, he'd return to the deck to promptly shake out his fur—drenching Sam and the boys. After Sam and the boys expended all their energy drying him off, Ralph would jump off from the end of the dock *again*, replaying the whole scene over and over.

"Sam took on the Benet brothers and Ralph—all on the same weekend."

Obviously aware of Ralph's lack of discipline outdoors, Penny turned to Sam with a mischievous grin. "Bet you were tired on Monday."

Sam admitted sheepishly, "I was *exhausted*!"

Everyone broke into laughter.

Still somewhat distracted, Sam studied the security camera mounted in the upper corner of the restaurant thoughtfully. "Jake, can I speak with you for a minute?" Smiling at Penny reassuringly, Sam stood up, motioning at Jake.

Once Sam had steered Jake into the privacy of the breezeway, Jake frowned. "What's up, Sam?"

"Would I be able to take a look at your reservation list? And maybe study some of the inn's video footage?"

"Sure, why not? Just talk to Grace, my assistant. What's the problem?"

"I thought I saw someone I used to know. Twice. It could mean trouble. I figure with all the weird stuff that's gone on around here over the last nine months, I'd rather be safe than sorry."

"I can understand that," Jake responded, grimly. "Danny doesn't know about the extra security people I've brought in. The video footage should be here for another week. I've got a company secured to view and file it. We won't be deleting *anything*, either. I've heard about some new scanning technology that'll shortly become available through the FBI."

It'd indeed been a rough year. Dragonfly Pointe had held a tragic secret, and it'd come as a complete shock for the residents of Crystal Rock. Sometime in the far past, an extensive tunnel system had been incorporated beneath Dragonfly Pointe. As of yet, it hadn't been entirely determined what other illegal activities had taken place underground. But the most recent use of this hideaway had been to conceal several women and children, apparently kidnap victims for a ring of human traffickers. Uncovering the scheme the previous September, Jake, as a special agent for the FBI, had managed to save the lives of the most recent victims. Despite the diligent efforts of the task force, the kidnappers had managed to evade capture, leaving numerous unanswered questions. Because the kidnappers still remained at large, Jake had set up extra video surveillance throughout the entire point.

With their moods still somewhat grim, Sam and Jake returned inside the restaurant, and sat back in their seats.

"How's Lucy doing?" Sam asked Danielle abruptly.

"Not as well as I'd hoped. I think her mom's going to send her out to Arizona for the summer to visit her Aunt Maura—Mike's sister. The doctor suggested that some time away from here might do her some good." Most obviously recalling the horror of the previous September, Danielle's eyes suddenly filled with tears. Lucy Callahan, now nineteen, had been one of the kidnappers' targets. Held hostage along with a six-year old girl, Lucy had been sexually assaulted after attempting to escape.

"The wedding seemed to distract her," Penny added. "She was great with the flowers. She picked up on everything I taught her right away."

"I knew she'd love being my maid-of-honor. I'm hoping she'll finally go back to school this fall. She was supposed to return in January, but she didn't think she could handle it. I just wish she weren't so lost. I *really* miss her." Danielle blinked, attempting to hold back her tears. "But, as usual, life goes on," she observed resignedly.

For a moment, there was silence.

"Well, *Mrs. Loughlin.*"

Danielle blinked, before shaking her head and muttering, "I wonder how long it'll take for me to get used to being called *Mrs. Loughlin?*"

Jake grinned. "The limo driver's already waiting to take us to the airport. I need to make some arrangements for Sam before we take off. How about I meet you out at the car in about ten minutes?"

Sam stood up with Jake, shaking his hand. "Have a great time."

"*You, too.*" Grinning, Jake waggled his brows, and then he winked at Penny deliberately, before turning and making his way through the restaurant.

Danielle was smiling, apparently noticing both Sam and Penny's discomfort. She drolly took charge of the conversation. "I'm sure glad Brian's moving into my apartment in New York. Now I can wait until after the remodeling is finished at the lakehouse to ship in the rest of my stuff. Penny, when I get back to New York next week, I'd like to come by and talk to you. Okay?"

"Sounds good. Jake warned me that something was up."

After reassuring Penny with a smile, she gave her a hug before standing up. "It's been long and complicated, but our plans should be finalized next week. And then I hope to have some really good news. Maybe for both of you," Danielle added quickly, studying Sam. "Make sure you get her to the airport on time tomorrow, Sam." Before Penny could even react, Danielle was retreating through the restaurant, on her way into the lobby.

Penny appeared troubled when her eyes met his. "I didn't realize that you were taking me to the airport."

Frowning, Sam was suddenly concerned by Penny's lack of enthusiasm. "You don't mind, do you?"

"No, of course not." Although Penny seemed visibly to relax, she was still staring distractedly through the window. "It's almost two. Are you sure you really want to help?"

"That's why I'm here." Smiling reassuringly, he took her hand when she stood up from the table.

Within a few hours, Sam and Penny, along with their large group of assistants, had successfully removed all the miniature lights, greens, and fresh flowers that had decorated each and every window, encompassing the lower level of the inn. By the time they finally finished with their cleanup, it was close to four.

Penny officially dismissed her employees with a wave and a smile. "Thanks, everyone."

Using the inn's bulky flatbed truck, Sam and Penny had hauled all the fresh greens and flowers over to the recycling center Danielle had set up on the opposite side of the road. A second dumpster was located on the bay side of the point, and a specific area had even been designated for compost. Danielle had deemed much of the soil unsuitable for the majority of the plantings and gardens she eventually intended on introducing at Dragonfly Pointe. Why not take advantage of some of the restaurant refuse? It hadn't been much of an effort to convince Jake.

The remaining members of the crew began to depart. Grabbing the final bag of trash from the truck, Sam dragged it over to the Dumpster.

After abandoning the flatbed truck in its parking place near the compost center, Penny and Sam strolled side by side, companionably along the road, eventually returning inside into the inn's lobby.

"I wouldn't mind going back up to my room for another shower before we take off. I didn't have a whole lot of time this morning," Penny observed, gazing down at her soiled jeans.

Sam lifted a brow. "Want some company?"

Unmistakably flustered at first, Penny laughed after a moment, rolling her eyes.

"Just kidding." Obviously enjoying her discomfort, Sam gave her a wry grin as his eyes met hers. "Well, maybe not." Finally, he sighed. "I guess I'll just go into the bar and have a beer instead."

Penny began moving silently toward the elevator.

"Penny. Hold on a minute." Wrapping an arm over her shoulders, Sam steered her away from the elevator. His voice was soft and husky when he asked, "It *is* okay if I stay with you tonight. Isn't it?" With a gentle tap at her chin, he gazed into glittering sapphire-blue eyes.

"I was actually going to make sure *you* really wanted to," she admitted, appearing sheepish.

"I wasn't sure what was going on. You've been acting kind of strange since lunch."

"I know. I'm just...I don't know...worried about getting in too deep with you—because of the circumstances, I guess."

Sam sensed her anxiety. "Please, Penny. I promise I won't do anything intentionally to hurt you. Let's just have fun and make the most of the time we have left. Alright?" Gently, Sam covered her lips with his.

At first, Penny squirmed uncomfortably. Probably because they were in a highly visible location in the lobby, Sam realized. But then, she seemed to disregard their surroundings suddenly, as she responded eagerly to the warmth and promise he was attempting to convey in his kiss. The elevator doors sprang open. Sam let her go reluctantly, but she was smiling radiantly when she boarded the elevator.

When she turned inside the elevator to face him, he winked, smiling broadly before the doors of the elevator closed.

Sam sighed. Knowing what little time they had left, he really hated letting her out of his sight. Deciding to return to the gift shop, he found Dawn busy with several customers. Excusing herself, she motioned to a glittering gift box laying near the register.

Sam brought out his wallet.

"Jake said he'd settle it up with you later," she murmured, handing over the small wrapped box.

"Thanks, Dawn." Slipping his wallet back into his pants pocket, he shoved the box into the larger pocket of his khakis.

She grinned, quickly returning to her customers.

Exiting the gift shop, he approached the reservation desk. Sam immediately recognized the attractive receptionist, turned manager, who'd relocated from San Francisco after her promotion as Jake's assistant. "Hey, Grace." Of Asian descent, Grace Lu was probably around twenty-five. With sleek black hair cut elegantly short, wispy bangs framed the delicate features of her face. After her move to town the previous September, Terry Lutz had found several excuses for visiting the inn on his off-time. She'd finally agreed to a date. As Jake's executive assistant and manager, Grace's primary focus was her job; although she and Terry were now an item.

"Jake told me that you needed to see our guest list. I went ahead and had it printed off for you. You have to promise me that you're the only one who sees this, though." Grace handed over the folder containing a lengthy, alphabetized computer printout. "We promise our guests that we'll keep their personal information private."

"I'll begin going through the names now. Is it alright if I hold onto this until the end of the week?"

Grace offered him a rare smile. "Just shred it for me when you're done. Jake trusts you, and that's enough for me."

Sam skimmed through the names thoughtfully. "The guy I'm looking for doesn't appear to be here."

"We do background checks on our guests, you know." Sam was startled. "Jake wanted to be careful because of all the trouble last fall. We have more security here, than we even had back in California."

"Can't say that I blame him." Carefully folding the list, Sam slid it back into its folder.

"Did you try the Riverbend? They took in a lot of the wedding carryover."

The Riverbend Lodge—it'd be much easier for Frank to remain unobserved if he were here for a specific purpose. And if Frank was traveling around by water, *that* would explain why Sam had only caught a glimpse of him near the dock. "That would make sense. Every time I've seen this guy, he looks like he's either arriving or departing. He *could* be staying at the Riverbend. Can I come back tomorrow afternoon to take a look at those security tapes?"

"Sure. Tomorrow would be better for me, anyway. It'll be a lot less busy around here on a Monday. And If I'm not here, just ask for a guy named Jeff Ballard. He'll be in charge of security at Dragonfly Pointe beginning tomorrow." When one of the housekeepers approached the desk with a large ring of keys, Grace was clearly distracted, when she turned away from Sam.

Raising a hand in farewell, Sam strolled through the lobby toward the entrance leading into the bar. The bar boasted a soothing tranquil atmosphere, primarily due to Jake's critical input. Although the seating areas around the booths and tables were dimly lit, warm natural light burst in through the long row of upper windows, lining the paneled mahogany wall behind the bar. After ordering a beer, Sam eased back contentedly into a leather barstool.

Gazing at the big screen television, Sam spent the next few minutes watching the end of a baseball game. It was rather amazing how many changes had taken place in Crystal Rock since he'd been a kid. There'd only been reception to two television channels back in the early sixties. Although Sam and his friends had always seemed to have better things to do anyway, it'd been *such* a big deal when cable television had finally arrived in town.

When the game ended, the bartender scooped up a small remote from atop the lustrous mahogany bar. Sam finished up his draft and gazed absentmindedly at the entrance of the bar as he prepared to depart.

Unexpectedly, Sam found his attention diverted by the echo of a familiar name. Surfing the channels, the bartender had swept past a channel that broadcast the nation's news.

Staring at the bartender, Sam ordered brusquely, "*Hold on*. I need you to turn that channel back to the news." Noticing her panic, he softened his voice apologetically. "I'm sorry. I think they're talking about someone I know."

Standing immediately in front of the television, Sam listened attentively once she'd turned the channel back to the news.

"*…apparently murdered. He was discovered yesterday morning by his housekeeper. Police are not releasing any details.*" The newscaster continued, "*Again, Louisiana State Representative and New Orleans industrialist, Peter Gerard, is dead, at age sixty-eight.*"

Sam's face was pale when he dropped back down into his seat.

"Is there anything I can do?" the bartender asked, sympathetically.

Glancing quickly at the tag pinned neatly on her white, buttoned-down shirt, Sam muttered resignedly, "Well, Theresa. I think I'm gonna need another beer."

Eleven

It was about ninety minutes later when the limo finally pulled to a halt. Taking in a deep breath, Vanessa attempted to calm her tattered nerves. With the barrier between the front and rear of the limo slowly descending, the driver signaled at John, who acknowledged him with a curt nod of his head.

The automatic locks snapped opened.

When John slid out from the limo and held open the door for Vanessa, she stepped outside apathetically.

Objectively, she studied her surroundings. Observing an odd assortment of warehouses and storage sheds, Vanessa caught a faraway glimpse of water. They appeared to be near a loading dock.

Maybe on a river?

"This way." Motioning her ahead, steering her towards a long sidewalk, John led her up into the entrance of one of the more updated warehouses. Boxy and blending into the background, the multi-storied, gray-sided structure appeared slightly familiar.

When her eyes met John's, she was startled to observe the same concern she'd recognized earlier. Quickly, John veiled his eyes, disguising his unmistakable sympathy. Hesitating as she moved slowly up the sidewalk, she was urged ahead with a gentle shove. Sighing resignedly, Vanessa forced her feet into motion.

As they entered the warehouse, cool air circulated throughout the vacant office. A large circular receptionist's desk occupied the center of the lobby. Escorting Vanessa down a long, dimly-lit hallway, John opened wide the set of double doors upon reaching the end.

Vanessa gaped, eyeing the familiar waiting room. Not only were the walls painted the same shade of gunmetal gray, but the contemporary furnishings of stainless steel and black leather were unerringly the same. With even the *placement* of the furniture appearing precise, Vincente DeMarcus's office here was an *exact* duplicate of his office in New Orleans.

Vanessa's apprehension was temporarily forgotten as she shook her head in disbelief.

"Have a seat." After waving her into a chair, moving over to another set of double doors, John knocked once, and then again, after an intentional pause.

"Come," a cold clear voice summoned with authority.

Hearing Vincente's detached emotionless voice, Vanessa's apprehension immediately returned.

Opening up one of the doors, John stepped inside the inner office.

Fifteen minutes later, perspiring and squirming with discomfort, Vanessa was still waiting. But mind games had always been Vincente's forte. She was painfully aware that he was purposely forcing her into a fearful state of anxiety.

Was he *unhappy* with her for rushing from New Orleans—and not going along with his previous plans?

Would he *punish* her?

Not only was she breathing irregularly, but her face had become exceedingly pale by the time John returned after opening the office door. He signaled her into the inner office with a curt nod of his head.

As Vanessa entered the office, John pulled the door closed and remained in the waiting room. Now becoming chilled, Vanessa wrapped her arms around herself, attempting to control her shaking and shivering. Another ploy of intimidation, the thermostat in Vincente's inner office was always set down low. For several long minutes, ignoring

Vanessa as she patiently stood before his desk, with slow deliberation, Vincente remained busy shuffling through his paperwork.

Eventually, as his eyes traveled upward and he studied her face dispassionately, his cold black gaze met hers. With a nod, he motioned her into a chair.

Dropping into her seat awkwardly, she attempted ineffectively to make herself comfortable in the chrome and leather sling back chair.

Outwardly, as usual, Vincente DeMarcus was immaculate. Wearing his favored suit of platinum, and a faultlessly tailored shirt to match, he'd elected a tie that was striped with gray and charcoal. He slid a hand back over his slick silvery hair—it was an unconscious habit of his that she'd become familiar with long ago. Easing back into his chair and crossing one leg over the other, he tented his fingers and silently stared. "Although I do not approve of your lack of communication, I am pleased you have followed our plans." Slightly accented, his words were spoken with emotionless precision.

Vanessa breathed in a sigh of relief.

Eyes narrowed, he inquired abruptly, "Did you kill him?"

"*Me?*" she squeaked. "No. Why would I do that? I thought you...?"

"Me? Why, my dear, your father was worth more...much more to me alive."

For several long minutes, he considered her coldly. "My sources have revealed the crime scene to be quite gruesome. And you did have reason to punish him, after all." He began to deliberately study the furnishings in his office, shifting his eyes intentionally toward the long low credenza standing isolated before the towering mirrored wall.

Following the direction of his gaze, Vanessa's face turned pale as she suddenly began to tremble.

Vincente seemed extraordinarily pleased by her reaction. "Ahh. But we have not had to use these measures since you were what...sixteen?" Deridingly, a half-smile crossed over his face.

Finally, he nodded resignedly. "Yes. I do believe you are telling me the truth." Turning his eyes downward, he began thumbing through his notebook purposely. "But now we must consider your inheritance."

His statement left her cold.

Pursing his lips, he lifted a brow as his gaze once again met hers. "What? I *am* your lawyer, after all. Do you not recall those papers you signed—on your eighteenth birthday?"

She nodded silently.

"Due to your recent ahh—*medical impairment,*" Vincente ignored her startled gasp, "we will possibly need to revise our plans. But for now, you will meet Frank at the," picking up and staring at his notebook, slowly and precisely, he continued, "Riverbend Lodge—at eleven a.m.—tomorrow. John will arrive at ten forty-five a.m. to accommodate you. You must be removed from your husband's home. You will find your luggage in the room we have reserved. We wish for no further discord between yourself and your husband—as it is imperative that you reconcile." He gazed at her coldly. "Or at least *appear* to reconcile. *We* will handle the other details."

After pressing a button on his speakerphone, he began writing in his notebook. It was an obvious dismissal.

As she awkwardly stood up from her chair, the door that led into the outer office opened and John reappeared. With a nod at Vanessa, he awaited her departure from the office.

Rushing down the hallway, Vanessa was nearly running by the time she escaped through the warehouse. Slowing down, she waited for John to catch up with her as she made her way through the parking lot. Struggling to keep her knees from collapsing out from under her, she slipped into the backseat of the limo gratefully when John held open the door.

Once they were on their way, Vanessa laid back her head wearily, contemplating Vincente's instructions. *What* did he want from Sam? From the beginning, Vanessa had only been interested in Sam's monetary value.

But now she was curious.

And *how* had Vincente discovered the results of her blood tests?

Closing her eyes, she considered her future despondently. Had she *actually* expected to gain control over her inheritance?

The return trip to Crystal Rock was surprisingly swift, and soon the limo driver was pulling into the parking lot of the park behind Sam's house.

When John held open the door, with a sigh of relief, Vanessa scrambled out from inside the limo.

"Wait. I should walk you back over to the house." Closing the door, he began to follow her.

She attempted to distance herself hastily. "It's not necessary." But when she stumbled into a rut awkwardly, John grabbed her elbow and continued to follow a few short steps behind her.

After a calm, cool precautionary side glance at the limo, John whispered succinctly, "He wants my family to move into one of *his* residences. He knows things about me and my family that he could only know by video surveillance. He specifically brought up information about my eight-year old daughter."

Vanessa gasped, squeezing his arm. "Don't. Don't let him near your daughter!"

John halted, staring into her eyes. "*Oh, my God.* It's true, isn't it?"

"How could you *not* know?" Vanessa spit out. "He survives on extortion and blackmail!"

Steadying her elbow, John continued moving forward. "I've never actually *seen* it. Usually, I escort individuals, mostly women, to and from his office."

"You're not his bodyguard?"

Grimly, he shook his head.

"Then *who* is?"

"Both Carlton and Trace."

"*Trace?*"

When Vanessa's face went pale, John seemed to recognize its significance immediately. "*What am I gonna do?*" he moaned, despairingly.

They silently approached Sam's door. "He'll find you. There's no way you can get away from him, once you're working for him, you know. He must have plans for you." Grabbing his arm, Vanessa hesitated on the front step. "There's only one way."

"That's what I was afraid you'd say." He sighed. "Witness protection?"

"Yeah. You might have to stay on with DeMarcus, though. If they put you in witness protection, they'd probably want information for their efforts. But they might be able to protect your family while you're helping them."

"There's only one problem with that." John admitted wryly, "DeMarcus has people in the FBI."

Vanessa was stunned momentarily. "I should've known," she admitted resignedly. And then, after a thoughtful moment, she said hesitantly, "You might be able to go to Sam."

"Your husband?"

"Yeah. He's on the up and up. And there's his friend, Jake Loughlin. Supposedly, he's with the FBI. If he's a friend of Sam's, he's gotta be straight."

Squeezing her hand with reassurance while nervously eyeing the limo, John slowly eased away. "Thanks."

"You're welcome. Just *don't* let them near your daughter. *Especially Trace.*" In an unsteady voice, she continued, "You can't even imagine what he's capable of."

Obviously shaken, after taking a few short steps in somewhat of a daze, John turned back and held her eyes. "I'm sorry," he whispered.

Blinking back her tears, she nodded as he squared off his shoulders and strode away briskly. After staring out at the street uneasily, Vanessa removed the key from her purse and unlocked the front door. As she marched into the living room, she quickly became aware a faintly familiar fragrance lingering in the air.

Sam's aftershave?

She crept through the hallway into Sam's bedroom, and then peeked into the bathroom. Sure enough, the towel she'd used that morning had been neatly rearranged, while another one was slightly damp.

Now relieved that she'd managed to avoid him, Vanessa considered her next move thoughtfully as she headed through the house and into the family room.

Would Sam return home *today*?

She'd worry about that a little later, she decided, settling into her seat and facing the computer screen again. Retrieving her documents, she began typing frantically. Maybe she wouldn't be able to do anything about her inheritance now. But recalling the disturbing premonition she'd been having, if anything should happen to her in the future, she'd be damned sure that her assets were accounted for.

Twelve

Far out in the distance, fishing boats dotted the sweeping shoreline across Crystal Rock Lake. Showing off nearby, an enthusiastic skier, towed by a powerful cruiser, sped effortlessly through its wake.

As the waves swept in from the speedboat's wake, gently jostling their pontoon, Penny studied Sam as, apparently lost in his thoughts, he stared out across the lake from behind the wheel of the pontoon. "Is something wrong?

With a start, he refocused his attention on Penny. "I'm sorry, Penny. I got some really bad news this afternoon."

Since meeting Penny in the bar a few hours earlier, Sam had been strangely quiet. After arriving at the Edmonds' home, they'd all enjoyed a simple grilled fare that'd included hamburgers and hot dogs. During supper, Nat and Olivia, along with Craig, had carried the conversation. Most likely worn out after spending the previous day at Dragonfly Pointe, Jarrod and Rodney had both been rather quiet as well.

With the exception of Shirley and Craig, they were all presently touring Crystal Rock Lake on the Edmonds' pontoon boat. Earlier, Jarrod and Rodney had each taken a turn steering, but now, with Sam at the wheel, attempting to avoid the blinding glare of the sun reflecting off of the lake, he was maneuvering expertly along the shoreline. As Jarrod and Rodney tugged their fishing lines in and out of the water, soft laughter echoed from the other end of the pontoon.

Although an hour earlier they'd plowed through choppy water, the shifting of the wind had left the surface of the lake a mirror, reflecting the vibrant ocher colors of the leisurely descending sun. Lifting her face into the air, Penny found the gentle invigorating breeze both soothing and refreshing. "Anything you'd like to talk about?" she asked, quietly.

"Not really. I just discovered that someone I used to know was killed. And rather tragically as well. But I've been trying to put it out of my mind."

Startled, Penny answered quickly, "I'm sorry."

"Well, I know it's an odd thing for me to say, but I'm not so sure that *I am*." He frowned, unmistakably sheepish. "It was my ex-father in law. I found out after I left New Orleans that he wasn't the fine, upstanding man he'd portrayed himself to be. I guess it's not much of an excuse for not feeling sorry about his death, though. But enough of that." His eyes were traveling over her with obvious appreciation. "Have I told you how beautiful you look tonight?"

Only a light touch of makeup accentuated the features of her face. Wearing a slim-fitting haltered sundress and sandals, Penny had drawn back her hair with a purple headband. She wasn't unaware that the color brought out the blue of her eyes.

She laughed softly, turning away self-consciously. "Only about three or four times since I met you in the bar. After I got you away from that bartender, that is."

Sam grinned, as he raised a brow. "Jealous?"

Penny *had* been jealous. Obviously believing she'd made a conquest, the bartender had actually glowered at her when Penny had taken a seat next to Sam.

"You shouldn't be. You look good enough to eat," he growled, bending over her ear. "And yes. I meant that *just* as it came out. I don't know how much longer I can keep my hands off of you," he muttered, softly.

Penny's jaw dropped inanely.

Sam seemed to be pleased by her reaction. He was definitely wearing a self-satisfied smile on his face when he settled back into his seat.

Penny attempted to reign in her chaotic emotions, sensing the intensity of Sam's heated gaze. Trepidation mixed with anticipation. Just when she finally began to relax around Sam, he'd say something totally unnerving that'd throw her completely off-balance.

"I wonder what's going on over there?" Relieved for a break from her muddled thoughts, Penny pointed at the shoreline.

Sam slowly began steering near the beach of the Crystal Rock Campgrounds. Loaded up with a wide range of construction materials, groupings of pallets were laid out in a clearing beyond the beach. "Somehow, Jake and Danielle finally convinced Bart Bradshaw to sell them the property. All of these renovations have something to do with a new charitable organization Jake's created. I know that they're restoring the campground—but I'm not exactly sure what they're building back there, where the recreational center used to be." Studying the recently renovated cabins that were staggered along the edge of the property, Sam shook his head in amazement. "You know, they've been so busy with the wedding, I can't figure out *when* they had time to come up with plans for all of this."

"It's gonna to be beautiful. The kids are sure gonna love it. I wonder if they've remodeled our old house?

Sam raised a brow. "House?"

"Yeah. I think I told you—my family used to live here—on the other side of the recreational center."

"*Here? Back in high school?*" Appearing slightly uncomfortable, Sam turned a discomfited gaze at Penny before studying the grounds and beach. "I never realized anyone was living on the grounds back then," he added. Somewhat uneasily, he studied her face before finally clearing his throat. "I guess I had the impression that the grounds were vacant over the weekends during the summer."

Purposely, Penny kept her eyes averted. *She'd* never confess that she'd actually caught him in action at the same beach they were traveling by now. Let him wonder. But it'd sure be nice if it still didn't bother her so much. In fact, all of a sudden, she was feeling rather deflated.

Tomorrow, she'd be on her way back to New York, and that would be it.

Sam would move on to someone else.

Maybe that pretty bartender.

It was amazing *how much* the idea bothered her.

As her eyes appreciatively followed the length of his long muscular legs and traveled over his narrow hips, before moving to admire his sturdy broad shoulders, Penny realized that, even at forty years old, Sam had a body that was close to perfection.

Suddenly catching her eye, he waggled his brows and grinned.

Had he *really* been able to figure out exactly what she'd been thinking?

She knew she was blushing when she shook her head with pretended frustration. *Blushing? At her age?* She *really* needed to quit thinking so much, she decided, settling back into her seat.

She smiled resignedly when Sam began to laugh softly.

About an hour later, after a series of long farewells to Nat, Olivia, and the boys, Penny was seated next to Sam in his truck. They both remained silent as they traveled back to the inn.

And she was nervous.

Again.

When they finally reached the parking lot of the Dragonfly Pointe Inn, this time, Sam was able to park nearer to the entrance.

"Looks like a lot of the guests have taken off," Penny observed, stepping down from Sam's truck.

With one hand gripping the handle of his bag, Sam used his other hand to gently guide Penny through the doors into the lobby.

As Sam and Penny approached the elevator, Grace Lu came rushing through the lobby, obviously attempting to catch up with them. "Sam—Penny—hold on! Danny and Jake wanted me to escort you two upstairs."

Both Sam and Penny stared at Grace curiously as, slightly out of breath, she held down the button for the elevator. "No one was using the Peacock Suite, so they thought you two might like to use it tonight." She laid a hand over Penny's. "Don't worry," Grace reassured her. "Danny packed up your stuff personally this afternoon." Obviously distracted, Grace frowned. "She and Jake didn't end up leaving here until almost six. Some kind of problem came up, so they were planning on departing from Eau Claire."

"*Peacock* Suite?" Sam barked suddenly, his reaction delayed.

Grace laughed, rolling her eyes. "We've got a serious nature theme going on here at Dragonfly Pointe. Somehow, Danny talked Jake into labeling all the suites with the names of birds," she answered dryly. Half covering her mouth, with a smile, she whispered, "I've delayed ordering all of the door plaques, though. I mean Cardinal, Blue Jay, Goldfinch— all of those seem appropriate. But *Peacock*?" Grace grimaced.

Both Sam and Penny burst into laughter.

When Grace exited the elevator onto the fourth floor, they followed quietly behind her. From the elegantly appointed walkway, Sam peered down at the beauty of the open lobby below. "Cool," Sam mumbled as, with widened eyes, Penny nodded her agreement.

When Grace unlocked the door for the suite, Penny caught her breath. Airy and elegant with high ceilings and skylights, the suite was reminiscent of a stylish loft. Wandering through the fully-equipped kitchen and following Grace into the dining room, Penny couldn't help but admire the antique mahogany dining set arranged for serving up to twenty guests. Throughout the open concept suite, mahogany wainscoting and rich crown molding kept in character with the historical Dragonfly Inn of the 1920's. Dark recycled wooden floors were set off by lovely area rugs of pale creamy yellow, patterned with smoky greens and blues.

"Peacock colors," Penny observed, standing in the living room. "Oh. Look at that couch." A graceful antique mahogany settee had been covered with a bold floral print, embracing a fusion of dusty greens and blues."

"Although over half of the rooms and suites have been set up with the more casual shabby-chic décor that's suddenly becoming popular, Danny and Jake prefer the more traditional décor. All of the suites have been decorated with an abundant use of antique furnishings. And this particular suite has three fireplaces," she added, motioning to an ornate, mahogany mantelpiece, framing the fireplace in the living room. "But each suite is decorated uniquely." Grace grinned. "That's psychological, you know. If our guests become attached to one particular suite, chances are they're gonna make reservations again for the following year."

Sam expelled a long, low whistle. "Is that a hot tub?"

Grace laughed softly. "Nice. Isn't it? They're only available in the lakefront suites. *And* they can be covered and locked away from kids." Tastefully tiled with mosaic, the distinctive rectangular hot tub was inset behind fold-away French doors, and optimized the view of the lakefront.

"What are there—four separate bedrooms?"

"That's right. Our renovations were designed to target family vacationers."

Penny turned to Sam. "This suite is beautiful. Isn't it?"

"*Very* impressive," he acknowledged, smiling.

Grace swept open a pair of double doors. "We moved your things into this room, Penny, because its Danny's favorite."

Penny peeked into the bedroom. Creamy walls enhanced the richness of the mahogany wainscoting and crown molding. The four-poster, king-sized bed was stylishly appointed with a thick down comforter, featuring accents of smoky, blue-green and turquoise. Rows of throw pillows of assorted styles and sizes invited you to jump into the bed. "This reminds me a little of your bedroom at the cabin," Penny observed, turning to Sam.

Dropping his bag onto the luggage rack, Sam laughed. "I told you that Danny helped me decorate. These must be some of her favorite colors."

"Oh. Look at the botanicals." Strolling through the room, Penny couldn't help but admire the framed collection of delicate floral etchings, lining the walls alongside a second set of French doors.

"Those are from an auction," Grace observed. "Aren't they beautiful? I think they're genuine."

"Yeah, they are," Sam added. When Grace appeared startled, he mumbled, "I just happened to be along with Jake that day for the auction." Sam stepped over to study a rosy-polished armoire. "I see that he had this armoire refinished, too."

"Oh. What a beautiful piece of furniture." Artwork was carefully arranged on exposed upper shelves, along with an assortment of books. While Penny ran her fingers appreciatively over the detailed carvings, running along the edge of the armoire's facade, Grace quietly slipped from the room.

"It's walnut. I can't believe that Jake actually followed my advice and had the damaged doors removed. You should've seen what it looked like before. I don't think he would've even bid on it if I hadn't talked him into it."

"So, you're into antiques *too*?"

Sam shrugged, appearing sheepish. "I guess. I've been picking up stuff for the cabin, and just started refinishing a few things here and there.

"Here, you two."

Penny noticed that Sam was as startled as she was, when they turned to Grace, who was holding two flutes of champagne.

"Jake wanted me to be sure to mention that room service is on him. He and Danny left you a bottle of champagne. I'm getting out of your way now." Grinning, she handed over the champagne before exiting the room. "Have fun. I left your keys in the kitchen," she called out.

Penny eyed the champagne in her hand with a grimace. "I was trying to avoid drinking any alcohol tonight."

"Yeah, me, too," Sam responded, grinning. "How about relaxing out on the balcony for a while?"

Sam must've sensed her nervousness. Maybe a little champagne would be just what she needed?

A white wrought iron glider and chairs were invitingly arranged outside on the balcony. As they eased down beside one another on the glider, Sam and Penny kept their conversation light while sipping on their champagne.

The view across the lake from amidst the treetops was spectacular. Swaying rhythmically side by side, they gazed out at the lingering remains of the vibrant sunset. A blazing ball of fire, the sun appeared to be dropping off the edge of the horizon.

As darkness slowly descended, their eyes finally met in silent accord. Grabbing Penny's hand, Sam tugged her gently up from her seat. Leaving the French doors open wide, they moved silently inside into the suite.

Sam raised a questioning brow, as he glanced hesitantly over at the hot tub.

With an unconsciously seductive smile, Penny reached back over her shoulder and untied her sundress, allowing it to drop onto the floor.

Somewhat dazed, Sam shook his head. He'd always had the impression that Penny was *shy*. Aware of the rapid beat of his heart, he gazed appreciatively over the lovely curves of her body. Reaching out, he ran a finger along the lacy edge of her bra. "Penny. You're so beautiful," he muttered, hoarsely.

Penny closed her eyes, as Sam's gentle touch sent heat coursing through her veins, and she was suddenly swept away by the force of her desire. "I've always kind of thought the same thing about you," she admitted, in a shaky voice.

With a rueful shake of his head, Sam laughed softly.

Opening her eyes to meet his, solemnly, she reassured him, "Really."

Still shaking his head in amusement, Sam growled, "I guess you know, by now, what you do to me." As his gaze became heated, the chocolate color of his eyes transformed, becoming deeper and darker. Reaching gently for her hand, he brought it up to his racing heart. Momentarily, he hesitated. But as his eyes held hers, he reached for her other hand, pressing it firmly against the thickness of his rigid erection.

"Oh, Sam," she whispered, unsteadily.

Suddenly losing all control, Sam pulled her into his arms.

Where she responded passionately, urgently, opening her mouth to his. Their kiss was long and slow and deep as the desire they'd both been denying exploded into a hunger that wouldn't be satisfied merely by kissing. Their tongues tangled frantically while their hands feverishly explored.

"Okay," he gasped, pulling away shakily. "We need to slow down a little." Sam's fingers brushed lightly through her hair as he tucked her head gently under his chin. Inhaling deeply and unsteadily, he became dimly aware of the tantalizing scent of roses and lavender drifting through his senses. Numbly, Sam acknowledged how absolutely *right* Penny felt in his arms.

When the beat of her heart finally began to steady, Penny eased away silently. Reaching for Sam's T-shirt and pulling it out from his waistband, she slowly drew it over his upraised arms.

In quiet acknowledgement, both Penny and Sam eyed the hot tub. With a rueful grin, Sam began to unfasten his belt. And then, in one swift motion, he quickly slipped off his khakis and briefs.

Penny's eyes widened unconsciously as she stared at Sam, fully aroused. And she swallowed nervously.

When she fumbled in her attempts to remove the remains of her clothing, Sam reached over. "Let me," he whispered hoarsely. Lightly fingering the centered clasp of her bra, Sam slid the bra from her arms, dropping it down onto the floor. Heatedly, he turned his gaze on her lovely bared breasts. Reaching out and lightly cupping each breast, he was dimly aware of Penny's startled gasp of pleasure when, using his thumbs, he rubbed gently over her perfect rosy-pink nipples.

Immediately aroused by his touch, Penny felt her body respond to the onslaught of desire that slammed through her senses. And, closing her eyes, she began to tremble.

Sam suddenly abandoned his affecting exploration of her breasts. With his touch seductive, he slid his hands down over her hips to remove the remaining swatch of lace. Pulling her back into his arms and moving his hands slowly down over her buttocks, he purposely ground his hips into hers.

Sucking in a deep unsteady breath, she moaned, gradually becoming aware of the heat and silky firmness of his erection.

Slowly pulling away, Sam released a shaky breath. "Okay. That's enough of that for now," he whispered. Reaching for her hand, he escorted her down into the lightly churning water of the hot tub. Anchoring an arm over her shoulders, he settled in beside her.

Still languishing under a spell of sensual haze, Penny glanced up at Sam. With his eyes tightly closed, he appeared to be attempting to steady his ragged breath.

"Penny," he groaned, as if in pain. Half opening his eyes, he gave her a rueful smile. "*No one's* ever made me feel like this."

His words initiated a sudden burst of confidence. Turning slowly, she slid a knee over Sam's outstretched legs, determinedly settling into his lap. As her hands began exploring, she observed the emotions playing on Sam's face with intense satisfaction. Moving lightly down over his hard muscular shoulders, her fingers delightedly tangled in the tawny hair covering his chest. When her fingers began circling unconsciously over Sam's flat brown nipples, mimicking his earlier attention to hers, with a helpless shudder, Sam groaned.

And then his control finally seemed to snap. Stealing her closer, Sam's mouth covered hers abruptly. With an enthusiasm that was immediately, delightfully arousing, Sam used his tongue to explore.

When Sam's kiss suddenly turned deeper and more intense, Penny crushed herself against him urgently...achingly...longingly.

But immediately, she realized, she desperately needed *more*.

Her hands reached out to surround his throbbing erection.

When adept fingers tantalized, exploring its length, Sam gasped, sucking in an unsteady breath. He opened his eyes dazedly, reaching out a staying hand. "Penny. What about *protection*?"

"Sam. We really don't need—I—I mean I had an accident several years ago," Penny whispered, appearing agonized as her eyes met his. "I was told I probably wouldn't be able to get pregnant again."

Taken aback, Sam murmured, "Oh, Penny. I'm so sorry."

With a rueful twist of her lips, she sighed. She laid her head on his shoulder as her body turned limp.

"Come here," Sam growled. Tenderly, he cupped her face within his hands, gazing reassuringly into her eyes. Waggling his brows, he grinned. "Now. Where were we?"

As her desire gradually came back to life, still somewhat uncertain, Penny drew in a steadying breath. Taking Sam's erection back into her hands, she slowly took him in, inch by throbbing inch.

Panting, Sam moaned, quite audibly, when she finally rested down on his lap, fully seated. "Oh, God. Just stay like that, Penny." Sam's voice was hoarse and gravelly as he attempted to hold steady.

But raising his knees behind her in an effort to get closer, without warning, he set her body off into the most intense and shuddering reaction of pleasure she'd ever experienced.

He groaned, as his forehead dropped against hers. "Oh, Penny. That was *way* too fast."

"It's been so long," she admitted, rather sheepishly. She buried her face into his shoulder again.

"You're just too damned responsive," he whispered, laughing softly into her ear. "But at least we've got the rest of the night. I guess we can take more time later," he growled, slowly beginning to thrust his body into hers.

Limply sated, she began to increasingly sense her returning pleasure as Sam rhythmically thrust and pumped into her. Urging him on, beginning to match his rhythm, she used her knees to ascend higher while Sam gripped her hips for balance.

As his brown eyes filled deeper and darker with passion, Sam gazed sightlessly into hers. Helplessly, she began to shudder at the exact same moment Sam stiffened, releasing a harsh ragged sigh.

Pulling her in closer, Sam closed his mouth desperately over hers, feverishly tasting her...and savoring her.

While becoming one with her.

For several long breathless moments, Penny kept her eyes closed as she struggled to steady the racing beat of her heart. With her head tucked up under his chin, Sam held her reassuringly in his arms.

Everything about this entire experience had been amazing.

And so totally unlike anything she'd *ever* experienced before.

They remained contentedly silent. Would her heartbeat *ever* return to its regular rhythm? With her palm resting over Sam's chest, she became immediately aware of the racing beat of *his* heart, and considered dazedly—*could Sam be just as affected as she was?*

But, taking into account all the women from his past, how could this experience *possibly* be as earth shattering for him as it'd been for her?

And with that thought, she slowly began pulling away.

Suddenly sensing the gradual change in Penny's contentedness, Sam refused to let her go. Realizing she'd been much more inexperienced than he'd even anticipated, Sam had a vague suspicion of the misguided direction that her thoughts were taking. "Penny. Don't you realize how *incredible* that was?" Sam whispered soothingly. He felt the tension slowly ease from her body. Gazing down tenderly at her face, taking in her sweet wistful smile as a sign of self-assurance, he finally let her loose from his arms. "I don't know about you, but, *after that*, I think I could use a little more champagne."

She nodded silently, and Sam pressed a sweet lingering kiss to her lips before climbing out from the hot tub, unabashedly at ease with his nudity.

Wandering around the room, discovering the built-in stereo system, Sam promptly switched on some music. Echoing through the suite, the same muted rock ballad floated up from the bar. When Sam turned back to Penny and suddenly caught her eyes roving over his body, he grinned. Grabbing the bottle of champagne and the empty flutes, he rested them on the ledge of the tub. After snatching up a couple of fluffy white towels and laying them over the ledge near Penny, he eased back down into the hot tub.

Waggling his brows, he grinned.

Her lovely face was flushed when she focused her eyes hastily up at the stars. "Sorry," she mumbled.

"For what? Don't you think I'd be staring at *you*, if you were prancing around naked?" Still grinning after pouring her champagne, he held out her flute.

Her eyes were wide when they met Sam's. Suddenly, they were both laughing as she reached for her champagne.

Studying Penny discreetly, for a brief moment, Sam considered— *what'd her marriage been like?* There was something both shuttered and indefinable about her behavior.

And then there was that scar at the base of her spine.

Settling back into the warmth of the hot tub, he stilled, immediately sensing the truth. *Penny exhibited the distinctly familiar behavior of someone who'd been victimized.*

Penny attempted, with difficulty, to become at ease again with Sam, when he wrapped an arm over her shoulders. She'd never had casual sex before. But this experience had been far from casual.

At least for her.

How was she ever going to be able to go back home and forget about Sam?

Thirteen

fter dragging the kitchen stool back into the house from the deck, Sophie grabbed a broom from the closet in the breezeway. "So. Let me get this straight—you need to find a lawyer?" Vanessa had briefly summed up the contents of her paperwork, but Sophie still seemed to be slightly confused.

"Well, yes, if you can recommend one. But I also need a witness for my will. As soon as possible, that is. Like right now."

Sophie returned outside and began sweeping the remains of her haircut from the deck. When she came back into the house, she appeared to be thoughtful. "Well, I'm a notary," she admitted, looking uncertain.

"That would work out perfectly, because all I'll need is a witness, then." Vanessa rinsed and dried off the shears that she'd used to cut Sophie's hair, before slipping them back inside the kitchen drawer. "Your lawyer here in town wouldn't be in his office on a Sunday, anyway. Would he?"

Opening the closet door, Sophie hooked the broom inside. "No. And, actually, he's only here one or two days a week. His law firm is based in Madison. The only reason Wes Stanton has an office here in the first place, is because his family has a vacation home on Pebble Lake."

Vanessa tapped her finger on the pile of unsealed envelopes, stacked up on the kitchen counter. "I'll need a witness for these, too. I want my instructions to be airtight.

"Well—my mom is home."

"If I weren't so worried about some pretty powerful people trying to question the validity of my paperwork Sophie, your mom would be fine. But I think I need someone whose word would hold more weight. Maybe someone like Sam. But it can't *be* Sam, since he'd most likely be administering my will."

Sophie wore a worried frown as she listened. She was obviously becoming concerned for Vanessa. After a thoughtful moment, she asked hesitantly, "What about Sam's deputy?"

"You know what, Sophie? That's a great idea. Let's go do it." Vanessa began gathering up her envelopes.

"*Now?*" Sophie appeared uncertain. "I'm not sure whether Terry's home today."

"Can't we go check?"

Sophie smiled. "Sure. Why, not? My notary stuff is at the office anyway, locked in my desk. So we need to stop by there first."

Turning her attention to Sophie's neatly-cropped hair, Vanessa reached out and rearranged a few stray curls. "*Well?*"

"Well, what?"

"Honey, I *know* you're dying to see yourself. Go look!"

Sophie rushed into the bathroom. Moments later, Vanessa began laughing softly when she heard Sophie's shriek of pleasure.

Wearing a radiant smile, Sophie strolled back into the kitchen. "Vanessa, when I noticed all the hair that you were cutting off, I was scared *to death* about what I was letting myself in for. But it looks great!" Sophie reached for Vanessa and embraced her tightly.

Vanessa became strangely emotional. Suddenly clearing her throat and rapidly blinking back tears, she reached for her purse as she pulled away. "Sit down, honey. We might as well finish you off right."

Sophie sat patiently as Vanessa proceeded to brush a light dusting of a smoky, blue-green shadow over her eyelids. Lining her eyes with a deep, kohl black, she generously swept mascara through Sophie's long, lush lashes. After applying a light dusting of powder and blush on

Sophie's cheekbones, and finishing off her lips with a shimmering coat of copper, Vanessa handed over the mirror from her compact.

"Wow." Sophie shook her head with amazement. "How do you even *know* all this stuff?"

Vanessa smiled. "Well, honey. When you're regularly sending out models on a runway, it really helps to know what you're doing."

Studying her face in the mirror, Sophie lightly fingered her hair. "I don't think I've ever worn my hair *this* short."

The cut emphasized the lovely turquoise-blue of Sophie's eyes, Vanessa thought. Although Sophie's long leggy body was clad in tight blue jeans and a T-shirt, with her hair styled skillfully into loose raven curls, her appearance was transformed from frumpy to chic. "You look adorable, honey. Why you could be a model yourself."

Sophie rolled her eyes, and responded dryly, "I sincerely doubt *that*."

With a frustrated shake of her head, Vanessa glared at Sophie. "Honey—that husband of yours sure did a number on you. Didn't he?"

Sophie seemed slightly shaken as her eyes met Vanessa's. "You know. You might just be right," she admitted in an unsteady voice.

Immediately disassembling, Vanessa packed up her purse. "Are we ready?"

"As ready as we can be."

Following Sophie through the house and out through the front door, Vanessa locked it quickly behind her.

Sophie pointed out the car that was parked in her parents' driveway. Digging through her pocket as they strolled across the street, Sophie pulled out the keys for her silver Camaro.

"Nice car," Vanessa observed, sliding into the passenger seat.

"I got it as part of my divorce settlement," Sophie answered dryly.

"There was a decent settlement, then?"

Sophie averted her eyes as she started up the engine. "Not really. Why?"

"Because if your husband had this much money to spend on a car, he probably had lots of extra put away."

"Well. We kept our finances separate. I took what I earned." Sophie pulled out from the driveway, and drove slowly along Pine Street. Other than a man who was mowing his lawn, and a couple of kids riding along on their bikes, there wasn't much activity in the neighborhood.

"Did you have a pre-nup?"

"Nah."

"Honey. Was your lawyer, by any chance, anyone of *your* choosing?"

Sophie answered defensively. "No. We just used the same lawyer, since it was an amicable divorce."

Vanessa groaned. "Honey. Something tells me you got *screwed.*" Studying Sophie intently, Vanessa did something totally uncharacteristic—she pleaded. "Do me a favor. Will you?"

The concern in Vanessa's voice must've registered. Sophie held steady at the stop sign, and turned to gaze at Vanessa from behind the wheel. "What?"

"Talk to your own lawyer. Maybe this lawyer here in town? Has your divorce been finalized?"

"No. At least I haven't signed anything yet."

"I'm willing to bet that your husband has hidden assets. And didn't you tell me that you paid for *his* law school with *your* income?"

Sophie answered with a tight nod of her head. Finally making a left, she remained quiet as they drove along Main Street.

"I've spent most of *my* life getting screwed over. I'd hate to see it happen to you." And where had *that* come from? How in the hell had she become so attached to Sophie in less than *two days*? Although Celeste DeVoux was a close friend, Vanessa had never felt this kind of a personal connection to another woman before.

Except maybe once, she admitted. Oddly enough, she'd spent more time thinking of her mother over the last few days than she had her entire life.

Sophie pulled into an open parking space immediately in front of the police station. Slipping her keys from the ignition, she opened the car door. "I'll just be a second," she said, slamming the door. Strolling over to the side entrance of the station, she unlocked the latch and went inside.

The town was a little more active today, Vanessa observed, noticing a group of teens hanging out down the street. She flipped down the visor to shade her eyes from the sun. Surveying the street through the mirror on the visor, Vanessa did a quick double-take.

DeMarcus had someone following her.

Damn. She hoped she wasn't setting up Sophie for trouble.

What'd made her think DeMarcus would only focus his surveillance on Sam's house? With so many strangers around town this weekend for the wedding, his goons were probably considering themselves safe from observation.

Vanessa's thoughts were interrupted when Sophie returned and quickly slid back into her seat. She started up the engine. "I tried to call Terry, but I didn't get an answer. Since he lives right near the lake and it's a beautiful day, he might just be messing around outside."

After pulling back out onto the street, Sophie drove along Main Street heading out of town. "I haven't been this way in a while, but I think I know where he lives."

Driving out of town and hugging the curving access road that led around Crystal Rock Lake, Sophie eventually traveled over an extended narrow bridge, before heading north along a newly-paved road. Settling back into her seat, Vanessa focused on enjoying the scenic view of the chain-of-lakes surrounding the town of Crystal Rock.

Sophie pointed out landmarks along the way. "They're finally updating our golf course." Obviously a clubhouse in the early stages of construction, a long low structure stood on the west. "Someone recently bought the course. He's converting it from nine-holes to eighteen-holes hoping to attract customers from Dragonfly Pointe."

"Yeah. My daddy was into golf. But I could never see the point of chasing a little white ball around over and over again."

Sophie began to laugh. "Well—I wouldn't mention it to Terry. He loves to golf."

When they came to a V in the road ten minutes later, Sophie veered off to the right. "I think this is the way. I've never actually been here. It's kind of odd that I haven't since Terry and I were really close friends when we were growing up.

Hearing an unsteady thread of melancholy weaving through Sophie's voice, Vanessa shifted her gaze to Sophie's face. "Okay. Tell me about it."

Sophie cleared her throat. "What do you mean?"

"Honey, it's written all over your face."

Sophie's sigh was resigned. "Alright. I mean, this was a *long* time ago. But Terry used to have a crush on me."

"How did you feel about him?"

"Well. He was Terry—my friend. And then I met my husband in high school—and I never really looked at anyone else. But I'm pretty sure that Terry never dated. I mean he was really, really skinny and his acne was awful. But he was *such* a nice guy. I used to get so mad because other kids made fun of him."

"Ah. I get it. So what's he like now?"

"Well. That's the thing. He's the same. But then, again, he's not. It's hard to explain. He went into the Navy—and then he ended up back here. I almost didn't recognize him when I saw him again."

They began travelling up a long graveled driveway. Eventually taking a left, Sophie seemed surprised when they finally pulled the Camaro near the garage of a homey and modernized two-story cottage. "Wow," she breathed out, enthusiastically. Jumping out from the car, she raced over to the edge of a cliff, and gazed over the extensive shoreline with its breathtaking view of Stone Lake.

How beautiful—Vanessa thought, following behind Sophie at a much slower pace. Somewhat isolated, Terry's home was situated only twenty or thirty feet from the water's edge. With a narrow flagstone trail leading down to the water, tiers of charmingly landscaped gardens were strategically spaced along the rambling pathway. She turned back to look at the cottage. With the doors and shutters vibrant in shades of rosy watermelon, the house was painted a lovely sage green. Bursts of lively colors popped out from the rows of planters lining the windows of the front porch.

Vanessa raised a brow. "Not what you expected?"

"No, not at all. I remember his parents had a nice home over on Crystal Rock Lake. But it was more modern and a lot larger.

Finally, they returned to the car, where Vanessa began systematically organizing and gathering up her paperwork.

As they approached the back door of the cottage, Vanessa observed that the grounds adjoining the cottage were immaculate. With a large fenced-in garden that was situated and centered, the growing grass surrounding the garden and edging the dense wooded lot was green and lush.

Vanessa turned to Sophie. "Better just introduce me as your friend, Vanessa Gerard. I'd rather not let anyone else in town know I'm here until I talk to Sam in person."

Nodding in affirmation, Sophie tapped lightly on the door of the screened-in porch. "We'd better just go on up to the other door."

Lined with a collection of white wicker and decorated with a whimsical assortment of Knick-knacks, the interior of the porch was enchanting. Stepping inside, they were greeted by a friendly white calico cat, patterned with patches of black and gold. Rubbing enthusiastically against Sophie's legs, the cat emitted an audible frenetic purr. Reaching down to stroke soft fur, Sophie laughed softly as her fingers were rewarded with a gentle nip.

"Sophie." With wide eyes, Terry Lutz appeared at the door leading into the entryway, looking rather anxious. Rushing by Terry, the calico cat scrambled into the cottage through the open door. "Hi. I didn't even know you knew where I lived. Is something wrong?"

But Sophie was clearly distracted. Shirtless and barefoot, the man who answered the door was only half-dressed. Since his longish hair was slightly damp, evidently, Terry had just stepped out from the shower.

Not so skinny anymore, Vanessa observed drolly. Not exactly handsome, but attractive nevertheless, Terry Lutz had dark-blonde hair and intense silvery-blue eyes. Maybe about five foot-eight or nine, he wasn't too tall. But his body sure made up for it, Vanessa couldn't help but notice.

And, most obviously, so had Sophie, Vanessa observed with amusement.

Her eyes had unconsciously widened, as she studied Terry's broad muscular shoulders, before appreciatively turning her gaze down over his long lean torso, lightly dusted with soft, dark-blonde hair. Moving her eyes down lower to his waist, she appeared to be hypnotized by the cut of his jeans, slung low and unbuttoned over his hips.

It was if she'd never really seen him before.

And he was *definitely* aware of Sophie. Vanessa noticed that his eyes roved over her with a deep heated gaze of yearning. "Your hair looks great," he observed, rather numbly, when Sophie's eyes finally met his.

Vanessa cleared her throat.

Sophie seemed to be battling some deeply unsettling thoughts, when she shook her head distractedly at Terry. "I—I'm sorry to just show up here. I tried to call first."

Sweeping a hand inward, Terry stepped away from the door. "That's okay. I don't mind. I must've been taking a shower." He hesitated, obviously uncomfortable. "I'm having a friend over for dinner."

"It won't take long. My friend Vanessa, here, is in a hurry for me to notarize her will. Since Wes Stanton usually isn't in his office until the end of the week, she needed a credible witness."

"Sure." Motioning them through the hallway, he led them into a large airy family room with windows wide open on the lake. He seemed to suddenly become aware of his state of undress, and he was obviously self-conscious when he cleared his throat. "Let me just go put on a shirt."

"Not on my account, honey," Vanessa drawled, her eyes deliberately roving his body.

Terry actually blushed when Sophie began laughing. "I'll be right back," he muttered. He was definitely uncomfortable when he scrambled from the room.

Vanessa studied the warm open space. Along with a pair of rocking chairs that were definitely antique, a mossy fabric-clad couch and loveseat were grouped invitingly around a red-bricked fireplace. "What a nice room."

"It is, isn't it?" Strolling through the room, Sophie gazed at the family pictures and collection of books lining the shelves on either side of the fireplace. Moving to study the lovely oak coffee table resting before the sofa, Sophie swept her fingers lightly over its carvings. "I recognize some of these pieces."

"Since Mom and Dad downsized when they moved to Eau Claire, they left most everything in storage," Terry observed, returning to the room. "I had my pick of the furnishings. My sisters aren't really into antiques." Not only had he pulled on a light blue T-shirt, but he'd slipped on some sandals as well. "Okay. What'd you need me to sign?" he asked, easing down onto the loveseat.

Vanessa had spread out her paperwork on the coffee table. "This is my will. Let's get this signed first."

Seating herself on the larger sofa next to Vanessa, Sophie pulled out her notary tools from her purse. Signing and dating the pages, Vanessa began handing them over to Sophie. Quickly, she crimped and signed, leaving it up to Terry to sign and date the bottom of each page.

"These are specific instructions for the lawyer, my husband, and some friends. Let's go ahead and notarize these too, just so they're on record. Okay?"

"Sure. It's probably best that way anyway," Sophie answered. Repeating the notary process, after she and Terry had signed and witnessed each of the letters, she handed the papers back to Vanessa.

"Well," Terry said, slowly rising up from the couch, "I'd invite you to supper but..."

Sophie stood up, reaching for Terry's hand. "I'm sorry to just show up like this. I *really* like your house. And I miss being friends. I guess I've been in a different place since Matt and I split."

"I understand, Soph," he admitted, clearly sympathetic as he squeezed her hand. "To tell you the truth, I've been kind of busy myself."

"Hello?" a low female voice called out from the hallway. When a lovely Asian woman appeared in the doorway, Sophie appeared to be curiously taken aback.

"Grace." Dropping Sophie's hand, Terry slowly made his way through the living room. Turning back to Sophie with Grace's hand in his, he continued, "Sophie. This is my friend, Grace. She's Jake Loughlin's assistant over at the Dragonfly Inn."

Sophie was definitely brooding, studying the petite woman standing guardedly near Terry. Sophie nodded at Grace with a tightened smile, before turning to Vanessa. "And this is my friend, Vanessa. Well. We should be on our way," she mumbled stiffly. "Thanks for your help, Terry. I'll see you tomorrow."

Vanessa smiled. "Yes. Thank you." After stuffing her paperwork into her purse, Vanessa smiled at Grace as she shook Terry's hand. With a casual wave of her hand, she followed quickly behind Sophie, who was rushing down the hallway and out through the door.

Moments later, Vanessa caught up with Sophie. "Honey. I think it's time for you to face facts," she drawled, sliding gracefully into the car.

Obviously miserable, Sophie turned to Vanessa from the driver's seat. "What?"

"You're jealous."

Sophie froze, obviously stunned. But finally, she challenged Vanessa's statement. "*No.* Terry and I have *always* just been friends."

"Well, honey. Sometimes that's just the way it works. You obviously care for one another, and it's natural to unexpectedly fall in love. Believe me. I know this."

"You mean it happened that way with Sam?"

Vanessa answered solemnly, "No, honey. *Not* with Sam."

"Your *friend?*" Grace questioned ruefully.

Yes, Terry realized, Grace was hurt. Closing his eyes, Terry drew in a deep unsteady breath. Sophie had never looked at him like she had today. And suddenly, he'd been embarrassed about his relationship with Grace. Why, he couldn't say. Sophie had forsaken him to marry a guy who hadn't nearly been good enough for her.

Even after discovering Matt Ruston had been unfaithful, she'd stuck with that jerk.

Terry had been crushed. He'd been *so* in love with her. Beginning back in grade school, Sophie had defended him from the jerks who'd tagged him with the memorable name of *scarecrow,* because he'd always been awkward and scrawny. He'd been such a geek back then. Although Sophie was pretty and popular, she was kind and compassionate, and she'd always been there for him.

Even after she'd, most obviously, become aware of his unrequited feelings for her.

"I'm sorry, Grace," he answered, sheepishly.

"Me, too," she whispered softly.

"Let's eat." Abruptly, Terry led her back into the kitchen.

An hour later, following the routine they'd established over the previous nine months, they fell into companionable silence. After loading up the dishwasher and snatching up a sponge, Grace proceeded to thoroughly scrub down the kitchen counters, while Terry stashed away potato salad and jello in the refrigerator.

Grace smiled. "The steaks were great, Terry."

Still distracted, he moved around the kitchen. "Tell Jake that I said thanks." With his thumbs tucked into his pockets, he stood staring thoughtfully outside through the kitchen window.

"It's time for us to talk," Grace whispered softly. Snatching his hand in hers and leading him over to the kitchen table, she maneuvered him into a chair before taking a seat beside him.

She was visibly nervous when she cleared her throat. "She's lovely, Terry."

Terry's eyes shot to hers. "Who?"

"Oh, Terry—*come on*. You even named your *cat* after her!"

He closed his eyes, definitely feeling guilty. Resting his elbows on the table, he buried his face into his hands with resignation.

"It's okay, you know."

Terry's eyes finally met hers.

"I've always known there was someone else. And she's not entirely indifferent to you, you know."

He hesitated. "But, Grace. You and I…" His voice trailed off.

"We've been on and off for about nine months now. But I've always known you're not in love with me. I want more, too. You know?"

He nodded resignedly. "We'll still be friends?"

"Of course. But if you really want a chance with this girl, it'd probably be better for us to make a clean break right now."

Feeling miserable, he pleaded for her understanding. "I really thought I was over her, Grace."

"Something happened between you two today, though. I could feel the tension from the moment I walked into the room."

Terry sighed wearily. "Definitely."

"Time for me to go."

Terry was taken aback. But pulling himself up from his chair, and following her through the cottage and outside through the door, he escorted Grace out to her car. After a sweet final kiss, he reached for the handle of the door. Terry quietly watched her settle into her seat.

After starting up the engine of the car, she waved at Terry. Wearing a tense smile, she was on her way up the driveway.

Finally exiting the graveled road, Grace was heading back to the main road when her helpless sobs began. Contrary to the impression she'd left Terry, she'd never entered a relationship lightly.

He hadn't even attempted to stop her.

I think I've spent enough time in the water. How about you?"

Penny nodded hesitantly.

Slowly lifting himself from the tub, Sam eased out from the water. Picking up a towel and holding it open, he nodded at Penny, giving her a brief tender smile.

She was feeling shy when she stepped out from the water. But quickly wrapping the towel around her, Sam picked up another and swiftly began drying her arms and legs. Finally, he wrapped the towel around his own waist.

Sam laid a palm gently to each side of her face. Slowly sliding back her headband, he tangled his fingers in her loosened hair. "Your hair smells great. I'd know your scent anywhere," he whispered gruffly, gazing into her eyes. "Are we ready for bed?"

Again, she nodded her agreement.

Taking her hand, he steered her slowly into the bedroom. Observing the eerily darkening sky, Sam tugged her gently through the French doors onto the balcony, and, after wrapping her in his arms, together, they stared upward at the threatening sky. When a flash of lightning jaggedly lit up the horizon, Sam pulled her quickly back into the bedroom. "Should we close the doors?"

She cleared her throat, still feeling nervous. "I'm comfortable if you are."

Turning her gently, he brushed his lips over hers. "C'mon." Quietly, Sam maneuvered her through the room until they were standing beside the bed. Reaching for her towel, after observing her nod of acceptance, he tugged it off.

Recognizing the appreciation in Sam's eyes, Penny immediately became much more confident. But when she reached for Sam's towel, and pulled it off from around his waist, Penny was surprised to discover that Sam was once again aroused. "That was awfully quick," she muttered.

Sam laughed softly, drawing her closer. "I've got news for you." Raising one hand in the air, he snapped his fingers. "All I have to do is look at you, and it happens just like *that*."

Penny blinked, startled by his words. Suddenly, she began laughing as she collapsed onto the bed. It was just so absurd, this idea of being so arousing to Sam. And when Sam began laughing as well, Penny was totally at ease when he dropped down beside her onto the bed.

All of a sudden, after he'd rolled and tumbled her dead center into the middle of the enormous bed, she found herself wrapped within his arms "Better, now?" Sam whispered.

Nodding, she smiled. Amazingly, she really *was* feeling better. Making love with Sam just felt so *right*.

"Now it's my turn. Don't move," he growled. His mouth began worshipping the curves of her breasts, before he slowly eased up onto his knees.

When she self-consciously covered her breasts with her hands, Sam pried her hands apart calmly. He laid a tender kiss to the palm of each hand before resting them wide on the bed.

As his eyes roved slowly over her body, the molten depths of his dark brown eyes intensified. "God, you're so beautiful." He bent down, covering her lips with his. When his mouth left hers in gentle exploration, nipping and sucking and savoring, she shivered in eager anticipation. After Sam found a particularly sensitive spot in the hollow of her throat, his tongue lingered, swirling, before seductively trailing down to her breast.

Penny sighed restlessly.

When he took her nipple into his mouth, first nipping and then sucking, Penny began moaning feebly, attempting to reach out for Sam.

Rising up slowly from his eager ministrations, he growled, "No. Just lay back."

Restively, she followed Sam's command. Once Penny's hands finally dropped away, Sam returned his attention readily to her other breast. Taking her nipple into his mouth, he sucked and nipped repeatedly until her nipple was as firmly aroused as the other.

And when Sam's hand gently cupped her breasts, purposely circling his thumbs over her moist, aroused nipples, Penny began to tremble.

Sam's breath was ragged when his mouth dropped down, caressing the silky soft skin at her waist. Moving down further, his tongue lightly circled soft skin, before settling on the delicate skin of her inner thigh. Kneeling with his hands resting on her thighs, he gently spread her legs apart. His mouth began exploring lengthily, before he purposely traveled inward toward the delicately sensitive channel at their apex.

"Oh, Sam," she moaned, shivering as his tongue thrust and swirled, plunging deeper into her folds.

And then he stopped.

Penny stilled. "Sam?" she asked, hesitantly.

Raising his head, his eyes met hers heatedly. "I just wanted to make sure you were paying attention," he growled. "Do you like that?"

"*Of course, I do,*" she muttered, impatiently.

Laughing wickedly, he returned to his ministrations enthusiastically. Kissing, licking, and then kissing again, he blew a soft breath before plunging his tongue deep into the depths of her folds.

"Ohhh, Sam," she whispered, gasping. Once his mouth had deliberately guided her into a series of delightful sensational shudders, all of a sudden, Sam set her off abruptly into an astonishing explosion of exquisite torture.

"Penny," he groaned. Sliding upward and over her, he plunged hastily inside of her.

Limp and sated, at first she was unresponsive. But with the friction of his movements, she delighted in the sensations invoked by the movement of Sam's muscular, hair-roughened chest against the still tightly aroused nipples of her breasts.

Soon she was urging him on. Wrapping her arms around him, with each purposeful thrust into her body, Penny met up with him eagerly.

Urgently.

Slightly dazed, Sam became aware of Penny's legs locking around his waist. Setting up a slow powerful rhythm, interpreting each and every response by the degree of exquisite ecstasy appearing on Penny's face, Sam deliberately positioned every thrust to respond to her need.

And then, powerless, he lost all control. Hearing her frenzied moans of pleasure, Sam plunged faster and deeper and harder.

With a helpless shudder, Penny's body, once again, began to convulse. Reaching out, Sam wrapped his arms around her as he pulled her up against him, closer and tighter, grinding his hips into hers. Moaning her name, while covering her lips with his, suddenly exploding, Sam convulsed...and shattered.

Sam's breath was harsh and staggered when he finally collapsed on top of her. "Oh, Penny," he groaned. "*What are you doing to me?*"

Still breathing affectedly, Penny reached out silently to Sam. She ran a soothing hand over the curves of his lower back, while the other hand brushed his sweat-dampened hair from his forehead.

Gently disconnecting, he pulled her back into his arms as he settled in beside her.

Moments later, when Penny became aware of Sam's steady breathing, she finally closed her eyes and slept.

Sitting up quickly in the bed, Penny searched the unfamiliar room. She must've awoken to the crash of thunder, she realized, staring outside at the storm. Sliding out from under the covers and grabbing Sam's abandoned T-shirt from the chair, she slipped it over her head. Making her way to the opened French doors, she swiftly pulled them closed.

Sam came strolling in from the living room. "Sorry—I didn't mean to wake you."

"I think it was the thunder," she replied, still half asleep. Sam hadn't taken the time to pull on any clothing, before running through the suite and closing up windows and doors. Once again, Penny's eyes roved appreciatively over Sam's body. "Aren't you cold?"

"There you go again." Penny felt the warmth in her cheeks when Sam began to laugh. Strolling over to his duffel bag and pulling out a pair of boxers, he slipped them on.

After gazing at the bedroom fireplace, he turned to Penny. "It's kind of chilly in here. How about a fire?"

When Penny nodded her head, Sam reached over and flipped a switch. "Automatic fire," Sam observed, taking a seat in a comfortable wing chair resting near the fireplace.

"Yeah. I think I like a wood fire better. But this is sure convenient."

Penny began to settle into the matching wing chair. But reaching out and tugging her into his lap, Sam grinned, ignoring her startled squeak. "Let's just sit here for a couple of minutes and listen to the storm. Okay?"

"Okay." She grinned back, comfortably settling into his lap.

For several long minutes, aware of the whipping of the wind and an occasional crash of thunder, they stared silently at the fire as the storm outside began increasing in its intensity. About twenty minutes later, the wind suddenly died down. Finally, the heavy downpour began subsiding, transforming gradually into a gentle soothing shower.

"So. What time does your plane take off?"

"Ten."

Sam sighed. "We should probably be on our way by eight?"

"Yeah. I suppose we should get some sleep."

Sam nodded, appearing somewhat reluctant. "We'd better take Jake up on his offer of room service in the morning, then." He suddenly stood up from the chair with Penny in his arms.

Shaking her head in resignation, Penny actually began to giggle when Sam dropped her onto the bed. Quickly whipping back the covers, he jumped in beside her. "I suppose we *have* to sleep. Don't we?"

When she nodded her head, he gave her a wry grin. "I had a feeling you'd say that." He tucked the covers up to their chins before reaching for Penny and pulling her back into his arms.

"Good night, Sam."

Sam continued to hold Penny within his arms, savoring these last few contented moments together.

He heard her breath turn deep and steady. Pressing a gentle kiss to her brow, he whispered softly, "Good night, Penny."

Penny eventually awoke, becoming distantly aware of the surging sound of a shower. After a quick sleepy glance around the room, she stared outside through the window just long enough to recognize it wasn't raining.

Finally slipping from the bed, she quietly approached the bathroom, searching for Sam.

The room was warm and steamy, and Sam appeared to have been standing under the shower spray for a very long period of time. Was it only her imagination—or did he look just as miserable as she was beginning to feel?

God, she didn't want to leave him.

With his head bent down, Sam had his hands braced up against the shower wall. As Penny approached the shower, he turned to her with eyes that were openly exposed.

She stilled, gazing into those eyes. *Could he possibly care for her as much as she was beginning to care for him?* Quickly pulling the T-shirt she wearing up over her head, she stepped into the shower to join him.

Blinking, he suddenly smiled, wolfishly.

And then he snapped his fingers.

With wide eyes, she found her gaze dropping down. *Sure enough.* And laughing softly, she stepped into his waiting arms.

"I don't want you to go," he whispered fiercely, squeezing her into his embrace.

"I wish I didn't have to, Sam," she murmured softly, laying the side of her face against his chest.

He sighed, letting her loose from his arms. When she reached for her shampoo, Sam tugged it gently from her hands. "Let me." Squirting the shampoo into the palm of his hand, suddenly grinning, he held his hand beneath his nose. "Is *this* why you always smell so good?"

Startled, she grinned back. "Maybe.

Gently dampening Penny's hair under the spray of the shower, Sam began to slowly massage the shampoo into her scalp.

Closing her eyes, Penny steadied herself against the shower wall. "No one's ever done this for me before," she whispered quietly.

Slowing his motions, after a gentle brush of his lips to her brow, he responded, softly, "Would you believe that *I've* never done this for a woman before, either?" His hands resumed their seductive dance, traveling down lower, moving over her breasts and buttocks.

Turning and opening her eyes, gazing heatedly into Sam's, Penny released a ragged sigh. "Now, it's my turn," she muttered.

Widening his eyes, Sam smiled.

She ducked her head under the shower and rinsed first. Squirting a dab of shampoo into her hands, she reached up to Sam's dampened hair. Soaping up his hair, her hands began trailing down over his body, tangling through the soft, tawny hair on his chest. "It's funny. I don't remember *this* as a teenager," she murmured in a husky voice, running her fingers across his chest.

"The chest hair came a lot later. So, you *did* notice me back then," he muttered, obviously delighted. "I was never sure."

"I just thought that you weren't interested in *me*."

"Ah, Penny. I couldn't keep my eyes *off* of you."

And abruptly they stilled, gazing into each other's eyes.

"Can you wrap your legs around my waist?" Sam whispered urgently. With his hands traveling down over her body, he took hold of her buttocks. Leveling her, holding her up and then against him, Sam braced her against the shower wall while her legs tightened instinctively around his waist.

And then his lips covered hers, urgently nipping and tasting.

Sam was panting with unrestrained desire, when he swiftly plunged into her. Once he began surging and thrusting, he seemed unable to control his pace, as he frantically lost all semblance of control.

Recklessly inundated with need, Penny met each surge of his body elatedly, thrust for frantic thrust. Trembling, and then cursing, Sam muttered his relief with a muffled murmur of her name.

Delighting and savoring through each and every remarkably sensitized nerve in her body, with a helpless succession of shudders, Penny silently moaned—*oh, Sam*. She'd never felt so *alive*.

Still warm and steamy, the temperature of the water remained steady for the several long minutes they remained under the shower, wrapped within each other's arms.

Suddenly despondent, Sam clung to Penny. Letting her go today would be one of the most difficult things he'd ever had to do.

How was she ever going to be able to just go home, and go on with her life? When Penny stepped out from the shower, Sam grabbed a towel and guided her over to sit on an inset tiled bench. Kneeling before her, Sam began dabbing and drying her, almost reverently, with the towel before wrapping it around her body.

Grabbing another towel, he began drying himself. As usual, practically hypnotized by the sight of his naked body, she knew she was staring. But she just couldn't seem to help herself.

Giving her a rueful smile, he shook his head as he waggled his brows. "We're not gonna have time to eat breakfast if you keep staring at me like that," he muttered hoarsely, dropping his towel onto the bench. Turning his attention to his unshaven face, he sighed, with a regretful glance at her reflection in the mirror.

She smiled with resignation, before standing up from the bench and making her way into the bedroom.

Dressed in jeans and a creamy sleeveless blouse, Penny was in the process of slipping into her sandals when a knock sounded at the door.

With a towel wrapped around his waist, Sam appeared at the bathroom door. "That's probably our breakfast."

Penny shook her head dazedly. "When did you have time to order it?"

"I didn't sleep much," he admitted with a rueful grin.

Making her way through the suite to unlock the door, Penny was greeted by an upbeat teenager, dressed in a white T-shirt, sporting the logo of the Dragonfly Pointe Inn.

Rolling in a stainless steel cart, set up with an elegant service for two, the young man positioned the cart before the French doors, to optimize their view of the lake. Quickly whipping off the covers from the plates, he motioned with his hand to one of the chairs he'd acquired from the dining room.

"But…"

"Don't worry, Ms. Wentworth, the tip is already covered," he eagerly assured her, pouring her juice.

"I'm sure a little extra is always appreciated," Sam added, joining them. Also wearing jeans, Sam was smoothing out his pockets after tucking in his T-shirt. He slipped a folded twenty to the teenager inconspicuously. "I think I've met you before. Haven't I?"

"Yeah. I'm a good friend of Dan Callahan's, Chief. My name's Kevin. Kevin Holliman."

"Sure." Sam reached over, shaking Kevin's hand.

Kevin poured Sam's juice, resting the pitcher on the table. Assessing their needs discreetly, he poured them each a cup of coffee. "Anything else I can do, Ms. Wentworth? Chief?"

"No. We're fine. Thanks Kevin." Penny smiled as Kevin saluted before retreating efficiently through the door.

Sam took a seat at their makeshift table.

"Will everyone be giving you a hard time after spending the night with me?"

"Actually, I don't think so. I'm pretty sure Jake has rules that apply for their guests. Even me." Sam laughed. "Of course that doesn't mean that the employees won't gossip. Especially the teenagers."

For the next few minutes, they turned their attention to their breakfast.

"That was good." Penny observed several minutes later, dropping her crumpled napkin on the cart. "How'd you know what to order?"

"Easy. I was watching what you ate yesterday." With a grimace, Sam sighed, standing up from his chair. "I guess I'd better get my stuff together."

"I'll throw on some makeup and dry my hair—and then I'll be ready to go, too." With reluctance, Penny stood up from her seat and followed Sam.

After she and Sam packed up their clothing, Penny returned to the bathroom. Once she'd applied her makeup, she began gathering loose items.

Sam peeked into the bathroom. "I see you still haven't dried your hair. Why don't I load up your suitcases with my bag in the truck, and meet you down in the lobby in, what...about fifteen or twenty minutes?"

"Maybe quicker," she replied, following him into the bedroom. After glancing around the room, she latched up her suitcase and zipped up her clothing bag. "I can bring along my overnight bag and purse. I think that's it."

"No problem," Sam answered. After a long lingering glance around the room, snatching up her suitcase and hoisting her clothing bag over his arm, Sam gave her a wry smile as he gazed into her eyes. Bending down, he grabbed his duffel bag. "Did you want me to check us out?"

"That's fine." She escorted him to the door.

"Fifteen minutes, then." Obviously reluctant for their weekend to end, Sam gazed at Penny like he was memorizing her face, before he finally turned and walked out from the suite.

Penny sighed with resignation before returning to the bathroom.

Manipulating her dryer, Penny was in the final process of loosely curling and brushing her hair when the phone began to ring.

Could Sam be having a problem? She rushed into the bedroom to pick up the phone. "Hello?"

Although there was a jumbling of indistinct voices in the background, no one responded.

"*Hello?*"

"*Stay away from him. He's mine.*" Chilling Penny to the bone, the low, scratchy voice echoed through the receiver.

"*Excuse me?*"

"You heard me." Shrieking with rage, the female's voice became louder. "*Stay away from Sam!*"

Penny gasped, as the receiver of the phone dropped inadvertently from her hand. Recognizing numbly the genuineness of the woman's poisonous threat, she was suddenly gripped by fear.

Penny was unusually quiet as they drove on to the airport, and she was painfully aware of Sam's anxious stares. After a few struggled attempts to lure Penny into conversation, looking irritable, Sam became silent.

She was *totally* confused. Something restless and undefinable had come alive inside of her, after her amazing weekend with Sam.

It was a feeling she'd *never* experienced before.

Was Sam seeing someone?

The voice on the phone had come off half-crazy and delusional. Should she tell Sam about the call?

She sighed. Why? She was on her way back to New York. Besides, when would she have the opportunity to see Sam again, anyway? Her life and responsibilities were centered in New York.

They finally reached the airport. After quickly scooping up her purse and overnight bag, Penny remained silent as she jumped from the truck and avoided Sam's assistance.

Gathering Penny's luggage, lagging slowly behind her, Sam was attempting to control his frustration. *What was going on here?* After spending the most incredible night of his life with Penny, she was treating him like some kind of casual acquaintance.

While Penny approached the desk to check in for her flight, Sam stood off in the distance keeping his eyes focused on the revolving doors that they'd just come through. Dressed in a black suit, the man who strolled in through the revolving doors barely managed to conceal the weapon holstered under his arm.

Standing before a vendor, Sam turned his eyes on an assortment of reading material, and pulled out a paper. Digging some change from his pocket, he handed it over to the vendor. Turning away from the display, while attempting to remain inconspicuous, Sam studied the man who'd been following him. With his eyes still shaded by a pair of sunglasses, sure enough, he had his attention focused on Sam.

Penny was approaching Sam with hesitance. The plane would be ready to board in less than five minutes and they'd yet to say goodbye.

She wanted to cry.

"They're ready for my luggage, now," she told Sam. Remaining silent, Sam carried her luggage into the boarding area and assisted her with weighing it in.

When the flight began boarding, Sam appeared suddenly stricken. "Penny. This isn't it. I'm *not* saying goodbye."

"Sam. We have two different lives," she reproached gently, blinking the tears from her eyes.

"You'll call me. Right?" he asked, gruffly.

"Well..."

He set his hand on her chin, turning her face back to his. As he steadily held her gaze, Sam's expression was fierce. "*Right?*"

And when Sam covered her mouth with his, that unidentifiable something inside of her came alive again when his lips moved languidly over hers. As the kiss soon turned from gentle to passionate, but eventually became remarkably tender, Penny was powerless to resist him. When Sam pulled away, she bit down nervously on her lip and nodded her agreement.

A voice blasted out from the speakers announcing the final boarding call.

With obvious reluctance, Sam finally let her loose from his arms. Reaching into his pocket, he pulled out a small box, wrapped in shiny silver. "This is for you," he whispered softly. "Open it on your way home."

This time, Penny couldn't blink away her tears. "Oh, Sam. You shouldn't have."

"I wanted to. God, I'm gonna miss you," he muttered. Wrapping an arm around her shoulders, he guided her over to the boarding area. With a gentle shove, he sent her on her way.

Moving forward into the boarding area, Penny turned back to Sam with a shaky smile, and lifted her hand in farewell.

Looking decidedly grim, Sam waved back.

For the first ten minutes in the air, Penny had stared at the small box decorated with curly silver ribbons, until she'd finally built up the courage to open it. Returning to Missouri after a week-long visit with her grandchildren, Regina, the woman seated beside her, was certainly curious to discover its contents.

Carefully and methodically folding down the paper, Penny unwrapped the box. Inhaling a deep breath, she finally removed its cover.

"Oh, Sam," she moaned aloud.

"How lovely," Regina observed, quietly.

Penny held up the pendant. "It is. Isn't it?" A pair of delicate dragonflies, shaped from shiny silver, sheathed an exquisite blue sapphire. Meticulously detailed and precise, the setting for the heart-shaped sapphire had obviously been hand-crafted.

Regina smiled. "And that stone's the same lovely blue as the color of your eyes, my dear." As Penny fumbled with the clasp, Regina asked, "Would you like some help?" Silently, she pulled the pendant from Penny's hand. She turned Penny gently toward the window before attaching the clasp at her neck.

As her thoughts began churning through a multitude of emotions, Penny eased back into her seat.

"You must love each other very much."

Penny blinked.

But why was she so surprised? Indistinctly, she'd recognized her own feelings for Sam the day of the wedding. But what about Sam's? Could he possibly love *her*?

Penny and Regina continued to chat companionably. It was a shame she'd have to transfer in Chicago while Regina continued on to Missouri.

As Penny prepared to exit the plane, Regina held out a hand. "It was so nice to meet you, my dear."

Penny smiled. "Thanks for putting up with me."

Regina smiled back.

Once she reached the airport terminal, zeroing in on a line of pay phones, she picked up the receiver in one of the booths. Digging out her calling card, she carefully entered the numbers from the card before adding the digits for Sam's home phone.

He wouldn't be home. But at least she could thank him for the lovely pendant.

"This is Sam. Leave a message and I'll return your call as soon as possible."

"Sam. This is Penny. The pendant's *beautiful*, Sam. Thank you so much. I know I was acting kind of odd on our drive to the airport, but I had this really weird phone call before I left the suite this morning, and I know I should've probably told you about it..."

Unexpectedly, her call was interrupted by the cool, controlled voice of a woman. "Hello. I'm sorry. Sam's not here right now. Can I take a message?"

Penny suddenly became uncertain. Who was *this*? It definitely wasn't the voice of the woman who'd threatened her this morning.

"Well," Penny responded. "If you'd just see that he gets this message, I'd really appreciate it."

"Sure. I'll make sure my husband gets your message," the woman answered, seemingly indifferent.

Penny was shocked into silence. Wasn't Sam *divorced*?

"Hello?" the woman coolly inquired.

"I...thank you. I'd appreciate that."

In stunned confusion, Penny hung up the phone. Roaming through the airport, she searched out a quiet corner. Dropping down into a seat, she covered her face with her hands, feeling dazed.

After finally regaining control of her emotions, Penny stood up from her seat. Pulling her boarding pass from her purse with a shaking hand, she made her way through the airport and began searching mechanically for her flight. Locating the gate, Penny settled into a seat nearby and awaited her boarding call.

Fifteen

*B*etween the flashes of lightning and the continuous crash of thunder, Vanessa had spent a restless night tossing and turning. But most of her restlessness could be attributed to nerves, she admitted reluctantly.

How could she handle her situation with Sam yet still appease DeMarcus? There was no way she'd continue being used as a tool of manipulation.

She might just as well be dead.

After returning to Sam's to watch videos, she and Sophie had feasted on chicken from the local take out joint. Strange how she'd totally *enjoyed* it.

In less than two hours, John would arrive to escort her to the Riverbend Lodge. Her eyes roamed the interior of the family room. Sophie had helped her straighten up last evening before returning home. The dishwasher had been unloaded and, after wiping down the kitchen counters, Vanessa would return the kitchen to its usual immaculate order. She'd even remembered to take out the garbage.

The only chore that remained was sorting through her clothing for Sophie. Even though she hadn't discovered a whole lot of information about Sam's blonde, Sophie had been surprised to learn that the woman, as a teenager, had once been her babysitter. Apparently, as a child, Sophie had adored her.

Vanessa sighed. Yes—she admitted to herself grudgingly—this woman sounded exactly like the right kind of a woman for Sam.

Eventually.

But first, Vanessa had to play her part, attempting for reconciliation.

Grabbing a notepad and pen and then pouring herself another cup of coffee, Vanessa headed off into the bedroom. Once again wearing her navy slacks and tunic, Vanessa grouped the rest of her belongings in the closet. Stacking three extra purses on the shelf, she lined up her hangers immediately below.

"What the heck. She might just as well have the luggage, too," she muttered aloud. After all, she had three bags of clothing and accessories awaiting her at the lodge.

She'd hold on to Sophie's sandals for now.

The journal.

She'd forgotten about the journal *again.* Well, she couldn't bring it along with her today. What if they searched her?

She'd have to hide it.

But she couldn't leave it here at Sam's. Eventually, DeMarcus would realize it was missing and, most likely, suspect that she had it.

And she needed it for leverage.

Reaching up under the lining on the closet shelf, she pulled out the notebook. "Sorry, Sophie," she muttered. "I sure hope I'm not setting you up for trouble." Writing a short note, she slipped into the pages of the journal.

Pulling her largest purse from the shelf and carefully inspecting its interior, she breathed in a sigh of relief. Running back into the kitchen, she pulled out the shears she'd used to trim Sophie's hair from inside the drawer. Also noticing a roll of black electrical tape in a compartment of the tray within, she snatched it up as well.

Returning to the bedroom, she flipped on the overhead light. Holding the purse with a steady hand, she began neatly slicing and ripping its inner seam. The journal fit into the opening of the doubled lining perfectly. Still allowing the centered zipper to open and close effortlessly, the rigid panel dividing the interior of the purse appeared as an element of design. Cutting a precise length of electrical tape to match the panel, she patiently applied the tape along the inner seam and carefully folded it over.

Picking up her suitcase, she propped it open deliberately on the oversized chair. After removing her other purses from the closet shelf, she positioned her altered purse atop the others inside the open suitcase, hiding it effectively in plain sight.

Whipping off an uncomplicated note to Sophie, she laid it visibly on top of the purse. Sophie would arrive here on her lunch hour to pick up the clothes since, supposedly, Sam never bothered to come home for lunch. Suddenly noticing her bracelet and pendant abandoned on the dresser, Vanessa scooped them up decisively and placed the lovely creations of rose and purple amethyst in the suitcase.

A gift, she added as a side bar in her note. Envisioning Sophie's face when she saw the jewelry, Vanessa smiled.

Damn. What was wrong with her? She was becoming maudlin.

With a final, thoughtful glance around the room, Vanessa knew she could count on Sophie to straighten any obvious disarray.

Placing the shears and tape in their proper places in the kitchen drawer, Vanessa quickly cleaned out the coffee pot and dumped the grounds. She and Sophie had erased all of her personal documents from Sam's computer last night. Sophie had offered to drop Vanessa's will and paperwork at Wes Stanton's office, in his lock box, this morning on her way into work.

Suddenly, the phone began to ring. Vanessa became aware of the low husky voice of a female apologetically leaving Sam a long message.

Should she?

Why not? She had to start this campaign sometime.

And first, to effectively convince DeMarcus that she was following his orders, she had to logically eliminate Sam's girlfriend.

Interrupting the caller, Vanessa picked up the phone. "Hello. I'm sorry. Sam's not here right now. Can I take a message?"

"Well," the woman responded, obviously startled. "If you'd just see that he gets this message, I'd really appreciate it."

Seemingly indifferent, Vanessa answered, "Sure. I'll make sure my husband gets your message."

Obviously at a loss for words, the woman remained silent.

"Hello?" Vanessa inquired, innocently.

"I...thank you. I'd appreciate that." With a click, the line went dead.

"Damn," Vanessa muttered, staring at the receiver in her hand. "Since when did *I* develop a conscience?" Carefully returning the receiver onto its cradle, reaching over to the answering machine, she purposely pressed delete.

The doorbell rang.

And Vanessa jumped.

"Show time," she mumbled. Snatching up her purse, she made her way through the house to the front door. Vanessa peered through the eyepiece, and immediately became apprehensive. Taking in a deep breath, she hesitated before opening the door. "Carlton. Where's John?"

Frank Carlton's nephew was dressed completely in black. With his eyes concealed behind his mirrored sunglasses, tall, dark, and menacing, there was definitely no mistaking him for anything other than what he was—a bodyguard, as well as an enforcer. "Mr. DeMarcus had other plans for John today."

Shivering uneasily at the coldness in Jess Carlton's voice, Vanessa was instantly concerned. Had they noticed John's anxiety yesterday?

They strolled over to a black sedan parked along the street. Eyeing the darkly tinted windows, Vanessa recognized it immediately as the vehicle that had been following her and Sophie yesterday.

Sliding into the back seat, Vanessa remained quiet on their trek through town. Heading northeast and departing the town of Crystal Rock, they followed a long and winding road. After traveling across one bridge and then over another, they drove along a newly-paved access road. They finally approached another extended bridge that was completely modernized and sculpted from shiny steel. As they slowly began crossing over the bridge, Vanessa gazed down uneasily at the steep thundering falls of the Crystal Rock River.

Five minutes later, they drove into a sprawling parking lot. Carlton pulled alongside a compact car, wedged into a space near a deserted, wooded retreat. Leaving the engine of his car running, he stepped out from the car and opened her door.

He reached into his pocket, pulling out two keys. "One is for the rental car and the other for your room," he said, placing them into her outstretched hand. "Uncle Frank is waiting for you down by the water."

Turning abruptly, he slipped back into his car. After uneasily observing his retreat, Vanessa hopped into the rental car. Starting up the engine, she maneuvered the compact through the lot. After parking near the lodge in an area designated for guests, she stepped out from the car and locked it up.

Following a winding path around the lodge, she found herself on top of a spacious deck that boasted a magnificent view of both the lake and the river. Apparently, you could order meals out here. A bar was tucked in beside the entrance of the restaurant, while a few of the tables were filled with guests, who were shaded by umbrellas. Following the steep widened steps leading down to an extended pier, immediately, she noticed the luxury cruiser parked in an isolated slip near the end of the pier.

Frank Carlton leaned negligently against the railing of the cruiser, inhaling a long final drag from his cigarette, before impatiently flicking it into the water. The lines in his face appeared even more deeply etched than they'd been the previous week. With raven-black hair streaked abundantly with gray, today, he looked every one of his fifty-nine years.

Without a single sign of acknowledgement, he immediately growled, "You need to find a way to get this done—*right away*. We don't have much time."

Vanessa hesitated, before boarding the cruiser and joining him. It was time to figure out what they actually needed from Sam. "And exactly *what* determines that?"

Frank's eyes met hers. Staring at her lengthily and deliberately, he seemed to be making up his mind. With a shrug he answered, "Shirley Edmonds. She's dying. We need you to take charge of some property before Sam realizes it's his."

She asked quickly, with deliberate calculation, "What property?"

"That's all you need to know," he muttered. "Just think of everything you'll finally inherit now that Peter's gone. You'd better get a move on. I don't want anyone to see you here with me. I'm pretty sure Sam saw me following him the other day, so I'm getting out of town. In the future, you'll report directly to Carlton." With a nod, he dismissed her.

When Frank began fidgeting with a fishing pole that'd been resting against the rail, Vanessa retreated quietly onto the pier. Frank had his man start up the engine and, soon, the cruiser was heading out toward the center of the lake.

Well. It looked like she'd only had the rest of the afternoon to formulate a plan. Vanessa returned to the lodge's deck, seating herself at one of the tables. Eventually, a waitress appeared, handing her a menu. After ordering a sandwich and coffee, she considered her options musingly.

She'd appear at Sam's home this evening with dinner.

And a bottle of wine.

She'd discuss the death of her father.

And ask for Sam's help. After all, *she had* discovered the body. Sam had always been a sucker for the damsel in distress routine.

Her grilled tuna on rye was extremely tasty. With a satisfied smile, Vanessa made sure to include a generous tip when she charged the meal to her room. All she'd been doing since arriving in town was eating, she was somewhat surprised to realize. Now that she'd come up with a tentative plan, she'd walk off her lunch before retreating to her room, Vanessa decided.

Stretching leisurely and standing up, she headed back down towards the pier, but veered off along a pathway. Hoisting the long lengthy handle of her purse over her head and shoulder, she secured it in place.

Ignoring a sudden shiver of apprehension, she stopped along the path and stared at the steep turbulent drop foaming at the base of the falls. The beauty of it all was quite magnificent, she had to admit. Half-ripped from its anchoring, a trunk of an enormous pine had dropped across the more dynamic division of the river. Had the tree become uprooted in the storm last night? Surveying the area, Vanessa suddenly noticed an odd assortment of felled trees and ripped branches strewn across the path ahead.

It was certainly much cooler today, she observed, shivering. With the threat of additional storms forecast for this afternoon, Vanessa turned her gaze upward at the sky. Sure enough, the clouds were darkening.

Staring across the river, she noticed two teenagers in a canoe steering expertly through the current. But Vanessa became uneasy. The water alongside the opposite riverbank appeared to be deceptively calm, as opposed to the shoreline belonging to the Riverbend Lodge. The actively raging current of the river crashed turbulently against the outcrop she was standing on.

What the...? Suddenly aware of an intensely painful pinch at her windpipe, Vanessa was unable to scream in protest.

In a daze, she gazed down gradually in slow motion, observing a flowering bloom of red sponging through the white of her tunic.

Ah—she finally realized—*her premonition was actually coming true.*

Vanessa could feel herself fading from far, far away.

Releasing a strangled gasp, she silently collapsed, dropping to the ground...lifeless.

Sixteen

$\mathcal{H}$aving spent the last three months looking forward to this past weekend, now that Penny was returning to New York, Sam was feeling suddenly disheartened.

This weekend had lived up to every single one of his expectations. *And a hell of a lot more.*

After spending over an hour feeling sorry for himself, he sighed, eyeing the clock on his dashboard. It was time to confront his tail. With about twenty minutes remaining before reaching Crystal Rock, he pulled into the deserted rest area ten miles south of Northwest Community College.

Sure enough, once the gray sedan had followed his truck into the parking lot, the driver parked his car where he was clearly able to observe Sam's truck. Deliberately, Sam headed toward the restrooms, where, slipping out through the opposite door, he ducked into the common area. Stepping around a long row of vending machines, he pulled out change from his pocket. With his soda in hand, Sam slipped back into a darkened corner, observing the entrance.

Pulling off his sunglasses and raking a hand through his hair, the harried agent eventually scrambled in through the door.

Silently, Sam joined him. "FBI, I presume?

With a hand instinctively moving over his weapon, the agent sighed resignedly as his eyes met Sam's. "I should've known you'd figure it out," he muttered. "You know why I'm here?"

"I can guess." Sam motioned him over to a long row of seating. Estimating the man to be in his early thirties, he was an unfortunate redhead, with skin marked by a multitude of ruddy, faded freckles, so he was easily recognizable. Once the agent was seated, Sam dropped down onto the bench beside him. "Peter Gerard?"

The man nodded his head. "Coincidentally, my parents were in the process of moving here, and I was assisting with their move. I was asked to maintain surveillance in case your wife appeared. You were immediately cleared of any involvement in Gerard's murder, by the way. I'm Shane Donnelly," he added, pulling out an I.D. After shoving his I.D. back into his pocket, he reached out, shaking Sam's hand.

Suddenly, Sam picked up on Shane's words. "What do you mean by calling Vanessa *my wife?*"

For a moment, Shane shifted his gaze, looking decidedly uncomfortable. "I'm not sure I was supposed to tell you," he mumbled, returning his gaze to Sam. "But during the last year—in the course of our investigation—we found a few loose ends."

"Loose ends? You don't mean...?" Sam was shocked. "I signed papers!"

Awkwardly, Shane cleared his throat. "Look. I don't know much about this. I was mainly on surveillance in New Orleans. I'm not exactly sure what happened, but I think what you signed was a legal separation. There was no property settlement."

"*Damn, that woman.* I should've realized that our divorce went through *way* too smoothly. *But why?*"

Shane shrugged. "We haven't been able to figure that out yet, either." Hesitating, he continued, "Plus there's more."

Now livid with anger, Sam barked impatiently, *"What?"*

"Apparently, they found some tapes when they went through Gerard's personal effects."

"What kind of tapes?"

"Video. But of exactly what, I'm not sure yet. I think they want you down in New Orleans, with your wife, for routine questioning."

"But why *me?*"

"Since you knew Gerard, I think that they're looking for your expertise. Apparently, there's some pretty delicate stuff on those tapes."

"Ah. You mean my oh-so-perfect father-in-law, along with my wife, may have been using whatever's on those tapes for *blackmail?*"

In silent acknowledgement, Shane raised a brow.

Crunching up his empty soda can, Sam rose to his feet impatiently and tossed it into the trash.

"Nice shot," Shane remarked, dryly.

"Look. I know you're only trying to do your job, but it's not necessary to follow me. Give me a number. *If* she shows up, I'll call you immediately."

With a nod, Shane pulled a card from his pocket.

Pulling out his wallet, Sam shoved the card inside.

Side by side, they made their way into the parking lot.

Recognizing it was stupid to take his anger out on Shane Donnelly, Sam hesitated before reaching his truck. "FBI, huh? You wouldn't happen to know Jake Loughlin—would you?"

Shane snorted. "Everybody knows Jake. He's actually the reason I'm here, by the way—or, rather that my parents decided to uproot their lives and move here."

Sam was startled. "And that'd be *because?*"

"My dad's an M.D. They needed a doctor available for the nursing home, Whispering Pines, along with the special education facility that's being built in Crystal Rock."

"*Special Education Facility?*"

Shane was eyeing him oddly. "Apparently, the school's supposed to be completed within the next few months. But they're still raising funds for the residential center."

Sam smiled. "Well, I'll be damned."

Shane mumbled, "I don't know what I might've said to improve your mood, but I'm happy to see that you're being more cooperative."

"I'm still furious," Sam admitted with a sigh. "But it's not your fault."

After another brief handshake and a final nod of farewell, Shane made his way over to his vehicle.

Sitting for a quiet moment behind the wheel, Sam attempted desperately to control his frustration. Now he was an adulterer. He'd been only too willing to let Vanessa handle the details of the divorce, not even hiring his own lawyer. How could he have been so stupid?

So—*why* hadn't Vanessa wanted the divorce?

In other words, he considered thoughtfully, *what* would she gain from him by remaining married?

It was almost half past noon by the time Sam reached Crystal Rock. Immediately heading into the station, he decided he'd give Nat and Terry a much needed break before taking time for his own lunch. Still considering Vanessa's duplicity, he was moody and restless, and really wasn't ready to tackle food.

Greeted immediately by Sophie Ruston's bright, cheerful smile upon entering the station, Sam was instantly distracted when he noticed a frown cross over Terry's face.

Interesting. What was going on *there*? Shaking off his black mood, Sam smiled, nodding in Terry's direction.

"Hey," he called out to Nat. "You guys go for lunch. I appreciate you two taking over the weekend shifts."

"Hey, Sam. No problem. Think I'll set off early for patrol and cruise around the resorts."

"You go too, Soph."

"Are you sure, Sam?"

"I think I can handle any incoming calls. I'll probably just catch up with my messages, anyway."

With a nod of assent, Sophie opened up the bottom drawer of her desk, pulling out her purse. Terry was frantically motioning in her wake, but she failed to notice him approaching her as she quickly escaped through the door.

"Wonder what's up? She's sure in a hurry," Terry grumbled.

"Yeah. Kind of odd."

"I was gonna ask her out for lunch."

Startled, Sam raised a brow. "What about Grace?

"She kind of decided we should break it off."

"*She* decided?"

"Well, me, too," he admitted, ruefully. "She said she needed more. And to tell you the truth, Sam, I've always kind of had a thing for Sophie."

Sam sighed. "I can sure sympathize with you there."

"Sam. About Sophie...?"

Sam held up a staying hand. "Don't worry, Terry. I've never had, or never will have, any interest in Sophie other than as a friend."

"She's been in kind of weird place since her divorce."

"I figured that. What a jerk that ex was, huh?"

"The biggest," Terry acknowledged. "Well—I guess I'll hit the café." And with a nod of farewell, he was out the door.

Appreciating the silence of the station, Sam stepped into his office. Opening the closet door, he pulled out a freshly pressed uniform. Slipping off his jeans and stepping into his khakis, he buttoned the matching short-sleeved shirt over his T-shirt.

Turning around, he froze.

"*Diane*. What are *you* doing here?" he asked, impatiently. So much for peace and quiet.

"Why, Sam. Since your girlfriend's left town, I thought you might want some female companionship."

Picking up and sifting through his messages, Sam was extremely annoyed when he dropped into the chair behind his desk. "Diane. I'm pretty sure that I made it clear—I don't know *how* many times these past few months—*I'm just not interested.*"

Easing down into a chair and facing Sam, Diane crossed her shapely long legs deliberately to their best advantage. With shoulder-length, ash-brown hair, effectively framing her sultry-green eyes, at forty, Diane was still exceedingly attractive. But advertising her attributes quite blatantly, in a form-fitting skirt and a low cut top, her figure was a little more lush than it'd been in high school. Having been married twice, as well as divorced, she was obviously still an accomplished seductress. But Sam could easily understand why both of her marriages had failed.

She leaned forward purposely, intentionally exposing the enticing curves of her breasts. "Oh, come on, Sam. How about just meeting me for a drink tonight?

Damn. Didn't this woman ever take no for an answer?

Sam stood up from his chair, fighting to control his anger. "I'm sorry, Diane." Grabbing her arm, he yanked her from her chair before escorting her forcefully through the deserted office. Opening the door that led out onto the street, he shoved her ungraciously through the door. "Thanks. But, no thanks. Now, I've got work to catch up on. See ya around."

She was gaping when he closed the door in her face. Returning to his office, he sat back down behind his desk. Shaking his head with a humorless laugh, he muttered out loud, "Just what I need on top of everything else."

Promptly, he began sifting through his messages, returning the most important calls. Noticing, with disgust, several messages from Diane, he crumpled and discarded the notes.

Finally, Sam was able to focus his attention on the Peterson robbery. After sorting through a half-dozen other file folders, relating to the earlier robberies, he eyed the supersize dry erase board he'd purchased the week before. Neatly transferring pertinent information from each of the files, he began creating a calculated inventory across the board.

Returning from lunch, Terry entered the office quietly and studied the board.

"I probably should've had Nat come back here this afternoon. But I suppose it can wait until the morning." Thoughtfully, Sam added, "Maybe I should talk to Mike and Jenny Callahan, first, anyway."

Terry raised a questioning brow.

"I forgot. You weren't around when Nat and I discussed recruiting Dan Callahan, to help us identify any teenagers we should be looking at more closely."

"Good idea. Dan will have eyes and ears where we won't."

"And whoever's behind these robberies is getting bolder. But now that they've stolen merchandise that's more easily identifiable, we might be able to work with the area resale shops."

Still considering the board, Terry nodded his agreement.

Sam heard the sound of activity in the outer office.

While Sam continued to study the files, Terry strolled out from Sam's office.

Wearing a strangely pleased smile on her face, Sophie was settling in front of her computer with an open folder in her hands.

"Hey, Soph. You sure cleared out of here fast enough, when Sam said we could go for lunch."

Sophie glanced up from her files. Oddly, Terry had attempted to speak to her more today than he had in the previous three months. And it didn't help that, for the first time in her life, she felt vulnerable in his presence. "Uh, yeah. I had something to do for Vanessa today."

Terry's eyes met hers uncertainly. Taking in a deep breath, he decided—*why not just go for it?* "I was gonna ask you to have lunch with me."

Sophie was obviously startled. "I don't know if that's such a good idea, Terry," she answered wryly. "I mean, contrary to what your girl-friend actually says, most women don't like it when their men hang out with other women."

"Sophie—about me and Grace..." But before Terry could continue, he was interrupted by Nat's voice, crackling on the radio.

Quickly, Sophie responded, rolling her chair from behind her desk to face the radio. "Excuse me, Terry." Picking up the headphones, she flipped on a switch. "This is base, Nat."

"We have a situation, Sophie. I need Sam and Terry, here, at the Riverbend Lodge, *ASAP*. There's been a homicide. I repeat—there's been a homicide."

Sam came rushing from his office, grabbing the headset from Sophie. "This is Sam, Nat. Give me the details."

"It's a woman, Sam. Caucasian. Probably mid to late thirties. She was in the water. I can tell by looking at her neck that it wasn't an accident. A couple kids in a canoe found her hooked within a fallen tree, and pulled her out thinking she might still be alive. She was only minutes away from being dragged by the current over the falls, and disappearing downstream. It's pretty bad, Sam. I don't recognize her face but, then again, she's faced downward. I'd rather not reposition the body before we process the crime scene."

"After I contact the state police, Nat, Terry and I are on our way. Over and out."

Grabbing back the headphones, Sophie was grim when she reassured Sam. "I'll make the calls. Just go ahead and get moving."

Rushing through the door and into Sam's truck, Sam and Terry were promptly on their way.

Twenty minutes later, Sam was approaching the lodge. Veering the wheels of his truck from the parking lot, he travelled over gravel and grass to get nearer to the water's edge.

Jumping from the truck, Sam turned his gaze nervously upward, studying the darkening sky. "Damn it, Terry. It's gonna be rough getting the scene processed with the weather coming in."

With a grim nod of acknowledgement, Terry gathered the processing equipment from the back seat.

Although Nat was attempting to preserve the crime scene, a small crowd had gathered along the riverfront.

Sam approached a young woman videotaping the scene. "I'm sorry, ma'am. I'll need that tape."

Obviously reluctant, she pressed a button, popping out the tape. "There's some family video on there, too," she added, ruefully.

"Leave your name and number. I'm not sure you'll be getting it back, though. It depends on what's there."

With a sigh, she nodded.

Sam motioned at the crowd. "Please," he shouted, loudly. "It's important that all of you return to the lodge. Do *not* check out. We need everyone away from this area so we can process the scene properly."

Although Sam heard some grumbling, the majority of the crowd began moving away with reluctance. Grabbing the throw away camera from the box of processing equipment, Sam took a few discreet pictures of those in retreat.

After surveying the area, Sam turned to the owner of the lodge. "Steve, I don't know if you still have those portable ice-fishing tents?"

"Sure do, Sam. We've got three."

Sam sighed wearily, studying the sky. "We'd better have them all."

"Anything else?" Steve Jacobs asked.

"Well. I could use a video camera."

"No problem there, Sam. With the new baby, Sherry keeps ours at her desk."

"I'd appreciate that, Steve."

Ordering two of his employees to retrieve the tents from the storage shed, Steve rushed up to the lodge so he could borrow the video camera from his wife.

After signaling for Nat to remain with the woman's body, Sam motioned for Terry to follow as he traveled north along the riverbank, carefully inspecting the pathway.

Snapping an occasional picture with his disposable camera, Sam studied the ground along the path intently. Eventually signaling for Terry to hold back, Sam began snapping a series of pictures of the compacted surface of a wide grassy outcrop along the riverbank.

Scoping out the area efficiently, with a sweeping hand, Sam finally motioned at Terry. "This is where it happened." A path of bloodied matted grass led down to the river. "She was dragged into the water after she was killed right here." Sam pointed down at the peak of the outcrop. Rubble and grass appeared to be layered with a wide pool of dried blood.

As he followed Sam's line of vision, Sam noticed that Terry's face looked a little green.

Approaching them from along the path, two employees in a golf cart pulled up with the tents piled high in back.

"We'll need to protect this area." Sam was still standing on the outcrop. "Maybe pop up the tents first, guys, and then Terry and I can secure them in place." Looking at Terry, he added, "I was gonna wait for the state police, but I think we'd better begin processing because of the weather. We'll tent over the body, too, and use the third tent to protect our equipment. I just hope we don't get much wind."

Jogging down the path with the video camera loaded and ready in his hand, Steve Jacobs handed it over to Sam as he stepped down from the outcrop.

Sam began filming the entire area methodically. Being sure to encompass all the vehicles in the parking lot, Sam even focused the camera out across the river and lake to include any traffic on the water.

Then, slowly, Sam moved in closer toward the body. Observing the remaining bystanders, while approaching the scene cautiously, for a moment, Sam was suspended in time.

Viewing the dismal scene before him now, despite his previous extended career as a homicide detective, there'd only been one other time Sam's senses had been identically affected. His mind summarily travelled back almost twenty-three years before, when the remains of six-year old Anna Ivers had been discovered at Dragonfly Pointe.

The moment in time that'd changed Sam's future, urging him to shift his priorities.

Slipping on a pair of gloves, Nat bent down while attempting to study the face of the victim.

He suddenly gasped.

Sam finally took a look at the body. Immediately recognizing the obvious widow's peak and ivory-white skin of the woman's partially exposed face, Sam realized that this murder was personal. Overwhelmed by shock, Sam moaned despairingly, "*Vanessa!*"

Seventeen

"Chad." Penny hugged him tightly. "It's not that I'm not happy to see *you*, but where's *Mom*?" Her assistant manager at Sander's Floral Innovations, thirty-year old Chad Ashton, and his partner Greg Marston, were two of Penny's closest friends.

He hesitated. "Penny. Your mom came knocking at our door early this morning. She was having some pains in her chest—so Greg and I insisted she go see a doctor. He checked her into the hospital to run some tests."

"*Oh, no,*" she moaned. "It had to be Alex. He was too much for her. Wasn't he?"

"Maybe," he agreed, with hesitance. "But Greg has Alex in hand right now. I thought you might want to go visit your mom."

After finally retrieving her luggage, they were soon on their way outdoors, rushing through the enormous parking lot. It seemed like forever before they reached Chad's car. Finally, he was shoving her gently into the passenger seat of his Volkswagen before stowing away her luggage.

Penny swiped the tears from her eyes. "I don't know how I would've survived these last few years without you and Greg."

As he slipped inside the car, Chad reached over and gently patted her shoulder, nodding reassuringly.

Once they'd battled the traffic exiting LaGuardia, they began battling the traffic on their way to the hospital. It was nearly an hour later when Chad pulled into the hospital parking lot.

As they exited the elevator onto the floor of the cardio care center, she muttered, "I sure would've hated to arrive at eight in the morning or five at night."

"Sometimes, I feel sorry for our delivery drivers," Chad answered.

Promptly checking in with a nurse at the reception desk, they were directed to her mother's room.

"Mom." Rushing into the hospital room, Penny leaned over the bed and pressed a quick kiss on her mother's cheek. Penny couldn't help but notice the distinct shadows under Monica's eyes. *"How are you?"*

"Oh, Penny. I'm fine. I guess I kind of overdid it a little with Alex. I should've asked for a little more help from Greg and Chad, but they were both so busy. I never really realized just how much you had to deal with every day, sweetheart. I'm sorry I haven't been around as much as I should've."

"Oh, Mom. It's not like I actually have places to go. I should've made other arrangements for Alex, though."

"Don't be silly, sweetheart. He's my *grandchild*. And I wanted to do this for you. I know that you're lonely. You don't have the opportunity to get away from Alex very often."

Penny sighed, shaking her head in frustration. "Well, this is it. I'm home for good, now."

Nodding their heads in reluctant agreement, both Chad and her mother remained strangely silent.

Penny studied each of them suspiciously. "Okay. What's going on?"

"Nothing we can tell you about yet, sweetheart. We'll leave that up to Danny," her mother answered, somewhat smugly.

"You guys are all in on whatever Danny and Jake are planning. Aren't you?"

"Yep," Chad answered. With a figurative twist of his fingers, he buttoned his lips.

"Now—go home sweetheart. Grandpa's ready to pick me up when they're done with the tests. I'm sorry to say your apartment's kind of a mess, since all of this happened while I was straightening up. I'll call you when I get my test results. I need a little rest after dealing with Alex for the last five days," she admitted, ruefully.

"Oh, Mom." Penny swiped away tears from her eyes.

"I'm fine. I promise. Now go!" she ordered.

"Alright." With a misty smile, Penny nodded. Still sniffling, Penny clung to Chad's hand when he tugged her gently through the door.

An hour later, Penny stood in her apartment surveying the damage. Asleep next door in Chad and Greg's apartment, Alex had apparently run himself down after running his grandmother ragged.

"God, Alex," she muttered. With the majority of his toys strewn throughout the room, Alex had obviously taken advantage of his grandmother's good nature.

And Monica clearly hadn't escaped his temper. Two lampshades hung ripped and tattered on the sofa table behind the couch.

Unplugged, the VCR lay broken on the floor.

And sometime in the last five days, Alex had punched another hole in the drywall.

Well, at least he hadn't smashed through the windows of the sliding doors leading out to the terrace again. It'd taken hours to clean up the broken glass.

Not to mention how unbelievably expensive it'd been to replace the doors.

Penny sighed wearily, suddenly becoming depressed. No matter how much she attempted to regulate Alex's blood sugar, puberty was supposedly affecting him as well. Once she found another doctor, she'd have to experiment with different medications and attempt to better control his behavior.

With insulin shots twice a day and frequent blood sugar testing, Penny had managed to control Alex's diabetes. But because he couldn't communicate his needs, it'd always been a long and difficult process.

Alex wanted to eat when his blood sugar was low.

But Alex also wanted to eat when his blood sugar was high.

And when he wasn't disoriented, he was angry.

And now, if they added medication into the mix?

Sighing resignedly, Penny began tackling the chaos in the family room.

After checking in downstairs at the shop, discovering that, as usual, Chad had the workplace under control, a few hours later, Penny was settled cozily in Chad and Greg's apartment. Several months before when Alex's caregiver had quit, Chad's partner Greg had insisted on taking over.

Skipping through the room in precise, repetitive circles, Alex brushed his fingers continuously through her hair. He'd obviously been pleased to see her. When she'd entered the room and her son had immediately rewarded her with a gut-wrenching hug, it'd been an effort for Penny to hold back her tears. She'd never been away from Alex for more than a single night. And that'd always been for work.

The four cramped apartments above Sanders Floral had been converted into two, and completely remodeled ten years before. The larger apartment had allowed Penny and Alex their own luxurious space, while the smaller apartment had been purposely left vacant so that Penny could select a desirable tenant. Seven years earlier, Penny had hired Chad as her assistant and had offered him the apartment when they'd become close friends.

Penny had supported Chad through years of romantic struggles. She'd been pleased when he'd finally met Greg, a CPA who currently worked from an office set up within their apartment. Although Greg was ten years older than Chad, as well as independently wealthy, they appeared to be well-matched. Greg was handsome with his neatly cropped hair of gray, complementing his intense silvery-gray eyes. He towered over Chad, who, with raven-black hair and deep-blue eyes, was only five-foot eight.

Although she'd recently halved their rent as a management benefit for Chad, when Greg had refused to accept any payment for his invaluable assistance with Alex, Penny had insisted on completely eliminating their rent.

"Okay, sweetie. Time to give Greg the scoop." Pouring two goblets of wine, Greg approached the couch and handed her one of the goblets. Curling up on the other end of the couch, he sipped on his wine.

"Well. He's really good-looking," Penny admitted, sheepishly.

"As handsome as Chad?" Greg waggled his brows.

She laughed. "Almost. When I met Chad, I thought he was the best-looking man I'd ever met."

"Sorry, sweetie." He dropped his voice, half hiding his mouth behind his hand. "He's taken."

Penny giggled.

Greg grinned. "At least you're smiling now. So," he hesitated, sipping more wine, "what's the problem, then?"

"I think he might still be married," she acknowledged, ruefully.

Suddenly appearing indignant, Greg bolted upright. "That jerk!"

"And then I had a call from some crazy woman, as I was leaving the inn this morning, screaming at me to leave Sam alone."

"Oh, sweetie." Thoughtfully, he sat back, resting his goblet on the table. "But let me get this straight. Didn't Danny mention that this Sam was divorced?"

"Yeah."

"And didn't his own mother call her his ex-wife, when you were discussing his skill on the dance floor?"

"Oh, yeah. I forgot that I mentioned that, when I talked to you on the phone yesterday. Hmm. I wonder what's going on?"

"Only one way to find out."

"Well. I already called him in-between flights. I was leaving him a message when this woman answered the phone—claiming that Sam was her husband. I wanted to thank him for this," she admitted, holding out her pendant.

Taking the pendant in his hand, Greg studied the detail. "Oh, sweetie. Isn't it beautiful?

"Yeah. It is, isn't it?" Penny sighed.

"Well. He wouldn't have given you *this* if his intentions weren't honorable. Just give him a day or two. Then you can ask him what's going on, cause he'll probably call you. Absence makes the heart grow fonder—or, so, they say. Now—drink your wine."

*N*umbly, Sam remained on the sidelines. Fearing repercussions from their superiors, Nat and Terry had finally convinced Sam to let them take over the crime scene.

After a call to Jim McClellan, who'd coincidentally remained at the Dragonfly Pointe Inn to handle a delicate matter for the Loughlins, Sam had whipped out his business card for FBI agent Shane Donnelly.

Jim had contacted the appropriate authorities and arrived to take charge of the scene. At one time Jake Loughlin's superior, but now his partner, FBI agent Jim McClellan had been Jake's best man at his wedding.

Approaching the state's coroner, who'd recently arrived, Jim briefly studied the crime scene while Wendell Currie meticulously examined the woman's body.

"Rigor mortis is just beginning to set in. She couldn't have been in the water long," Wendell informed Jim. "I'd estimate she died close to noon. Probably no later than twelve-thirty," he added.

Jim McClellan glanced objectively over the woman's body. After turning and observing the raging river's current, he motioned at the woman's head, nearly decapitated from her body. "Before or after?"

"Before." Wendell Currie nodded, decisively. "Something serrated—most likely a knife—sliced across her throat and severed the artery immediately. She bled out. Pretty brutal way to die."

"Tell me about it," Jim observed, grimly.

Dark threatening clouds covered the sky. A light sprinkle had begun only ten minutes before. Making his way toward Sam, Jim eased down onto the ground beside him. "Good idea to bring in the tents, by the way."

"Looks like all hells about ready to break loose."

"Just for my information Sam, tell me about your day," Jim asked, quietly.

Sam's eyes met Jim's. "I left town this morning about eight. I dropped Penny Wentworth off at the airport, in Eau Claire, at about nine-thirty. I left the airport when her flight took off at ten. I got back to Crystal Rock at twelve-thirty and drove immediately over to the station. I was in my office when Nat called in."

Jim hesitated. "Why so long getting back from Eau Claire?"

"I stopped at the rest area to confront my tail."

Jim raised a brow.

"Shane Donnelly. He was following me in case Vanessa showed up. Guess she was already here, though," Sam added, with a humorless smile.

"Speak of the devil." Jim nodded. After grabbing a briefcase from the interior of his car, Shane Donnelly vaulted down the path from the parking lot.

"You've met him before, then?"

"Yeah. He's a good kid. Looks like you're off the hook."

"Well. My ex-father-in-law was killed last week, and I've apparently been cleared of that murder, too," he muttered, mockingly.

Jim held up a staying hand. "Hey. I'm only trying to help."

"Sorry, Jim. I just found out that, apparently, I was still married. I was furious. I probably *could* have killed her. And now that my wife's turned up dead, I feel like crap. I never wanted her to *die*." As delayed grief kicked in, Sam covered his face with his hands despairingly.

After reassuring Sam silently with a pat on his back, Jim stood up from the ground.

Shane approached them, and shook Jim's hand. Staring down at Sam, Shane mumbled quietly, "Let me go take a look at the victim. I'll be right back."

Keeping his eyes covered, Sam nodded his head.

A few minutes later, still rubbing his eyes, Sam stood up resignedly from the ground. Lightning ominously split up the horizon, as the rain began pounding down harder.

Once he'd returned, Shane discreetly pulled Sam aside. "It has to be confirmed, of course. But I think we're dealing with the same killer. Let's discuss this somewhere private."

"May I see my wife first?"

Obviously startled at the intensity in Sam's gaze, Shane seemed suddenly uncomfortable. "Give the coroner about five more minutes at the scene. They're almost ready to move the body."

Quietly, they stood in the rain. Two attendants eventually travelled down the path carrying a portable gurney. Carefully following Wendell Currie's instructions, they loaded up the body.

After guiding Sam over to Vanessa, Shane stood off deferentially in the distance. Oddly enough, in death, Vanessa appeared at peace. Carefully tucked in to disguise her severed neck, a sheet had been slung loosely over her body. Although dampened from the water from the river, Vanessa's raven-black hair was still sleekly slicked back, and had managed to remain tidily arranged in her trademark chignon.

Sam's eyes caressed her face with remorse. "Vanessa," he whispered, softly. "You're still so beautiful. Even now." For a few short minutes, he remained respectfully silent.

With a final nod at the attendants waiting to remove the body, Sam followed Shane away from the crime scene. "Let me know when you're ready to release the body. I'll be making all the arrangements," Sam added, approaching the gathering of law enforcement hovering near Jim.

Strolling alongside Sam, Shane nodded.

As several members of law enforcement began methodically documenting the crime scene, Sam studied the riverbank glumly. "Too many curious onlookers." He sighed. "Let's meet up with the task force at the station."

"Sophie." With trepidation, Terry entered the police station through the door. Since the FBI was taking charge of the federal investigation, Terry and Nat had mostly worked along the sidelines. Once he'd managed to get the okay from Nat to take off, he'd rushed here to the office.

He needed to be the one to break the news to Sophie.

"There've been so many calls, Terry. I finally quit answering, since everyone just wanted information about the murder. What can you tell me?"

"Sophie. Sit down."

Tugging at her elbow, Terry led her back to her desk, gently shoving her into her seat. Gazing intently into her eyes, he leaned on the edge of her desk and reached for her hand.

Recognizing something was dreadfully wrong, Sophie searched Terry's eyes. "Terry. *You're scaring me.* What's going on?"

"The woman who was killed. You know her," he relayed, softly.

With widened eyes, Sophie squeaked, "But…but *who?*"

"It was Vanessa, Soph. Sam's *wife.*"

She gasped. *"Oh, my God."*

Barely comprehending the significance of Terry's words, Sophie covered her face with her hands and began sobbing inconsolably.

Moving in closer and gently pulling her into his arms, Terry rubbed his hand soothingly over her shoulders. "You need to tell Sam about what's been going on. The stuff about notarizing her will, or anything else that might help. Her murder is part of a federal investigation, Soph. Someone killed her father, only four days ago, down in New Orleans. *How in the hell did you two even meet?*"

"At Sam's," she spit out, sniffling. "There were lights on his house, when I knew that he was gone for the weekend, and I went over there to check things out."

"Well. Just save anything else you need to say, for Sam and the FBI task force. You're gonna have to answer a lot of questions. I don't want you to be burned out before everyone arrives. They're on their way here, now. Let's get some coffee brewing, so you're a little more prepared. Just make sure you talk to Sam and Jim McClellan *first.*"

"Thanks, Terry. *I can't believe that she's gone.* I loved being around her. Vanessa was just so *alive.*"

"Why didn't you say anything to Sam, about his wife being in town, Soph?"

"Vanessa wanted to talk to him personally. She asked me not to tell him that she'd been staying at the house. She was planning on explaining everything to him tonight."

Terry nodded wearily.

Fifteen minutes later, Sam and the FBI task force arrived on the scene. Retrieving the conference table from the basement, Terry set up the table in Sam's office for privacy.

Sophie was amazingly composed when she asked to speak with Sam and Jim McClellan.

With Shane Donnelly and the other three members of the task force settled in Sam's office, Sam sighed, turning to Sophie when she pulled him aside. "What is it, Sophie?"

"It's about Vanessa, Sam," she whispered. "I met her after the wedding on Saturday. She was staying at your house."

Sam stared at Sophie with consternation, before gazing over uneasily at the individuals seated around the table in his office. Turning to Jim, he uttered softly, "Think we can get away from them for a few minutes, Jim?"

Jim strolled up to the doorway of the office. "Be back in five," he announced. "Sam needs a moment with his staff." Turning back to Sam, he inquired discreetly, "Alright if I join you? Like I said before, I only want to help."

Sam signaled Sophie and Jim down the basement stairs. Once they'd traveled down into the basement, Sam began unfolding some of the remaining chairs that were stacked against the wall.

Motioning Sophie into a chair, Sam settled into a seat beside her. "Okay, Sophie. Start from the beginning."

"Well, on Saturday, I came home for a while, in-between the wedding and reception. When I was leaving to head back to the reception, I noticed a light switched on in one of the bedrooms of your house. I just figured you were home and your truck was parked in the garage. Anyway, when I arrived at the reception, I noticed that you were *there.* So, when I finally came home at midnight, I was a little buzzed," she admitted, ruefully. "But I noticed that there *weren't* any lights on in your house. So I just went over there. I mean, in the back of my mind, I was kind of thinking about those robberies that we've been having around town."

"You should've just called me at the cabin, Sophie."

"Well." Blushing and turning her eyes away from his, she cleared her throat. "You appeared to be busy at the wedding, and I didn't want to bother you."

Reaching for her hand, Sam squeezed it gently. "I understand, Sophie," he reassured her, softly. "So. What did you find?"

"Luggage—and some clothing hanging in the closet of the small bedroom at the front of the house. Anyway, I was standing in the bedroom when Vanessa popped in on me. I guess she was resting in your family room on the couch. She'd thought you'd come home."

"How'd she get in?" Jim McClellan asked.

"Easily." Sam grimaced wryly. "I leave a key under the mat. Why not? I don't have much, and I'm having construction work done inside."

Jim nodded.

"So what'd she tell you, Sophie?"

"Actually, not much of anything. She didn't even tell me about her father's death. But she did admit that she was still your wife, Sam—you just didn't know it."

"So *what* did you even talk to her about?"

"Fashion, mostly. I sew a lot of my own clothes, and Vanessa loved my sketchbook. She kept on insisting that she was gonna sponsor me."

Sam was taken aback. "You must really be good, then, Sophie. Vanessa was a perfectionist when it came to her business," he reassured her, gently.

Sophie drew in a deep breath. "But there's more."

Sam raised a brow.

"She wrote a will, Sam. And she wrote some letters that she had me notarize. One was to you. I think she wanted you to make sure her instructions were carried out. Whatever else happened between you two, she trusted you."

Sam was stunned.

Noticing that Sam was at a loss for words, Jim took over the questioning. "Have you still got the will, Sophie?"

"No. I dropped it into Wes Stanton's lock box this morning. Vanessa wanted it secure once I notarized it and had Terry witness it."

"*Terry Lutz?*"

This time Sophie squeezed Sam's hand with reassurance. "He didn't know she was your wife, Sam. I introduced her as my friend."

"Did you read the letters or the contents of her will?" Jim inquired.

"No. Contrary to the opinion of several of my colleagues, I believe the contents of what I notarize are private. I only witness and verify my client's signature."

With an indulgent smile for Sophie, Sam added, "*I* could've told you that, Jim."

"But," Sophie began excitedly, "she typed it on Sam's computer— and even though we deleted it..."

Jim continued where Sophie left off. "Nothing can *actually* be deleted from the computer's hard drive." He added thoughtfully, "I'd sure like to get a look at those letters and that will."

"No reason Sophie needs to tell these guys *where* Vanessa typed up the will. Is there? You two could go to the house now and make copies. They can get a court order for the originals from Wes Stanton. That gives us a few days to consider their contents." Sam continued, "Jim—why don't you and Sophie take off to get everyone food? I don't know about the two of you, but, all of a sudden, I'm starved."

Jim nodded. "If I call ahead to the Dragonfly, that'll give Sophie and me plenty of time to swing by your house."

"I should be able to keep the task force occupied for at least an hour before revealing Sophie's role in all of this. Standing up from his chair, Sam sighed wearily, shaking his head. "*Damn, Sophie.* Exactly *what* did Vanessa get you into, I wonder?"

Then he eyed her oddly.

She blinked. "What?"

"It's just that, besides Celeste Devoux, I can't recall Vanessa *ever* having a female friend," he observed, dryly.

"Her purse was found in the dumpster. They're checking it for prints. The standard components were found inside. Wallet, ID, credit cards, makeup. Keys. A set for the rental car parked in the lot. A key for her room at the lodge. And a single, unidentified key. Probably a house key. No cash in the wallet. I doubt she'd visited her room yet. There was a thousand in hundreds and twenties tucked into an envelope and stashed in her luggage. Not unpacked, by the way."

Knowing Sophie and Jim would most likely be returning soon, Sam finally eased back tiredly in his chair. "Alright if I take a look at that unidentified key?

Popping open the latch for his briefcase, Shane Donnelly carefully removed an evidence bag.

Briefly, Sam studied the key. "That looks to be my house key." Aware of the calculated glances from the other members of the task force, Sam continued, "And, no. I didn't know Vanessa was staying there. My neighbor, who's coincidentally a member of my staff, only just told me. I have a cabin on the lake, and I spent my time over the weekend traveling back and forth from my cabin to the inn—since I was part of Jake Loughlin's wedding party."

"I can second that," Shane Donnelly added.

"Sophia Ruston lives across the street. Her family usually keeps an eye on my house for me. Sophia saw lights on. Vanessa specifically asked her not to tell me she was there because, supposedly, Vanessa wanted to talk to me personally. I suspect she wanted to explain why we weren't divorced." Sam added, dryly, "But I doubt she would've actually told me the truth. Sophia should be back momentarily, and she'll be ready to answer any of your questions.

"Since you're the next of kin, you'll be receiving Vanessa's personal effects," Shane observed, handing a list over to Sam. "We found something strange in the side pocket of her purse," he added, pulling out a copy of a business card.

Staring at the copy of the card, Sam was puzzled. "Sean Murphy. For some reason, that name sounds vaguely familiar. But how would *I* know a D.A. in Chicago?" He muttered musingly, "Come to think of it, how would *Vanessa* know a D.A. in Chicago?"

"I'll make another copy of the card and attach it to the file."

"File?"

"We want you to handle the case from here, of course, along with Jim and myself."

"Wouldn't that be a conflict of interest?"

"Not if I coordinate the investigation. I was planning on staying in the area for at least the next few weeks, anyway," Shane added.

"Maybe I can recruit the retired chief of police, Jim Callahan, to take over my office for a few days. If you still need my help in New Orleans, that is."

"Definitely. Gerard's personal effects will most likely be handed over to *you*."

"God," Sam muttered, grimly. "I hadn't even thought of that."

Returning with food from the Dragonfly Pointe Inn, Sophie and Jim settled in at the conference table alongside Shane Donnelly and the other members of the task force. For the next hour, Sophie was drilled with questions. Apparently satisfied with her answers, the task force decided to adjourn to Sam's home on Pine Street to search through the house.

Sean stood up. "I'd prefer you stay here, Sam."

"Don't worry, Sam. I'll accompany Sophie," Jim McClellan assured him.

"I'll stay here with Sam." Terry Lutz added quietly, as Sophie, Jim, and the members of the task force lined out from the station.

Taking a seat behind his desk, Sam studied the list of Vanessa's personal effects somewhat distractedly. "What a hell of a situation."

Terry entered Sam's office, dropping into a chair. "Nat decided to hang around the crime scene. He said he'd let you know if any contrary or unusual evidence was discovered."

"Hello?" A voice called out from the outer office.

"Jim. I was just gonna call you." When Jim Callahan strolled into his office, Sam stood up and reached for his hand, shaking it firmly.

"Figure since I'm the former chief, I'd be able to get the scoop on what's going on." After eyeing the grim faces of Sam and Terry, Jim dropped his inquisitive smile. "Okay. I can tell that it's bad," he muttered, easing down into a chair facing Sam.

"They discovered a woman murdered at the Riverbend—it was my ex-wife, Jim."

"Only she really *wasn't* his ex-wife," Terry added.

"And my wife's father was also murdered last week, down in New Orleans," Sam continued. "So the FBI wants me to work with them."

Jim looked dazed. "It all sounds pretty damned confusing."

"Tell me about it. They're searching my house, now, because Vanessa was apparently staying there over the weekend."

Jim held up a hand. "This must be awfully difficult for you, Sam. I'll come by and you can fill me in tomorrow. Meanwhile, I think we could all use a drink."

Sam blinked.

"Where's my old file cabinet?"

Sam pointed a thumb toward the outer office.

"This office sure cleans up well. Fresh paint, too? Looks good." Jim made his way into the outer office. Pulling open the bottom drawer of one of the file cabinets, he slipped out a box from the very back of the drawer.

Dragging out a bottle of whiskey and a shot glass, after returning to Sam's office, he poured out a shot for Sam and Terry, before quickly chugging down one of his own.

Roaming restlessly through Sam's office, Jim glanced over the files laid out across the conference table. *"Sean Murphy?"*

"Yeah. They found his card in Vanessa's purse. I thought the name sounded familiar. But I couldn't remember why."

"*Of course* his name should sound familiar to you, Sam, since I've introduced you to him. He's my *nephew*. I just left him up in Hayward—not more than two hours ago!"

Sam groaned, dropping his head tiredly into his hands. "Oh, man. *This is getting too damned complicated*. I hate to interrupt his honeymoon, but I really think we could use some extra help from Jake Loughlin."

"It feels pretty damned nice, getting special treatment," Sam observed, turning to Danielle.

She grinned wryly. "Yeah. Flying on a private plane can be pretty convenient. Jake sometimes has trouble hiring a pilot spur of the moment, though. But fortunately Cam was booked for our beck and call because of our honeymoon."

"I'm sorry that your honeymoon was interrupted, Danny."

"If Jim hadn't called us, we would've come home anyway, Sam. The story about your wife's murder was all over the news. I'm just glad we were returning to the Bridgeport Bay Hotel. No one would've been able to get a hold of us if we'd stuck with our original schedule."

With a sigh, Sam nodded. "Maybe I'll try for a nap. I haven't had much sleep over the last few days," he added. Reflecting much upon his life with Vanessa, a guilty conscience had left him remarkably depressed. And it hadn't helped that he hadn't heard from Penny, at all, since she'd returned to New York. Finally giving in and calling her this morning, Sam had been disappointed to discover she'd had the morning off. After leaving a message for her to return his call, he'd hung around home, hoping she'd call back, before finally heading off to the airport.

"Same here. Jake and I did a lot of traveling this past week." Settling back into her seat, Danielle yawned. "G'night."

Vanessa's body would be returning home for burial today. After a one-night detour in New York, Sam would catch a commercial flight for New Orleans tomorrow. Attending Vanessa's funeral, and then assisting with the murder investigation, Sam would remain in New Orleans for as long as he was needed.

Still curious as to the contents of Vanessa's will, Sam had been advised by Jim McClellan that is was better he remained uninformed. Jim had been somewhat shocked by the contents of her will, he'd admitted to Sam. But since there was another will on file in New Orleans, the validity of Vanessa's latest will might be questioned. With her letters and updated will now in the hands of the task force, Sam should allow them time to research its legality before they disclosed its contents.

Since the task force had been created long before Peter Gerard's murder, Jim had warned Sam to be prepared for some pretty surprising revelations once he reached New Orleans. And with some vital information revealed in Vanessa's letters, Shane Donnelly was in the process of revising his task force's strategy.

After being asked to stay clear of the immediate investigation of Vanessa's murder, Sam had recalled the surveillance tapes awaiting him at the Dragonfly Pointe Inn. Working with Jake's head of security, Jeff Ballard, Sam had painstakingly gone over the tapes from both the week before and after the wedding. Frank Carlton had, indeed, been in Crystal Rock.

But Sam had been exasperated to discover that the FBI were already aware of it.

Something else on those tapes had struck him as odd, though—he just hadn't been unable to figure out *what*. Since the FBI had requested copies of the surveillance, Sam would probably go over the tapes again once he reached New Orleans.

He must've dozed off, he realized, when he found himself awakened by the stewardess as they approached the airport. He reattached his seat belt.

Danielle came strolling down the aisle from the rear of the plane, and returned to her seat. "I got the munchies," she admitted, sheepishly. "There's an assortment of junk food available back there in the break room."

Sam grinned. "I'm kind of hungry, too. Maybe we should get some lunch at the airport before we catch a cab?"

"Sounds like a plan. Penny won't be back in her shop until at least two. Her mom's surgery on Tuesday was a breeze she told me, according to the surgeon."

"Her mom's *surgery*?"

Danielle appeared taken aback. "Didn't Penny tell you? Her mom had to have a shunt inserted into one of the valves leading into her heart."

"I'm glad her mom's okay. I haven't even *talked* to Penny since Monday," Sam grumbled. "I left her a message this morning, but she never called me back."

Danielle laid a hand over his. "I talked to Penny last night. Her mother was going to be released from the hospital this morning, Sam, and Penny was planning on taking her home. Monica lives with Penny's grandparents on the outskirts of New York, but she lives in a guesthouse on their property."

He nodded, still feeling irritable.

Once the plane had landed, Sam and Danielle began gathering their belongings and worked their way to the exit. With a smile and a wave to both Cam and their stewardess, Danielle steered Sam ahead to a parked cart, ready and waiting to escort them over the runway and into the airport terminal.

Almost two hours later, traveling somewhat ineffectually through the busy, traffic-jammed streets in their cab, they finally arrived at Sander's Floral. "This neighborhood's changed quite a bit," Sam observed, motioning with his hand. "There used to be an enormous parking lot here, attached to the alleyway."

After unloading their bags, Sam turned to the driver, pulling out his wallet.

"But you paid for lunch, Sam."

Glaring at Danielle, he pulled out a couple of bills. "It's the least I can do. You and Jake are always taking care of everything for me," he muttered.

"I completely forgot that you used to live in New York. Where was your precinct?"

With a rueful grin, he nodded at the clearly marked station house standing across the street on the corner.

For a long startled moment, Danielle gazed perceptively at him. "Oh, Sam," she whispered, softly. "Does Penny even *know?*"

Hesitantly, he shook his head. "She was married, Danny. And I barely knew her," he admitted, wryly. "But she was always on my mind. I just presumed that she was *happily* married, and I was okay with that. But she wasn't. Was she?"

"Sam—that man was a *monster*," Danielle admitted, practically in tears. "*What he did to her...*"

Closing his eyes, Sam groaned. "God. *If I'd only known at the time.* This past weekend, I kind of suspected that she might've been abused. " Clearly shaken, he growled, "To tell you the truth, if he wasn't already dead, I probably would've killed the guy. I intentionally tried to forget about Penny when I met Vanessa, Danny."

"Well. You and Penny *really* do need to sit down and talk." Drawing in a steadying breath, she turned her attention to the shop, with its clean brick façade. Planters under the huge shuttered windows were filled with flowers, framing the arrangements and antiques displayed inside. "It looks great. Doesn't it? Penny helped design the remodel. She's increased the business's profits by over thirty percent, according to her grandfather."

With a startled glance at Danielle, Sam felt oddly proud.

Studying Sam's face, Danielle grinned. "Well, let's get inside. I take it you didn't mention you were accompanying me in the message you left for Penny?"

He nodded sheepishly, and rolled his eyes. "I was waiting for her to call me back."

With a glance at her wristwatch, Danielle tugged on Sam's elbow, and led him into the shop. "You've got thirty minutes. I'll keep myself busy until then."

Sam smiled. Retrieving the remainder of their luggage from outside, he neatly piled up their bags in the breezeway of the shop. Looking around, he realized that even the floor plan of the shop had been altered since he'd been here last. Chairs that were clad in muted floral fabrics were tucked around a couple of painted tables. In the style of shabby chic, the walls were painted a pale shade of green, while the wooden floors had been bleached to a creamy white. Filled with masses of colorful flowers, as well as a variety of previously put together creations, a row of flower coolers, lining the entire wall, displayed a unique assortment of contemporary and traditional arrangements.

Smiling, Danielle approached the huge antique desk that served as a check out for customers. "Hi, Chad. How are you? Sam. This is Penny's friend, and manager, Chad Ashton."

And then Sam got a glimpse of the man who was studying the screen of a computer behind the desk. With raven-black hair and deep-blue eyes, his face could've been etched by a sculptor. Observing the man's lean fit body, Sam frowned.

This was Penny's *friend?*

Mechanically moving forward, Sam firmly shook Chad's hand.

With eyes that were twinkling, Chad's smile was subdued as he looked Sam over. "Nice to finally meet you, Sam. Penny's going to be surprised." Nodding at a staircase that was located near the rear of the shop, he continued, "Just go on up the two flights of stairs past our apartments. At the end of the hallway, there's another staircase leading to the rooftop. She's working up there right now.

Our apartments?

With a curt nod of his head, Sam moved through the shop and began climbing the staircase.

Lifting a brow, Chad turned to Danielle. "The quiet type?"

She laughed. "I think that he's jealous," she murmured.

Chad blinked, before he grinned. Returning to his work, he shook his head ruefully. "Little does he know."

Danielle snorted.

Making short work of the two flights of stairs, Sam approached the final steps. Taking in a deep breath, he climbed slowly up the staircase. The heavy metal door was propped open, and Sam quietly slipped through the doorframe.

Sam was amazed. *The rooftop was an oasis.* Lined in rows along the fenced-in edges of the deck, raised beds were filled with an assortment of colorful flowers and vegetables, creating a beautiful intricate maze. When he finally reached the center of the rooftop, Sam was surprised to discover an enclosed gazebo. Along with wrought iron furnishings consisting of tables, chairs, and gliders, the spacious sanctuary was outfitted with an outdoor kitchen and grill.

Realizing he was still irritated with Penny for ignoring him over these past five days, he wryly acknowledged his reaction as churlish. He really needed to put aside his irrational annoyance, he decided, as he began searching for Penny.

Strolling along a pebbled pathway, he finally found her. Unripened tomatoes spilled abundantly over the edges of an upraised planter, and Penny was plucking out weeds from inside.

His irritation immediately vanished when he noticed the silver chain around her neck. *She was wearing his pendant.*

But then he suddenly became aware of her attire.

And his mouth went dry.

Short tatty jean shorts fit snugly around her bottom, while her brief skimpy halter top left little to the imagination.

Raising his hand in the air, Sam snapped his fingers.

Penny's head jerked up. *"Sam!"*

Her smile took his breath away.

Quickly standing up on her feet, she rushed along the path and fell into his waiting arms. "I just left you a message," she murmured.

"There's been so much going on," he muttered, pulling her closer.

"I know. I'm so sorry about your wife, Sam."

"Penny," Sam began, gazing into her eyes. *"I swear I didn't know."*

"I realized that pretty quick after I talked to her, Sam."

"You *talked* to her?"

"In-between flights. I called to leave you a message, after I opened your gift. It's beautiful, Sam," she added, lightly fingering the sapphire pendant.

"I never got the message, Penny." He sighed, and grimaced. "Knowing Vanessa, she probably erased it."

"But why?"

"I haven't got a clue about what's been going on, Penny. But I'm on my way to New Orleans tomorrow to try and find out. We can talk about all of that later." Grabbing her hand, Sam led her into the gazebo. He thoughtfully studied a cushioned, wrought iron chair. "We've got about fifteen minutes left before Danny shows up." And then he gave her a wolfish smile.

"*Now?*" Penny rolled her eyes. But following the direction of his gaze, she appeared intrigued.

"You're so damned lovely." Pulling her into his arms, Sam's mouth impatiently covered hers.

"Oh, Sam," she finally sighed. "It's only been five days. But I can't believe how much I've missed you."

Closing his eyes, he embraced her tightly, taking comfort in the feel of her soft bare skin, warmed by the sun. "Same here. These last few days have been awful. I didn't want her to *die*, Penny."

"I know, Sam," she murmured. But when she guided him into the gazebo and gently shoved him into a chair, she frowned, obviously becoming aware of the weapon holstered under his leather jacket. "I was wondering why you were wearing a jacket, when it's at least seventy-five degrees outside."

"I had to bring a weapon along, since I'll be working in an official capacity down in New Orleans." He grimaced. "Let me get everything off." He yanked off his jacket impatiently and unclipped his holster. Laying them neatly aside, Sam covered his belt buckle with his hands.

"Let me," Penny whispered, shoving his hands away.

"Penny. I'm afraid this is gonna have to be quick," he muttered.

With shaking fingers, she began working on the buckle determinedly. Balancing over his knees, unbuttoning and unzipping his jeans, after running a hand tentatively down its length, soon, she was holding his rigid erection in her hands.

With an audible hiss, Sam made a frantic move, reaching his hands to her waist. After unsnapping and unzipping the fastenings of her shorts, he pulled her into his lap. Penny finally managed to wriggle out from her shorts. He became distantly aware of her contented sigh when his fingers began to gently ready her. Finally pushing into her warm wet entrance, he slowly and steadily brought her down over the length of his rigid erection.

When she was fully seated, he held himself motionless. For several long heart-stopping moments, Sam gazed tenderly into Penny's eyes as, filled with passion, they gradually transformed into a deeper, darker blue.

Reaching for the tie at her neck, he impatiently pulled away the straps of her halter, exposing her breasts. Cupping, caressing full breasts with both hands, Sam gently circled her rosy-pink nipples with his thumbs, until both were rigidly aroused. "You have the most beautiful breasts I've ever seen," he whispered, hoarsely.

She laughed softly. "I'm not so sure about *that*." Now that she was practically naked, Penny's face was rosy, as her gaze swept nervously over the other buildings, surrounding the rooftop.

"I am," he muttered, fiercely. And with that, he began moving. Thrusting, rolling his hips in a rhythmic grinding motion, Sam set about arousing every single one of Penny's senses.

And, in turn, arousing his own.

Thrusting, grinding, and thrusting again, Sam set his stroking fingers near the sensitive skin where they were joined. She was shuddering and shaking when Sam explosively erupted, as one with Penny.

Burying his face into hair, infused with the soothing familiar fragrance of rosy-lavender, Sam swept Penny fiercely into his arms.

"Oh, Sam," Penny moaned, looking somewhat dazed. "That was...*incredible*."

God, how he *loved* this woman. *Should he tell her?*

Gently pulling away, he lightly cupped her face within his hands. After clearing his throat, Sam began hesitantly, "Penny...I..."

Obviously banging the door purposely, all of a sudden, Danielle called out from the entrance of the roof garden. *"Sam? Penny?"*

"Has it been thirty minutes *already?*" Sam mumbled irritably. Reaching out and pulling up the straps of Penny's halter to cover her breasts, he quickly knotted the straps around her neck.

Penny laughed softly, clearly reluctant to move off from his lap.

Quickly rearranging and righting their clothing, they were amazingly composed by the time Danielle appeared at the gazebo.

Studying their faces, Danielle grinned. "Ah. A little too soon, huh? If I didn't need to catch Karen at the office, I probably would've waited a little longer. Where can we talk?"

"How about right here. There's some iced tea and soda in the fridge." Penny reached a hand into the mini-fridge, installed under the countertop of the outdoor kitchen. After handing out their drinks, she settled into the glider next to Sam.

"Okay. Let me get it all out at once, Penny. Save the questions," she added, taking in a deep breath. "For the last nine months, Jake and I have been soliciting donations, after we finally forced the Bradshaws to sell us the Crystal Rock Campgrounds. And we've built a school." She studied them with obvious calculation, before adding, "For special education."

Penny blinked.

"Sam. You don't seem surprised."

"I've met Shane Donnelly. Since his father was the doctor Jake hired to oversee the school, I just put two and two together. At least about *that* part of your plan."

Danielle smiled. "The school is scheduled to open in late August. Jake has an experienced friend from college coming in to take charge. We've hired five well-qualified teachers so far, and we're looking to add more as we recruit students and funding for each student. Right now we have ten students," hesitating, she added, "including Alex Wentworth. That is, with your permission, Penny. Our director has his records—courtesy of your mother."

Penny appeared to be stunned.

Danielle held up a staying hand. "Now. No questions, yet. Jake and I have purchased the entire building block of Main and Oak Streets in Crystal Rock. We have an architect hired to plan an overhaul of the buildings. We'd like to keep the buildings intact on the outside, but reinvent the building block into a mini-mall for tourists. In that building, along with a shop offering crafts and antiques, we'd like to display Dawn's artwork and jewelry and, possibly, take on other area artisans. And, most importantly, Penny, we want you to not only open and run a flower shop, we'd like *you* to take charge of the whole project."

Danielle became silent, allowing Penny to absorb the information.

With an all-encompassing motion of her hand, Penny finally spoke. "What about here? Sander's Floral?"

Whipping out a contract from her purse, Danielle prepared to explain. "Well, this is where it gets complicated. It'll only happen if you agree to this, Penny. Your grandfather wasn't comfortable turning over his shop to you, because he didn't want to leave you saddled with a massive mortgage after your recent renovations. So far, because of your excellent management, the mortgage has been reduced by fifty per cent in the last five years. So what we've proposed is this—Jake and I will take over the mortgage, and become owners, holding thirty-five percent control. Chad would also like to invest his savings, to become an owner, with fifteen percent control. You would be the primary owner, of course, with fifty percent. You and Chad wouldn't have to begin paying into the back mortgage until our newly formed company, as a whole, shows a profit. Don't worry. Jake assures me that there are several tax advantages built into this proposal."

"But wouldn't it be more beneficial for Jake to invest as a primary owner?"

"No, oddly enough. Jake has so many investments, if we set this company up with you as an owner, and Jake as an investor, your company will receive several financial incentives as a small business. But it's complicated. Your grandfather's lawyer and accountant already went through everything with Jake and his accountants. Your grandfather wanted to insure Sander's Floral will remain in the family—so any money after profits will pay off the mortgage on Sanders Floral first, since this property is worth so much more than the property in Crystal Rock is. And, of course, the property taxes here are a lot higher than in Crystal Rock."

"So—Chad wants to stay here and run the shop?"

"Exactly. And your apartment will be here when you need it. You'll probably need to return for inventory. And maybe to help out during some of the holidays."

Penny seemed dazed as she shook her head. But then a question arose. "If we moved to Crystal Rock, where would we live?"

Shrugging, Sam finally broke in to the conversation. "At my house, of course."

Penny hesitated, appearing thoughtful, yet indecisive.

Sam gazed into her eyes. "I'm not rushing you into anything, Penny. Don't worry. I'd live at the cabin," he added, reassuringly.

"But your house is a little small for Alex and me. I know that there's a big yard. But the inside..."

"You haven't seen my addition, have you? The house has an entirely new family room, and a finished basement, too. The kitchen's been updated, and its open concept along with the family room. And I'm even adding a privacy fence around the yard."

Turning her eyes quizzically to Sam's, Danielle mouthed silently, "*Fenced-in yard?*"

Sam glared.

Unaware of their exchange, after reading over the contract, Penny made a statement, matter-of-factly to Sam. "I'll pay you a fair rent, then."

He smiled. "Of course." *She was gonna do it.*

"Let me talk about all of this with Chad and Greg, first. I'll need a few days to think about it."

Sam stood up impatiently.

Penny looked startled when she glanced at Danielle, who gave her a subtle encouraging nod when Sam began to walk away.

Sam followed the path until he reached the edge of the rooftop. He could hear the crunching gravel under Penny's feet as she trailed behind him. Leaning beside him along the railing, Penny reached for his hand and squeezed it reassuringly. "Sam. I'm probably gonna do it. It's just such a change for Alex. And he's not very good with change, I'm afraid," she murmured, softly.

Sam stared at the breathtaking view of New York City. "It just scares me to realize how important you've become to me," he whispered.

Obviously overwhelmed by his surprising admission, she moved silently into his arms.

Twenty

$\mathcal{C}$ onfident now that Penny was seriously considering relocating to Crystal Rock, Danielle was on her way into her office twenty minutes later. Since it was mid-afternoon, Karen should still be working for at least a few more hours.

Located with several other businesses, in the towering office building once housing Brian Johnson's struggling architectural firm, their thriving landscape business, *A New Leaf,* had the advantage of location with a ground floor suite.

After paying the cabbie, Danielle hiked up the steep rows of concrete that led into the grand entrance of the office building. Approaching the office through the lobby, she halted, and gazed into the darkness through the beaded glass doors.

Where was Karen?

Dropping her bag to the ground, Danielle dug through her purse for her keys. Unlocking and entering the office, she turned on the lights. Briefly studying her surroundings, she was relieved to realize that *almost* everything appeared as it should be. On a workday, she normally wouldn't expect to find Jess and Rosie here. But their desks appeared remarkably clear.

Too clear.

And then her eyes fell onto the uncluttered surface of Karen's desk. The only item lying on top was a phone. None of her office equipment, or even her pictures and Knick-knacks, was visible.

What in the hell was going on?

Slowly moving around the desk, Danielle circled the spacious empty workplace, eventually approaching her private office.

Reaching for her key, Danielle was surprised to discover that her office was unlocked. Opening the door and glancing inside, for a moment, she was puzzled.

This *was* her office. *Wasn't it?*

The desk was positioned in the corner, and her entire office suite had been rearranged. Ordinarily packed full with her landscape books and manuals, some of them at one time belonging to her parents, the mahogany shelves stood stark and empty; although they were sparsely littered with a few unfamiliar pictures and books. Removed from the credenza, her computer now rested on an oddly vacant desktop that was lined with a calendar and a hodgepodge assortment of office paraphernalia. The desktop had been stripped of every single one of her personal belongings.

Having always proudly displayed her work-related awards beside her diploma on the office walls, the plaques appeared to be missing.

Along with her diploma.

And where were her botanicals? The set of nearly a hundred had been purchased from an estate sale the previous summer, and had been a wedding gift from Jake. After choosing several favorites to display here in her office, Danielle had temporarily hung the remaining watercolors in the more prestigious suites of the Dragonfly Pointe Inn, while awaiting the renovation of the lakehouse.

Easing down into the chair behind her desk, she unlocked the top drawer. And realizing that even her *locked* desk drawers had been stripped of their contents, Danielle suddenly became furious.

She'd have to call Brian. But, *first*, she'd search for her belongings. Before calling in a locksmith.

Rushing into Brian's office, she briefly but unproductively searched, before finally locating a large box containing her diploma and awards, shoved into a small closet. After examining the outer office and finding nothing, Danielle followed the hallway that led out to a rear second exit into the lobby. Eventually, she discovered her books and manuals stacked sloppily in a tattered assortment of boxes, in the dingy closet of the breezeway immediately outside the exit.

When Danielle opened the door into the janitor's supply room, and suddenly noticed her botanicals propped against a grimy wall, she swore out loud. Enmeshed in silent fury, Danielle began grabbing up the boxes.

Thirty minutes later, she was still hauling the boxes into the outer office when the security company's locksmith arrived. Escorting him through the office, she pointed out the locks on Brian's office door as well as her own.

"All new locks then? And you want cameras installed in your outer office?"

"Yeah," she acknowledged. "Only the lobby was set up previously. Apparently, we're having some trouble with one of our employees," she admitted wryly. "And let's change both entrance locks from the lobby too. I'm not sure we'll be retaining our office manager."

She promptly set to work reorganizing her office, while the locksmith replaced the locks and rewired the security cameras. Luckily, her shelves hadn't been moved. Clearing and boxing up Karen's clutter and office equipment, she began stacking Karen's books and belongings on top of the desk in the outer office.

Danielle was almost in tears when she realized that some of her more valuable manuals—the ones that had once belonged to her parents—had been damaged. Ripped and frayed, some of the more delicate books were now missing their covers.

Once the locksmith was finished, Danielle decided she'd better call Brian. Who would they put in charge of the office, if they had to fire Karen? Brian was supposed to remain in Crystal Rock for several more weeks, to supervise the remodel of the lakehouse for her and Jake.

"She did *what?*" Danielle could hear the shock in Brian's voice, over the phone. "I told her she could make calls from your office—but only when Jesse and Rosie were working the phones. What the *hell* was she thinking?"

"I don't know, Brian. I mean we did a background check, and Karen came with the highest of recommendations. Maybe we gave her too much authority?" Danielle was still struggling to hold back her tears.

And then a thought suddenly occurred to her.

"Brian," she moaned. *"You didn't?"*

Brian began clearing his throat uncomfortably. "Didn't what?"

"*Sleep* with her?"

The line remained silent.

"Brian. How could you?"

"Danny. I swear it was only a couple of times last summer. Before I met Dawn. It was over before it even began."

Before he'd met Dawn? She'd definitely have to think about *that* slip later.

Resignedly, she sighed. "Well. What can we do about it now? The locksmith's already been here. All the locks have been replaced. And, now, along with the alarm installed in the lobby, there's an alarm that'll go straight through to the security company, if anyone attempts to enter either your office or mine."

"Good move. What else *could* you do? I'm not sure we can afford to fire Karen, Danny. You can't stay there in New York, and I can't get back there yet."

"Yeah, well, I'll probably stay late tonight, setting my office back up."

"Have her call me when she comes in. I'll set her straight. Something strange is going on."

"I definitely agree. Well, *if* she comes in, I'll have her call you."

"I'll be working here the rest of the night. I'm really sorry, Danny."

Karen eventually strolled in an hour later. At age twenty-four, she'd initially impressed Danielle with her intelligence and maturity. Stylishly cut light-brown hair showed off her big brown eyes to their best advantage. Observing Danielle struggling to shove her desk back into its former position, she froze, gawking indecisively.

"Don't just stand there," Danielle growled, amazingly composed. "I could use some help."

Silently, Karen dropped her purse. Taking a hold of one end of the massive mahogany desk, she began pushing and shoving until Danielle signaled her to stop with a wave of her hand.

Karen must've finally realized that Danielle was furious.

"You've destroyed several of my manuals. I presume you didn't know that they once belonged to my parents, making them priceless to myself." In a monotone, Danielle continued, "If you search the city for another job like you have now, you'll realize that you're making thirty percent above anyone else who's holding the same position." Before Karen could react, Danielle held up a staying hand. "I should fire you. But I realize, right now, it'd be hard to replace you." She snorted. "And my botanicals." She motioned to the wall. "They're worth several thousand dollars." Enmeshed in her anger, Danielle was faintly aware of Karen's gasp of shock. "And you had them stacked in an unlocked janitor's closet. I can't believe I'm giving you one more chance. But you'll never again enter our inner offices unless Brian or I are here. I've had new locks and security cameras installed."

"We'll see what Brian says about that," Karen said.

Danielle was somewhat surprised to hear the contempt in Karen's voice.

"He said I could have your office."

"Brian told me that he gave you permission to *use* my office for calls. That was it." Danielle added, indignantly, "I don't know *where* you got the idea, that you could move into my office, since I'm his *partner*."

"But, I thought...?" Karen appeared deflated, and suddenly seemed doubtful. "Since it was *his* firm?"

Shaking her head wearily, as she returned to unpacking her books, Danielle waved at the phone in the outer office. "Call Brian. *Now*. And put it on speaker," Danielle ordered.

Karen's look was mutinous as she eyed her cluttered desktop. She picked up the phone and determinedly began punching in numbers.

"Brian. This is Karen," she said, acknowledging his hello.

"Karen. What the *hell* is going on there? *Danielle told me you moved into her office.*"

"But...I thought..."

"You thought *what*? I know that you understood me—when I said you could make *calls* from Danielle's office. *Nothing more*."

"But since you're the boss...?"

"Karen. Where in the hell did you ever get *that* idea?"

"Danny's never at the office."

"Who do you think goes over all those landscape plans? And okays the plant selections? *Danny.* She's been working from Wisconsin. I just come up with architectural and structural plans. She's a *partner*, Karen, for Christ's sake. In fact, she's *more* than a partner, now, since Jake Loughlin, her new husband, has been our silent partner from the beginning."

"I never knew—maybe since I don't handle the financials..."

Ignoring her words, Brian continued, "And, by the way, what happened with the wedding guest list? Why in the hell was Todd Shelton at Danny's wedding, after we *specifically* asked you to axe his invite? If you still want your job, you'd better prove it to Danny, Karen."

Through the speaker, Danielle could hear the buzzing of the dial tone. Brian had apparently disconnected the conversation abruptly, by slamming down the phone.

Karen looked visibly stunned, as she stared at the receiver. Finally, she rested it gently in place. Taking in a deep breath, she approached the door of Danielle's office.

Danielle had been watching and listening, but now she was studying one of her damaged manuals. When she turned her eyes on Karen, she knew she was blinking back tears. She just couldn't help it. It'd been such a busy week, with the wedding and honeymoon, before they'd rushed home because of Sam. Then, to arrive at her office and have to deal with *this.* "Well. Do you *still* want your job?"

Karen nodded hesitantly, refusing to meet Danielle's eyes.

"Be back here in the morning at eight, sharp, and we'll go over the new rules. Go. Right now. I'd rather be alone." Danielle turned away dismissively.

Quietly, Karen left the office.

Still shaken, walking determinedly for several long blocks, she finally reached a towering apartment building. Entering the lobby, she greeted the attendant at the reception desk. "Could you please ring the penthouse? Tell him Karen is here to see him."

Soon, she was riding up the elevator. Once the doors slid open, she approached the entrance of the penthouse suite. After her brief knock, he answered the door. He was grimly unenthusiastic, while the look in his intense silvery stare confirmed his displeasure. "*Why* are you here?"

Suddenly fearful, Karen stepped back from the door. He was dangerously handsome. But for the first time since they'd met, she was actually *scared* of him. "I almost lost my job."

Obviously reluctant, he stepped aside from the door, motioning her inside with a sweep of his hand.

A few hours later, Todd Shelton stared distractedly out at the brightly lit skyline of New York.

She was becoming sloppy.

And annoyingly demanding and possessive.

Had Karen outworn her usefulness?

Twenty - one

Once Danielle had departed, Sam had retrieved his luggage and returned to Penny's apartment, where they'd showered and dressed quickly. Already guilty about leaving Alex with his caregiver for as long as she had today, Penny needed to spend some time with Alex, she'd explained to Sam.

Suddenly, the phone rang. After a brief conversation, Penny laughed softly before returning the receiver to its cradle. "We're having drinks and dinner with Chad and Greg. If that's alright with you, that is?"

With a shrug of his shoulders, he nodded his acceptance. "Who's Greg?"

"He's Alex's caregiver. And he's also a CPA. That's why I hate leaving him saddled with Alex for too long. I know that it *has* to interfere with his work. He and Chad live right next door. Are we ready?" Wearing only a touch of makeup, her hair was loose over her shoulders, and Penny looked lovely in a sleeveless lavender blouse, paired with a short denim skirt.

"No shoes?"

She smiled. "They've got these gorgeous, high-piled area rugs, covering most of the wooden floors in their apartment. Everything in my apartment is totally utilitarian. In fact, I had to make Greg promise to bring Alex over here when he acts up." Gazing around the room, she sighed resignedly. "They have some really beautiful collectables I'd hate to see broken."

Preparing for changes he'd probably have to make in his own home to accommodate Alex, Sam had studied the interior of Penny's apartment. Admiring the style and color scheme of her furnishings, he'd been pleasantly surprised to realize that Penny's taste and preferences were similar to his own.

But devoid of any accent pieces, Penny's apartment was rather stark.

Plus, there appeared to be several holes in the walls. "Alex?" Sam nodded, eyeing the largest hole punched into the drywall near the door.

She nodded, ruefully. "He didn't want to go to bed that night. Most of time, I'm covered with a few bruises, myself," she admitted.

Sam frowned. *Just how bad did Alex get during his episodes?* Somehow, he got the feeling Penny was purposely brushing off Alex's incidents rather casually.

"That's the first thing I'll have to do when we move—find a good doctor. I'll need to experiment with some medications, to try and regulate his behavior. It's time. But it could be a long, difficult process—or, so, I've heard."

"But *I'll* be there to help you," he added, reassuringly. *When* we move, she'd said. Had she even realized it? With a gentle shove, Sam pushed her through the doorway.

Reaching the door at the end of hallway, knocking softly, Penny opened the door and stepped into the apartment.

Following Penny, Sam halted. At first glance, he was stunned. *This* was Alex? Only a few inches shorter than Sam, he was powerfully built. Somehow, Sam had envisioned him as a *little kid*. And because he was mentally impaired, Sam had assumed he'd have the mongoloid features associated with Down's syndrome. With blonde hair and blue eyes, although appearing most obviously unaware and distant, Alex was exceptionally *handsome*.

He looked so much like Penny.

With a shake of his head, Sam was visibly bemused as he finally became aware of his surroundings. Filled with antiques and assorted displays of collectables, the apartment was a showplace.

As Penny's silver-haired *friend* approached him with a smile, Sam frowned. Did *every* friend of Penny's have to look like a male model?

In a purposely higher than average octave, shaking Sam's hand, Greg observed, "You were right, Penny. He *is* handsome. Isn't he?"

Sam blinked, and scowled. Decidedly uncomfortable, he became aware of the man's eyes traveling over him with, what appeared to be, lingering appreciation.

When Penny began sputtering with laughter, Sam's comprehension finally kicked in.

And he began to grin.

"Yep." Greg chuckled. "I'd say that Danny got it right, when she was talking to Chad. He *was* jealous."

"Well." Eyeing Penny, who appeared to be taken aback, Sam growled, "When every guy surrounding her is so damned good looking, can you blame me?"

"Now *that's* a good answer." Mischievously, Greg waggled his brows. "Now. If you ever get tired of Penny..."

Sam laughed, turning back to Greg. "Sorry. But *that* I can never imagine.

"Well, that's good to hear. It's about time Penny found herself a nice guy," Greg answered, gruffly. "What can I get you to drink, Sam? Wine, beer, scotch?"

"Beer will be fine. Thanks."

And for the next several hours, they continued to converse. With Chad eventually joining them for dinner, they feasted on a delicious meal of pot roast with carrots and potatoes.

Alex was surprisingly well-behaved throughout the entire evening. But with Penny scooping and regulating the amount of food going into his mouth, his table manners definitely needed some work. Eventually, he began pacing the room, always circling around Penny. It was obvious she was the center of his universe.

And Alex was definitely scoping out Sam. Although his eyes never met Sam's, he was slowly slipping in closer. By the time Sam and Penny were seated on the couch in the living room, sipping their after-dinner drinks, Sam was increasingly aware of the light, soft touches of Alex's fingers as they brushed curiously through his hair.

Finally, it was time to return to Penny's apartment.

"You've been a really good boy tonight, Alex."

Turning to Penny, wavering for a moment, Alex smiled before resuming his routine.

And when Sam reached hesitantly for Alex's hand, Alex willingly conceded it. After thanking both Chad and Greg with a smile, Sam walked Alex through the door.

Penny observed, "Alex is tired tonight." She entered her apartment with Sam and Alex trailing closely behind her. "He's been a terror this entire week, since his routine's been upset. It's finally caught up with him. I should get him into bed."

Sam smiled, squeezing Alex's hand. "I'll help."

She grinned. "Enter at your own risk," she added, moving down the hallway toward Alex's room.

When Alex began dragging him into his bedroom, Sam entered, feeling slightly bemused. With shelves and storage lining all four walls of the room, Alex's room was stuffed with every toy imaginable.

Watching Penny pull out his pajamas from a drawer, Alex began to strip with no inhibition. "Just put your bottoms on, Alex. Hurry into the bathroom so we can brush your teeth."

Sam grinned, watching Alex follow Penny's orders. "I was never very shy, either."

Penny snorted. "Then you haven't really changed, much. Have you?" she observed, dryly.

With a mischievous grin, Sam caught her by the waist. Brushing a kiss on her lips, he pulled her into his arms. "I've wanted to do that all night," he whispered, softly.

Surprisingly, she waggled her brows. "Just a few more minutes, then, and you'll have the rest of the night to prove it."

Sam stood back as Penny and Alex continued their nightly routine. After observing her testing Alex's blood sugar earlier, Sam had flinched when she'd given Alex his insulin. Sam was definitely squeamish—he'd need a little more time to become comfortable with the procedure.

While Alex had acted like he hadn't even felt his insulin shot at all.

Pulling out the monitor and pricking his finger, Penny tested Alex's blood sugar again. "Ah. One-twenty. Perfect, Alex."

Urging him to the toilet, she retrieved his toothbrush and set to brushing his teeth. Scrubbing his face with a washrag doused with soap and water, she finished up with his hands. Penny observed dryly, "He *can* do everything himself. But I prefer to do it for him, at least at bedtime, since he doesn't ever seem to do it as well as he should."

When he was sure his mother was finished, without any directive, Alex quickly flushed the toilet. Yanking his pajama bottoms up, he rushed back into his bedroom.

"That's the thing, Sam," Penny muttered, softly. "He knows a lot more than he lets on, you know.

They followed behind Alex. After stuffing his dirty clothing into his hamper and pulling on his pajama top, Alex jumped into bed.

Penny adjusted the dial of the radio on the nightstand, and grinned, as Alex smiled, when soft music echoed through the room. "He *loves* light rock." Once she'd covered him with his quilt, Penny bent over Alex and kissed him gently on his cheek.

Sam grinned. Moving over to the bedside, he reached for Alex's hand.

And then suddenly, powerfully, Alex yanked on Sam's arm, bringing him closer. Stretching up from his bed, Alex wrapped his arms around Sam, hugging him tightly.

Rather numb and emotionally drained when he left Alex's room, Sam was aware that his eyes were suspiciously moist.

As Sam began to awaken, he became aware, rather dazedly, that he wasn't alone.

It took only a moment to remember where he was. Boasting warm creamy furnishings, accented by delicate floral fabrics of rose and green, Penny's bedroom was warm and inviting. Curling over on his side, slowly stretching his arm over the width of the queen-sized bed, with a sleepy gaze, he finally realized that the other half of the bed was empty.

Where was Penny? Sam grinned with satisfaction. It'd been quite a night.

And, then again, he sensed movement in the bed. Sam scrambled upright when he realized Alex was sitting patiently at the foot of the bed. He was humming, most obviously off in his own world, as he tapped two Lego blocks together repeatedly.

Sam eyed the alarm clock; it was only eight o'clock. "Alex. Where's your mom?" Sam asked, attempting to gaze into Alex's eyes.

Sam finally spotted the note on the nightstand. *Am working—had a funeral. Breakfast in fridge. Alex's insulin shot is ready to go. Go to Greg's if you need help.*

"Your mom wants me to give you your shot and breakfast, Alex. I hope I can handle it," he mumbled.

Tapping his blocks together faster and harder, Alex answered Sam with a giggle.

Sliding from the bed, Sam slipped on his shorts. After taking Alex by the hand, he tugged him into the hallway. A tall, wrought iron gate barricaded the kitchen from the bedrooms and bathroom. "Hmm. This wasn't closed up last night, kiddo. It must be here to keep you away from the food—because of your blood sugar. Huh?" Noticing a key ring looped up high on a hook, Sam pulled down the keys. Going through each key one at a time, he finally discovered the one that fit. "Tricky. Your mom must've added a bunch of keys to the ring—probably to stop *you* from finding the right one."

Sam led Alex into the kitchen. After pulling out a pre-poured bowl of cereal from the fridge, Sam discovered a syringe loaded with insulin, lying clearly visible in a marked container.

"Okay. You'll have to be patient with me." Turning Alex to the wall for leverage, Sam ripped open an alcohol swab. Without prompting, Alex pulled the waistband of his pajamas halfway down over his buttocks.

Sam snorted. "You're a hell of a lot less nervous about this, than I am, kid. Shivering with revulsion, Sam mumbled, "Your mom says that she usually gives you these shots in your tummy. I can't even handle getting a shot in my own *butt*."

Swabbing a patch of Alex's skin with alcohol, pulling the cap from the syringe, Sam awkwardly inserted the needle.

Eventually pulling out the needle, he muttered with relief, "I did it!"

Alex giggled.

Pulling up his waistband, Alex promptly picked up the bowl that Penny had left filled with cereal, and shoved it into the fridge. Slowly and carefully, he set about pulling eggs from a drawer inside the refrigerator.

"Ah. I don't blame you. I suppose it'd be okay. Your mom kind of explained everything to me last night. Since you're out of school, you burn off a lot more calories, and you can't seem to get enough to eat, anyway. And I wouldn't mind eating something a little more satisfying, myself."

Attempting to assist, Alex followed Sam around the kitchen as he gathered up food and utensils.

And when Sam served up his breakfast, Alex finished up every single crumb on his plate; laughing and giggling exuberantly during their entire breakfast.

"Hello?" Breezing quickly through the living room and then through dining room, Penny halted, as her eyes widened. She was obviously dazed as she took in the scene before her in the kitchen.

Sam raised a brow. "Breakfast?"

"Sure," she replied. Dropping down onto a stool, she began to laugh softly.

"Alex might've had a little too much to eat," Sam admitted, ruefully. "He decided he wanted eggs, and I was kind of hungry myself."

"Oh—he'll be fine." She smiled when Alex picked up his empty plate, and handed it over to Sam. "His blood sugar was perfect earlier when he was still asleep. We can go for a walk later if his blood sugar gets high. I haven't had a chance to eat, either, since I've been up since four."

"*Four?* No wonder why I didn't hear you." Sam scooped the remainder of bacon and eggs onto a plate for Penny. Motioning at the toaster, and acknowledging her nod, he popped in some bread.

"My beeper went off. We had a *huge* funeral order. We get referrals since we work in conjunction with several area funeral homes. Our shop handles the majority of funeral work for this part of the city."

After Penny finished up with her breakfast, Alex ran off to play in the family room. Sam and Penny began to companionably straighten up the kitchen. After pouring them each a cup of coffee, Penny tugged on Sam's arm, and led him off into the family room. Settling together on a sofa, they sat contentedly sipping on their coffee while observing Alex.

"What time do you need to be at the airport?"

He grimaced. "Probably by noon. At least I have a direct flight. I have a meeting with the task force in New Orleans immediately after my flight arrives this afternoon."

"We don't have much time left," Penny observed, softly.

Taking in a deep breath, Sam finally dared to ask, "Well?"

"*Yes,*" she answered, with emphasis. "I'm moving back to Crystal Rock. It would be the best thing for Alex." Gazing into Sam's eyes, she added, "And it would probably be the best thing for me, too.

"I'll go along with that," Sam muttered, pulling her into his arms.

Twenty - two

ne month. Sam would return to New York and drive Penny and Alex back to Crystal Rock. He'd insisted. But he had a hell of a lot of work to do at his house on Pine Street. After he childproofed the interior, he'd need to finish off the basement with drywall and flooring. Plus, he'd have to hire someone to install a privacy fence. Once he reached New Orleans, he'd call Mike Callahan to get things started.

It was close to four when the plane finally arrived at the airport. Negotiating the crowded terminal, Sam was awaiting his baggage when Shane Donnelly appeared.

"I thought you were in Wisconsin?" Sam asked, taken aback.

"The situation is pretty delicate, Sam. Even more so than before. I'd prefer to be the one to show you the videos and go over the autopsy with you," Shane answered, quietly. "I'll fly back to Wisconsin sometime tomorrow after the funeral."

As he uneasily studied Shane, Sam nodded his acceptance.

Retrieving his luggage, Sam followed Shane through the airport terminal and out through the parking lot. After loading his luggage in the trunk of Shane's black sedan, Sam slid into the passenger seat.

Exchanging only a few brief words on their drive from the airport, Shane eventually pulled into the parking lot of Sam's former precinct.

"We thought you might be more comfortable working with some of your previous colleagues, Sam. This investigation began immediately after you left New Orleans."

Sam gazed sharply at Shane, but remained silent.

Following Shane into the station and through a door into one of the conference rooms, Sam acknowledged the familiar faces as his eyes searched the room. "Pete, Brent, Linda. Good to see you guys again."

A murmur of solemn voices returned his greeting.

"You remember some of our task force?" Shane reintroduced Ben Greaves and Cal Donner. "Sherry Simpkins is coordinating the surveillance." Sam shook hands with the tall, slim agent who appeared to be second in command. Taking a seat next to Shane, she anxiously thumbed through her notes.

Abruptly, Shane began, "Only a few months ago, Peter Gerard agreed to testify to avoid prosecution. At first we believed his murder was retribution. But now we're not so sure. Evidence has turned up to suggest that his agreement to testify was a setup by Frank Carlton, to allow them to restructure their trafficking ring. Gerard was more valuable to them alive."

Shocked by this information, Sam dropped down into his seat at the conference table.

For the next few hours, as several individuals deliberated and reported on updated information, silently absorbing, Sam observed the task force at work.

Although Gerard International had been a profitable conglomerate that'd packaged and distributed seafood throughout the entire United States, from practically the moment of Gerard's inception as CEO of the business, the members of the task force strongly suspected that the company had been a front for human trafficking.

After running through his wife's fortune, Peter Gerard had joined forces with Frank Carlton. With thousands of shipping channels available in the air and on the water, Frank Carlton's international enterprise had allowed worldwide distribution of fresh and frozen seafood.

And for his investment, Frank Carlton had required a crucial, inexhaustible price: Gerard International would forever serve as a legitimate front for their trafficking.

Going over a list of Frank Carlton's recent associates, after finally citing additional key players who would require immediate surveillance, the task force concluded their meeting.

Shaking several more hands, murmuring words of farewell, Sam was finally alone with Shane Donnelly.

Wordlessly, Shane rose to his feet. Approaching a previously set up VCR and television combo, he pressed a button. For five minutes, Shane anxiously paced the floor, allowing Sam to view the first few minutes of a video tape.

Finally approaching the VCR, Shane discharged the tape and inserted another. He repeated the process several more times.

When Sam finally held up a staying hand, Shane shut down the VCR. Dropping his head into his hands, Sam came to gradually recognize the depth of his own anguish, miserably and profoundly.

While Sam attempted to contain his grief, Shane spoke gruffly, "I'll give you a minute." Quietly, he left the room.

Dazed and confused, Sam struggled to come to terms with the revelations on the tapes. He stood up on his feet, reluctantly approaching the box containing the videos.

There were over twenty-five tapes inside.

A few minutes later, Shane quietly reentered the room, speaking softly, "We believe it was blackmail, Sam. And not something Vanessa *ever* wanted to do. We think she was manipulated from the time she was a teenager." As Sam self-consciously scraped away his tears with the back of his hand, Shane's eyes met his. "But it may have begun earlier, Sam. We have evidence suggesting Peter Gerard was a pedophile."

"That bastard." Stunned, Sam's legs collapsed as he dropped back down into his seat. "Oh, God. I never really knew her at all. Did I? I knew there was something strange about their relationship, but I totally misread it," Sam whispered, hollowly.

Shane hesitated, but then squaring off his shoulders, he continued, "I'm afraid there's something else, too, Sam."

Attempting to avoid Shane's troubled gaze, closing his eyes, Sam asked quietly, "What?"

"The autopsy results were pretty much what we expected, Sam. Her throat was slashed by a serrated knife, identical to the knife used on her father. But, meanwhile, after searching her townhouse, we came across some paperwork for some blood work she had done a few months ago. And we double-checked with the lab." Breathing in deeply, he continued, "She was HIV positive, Sam."

Shaking his head wearily, Sam released a ragged sigh.

"So you may want to…" Shane's voice faltered, as it faded away.

Laughing humorlessly, Sam responded, "I'm clean. I decided to get tested with my last physical, just as an afterthought. Although, *everyone* would probably be surprised to know that *I* was faithful to Vanessa. At least until I signed the papers and believed I was *divorced*."

With his hands in his pants pockets, Shane turned his gaze uncomfortably from Sam's. "We've made arrangements for your rental car. I think you've been through enough today. And you still have Vanessa's visitation to get through tonight. After the funeral tomorrow, we can talk about the will and some of the options we've come up with to move forward. Come on. Let's pick up something to eat and get you to your hotel."

After tossing and turning for half the night, Sam had given up on sleep. Eventually, he pulled out his black suit. Having faced the curiosity of a grieving crowd last night at the visitation, Sam had been surprisingly pleased by the number of individuals attending who'd, most obviously, sincerely, respected Vanessa.

Efficiently knotting his black and maroon tie, Sam was startled by a knock at his hotel room door. It was probably a member of the task force arriving, to escort him to the funeral, he assumed, before answering.

"*Celeste.*" An exceptionally successful fashion designer, as well as an icon of fashion here in New Orleans, Celeste DeVoux was currently in charge of Vanessa's string of Le Chic boutiques, scattered throughout the county. And she just so happened to be the only friend of Vanessa's that Sam had actually *liked*. "It's good to see you," he muttered, when she swept in through the doorway.

"I weel go weeth you, of course," she announced, lifting a brow in challenge.

"Of course," he answered, meekly. "Thanks."

With hair of rich mahogany, sleekly styled into an upsweep, Celeste, as usual, was lovely in a trim black suit. Estimating her age to be around fifty-five, Sam knew better than to *ever* make the mistake of asking.

She'd been Vanessa's one true female friend.

Sam frowned, suddenly recalling Sophia Ruston. Maybe he should've flown her in for the funeral?

"What eez wrong, Sam? I mean besides zee obveeous?"

"Vanessa made a friend in Crystal Rock. She probably should've been included," he admitted ruefully.

"*She?* Now that eez unusual," Celeste responded, smiling.

"I think that Vanessa might've found you a protégée, Celeste."

After slipping on his suit jacket, he held out his arm politely, to escort her down to the hotel lobby.

When they moved outdoors, Celeste signaled to a driver, who stood waiting near a long black limousine. "We weel take my leemo, of course, so we may follow zee procession. You must tell me more about zee girl."

With Sam eventually revealing some of the details of Vanessa's sordid past, they conversed in depth on their way to the funeral home.

It was a long demanding day. As the temperature climbed up to over ninety degrees, the humidity made it feel more like one-hundred. Surprisingly uncomfortable, Sam loosened his tie and unbuttoned the jacket of his suit. He couldn't recall being nearly as affected by the heat and humidity when he'd resided here in New Orleans.

Later in the afternoon, while a solemn minister spoke, Sam stood with the remaining crowd near the family burial plot. The casket would soon be placed in a vault belonging to the maternal branch of Vanessa's family. Buried on Wednesday, Peter Gerard had been interred in a secondary family plot on the outskirts of the cemetery.

Frank Carlton had made those arrangements.

Typically, a New Orleans funeral would conclude with a celebration of food and drink. But due to the circumstances of both Peter and Vanessa's violent deaths, Sam had deemed hosting a gathering after the funeral to be in poor taste.

Celeste suddenly shoved something into his hand. Shaped with sprigs of greenery, the fragrant bouquet was topped with creamy flowers. Baffled, Sam studied the nosegay. "What's this, Celeste?"

"Honeysuckle. Because she loved zee scent in spring." Celeste delicately dabbed at her tears with a lacy handkerchief. "She told me once that eet reminded her of her mother."

Sam sighed. Something else he'd never known about Vanessa. Closing his eyes, Sam held the sprig to his nose, inhaling its light, fruity scent. Approaching the casket, he carefully rested the ribbon-wrapped bouquet on top.

When the service ended, Sam assisted as the pallbearers carried the casket inside to the vault.

Finally escorting Celeste to her limo, he thanked her with a tender smile and a warm embrace. "Why couldn't I see what was really going on between Vanessa and Peter, Celeste? It's obvious now that I know. I had to have been an *idiot* not to see it. No wonder why Vanessa was always so discouraged—never having control of her own business. I just assumed that she was lazy when she spent less and less time at her office. But how could I ever think *that,* when her business was so successful?"

Celeste sighed. "She waaz very troubled, Sam. And I am sickened to finally know *why*. Let me know whaat will happen with zee business."

Squeezing her hand reassuringly, Sam promised to get back with her soon.

And then he saw him standing at the edge of the crowd.

Ryan Carlton.

Observing the pallor of his face, along with his sunken cheekbones, Sam was stunned by Ryan Carlton's visible weight loss.

And then it hit him. Assuming that Vanessa and Ryan had most likely been lovers, Sam had never seriously considered the whispered rumors he'd heard about Ryan's health before he'd left New Orleans.

As he determinedly approached Ryan, ignoring the unmistakable signs of the man's intense grief, Sam swore, bitterly, "*You son of a bitch.*"

Startled by Sam's accusation, Ryan Carlton's anger immediately surfaced. "*Damn you,* Sam Danielson," Ryan muttered, fiercely. "You're such an idiot. I *loved* her. I knew every single one of her faults, and I *still* loved her. You never even knew her." Turning away furiously, he stomped through the cemetery to the road, slipping into the passenger seat of his waiting vehicle.

Observing the retreat of the cobalt-blue luxury sedan, Sam seethed in silent fury.

But his fury gradually subsided as he grudgingly acknowledged the truth. And wearily, Sam sighed. Ryan Carlton was right. Sam hadn't really known Vanessa.

As he turned his attention on the remaining vehicles, Sam finally located Shane Donnelly, standing patiently beside Sherry Simpkins. Strolling to their car, Sam signaled he was ready to depart.

"We haven't a clue as to why they were killed. But the way they were killed was personal, Sam. That's why we need *you*. It's pretty damned difficult narrowing down suspects, if we can't figure out *why*," Shane admitted. "This updated will, that Vanessa came up with, is sure gonna put a big wrench in the running of Gerard International."

Back at the stationhouse, Sam and Shane were meeting with Sherry Simpkins, along with two members of the task force, not presently assigned to surveillance.

"So—whatever Vanessa's included in her new will is actually valid?"

Sherry Simpkins took over. "Most likely. Vanessa didn't kill her father, and she *was* his beneficiary. But the original will she signed, at eighteen, names the board of directors as her beneficiaries for the business, with Frank Carlton assuming Peter Gerard's control as CEO. Peter Gerard's will names Vanessa as his beneficiary, but leaves Frank Carlton in control of the company. *And* her income. Twenty years ago, Vanessa signed an acceptance of the terms."

Sam shook his head, silently attempting to process the information.

"In a letter to her new lawyer, Vanessa claims that she was forced to sign both the agreement and her will, and was never allowed to read either one. But what it means, now, Sam, since you two were never divorced, *you* control fifty-one percent of Gerard International."

Sam gasped. *"What?"*

"You know what the kicker is though, Sam? No matter what Peter Gerard attempted to do, he'd never be allowed to sell the business. The company was renamed when Gerard took over. It turns out Vanessa has always owned it. *She* inherited it directly through her maternal grandparents. Apparently, she never even knew," Shane reflected, grimly. "And if she *died* before Gerard, he'd lose it all. If she didn't marry, the company would've been sold, with the proceeds distributed to charity. But since you were still married, it's *yours*. We've been trying to locate Peter Gerard's lawyer, but he appears to have fallen off the face of the earth."

Sherry continued, "The rest of Vanessa's directives are pretty easy to fulfill. Her company, Le Chic, splits between Celeste Devoux, Sophia Barelli, and you. Now *that's* a highly profitable business."

Sam shook his head dazedly. "That's a shocker, too," he mumbled.

"The New Orleans properties are yours, too, but appear to be heavily mortgaged. They would, of course, be seized if we could actually prove illicit funds were used to purchase or maintain the properties. But they were all family properties before the trafficking began. So, according to the books, Gerard International is legitimate. Peter Gerard has money floating around somewhere. And he never replaced the money he stole from Vanessa's trust fund. Although he set up her business from her own trust, he was funneling the majority of her profits elsewhere."

"But what about Peter Gerard's prosecution?"

"It had nothing to do with the trafficking *or* Gerard International. Someone came forward about his sexual indiscretions. He liked young girls, Sam—most particularly, six to twelve-years old."

Agonized by the implications, Sam drew in a ragged breath. "Oh, God. And, as an informant, he would've been free to continue. *That sick son of a bitch*. What's wrong with me that I didn't notice? I mean I didn't even have a *clue*."

For a few tense moments, the conversation halted.

Sam finally spoke. "So, how much information did Gerard even have the opportunity to feed to you?"

"Not much."

"What do you want from *me*, then?"

"*Sam*. Think, man. You own the business. No court orders or subpoenas. You have immediate access to their paperwork. Think of all the time and effort you can save us in this investigation. We realize that you don't want to be here forever, so we want you to appoint someone to act in your stead. This investigation could go on for years. There are *thousands* who'd lose their jobs without Gerard International."

"Alright. What's the catch?" Sam asked, dryly. "*Who* do you want me to appoint?"

Shrugging helplessly, Sherry turned her eyes on Shane, before he informed Sam resignedly, "Ryan Carlton."

Sam gaped. *"Ryan Carlton? Why would I want to hand over the reins of the company to Ryan Carlton?"*

Clearing his throat uncomfortably, Shane answered, "Because Vanessa asked you to?"

With a stare of astonishment, Sam circled his eyes through the room. Studying the other members of the task force, Sam realized that none of them appeared to be surprised.

When Shane slid copies of two notarized letters across the table, feeling apathetic, Sam picked them up and begin reading.

Once he was finished, he stood up from his seat and began pacing the room. He studied Shane thoughtfully. "He's been working with you all along. Hasn't he?"

Seemingly hesitant, Shane nodded.

"And Vanessa was unaware?"

He nodded again.

"How would we handle it?"

"We'd rewrite the will. Make it appear Vanessa left Ryan in control of the company. How would Frank Carlton even have a clue that you discovered your divorce was invalid? Whatever the instructions were that he gave her, he knew Vanessa never had the opportunity to speak with you.

"How did Ryan Carlton come to be involved?"

"Besides the fact that he was in love with your wife? Frank Carlton is his uncle, and he's wreaked havoc on every life he's touched. Ryan's half-brother Jessie is Frank's right-hand man. Jessie was the favorite son. So, of course, Allen Carlton blames Frank for Jessie's defection, even though Jessie was nothing but trouble to begin with. Allen Carlton would, of course, be assisting us as well."

"All right." Sam sighed, wearily. "Let's do it."

With a curt nod, Shane sent the other members of the task force from the room.

"You need to find a way to get along with Rye Carlton. I'm not sure that you've realized it yet Sam, but we think Vanessa married you for a reason. Although, whatever that reason was, and is, we're still not sure. We went over all of your stepfather's businesses and investments, and except for the fortune you'll inherit when Craig Edmonds dies, there's nothing obvious that sticks out. Not for Peter Gerard and Frank Carlton to have gone through all their initial trouble—to conveniently have Vanessa available, for seducing you at the right place and time, that is."

Sam continued, "And whatever reason *that* was, it was probably the reason she never divorced me, either—and hid that fact from me, over the last four years." Sam stood up wearily from the conference table. "I need a little time to absorb all of this. Would you believe that I had absolutely *no* idea that my step-father had a *fortune*? And now it'll all come to *me*?"

"Give us a day to write up the new will, and get together the appropriate paperwork. Then we need to leak out the information, to just the right sources, that the terms in *our* will are valid. You should be able to have access to all of the household financials and records by tomorrow, Sam. We'd appreciate it if you could start there. Meanwhile, talk to Rye Carlton." Shane began gathering up paperwork.

Deciding he needed some time to think, instead of asking for a ride, Sam began walking the ten long blocks back to his hotel.

Twenty-three

$\mathcal{H}$olding Ryan Carlton's gaze, Sam attempted to convey his remorse. "I'm sorry for assuming..."

Obviously uncomfortable, Ryan shrugged. "You couldn't have known. I was really sick as a kid. It compromised my immune system."

"*Vanessa* gave you AIDS?"

"And Vanessa would've never known *she* was HIV positive, if I hadn't forced her to get tested. You see, she's been the only woman I've been with since you two split up. I refused to sleep with her while the two of you were still together, you know."

"You're right. I never saw the whole picture. I *was* an idiot," Sam admitted, ruefully.

"Whoa. I can't believe you're finally willing to admit it," Rye observed, dryly.

Sam snorted.

Sam had driven out to the Carlton estate, thirty-five miles north of New Orleans. With a magnificent view of the Gulf, the elevated manor spread out over several acres of oceanside property. After shaking hands and accepting a tumbler of iced tea, Sam had escaped to the poolside with Ryan, where they'd attempted to sort out their differences.

Hooking his thumbs over his jean pockets, standing near the edge of the patio, Sam gazed unseeing at the clear, sparkling water of the Gulf. Sighing resignedly, he finally began, "Okay. Tell me about your relationship with Vanessa. Better start from the beginning."

With a nod of acknowledgement, Ryan settled back on the lounger. "I think it was love at first sight," he admitted, with a quick smile. "I met Vanessa when we were only six-years old. Our parents were friends back in those days. Vanessa was happy and loving back then. Her momma used to take her everywhere." Sipping his tea, he continued, "And then everything changed. Evie Gerard became ill, and I rarely saw Vanessa. And that was only at school. And when her mother died..."

His memories were obviously becoming more emotionally charged, and Ryan's southern drawl became thicker and more difficult to understand. "When we finally became friends again, it was about six months after her mother died. The edge of their family estate lines up along the beach up with ours, so we began hanging out together again. She was different, though. She was so *sad*. She didn't laugh anymore, and most importantly, *she didn't cry*. And I couldn't let it go. She was only about eight then."

Ryan closed his eyes. "She finally told me. She said her dad... well...I never knew about things like that, Sam. I was shocked. I told my father. I tried to tell a teacher at school." His lips twisted into a bitter smile. "And *I* ended up in trouble for accusing Peter Gerard."

"That sick son of a bitch," Sam muttered. Aware that he was trembling, Sam began pacing the patio.

"So. We never talked about it. And then, when she was about twelve, something even worse happened." Turning his head sharply, Sam gazed at Ryan. Filled with pain, Ryan's eyes agonizingly met his. "She wouldn't tell me, of course," Ryan whispered. "But I suspect that's when her father began handing her over to other men."

With a groan, Sam dropped into his seat, covering his eyes.

"And eventually we fell in love. I wanted to marry her, you know." He added, resentfully, "But Daddy wouldn't let *that* happen. And she kept right on going along with his brain-washing. I suspect, too, that she was being threatened with her inheritance. Psychologically, I think, she associated the well-being of the company with her mother. And I know she looked at it as her rightful payment for prostituting herself for Peter Gerard. She always claimed that *he owed it to her.*

Startled, his eyes met Ryan's. "She used to use that same phrase, when I gave her a hard time about taking money from Gerard, and not living within our means," Sam admitted, with remorse.

"Don't beat yourself up, Sam." Ryan sighed, adding wryly, "He *did* owe it to her."

Taking a break, each sipping on their tea, they finally, reluctantly, resumed their conversation.

"Next thing I knew, she was moving to New York. The other men were hard enough, but when I heard she was going to marry *you*, I..."

Sam could see the tears glimmering in Ryan's eyes.

Somewhat self-consciously swiping his hand over his face, Ryan continued, "So, I moved on. I married. On the rebound, of course. Sarah and I stayed together, but we weren't happy. Although my father was. He'd always considered Vanessa a tramp. Long ago, he'd stopped associating with Peter Gerard, when Frank came into the picture. I think he finally found out the truth about Gerard, too." Ryan added bitterly, "But it always bothered me—that he wouldn't accept the truth from his own *son*."

"So, how did you come to be working with the task force?"

"Dad suspected Uncle Frank was using our hotels for money laundering. When Dad and Frank had their big falling out twenty years ago, they split up the company. Dad took over the hotels, and Frank took over the shipping and cruise lines. Dad got the raw end of the deal, but he didn't complain. He just wanted away from Frank. I got my business degree and stayed in school to get my master's and P.H.D. Dad was grooming Jess for the business, but Jess was lucky to graduate from high school. He was always getting into trouble—costly trouble, that is. When Jess turned to Frank, Dad finally figured he needed *me*," Ryan muttered bitterly. He shrugged. "And of course, I came running. I handle the books and a hell of a lot more. And I'm pretty damned good at it, too, so I should be able to whip Gerard International into shape. It'll put me in a perfect position to study what's been going on."

Sam cleared his throat. "What about your health?"

"I should still have a few good years left in me—as long as I take my meds and take care of myself. What else have I got now, Sam?" he observed, wryly.

Sam nodded decisively. "Alright. Let's get things started. We're gonna claim that Vanessa left you her controlling shares. If it should ever come out, that our divorce wasn't finalized, we'll say that I'm still allowing you to temporarily assist with the business since I can't be here."

Ryan nodded his approval. Studying Sam, he began hesitantly, "I *do* have an idea about Vanessa's in-town property. I mean if I can fund some money back into the mortgage?"

"Go ahead."

"A facility to assist children of abuse? How many of these children actually go on to have happy and rewarding lives? The estate here on the Gulf could serve as a women's and children's shelter, possibly, if we sell some of the attached property."

"Sounds like a plan. And I think Vanessa would approve," Sam answered, gruffly. Standing up from his chair, Sam pulled a letter from his pocket. "Here. You should have this."

Looking startled, Ryan nodded, accepting Vanessa's letter.

"Thank you, Ryan. I misjudged you," Sam admitted, wryly.

"Ah, Sam." Standing up and raising a brow, Ryan shook Sam's hand. "Wouldn't Vanessa get a kick out of this—the two of us getting along?"

Sam grinned. "That, she would."

For the next several days, Sam began sifting and boxing up paperwork he could send back to Crystal Rock and review in his spare time. He was getting nowhere with his investigation. Every file he discovered at the townhouse, as well as in their former home, Cypress Manor, appeared to be only relevant personally.

Discovering the suite of rooms in the townhouse where Vanessa's videos had been secretly filmed, Sam noticed that the contents of the hidden closet had been entirely stripped when seized by the FBI. Although the majority of the men featured with Vanessa in the sickening videos had been married, Sam presumed the videos filmed during Vanessa's childhood had been the most effective for acquiring information obtained for blackmail and extortion.

Sam decided to prolong the complete investigation of Peter Gerard's mansion and estate. Worried that Frank Carlton would be more suspicious of Sam's motives if he remained in New Orleans, he'd search and pack up the study first, and then return in the near future to further investigate additional rooms in the mansion.

The family of Genevieve Bovier Gerard, Sam was amazed to discover, had a long, historical link to New Orleans. Believed to be distant cousins of the former first lady, the family had been rumored to have connections to French nobility.

Probably out of jealousy, Sam suspected, Peter had never discussed his wife's family. It disgusted Sam to even consider what kind of a husband he must've been to Genevieve.

After borrowing a high quality camera from the coroner's office, beginning in the study, Sam began focusing and taking shots at various angles. Having felt guilty for his extravagance at the time, Sam wryly acknowledged that the darkroom he'd built at his cabin might prove to come in handy.

Constructed in the pre-Civil War era, Vanessa had claimed the mansion boasted several secret passageways, originating with the historical underground railway. Rather than take the time to search the entire home for passageways, Sam would attempt to obtain a copy of the mansion's blueprints.

After going through Peter Gerard's bedroom and snapping several more pictures, Sam finished up with a visual search of Vanessa's room. Strangely, through all their years of marriage, Sam and Vanessa had spent less than a dozen nights here as a couple. Although their wedding had taken place on the grounds, they'd left for their cruise to Mexico immediately following the reception.

Considering the circumstances, Sam decided he'd have Ryan Carlton go through Vanessa's personal effects. He had a feeling that Vanessa would've probably appreciated it.

Suddenly envisioning Peter Gerard slinking into this room, to take advantage of an innocent and grief-stricken, eight-year old girl, Sam was truly heartsick.

No, Sam admitted, with extreme remorse, he'd never really known Vanessa at all.

Twenty-four

S he did *what?*" Definitely shocked, Sophie dropped into a chair in Sam's office.

"She left you one-third interest in her company—with a few stipulations. You'll need to intern with Celeste DeVoux, down in New Orleans, before assuming the financials."

Looking dazed, she mumbled, "I've always wanted to visit New Orleans. But I'd prefer not to have to *move* down there, Sam. My parents are getting older, and I'm worried about how much longer they'll be able to keep up with the demands of the bakery."

"Well, that's not a problem. Apparently, Vanessa expected you to eventually open up a boutique *here* in Crystal Rock. And, in the few days that she was here, she decided that this town would be a perfect location for Le Chic's new catalog and mail order division," he added, dryly. Sam slid over an envelope containing a letter addressed to Sophie. "She wrote you a letter of introduction for Celeste."

"But what about my job here?"

"For the sake of the investigation, it'd be better if you didn't begin your internship until the first of the year, anyway, Soph. As a matter of fact, you can't tell *anyone* about this, yet. I wish I could tell you why, but it's confidential."

Shaking her head, and acting as if she was still in a daze, she stood up from the chair. "Whatever you say, Sam."

Sam studied her affectionately "Well. Now that you have a *career* to look forward to, you need to get used to the idea. Unless you don't really want it?"

"Are you *crazy*? Of course I want it. Designing has been my *dream*." Closing her eyes, she moaned softly, "Damn it, Vanessa."

Clearly understanding, Sam nodded. When Sophie escaped from his office, sighing wearily, he returned to his paperwork.

A few minutes later, Jim Callahan stepped into his office.

Sam looked up. "Thanks for pitching in while I was gone."

Dropping into the chair previously occupied by Sophie, Jim answered, "No problem, Sam. I talked to Mike and Jenny about Dan assisting the department with those robbery cases. They feel that Dan's responsible enough to make his own decisions."

"Good to know, Jim. Want to go along with me, when I talk to him?"

"Nah. No need. I'm counting on you to stress his limitations—as far as associating with anyone who might be suspect."

Sam nodded his agreement. "So. How's Lucy?"

"That's right, Sam. I forgot that you haven't heard. Jake wanted to keep it quiet. And then this murder happened."

Sam straightened up behind his desk. "What's going on, Jim?"

"That Sunday morning, after the wedding, Lucy was almost *killed*, when she was canoeing at daybreak. She's been off in another world since her assault, Sam, and she's been going out to the river *alone*—pretty regularly since spring, I guess. But, anyway, somehow she got overturned. Gabe Giordano and his daughter were moving into the old angel's manor on the cliffs. Luckily, they discovered her, and fished her out from the water—right before she was ready to plunge over the falls."

"*Damn it, Jim!* I can't believe no one told me about this. Who's Gabe Giordano?"

"He's a friend of Jake's, and former FBI. He retired when his wife passed away, so he'd be able to take better care of his seven-year old daughter. He and his daughter were at Jake's wedding. You probably didn't get a chance to meet them, since they weren't there long.

Lucy would probably be dead now, if they hadn't pulled her out from the river."

"But Lucy's okay, now?"

"Oddly enough, more than okay. I don't know what to make of it, but she claims Merle Hagenmeyer's been *stalking* her."

"*What?*" Sam growled. Leaning forward, he nearly knocked over his coffee cup.

"Jake's looking into it. They kept Lucy in the hospital that night—worried that she might have a concussion. The next day, Mike and Jenny put her on a plane to Arizona to visit her aunt."

"I'd better discuss this with Jake, soon." Sam stood up from behind his desk. Strolling over to the coffee pot, he hesitated, before pouring himself a refill. "What'd you mean by that comment—Lucy's *more than okay?*"

"She was so *damn mad* when she woke up at the hospital. You should've seen her, Sam. It was wonderful." Jim was fretful, as he ran a hand through his silvery-gray hair. "She's finally coming back to us," he added gruffly, sniffing suspiciously.

Sam smiled. "Good to hear that, Jim. Did Jake ever speak with your nephew?"

"Murphy made a detour to visit Jake while you were out of town. I gather there wasn't a whole lot to say. Your wife borrowed money from him. Someone was following her, but he never saw a face. He couldn't even be sure if the person following her was male or female."

"Yeah. Vanessa was booked on a flight out of New Orleans, two days *after* she actually left. Someone went in her place and delivered her luggage to the Riverbend, we've determined. Something made her leave town right away. At first, she was the primary suspect for her father's murder. But we believe that *she* discovered the body, and might've thought she'd be targeted next."

"Sounds likely." Jim sighed. "Since, unfortunately, that's what actually happened."

Sam nodded his agreement grimly.

Later that day, Sam was visiting Jake in his apartment. Between Vanessa's murder investigation, and the latest information he'd heard about Lucy Callahan possibly having a stalker, he figured it was time to compare notes.

But as he listened to what Jake was telling him now, Sam's jaw dropped. *"What?"*

"His wife was killed in an alleyway behind her parent's house in Chicago. She was brutally raped, tortured, and murdered. I think Merle Hagenmeyer hid out in the Murphy's camper, after killing Anna Ivers here in Crystal Rock back in 1965, and was still hiding there when Anne Murphy returned to her parents' house to clean it out, after the Murphys drove home to Chicago." Jake declared, grimly. "The camper actually belonged to Anne's parents."

"But you didn't voice this theory to Sean Murphy?"

"Hell, no."

"How do you plan to prove it?" Sam asked.

"Murphy was thinking about reopening the case, and requesting a DNA match, anyway. On my orders, he'll retrieve the original evidence and hand it over to the FBI. If we get a DNA match to Hagenmeyer, we'll have to tell him. But why feed his guilt?"

Sam nodded his agreement.

"Something else on your mind?"

Hesitantly, Sam began, "Todd Shelton?"

"Our wedding crasher?"

"Yeah. Penny says it's over. He's finally quit calling her. But I have a feeling there's something else she's holding back. Plus, he seems too obsessive to just give up on her so easily."

"You'll be relieved to know that I have someone checking him out already, Sam." Jake added, dryly, "The guy's an ass."

Sam snorted.

"But mainly, I'm worried about a breach of security. At least ten of the guests at our wedding were uninvited. So either Danielle's secretary, Karen, misunderstood, or something else is going on. I'll let you know, once I get something back on Shelton."

"Thanks, man." Settling back on the couch, Sam shifted his eyes across the jam-packed living room of Jake's apartment, located on the upper level of the Dragonfly Pointe Inn. "How's the remodeling going, over at the lakehouse?"

"Slow," Jake growled. "But we'll have the kitchen and master suite completed within a few weeks. Cal's crew is doing exactly what you're doing at your cabin with the addition, Sam—adding on and completing the finish work before cutting doorframes into the original structure."

"Did Cal say anything about finishing my basement?"

"Did he ever," Jake admitted, ruefully. "His crew's overloaded—between finishing up at the school and working on our remodel."

Sam sighed. "I was afraid of that."

At that moment, there was a tap at the door. Opening the door, Mike Callahan peeked in. "Am I interrupting?"

Jake laughed. "Speak of the devil."

"Uh, oh. Complaints?"

"Never, man."

"Oh, hey, Sam. I'm glad you're here. I came up with a few ideas, about getting all of that work done at your house."

"I'm willing to listen to any suggestions. I guess I went a little overboard, when I told Penny the basement was already finished, *and* I was planning on adding a privacy fence."

"Ah. It *must* be love." Cal grinned.

Sam grinned wryly.

"I've got three guys, from my crew, who'd be willing to work for you during their own spare time—for the extra bucks. So it'd be nights and weekends, to get your basement completed."

"I'd appreciate that, Cal."

"Now, the fence. I have two very competent kids, under my own roof, who'd appreciate the extra money—Dan and Kate."

"*Kate?*"

"Kate. I can't even believe how competent she is at *fifteen*. She began assisting me with our own home remodel back when she was nine. And she's the only kid of mine who's never lost interest. Mark my words, she'll be taking over the business someday," Cal added, smugly.

"Well. You're the expert, Cal. If you say that they can do it, then let's get them to do it."

"They might need your help, Sam, with the post-hole digger. You want wooden privacy panels, right?"

Sam nodded.

"Is tonight soon enough? They'll measure out the area. We can get your posts and fencing panels delivered within the week—same with the drywall and supplies we'll need for your basement. You'll need to get a permit, too."

"I'll be there tonight to answer any questions."

"I'll let them know." Cal turned to Jake. "Someone said you needed to see me?"

"This is about Lucy, Cal. Maybe it's good that Sam's here, too." Jake nodded at the sofa. "Sit down. Help yourself to coffee, if you want."

Cal gazed down at his dusty work clothes. "I'm kind of a mess."

Jake chuckled. "Haven't you noticed the throws, covering the furniture? Danielle insisted when she moved in."

Once Cal was settled on the couch with coffee, Jake began revealing his plan. "Okay. Here goes. Gabe Giordano didn't move here only because of his daughter. He's always been a really good friend of mine. He's got kind of a crazy background. He grew up on a vineyard in California, got his degree—pretty easily—in horticulture, and worked undercover for several years for the FBI. When his wife died of cancer, his mother-in-law took over the raising of his daughter. But then *she* died. His daughter's really fragile right now. And Gabe barely knows her. Gabe's gonna run the new horticulture department at Northwest Community College. Kind of convenient, huh, since Lucy's interested in horticulture? Gabe needs a live-in nanny for his daughter, as well as someone to do chores around the house."

Cal raised a brow.

"I suggested Lucy." Before Cal could comment, Jake held up a staying hand. "Now, just give me a minute to finish. They can go back and forth to school together. Lucy would be able to do whatever she wanted when Gabe was home. After all, he wants to get to know his daughter. And Gabe could be her bodyguard, Cal." His face turned grim, as he drew in a deep breath. "I studied the bank along the river where Lucy, supposedly, took a break, before returning to her canoe that day she overturned." Standing up from the couch, Jake entered his office. When he returned a moment later, he was carrying an evidence bag containing a single cigarette butt. Dropping it on top of the coffee table, Jake eyed Cal with obvious apprehension. "We have a match."

Picking up the pouch, Cal gasped, staring at the name on the label. "Hagenmeyer? *Oh, my God, Jake.* She's been so troubled. I thought that, *maybe,* Lucy was just imagining it, when she said she'd seen him a couple of times. I mean, why hasn't anyone else? After all, he *did* assault her. *You mean all this time, he's actually been here, somewhere, stalking her?*"

"Could be, Cal. And if it's true, he doesn't appear to be at all concerned about our extra security around Crystal Rock and Dragonfly Pointe."

Troubled by the significance of Jake's words, all three men remained silent.

"Okay," Cal finally answered. "I'll go along with whatever you want, Jake. I thought Lucy should be with her family. But maybe you're right. After all, nothing's really changed since her assault, and she's become even more distant. And this little Giordano girl obviously needs *someone.* Maybe Lucy might need someone, too. Maybe they'll be able to help each other."

Twenty - five

am was late. Although Penny had offered to pick him up at the airport, Sam had insisted that she finish up with her packing.

Hearing a tap on the door, moving to answer it, Penny was relieved to discover it was Sam. Motioning at two men standing behind him in the hallway, Sam introduced her to Tim and Pete. "I've hired a moving company, Penny. I figured it'd be easier and more reliable than renting a U-Haul. You and I can take turns driving your van. The trip will be a lot less stressful for you and Alex.

"Oh, Sam," she whispered, almost in tears. "You always seem to come up with a solution for everything." Finally, she surrendered into his waiting arms. "Since your house is furnished, I wasn't planning on moving a whole lot of furniture. Just Alex's bedroom suite— along with a few of my favorite pieces. And most of our clothing, of course. But there still seems to be a lot more stuff here than I thought there was."

"It's really good to see you," Sam muttered softly, with a kiss to her brow. "Okay. Let's get started."

After several hours of trekking through the main thoroughfare of the shop, and down the awkward steps of the fire escape, the moving van was packed and ready, two-thirds full. Since they'd most likely arrive in Crystal Rock before Penny and Sam, the moving men had instructions to call Danielle Loughlin to coordinate the unloading at Sam's.

Sam, Penny and Alex would take off in the morning. Although the trip could easily be made in two days, Sam had decided to stretch it out over three for Alex's benefit. He'd reserved rooms at a couple of hotels along the way, since it might be a difficult journey with Alex.

After sending out for pizza, the three of them were sitting in the kitchen and eating it. Realizing something unusual was about to happen, Alex was definitely wired, and hopping up and down in his seat.

Penny grimaced. "I hope he sleeps tonight."

Sam grinned. "Has he ever slept in a sleeping bag before?"

"Once or twice—when we stayed overnight at a camping retreat. I think that he finally fell asleep from exhaustion. I can't really remember. It seems like it's been years since he's behaved well enough for me to take him anywhere," she admitted, with regret.

"Well. I'll be around now, to help you with that," Sam reassured her, laying a hand over hers.

Gazing into Sam's eyes, filled with warmth and sincerity, Penny stilled. If she hadn't already realized she was in love with this man before he'd connected with her son, she would've definitely fallen head over heels in love with him now. His actions proved he cared. But just how much? Since Sam had never revealed his feelings for her, she was hesitant to talk about her own.

Settling Alex in his room, Penny tucked him into the sleeping bag that was laid out upon the floor. When packing for the move, she'd decided to leave about a third of Alex's toys here in his room. Greg had mentioned he had a single bed in storage, and would move it into Alex's room for future visits.

After several wearing weeks preparing for the move, Penny was drained. Once they finally settled in for bed, Sam made love to her slowly and passionately. Curling up in Sam's arms afterward, comforted by his warm embrace, Penny drifted off eventually into a deep, exhausted slumber.

As his fist smacked into her jaw, she heard it crack, before he crushed his entire body hard on top of her and flattened her beneath him. Her limbs began thrashing when he flipped her over, slamming the back of her head against the floor.

Futilely, she struggled to get away.

He punched into her gut. With a groan, she fell back again flailing onto the floor. Shoving her legs apart, he fiercely dragged her into position.

Panting, groaning, she began gasping for air. Now she could barely move. This time he'd beat her more severely.

Accusing, demanding, she was a cheating slut, he screamed.

Holding her down, forcefully, viciously, he plunged into her. Thrusting, ripping her apart and then thrusting again, he clamped his hands around her neck, choking her…strangling her…

Penny let loose a blood-curdling scream.

"Penny, Penny, what is it? God. Please wake up, sweetheart. It's me, Sam."

Opening her eyes in confusion, staring sightlessly at Sam, Penny was trembling violently, with eyes filled with stark terror. And then, piteously, she began to cry, swallowing gulping, heart-wrenching sobs.

Caught up in her misery, she crawled into the corner of her bed, and wrapped her arms around herself. As she gradually became aware of her surroundings, Penny finally surrendered herself into Sam's comforting embrace. Rocking and soothing her, he murmured soft words of assurance while she continued to cry. It seemed to take forever before her wretched sobs began to ease.

"Oh, Sam. *I'm so sorry.* I had a nightmare."

"Oh, sweetheart," Sam whispered. "Can you talk about it?" Hesitantly, he continued, "Does it have anything to do with your husband?"

She stilled, and her heartbeat accelerated rapidly under the palm of his hand. Quietly, she asked, "How did you know?"

"You have all the classic symptoms, Penny." His fingers lightly feathered her hair. "Just go ahead and tell me. Please," he urged.

Impatiently wiping away her tears, and gazing into Sam's tortured eyes, she nodded resignedly. "Everything was kind of crazy when we moved back here with my grandparents. After my dad was diagnosed with his brain tumor, he had some really good days. But he also had some really *bad* days. So David Wentworth became his assistant. When my dad finally decided he couldn't handle working anymore, David would be the one to take over his duties at the church. Anyway, my dad kind of got it into his head that David would make me a great husband. My dad was kind of weird about things like that—probably because the tumor began distorting his memories. But it also might've been his way of trying to make sure my future was secure, since my parents married young—they were both in their teens. And they had a good marriage. I wasn't particularly interested in David Wentworth, but he was interested in me. *Too* interested, I came to realize later."

With a shaking hand, Penny scraped away a few more tears. "No one knew that I had a boyfriend. Jason was the sweetest, kindest man. But *I* was an idiot where he was concerned. He was an artist—a painter. And he was really *talented*, Sam. Anyway, he worked part-time with me at the shop. He had tattoos and an earring, and I let that affect the way that I treated him. I realized, eventually, that by not introducing him to my parents as my boyfriend, I must've really disappointed him. I treated him like I was ashamed of him." Penny released a ragged sigh. "And then it was too late. He was mugged and killed leaving work one night, only a few blocks away from here.

Reassuringly, Sam pulled her in closer.

"And then I discovered I was pregnant."

Obviously startled, Sam pulled away, gazing into her eyes. "Let me guess," Sam observed. "You didn't want to disappoint your parents, and there was David Wentworth, ready and able."

Penny nodded. "We were married within a few months. I'd told him about the baby right away. He said it didn't matter, and I thought he was my savior. He fooled *everyone*, Sam. He was so unreasonably jealous of everyone and everything in my life. On the outside, he appeared caring and loving, but on the inside..." Penny's voice faded away into a whisper, "*he was evil.*"

Although Penny could tell Sam was becoming angry, he pulled her in closer and rubbed a hand soothingly over her shoulders. Eventually clearing his throat, he asked, "So. He enlisted in the army?"

"Not because he wanted to. Grandpa forced him. One night, after beating and...well—*raping* me, David began kicking me, over and over again, and then he shoved me into our bedroom closet. We lived in one of the original apartments above Sander's Floral. Inside the closet, there was old fashioned, built-in shoe rack that was made with metal spikes. My kidney was punctured. If the neighbors hadn't called for an ambulance, I'm not exactly sure what David would've done. Grandpa threatened to file charges unless David disappeared from my life. I was almost killed, you see. He was MIA before we even had a chance to file for the divorce."

"You were lying face down on your stomach, when I began snuggling with you." Sam murmured, softly, "I must've done something earlier, to set off your nightmare."

"Probably. Everything I used to do with David felt degrading, Sam. His favorite move was to make me crawl on my hands and knees. He'd shove my head down, so he wouldn't have to look at my face when he forced me. He treated me like a prostitute. It probably had something to do with me being pregnant with Alex, before we were married. He was such a hypocrite. That last night, when he nearly killed me, *I'd told him I was pregnant with his child, Sam*. And he beat me. He claimed it wasn't *his*," she moaned, somewhat hysterically.

Penny's helpless sobs began again. Wrapped in Sam's arms, she could feel the tension of his rage.

Eventually, her sobs subsided, and Sam sighed, as he gently wiped away her tears. Grabbing her hand, Sam led her down the hallway and into the kitchen. Opening up the cabinet door above the refrigerator, he brought down the bottle he'd noticed on his previous visit.

"This'll make you feel a little better," he murmured. After pouring her a shot of whiskey, he handed it over. "Then maybe we can see about making you feel better in another way." He waggled his brows.

After sputtering down her shot, Penny struggled with a smile.

Sam squeezed her hand, staring at her with obvious concern. "Are we ready to go back to sleep?"

Penny nodded.

Once they'd both climbed back into bed, Sam pulled her into his arms.

"We're probably both going to be tired tomorrow. I'm sorry, Sam."

"I only planned for about six hours on the road tomorrow. Since we have reservations, there's no hurry for us to get out of here in the morning."

"Well, in that case..." Gazing steadily into his eyes, Penny quickly sat up, and stripped off her nightshirt.

Sam breathed out softly, "Tell me what you want." His hands stroked down over her shoulders to caress her bare breasts.

"I want you to lie back," she whispered.

Following her orders, Sam eased down onto the bed.

Slowly straddling Sam, she bent over him, and moved her mouth gently, subtly, over his. Feathering light wispy kisses over to his ear, she nipped at his earlobe with her teeth.

She could see he was becoming increasingly aroused, and he began to move his mouth over to hers. But she held him down firmly with the palms of her hand. "No," she murmured. "Now it's my turn."

While both hands tangled through the tawny hair covering his chest, her lips traveled slowly down from his mouth, lightly skimming over his skin. And when her mouth covered his nipple, licking, sucking, and finally nipping again, Penny became aware of Sam groans of pleasure with intense satisfaction. She moved her mouth unhurriedly over his chest to his other nipple, stroking with her tongue and nipping with her teeth.

And then she began moving her lips down further.

First stroking and then caressing, Penny finally wrapped both hands firmly around the length of his thick, rigid erection. Tentatively, she ran her tongue along its length.

Sam hissed, nearly jumping from the bed.

"Sam," Penny whispered. "It's been so long since I've done anything like this. And now I'd prefer to think of the act as something enjoyable rather than degrading."

Clearing his throat, Sam swallowed, looking rather nervous. "Well, you won't see *me* trying to discourage you."

With a mischievous grin, she observed, "That was awfully easy."

And when Penny returned her attention down, slowly taking his hard, rigid length into her mouth, Sam's incessant moan transformed into a tortured sigh of relief.

Licking and stroking, rhythmically running her hand over his length, Penny used her mouth to mimic the movements of her hand.

And Sam was enthralled. Seductively stroking, sucking and licking, Penny's every movement held him captive.

"Penny," he finally groaned. Trembling, reaching down with both hands, he brought her face up to his. Covering her lips with his, Sam's kiss turned gradually from needy to gentle. Breathing unsteadily, Sam murmured, "Let me make everything better for you, Penny. So you can forget about him. So *we* can forget about him. I don't ever want him to come between us again. I need you to trust me." He begged, "*Please.*"

Searching his eyes, she nodded, somewhat reluctantly.

"Turn over then."

Slowly and hesitantly, Penny flipped over, positioning her pillow lengthwise under her head. Reaching for his own pillow, Sam slid it gently under her hips. Moving down on his elbows, sliding down over the delectable curves of her body, he began his seduction by lightly running his tongue over the curve of her instep. When she began to shiver deliciously, he shifted his attention to the arch of her other foot.

By the time his fingers and tongue ran over her buttocks, working at the delicate skin of her inner thighs, Penny trembled with need, as every sensual stroke of sensation burned straight through to her core.

Gradually, Sam began moving upward, covering her body inconspicuously with his.

By the time Penny finally became aware that Sam was completely covering her, her mind and senses were absorbed by sensation. Shuddering and shaking in the throes of her bliss, Penny urgently called out for Sam.

"Oh, Penny," he moaned, entering her inch by torturous inch. "Making love to you is like *nothing* I've ever experienced before," he murmured, finally fully positioned.

Bracing one palm on the bed, Sam used his other hand to fondle her breast. Teasing and caressing, rolling and squeezing her nipple, Sam began moving with gentle, rhythmic thrusts.

Urgently wanting and needing more, desperately urging him on, Penny began meeting him, matching him, rearing back to absorb each powerful thrust. In a daze, she turned her head, peering over her shoulder.

Once his lips came down desperately to meet hers, she convulsed, delightedly and exultantly, while emitting what sounded like helpless, irrepressible cries of pleasure. The delicate taste of her essence lightly flavored Sam's mouth.

And then, hoarsely, Sam shouted her name. Alternately shuddering, cussing and muttering her name, Sam continued thrusting and
pounding into her, deliberately drawing out their intense moments of
staggering, mind-blowing pleasure.

Finally, they collapsed.

Slowly disconnecting from Penny, Sam groaned, burying his face
into his pillow.

Penny laughed wearily, settling in next to Sam. "I'm pretty sure
that technique of yours probably worked, Sam. Hopefully, I won't be
having any more nightmares."

Sam snorted agreeably.

Twenty - six

"Mrs. Sanders." Startled, Sam paused on his way into the kitchen. "I'd better go put some clothes on," he added, gazing down at his loose boxers.

"Not on my account, Sam," Penny's mother admonished, laughing. "And call me Monica. I just stopped by to say goodbye and drop off a load of snacks for your trip. I thought you'd be up and moving by now."

"We had kind of a long night." Strolling over to the coffeemaker, Sam began assembling a fresh pot. With a sigh, he turned back to Monica. Arms crossed, he leaned back against the counter. "Penny... well, she..."

"Had a nightmare?"

"Yeah."

"I'd hoped..."Monica sighed. "Well—I'm sure glad you're here, Sam. But I definitely expected you to pop back into Penny's life a lot sooner."

Sam stared at her, somewhat bemused.

"You seemed devastated when I told you she was married all those years ago. If you'd only appeared even a few weeks earlier—maybe she wouldn't have married that...*psychopath*."

"Do you really think that if I'd shown up before she married him, she wouldn't have gone through with it?"

"Ah, Sam. That's something we'll never know, now. Will we?" Monica sighed resignedly. "I was worried when she began dating Todd Shelton, too. I was so relieved when she broke *that* off."

"He showed up in Crystal Rock for the wedding, you know. And he didn't *act* like he thought it was over. Penny seemed almost terrified of the guy."

Monica grimaced. "I'm almost sure that *something* bad happened between them. But Penny tends to keep these things to herself."

"He kind of worries me. He doesn't appear to be the type of guy that backs off as easily as he did."

"Give Penny a little more time, Sam. And then ask her exactly what happened. Except for her grandfather, all of the men in her life have let her down at one time or another. She just needs to know that you're gonna stick around. I used to notice the way she watched you all those years ago. But I never knew that *you* felt that way, too, until you appeared here in New York."

"Yeah," he agreed, sheepishly. "They say things happen the way they do for a reason. I was scared to approach Penny when I was younger, Monica," he admitted, wryly. "I thought I was my father's son."

"Oh, Sam. You're definitely not like you father. From what I'd heard about him, your dad was too young and immature to be married. He didn't know the meaning of the word fidelity."

Aware of the sudden rustle of activity sounding from down the hallway, Sam turned to pour a cup of coffee. After adding a quick dollop of milk, Sam rested the cup on the counter for Penny.

Monica gave him a reassuring smile.

When Penny appeared in the doorway of the kitchen, she was obviously startled to discover that Sam was conversing with her mother, wearing only his boxers.

"*Mom.*" Penny coughed, clearly struggling to disguise her laughter.

Motioning Penny to the breakfast bar, Sam pointed at her coffee.

"Thank you, Sam. Alex is up and moving. He should be out here in a minute."

"I've got an idea," Monica began. "Why don't you and Sam get dressed and finish loading up the van, and I'll go ahead and make us some breakfast. I can spend a little time with my grandson before you all take off."

"You're not overdoing it, Mom, since your surgery?"

"No. In fact I probably need to get a little more regular exercise. I'm thinking about coming back to work."

"Sure, Mom. You know how much Chad would appreciate that. Even with all the kids we've hired to care for the flowers and coolers, no one's ever done the job as well as you. In fact we had to dump like six buckets of pom pom mums the other day, after they developed head rot. Chad thinks Ashley isn't bleaching the buckets when she changes the water and cuts the stems."

"I love tending the flowers, since I'm so clumsy at arranging them. My Penelope's *so* talented, Sam." Reassuringly, Monica patted Penny's hand.

Sam was startled. "*Penelope?*"

"She was named after her grandmother. But she could never pronounce her name as a child."

"So it turned into Penny," Penny admitted, wryly. "I still always wanted a *sexier* name growing up. You know, like Tiffany or Bethany..."

Monica snorted.

Chuckling, Sam observed Alex running through the hallway. "Now *here* comes trouble."

Seating himself at the breakfast bar, while affectionately eyeing Sam, Alex was smiling. And belatedly acknowledging Sam's words, he began to giggle.

With Sam at the wheel of the van a few hours later, by mid-morning, they were finally packed up and on the road.

"I couldn't believe it, when I came out into the kitchen and found my mother ogling your butt, Sam."

Sam turned his eyes from the road to meet Penny's uncomfortably. "*No?*"

"Well. It *is* a very nice butt. I've watched many women admiring that butt. Not just back in high school, but at Jake and Danielle's wedding."

After a short bark of laughter, Sam was sheepish as he shook his head, and turned his eyes back on the road.

"You know, I never really told her about *us*." She added, thoughtfully, "She had to have been shocked when you popped into the kitchen dressed in your underwear."

And when his wide eyes met hers, they both burst into laughter.

"Hmm—she didn't act uncomfortable," he finally said, still laughing.

"Well, she *was* a preacher's wife. She's always been able to talk to everyone about anything. I've seen her charm the pants off of a homeless man. Literally, that is. He was infested with lice and the shelter was encouraging him to bathe. You know, even after her operation last month, my mom *still* helps out at the shelter every week."

"You, too?"

"Not like I did when I was younger. I've been working so many hours. And then there's Alex. At least Greg will be able to concentrate more on his work now that Alex won't be around. My grandparents are really gonna miss him, though—but they're only able to handle Alex in small doses, anyway."

Penny's grandparents had shown up earlier, while they'd been packing up the van. Shaking Sam's hand and staring hard into his eyes, Mr. Sanders had obviously been giving Sam a clear warning about his granddaughter and great-grandson.

"Your grandfather couldn't have given you a more useful gift than this van," Sam observed, as he turned his eyes back on the road.

"He said that he could afford it, now, with the sale of the business." Penny's eyes filled with tears. "It *was* a great gift."

Not only did it have a large compartment for luggage in the rear, the full-size van had an additional set of cozy reclining seats behind the passenger and driver's seats. A long fold-over couch, with the potential to transform into a bed, seated Alex, who was gazing contentedly through the window, while sorting sloppily through his packed-up containers of toys.

"It'll come in handy for driving Alex back and forth to school as well as for work, once my shop becomes established."

Sam nodded.

The journey to Crystal Rock proved to be relatively uneventful. The only difficulty occurred in Cleveland, where Alex, having apparently observed the hospitality center when they'd checked into the hotel, unlocked and unlatched both locks on their hotel room door, to sneak from their room and retrieve a donut. At six in the morning, Sam awoke to the quiet snicks of an opening latch.

Observing that the door to the hallway was cracked, Sam jumped from the bed, grabbing his jeans. With one leg in and one leg out, Sam tripped down the hallway after Alex while pulling up his pants. Reaching the reception area, he was attaching the snap at his waist when the receptionist, who was startled as well as amused, pointed across the lobby at Alex.

The receptionist began laughing when, rolling his eyes upward in exasperation, Sam approached Alex, who was wolfing down a donut. Scolding loudly, Sam grabbed Alex's hand just in time to stop him from reaching for another.

Wrapped in her robe, Penny came scrambling into the lobby. She searched through the lobby frantically until she observed Alex, safely restrained by Sam. Shaking her head in frustration, Penny noticed the receptionist was grinning.

Attempting to get away from Sam, Alex began giggling when Sam hoisted him over his shoulder. And, recognizing the absurdity of the situation, when Sam's eyes finally met Penny's, they both burst into laughter.

"Now you know why I had to install a locked gate in my hallway, Sam. I'll never have to worry about him climbing out of his window, since he's afraid of heights. But when it comes to food, he can be so damned sneaky!"

Sam had made their second set of reservations at the Wisconsin Dells. He'd insisted that they spend a few hours, the next morning, taking Alex on a few of the rides.

"But everything is *so* expensive, Sam."

"Penny. He *has* to ride the ducks. It was the biggest thrill of my life, when I was a kid."

And it *was* the thrill of Alex's life. Hesitant at first to board the strange looking vehicle, that was a cross between a bus and a boat, he laughed and giggled exuberantly throughout the entire ride. As they travelled from land to water, that dumbfounded gaze of wonder and astonishment that lit up Alex's face pierced straight through to Sam's heart.

Rolling into Crystal Rock around six that evening, Sam sighed with relief to see the privacy fence had been completed. At least the project had allowed Sam the opportunity to talk seriously with Dan Callahan about the robberies around town. He'd had to emphasize, more than once, that at this point all they required was information. Whatever Dan found out, he shouldn't do *anything* out of character, thereby alerting any possible suspects.

Grabbing Penny's hand, Sam strolled up to the front door and unlocked it. With a gentle shove, he pushed her inside. "Take a look around," he ordered, gruffly. "I'll get Alex."

After pulling the side door of the van open wide, Sam grabbed a box of toys before escorting Alex into the house.

Penny stood admiring the empty living room and dining room, looking somewhat bemused. The floor had finally been stained and buffed to the sheen of an acorn, while the walls had been painted a creamy, buttery yellow. "I could've brought some extra furniture, Sam. There was room on the truck."

Sam laughed. "I thought that you'd like to choose the furnishings. I just finished these two rooms last week. We could either buy new, or pick something out at an auction or an estate sale, and bring Alex along, too. Danny and Jake have already been cruising the state for antiques that you'll be able to stock in the new mall."

Grabbing her hand, he dragged her through the dining room, pulling her through a swinging door.

Penny smiled her pleasure. "Oh, Sam. This is *wonderful*. I love French Country." Her eyes searched the warm, inviting space, obviously admiring the details. Creamy custom cupboards and brand new appliances lined the kitchen, while a long leather couch and chairs stood in the family room, over a patterned area rug, near a magnificent stone fireplace. "Everything seems comfortable and durable—and with easy to clean wooden floors—this room is *perfect* for us, Sam."

"I was hoping that it would be. Come on." Opening the door into the breezeway, he pointed at the basement door. "This will be Alex's hangout." Grabbing Alex's hand, he pulled him slowly down the staircase. When Alex reached the large open family room downstairs, he began circling the room excitedly with his hands and elbows in the air.

"Oh, Sam. You've thought of everything." An entire wall was lined with shelving. Centered over a small assortment of tapes, a VCR and large television held the place of honor. "I'm glad you thought of a VCR."

"It's a cheap one," he admitted, wryly. "I saw what happened to your last one.

Penny laughed. "That's why I brought along the durable leather furniture from my family room." Penny pointed at the loveseat and chair that the movers had unloaded.

"And it's familiar for Alex. So the whole space is his. And maybe yours, if you need to work from home. There's an empty room in the back that could be used as a bedroom or office, as well as a bathroom, so Alex doesn't need to go up and down the stairs. The laundry room is on the other side of the bathroom."

"Sam. I love what you've done to this house. And with the whole fenced-in yard to run around in, Alex will have more than enough space."

"I've got one favor to ask."

"Name it."

"I can't do my laundry at the cabin yet."

"Of course you can do it here."

And with that reassurance, returning outside, Sam pulled the van into the garage and began unloading it.

Sam deliberated over whether he should go or stay. He'd offered to move out to the cabin. But unless Penny acted like she actually wanted him to *go*, he'd stay.

Twenty - seven

To Penny's relief, Sam never attempted to move out to the cabin. And he was wonderful with Alex. Many mornings, Penny would awaken to find breakfast on the table, with Alex assisting Sam contentedly. Sam had learned how to test Alex's blood sugar, and even though he still couldn't help from grimacing uneasily, he frequently gave Alex his shot.

Working with the architect, Penny spent several long hours going over the requirements for the shops in the mall. With the walls and foundations stripped down to two by fours, a bunch of work was needed to transform and connect the inner structure. It would be at least six months before the extensive list of provisions and furnishings for even the flower shop could be ordered. Penny decided to search for storage space, so she could begin ordering supplies, as well as silk and dried flowers. Until the shop became established, Chad and Penny had agreed that this area of the country would be perfect for marketing and shipping prearranged silk and dried floral arrangements. After all, with no florist in town, it'd been years since fresh flowers had been available. Demand would be uncertain.

Along with Alex, Sam and Penny frequently visited Sam's mother. Although Shirley was brittle from her cancer, she was holding her own, and her health didn't seem any worse.

With Penny and Sam spending a lot of time with Jake and Danielle Loughlin, as well as Nat and Olivia Benet, they all became close friends. Penny was given a glimpse of Sam's marriage through Olivia's eyes, one day, when they were hosting a cookout at the house on Pine Street.

When they were alone together in the kitchen, Olivia said, "Sam and Vanessa never did anything as a couple, Penny. It was like they lived two different lives. I never really understood how they came to be married. And then the infidelity should've ended it. But they were still married another five years after that."

Sam had been unfaithful to his wife? It didn't bode well for the future of *their* relationship.

And when Penny dropped in for lunch one day at the station, she noticed a familiar female slinking out from Sam's office. *Diane.* The very same woman that Sam had been having regular sex with back in high school. When Sam appeared happy to see *her* that day, Penny had chosen not to think about it.

Until she ran into Diane.

Taking measurements outside of the blocks of Main and Oak, hoping to determine the most efficient placement for new display windows, Penny was studying the brick façade of the weatherworn buildings with the architect.

Penny couldn't help but notice that Diane still had a nice figure.

Although it was a bit more...lush.

With shoulder-length brown hair and sultry-green eyes, she was attractive.

In a sleazy kind of way.

Scolding herself, Penny wryly recognized she was jealous. It was time for her to sheathe her claws.

"Penny, I presume?" Diane nodded, brusquely. "I've just heard from Sam that you've moved back into town."

"Yes. I'm coordinating the plans for the new mall," she answered politely.

"Ah, yes. The little flower shop. That should be nice for the tourists."

"Well, it'll be a little bit more than a flower shop," Penny responded, dryly.

Dianne began abruptly, "Sam never mentioned you were *returning* to town. This last month has been very difficult for him. He and I have been seeing each other, you know, since his ex-wife was killed. Naturally, he turned to me since we're still very close."

Sam had turned to *this* woman for comfort? With her insecurities returning, Penny's blood went cold. Had he been with *another woman* after she'd returned to New York?

"Back in June, neither Sam nor I was aware I'd be moving back here permanently," Penny replied, mechanically.

"*Permanently?*" For a moment, Dianne seemed dismayed. "Ah. Well. I'm sure I'll see you around." With another nod of her head, Diane rushed off.

Sam stared at Penny as she pretended to be asleep in the bed beside him. For the last few days, she'd seemed to be insecure and indecisive.

And they hadn't made love at all.

Sam was concerned. Was he crowding her? He wanted nothing more than to wake up with Penny every single morning for the rest of his life.

But realizing he might be expecting too much, too soon, he began, "Penny. I'm moving out to the cabin tomorrow. I said I'd give you your space, but I really haven't. Have I?"

Penny was stunned. *Ah, Sam—no.*

But she couldn't say the words.

The next morning, when he was ready to depart, Sam was obviously miserable. "You know where to find me, if you need me."

Turning away, Penny's eyes became misty with tears. And when she failed to protest, Sam continued to silently pack his bags into the truck.

Two days later, Penny began to realize she was behaving like an idiot.

Sam wouldn't cheat on her. Even though he still hadn't opened up to her, she needed to trust him.

Once she'd decided on her course of action, the most difficult chore was finding someone who could handle Alex for the evening.

She called Danielle—who, in turn, called Olivia.

Appearing with Jarrod and Rodney, Danielle and Olivia walked in through the open door of the garage with their overnight bags.

"Thank you, guys." Olivia and the boys continued on into the kitchen to be with Alex, while Danielle stood in the breezeway with Penny. "I really appreciate this, Danny. I've given Alex his insulin and he's eating right now. There's a snack for bedtime in the fridge. And his syringe is ready for the morning, if I'm not back later tonight. I'll try to call you, one way or another. Help yourself to anything in the fridge."

"If we have any problems, we'll call you at the cabin, Penny. Just go ahead and go—don't worry. Wish Sam a happy birthday from all of us." With a gentle shove, Danielle pushed Penny out toward the van, parked in the garage.

After speeding to the grocery store, Penny picked up steaks and potatoes along with a few pre-made salads from the deli. Not exactly a feast, but Sam would most likely enjoy it.

Stopping at the bakery, she encountered Mrs. Barelli preparing to lock up for the day. It was amazing how Sophia looked so much like her mother. Still striking at age forty-five, Marie Barelli was, as always, cheerful and upbeat. She was a perfect balance for her husband, Sid, who was rather serious and sober.

"Penny. It's so good to see you. What can I get for you?"

"I know that it's kind of late in the day, but its Sam's birthday today."

"How about a freshly-prepared cream cake?" Pulling out an unfrosted yellow cake, she laid it on the counter. "It'll only take a minute for me to ice it. Chocolate fudge?"

"Anything you recommend, Marie. It's always such an effort having to walk by your bakery every day. I'd probably stop in here more often if it wasn't for Alex's diabetes."

Marie appeared thoughtful. "Hmm. Penny. You've just given me an idea about introducing some new items. I'll have to experiment."

Moments later, Penny was on her way to the cabin. It was strange, but she hadn't been back to the cabin, even once, since she'd returned to town. Although a small, red convertible was parked near the garage, when she pulled into the driveway, there was no sign of Sam's truck.

Luckily, she happened to have a key for the cabin on her ring for the house. Quickly climbing up to the porch and unlocking the door, she stilled.

Sam was living *here*? Nothing in the kitchen had changed in the past six weeks. Peeking through the door of the dining room into the living room, she was shocked to realize that not much progress had occurred at all on the entire renovation.

Thoughtfully, she began putting away the groceries. She'd even remembered to bring along a corkscrew and goblets. After popping the cork and pouring some wine, she decided to prepare the grill. Sam should arrive soon. Typically, he'd be home from work between six and seven.

Grabbing her goblet of wine, and moving through the living room, Penny unlocked and stepped through the door leading outside into the screened-in porch. Gazing across the deck through the screen, she halted.

With steps extending immediately up from the pier, an elevated deck had been built alongside the porch since her last visit.

And in it?

A brand new sunken hot tub.

But it wasn't the addition of the hot tub that'd stopped Penny in her tracks.

It was the naked woman lying inside of it.

Penny was stunned.

Definitely aware of Penny's gasp of shock, flaunting her nudity for its full effect, Diane eased up gradually from her reclining position in the tub.

"Oh. I thought you were Sam. What are *you* doing here?"

With her mouth gaping open, Penny slowly began coming to grips with the situation. After all, *Diane hadn't had a key*. Had she? "I'd like to ask *you* the same question?"

"I'm waiting for Sam, of course. I heard you two weren't together anymore." She shrugged. "Of course, Sam never mentioned you were together in the first place.

Penny couldn't remain here with this...*woman*. She had to get out of here. "Tell Sam that I was here."

Diane smiled slyly. Penny spun around on her heels, very much aware that Dianne must be viewing her departure with extreme satisfaction. Penny heard the splash from Dianne dropping back down into the hot tub.

Entering the porch, Penny made her escape through the cabin, locking up the doors securely. Diane had ruined *everything*.

She abandoned her wine and, after grabbing her purse, she rushed out to the van. Gravel went flying when she sped the van down the driveway.

Twenty - eight

$\mathcal{S}$am had almost stopped by to see Penny. Sure, he talked to her on the phone every day. But, damn it, he *missed* her. He sighed wearily. *And he missed Alex, too.* In fact, he'd been in such a foul mood over the last few days, everyone at work was avoiding him.

Pulling slowly into the driveway at the cabin, he instantly recognized the red convertible. Damn. *Diane.* It was just too much. This was his sanctuary. The only woman he wanted here was *Penny.*

Slamming the door of his truck, he hiked up to the door of the cabin and quickly unlocked it. Noticing the bottle of wine and goblets set up on the plywood table in the kitchen, Sam halted. Since plates and silverware were stacked on top of it, he peeked inside the fridge and noticed the groceries. Momentarily, Sam was confused. Diane *couldn't* have brought this stuff. She didn't have a key.

But then he finally recognized the obvious. And Sam became furious.

Making his way through the cabin, Sam strolled determinedly out onto the deck. Purposely slamming the door behind him, Sam stopped in his tracks when he reached the pier. "God, damn it, Diane. What the *hell* are you doing in *there*?"

She stood up from the hot tub.

"Put some clothes on!" he shouted. "Where's Penny? *What did you say to her?"*

Diane's mouth gaped open as she stared at him with widened eyes. She must've forgotten whatever story she'd concocted, to explain her presence here today, because she, obviously, hadn't anticipated his fury. "Ah. She left Sam."

"What kind of *crap* have you been feeding her? And how *long* have you been doing it? Just get dressed and get out of there. *Now.* I'm gonna go find Penny. When we get back here, you'd better be gone. And I'd better not *ever* find you here at the cabin again." Spinning on his heels, Sam slammed his way back into the cabin, closing and locking up doors.

This woman was after Sam. Slinking out from the cover of the trees along the shoreline, quietly withdrawing the knife from its sheath, creeping in closer and closer...until...

Dianne was half dressed when Sam returned unexpectedly to the deck. For a moment she stupidly thought he might've changed his mind and was coming back to *her*. But, as it turned out, he was even angrier. "You've got a flat tire, Diane. I'll drive you back into town and make arrangements for someone to come out here and take care of your car. *Hurry up and get dressed!"*

Penny ended up at home. At her old home, that is. She really needed some time to think. Parking the van on the outskirts of the campgrounds, after easing her way under the construction tape surrounding the beach, she finally dropped down on the sand.

There was *no way* Sam was interested in Diane. But Penny had been furious to discover her at the cabin.

In Sam's new hot tub.

Had that amazing night that they'd spent together at the inn, had anything to do with his purchase of the hot tub?

Maybe.

Suddenly, she realized that she didn't need Sam to confess that he loved her. He'd been showing her all along. Look at the way he treated her son; accepting his limitations, and loving him just the way he was.

And then, Penny began thinking about Danielle's mysterious remarks, regarding Sam's request for construction materials. She realized Danielle must've been attempting to clue her in. Sam hadn't made any progress at the cabin because he'd been too busy making improvements at the house on Pine Street.

For her and Alex.

Aware of a sudden rustling in the woods, she turned and peeked over her shoulder. Penny's heart stopped for a moment when a familiar figure emerged. *"Sam."*

"I *finally* found you—I've been all over town. Diane's been like a stalker, since she's returned to Crystal Rock, Penny. I swear there's *nothing* going on between her and me."

She answered calmly, "I know."

"I...*what?*" Sam's eyes widened.

She smiled. "I said, I know."

After dropping down onto the sand and settling in beside her, Sam wrapped his arms around his knees. Holding her gaze, he continued, "But at one time there was."

"I know that, too."

Sam gave her a rueful smile as he admitted, "I figured that you did—back in June, when we cruised by the beach on the pontoon. You wanted me to squirm, a little. Didn't you?"

She grinned. "Only just a little. But mostly, Sam, I was jealous."

He snorted. "You shouldn't be. Since age eighteen, even when I was at my worst, Penny, I've always been obsessed with *you*," he observed wryly. "I guess you've been open with me about your past—so it's my turn to do the same for you."

At a loss for words, Penny reached for Sam's hand, squeezing it reassuringly.

"My father was unfaithful to my mother, Penny. But it was more than just unfaithful. He slept with every willing woman available. I'm not exactly sure why my mother stayed with my father, but something happened when I was young that set them apart. My mother's never told me what. That's why she and I made several trips back and forth to Michigan, to my grandfather's resort, when I was young."

Sam pulled Penny in closer. "And I caught my father cheating. More than once. I tried to hide it from my mom, but I think she always knew. Hell, Penny. *He was seducing high school girls.*" Sucking in a staggered breath, he continued, "The weird thing about it was—he was still a good father to me. I mean we went fishing, and worked on building a boat together. He always tried to teach me right from wrong. And he never once talked about, or pushed me into, having sex. So that's why I knew, that with his behavior, he was somehow punishing my mother. He died right after I turned thirteen."

Sam became quiet when, letting out a squall, a gull landed nearby, immediately rooting through the sand. Apparently dissatisfied, the gull suddenly, widely, spread his wings, flapping with a short running start and gliding through the air.

Sam finally continued, "And after I turned thirteen, I began getting a lot of attention from women. I guess because I looked like my father. Women were always coming on to him." Slanting her a side glance, he was clearly attempting to gauge her reaction. "I was pretty young when I had sex for the first time."

"I understand Sam," she reassured him, softly. "You were— *you are*—really handsome. I mean, I thought so the very first time I met you."

"I thought I was just like my dad. I tried to be like him, I guess, with the women and the sex. But I *never* had a real girlfriend. When you came into my life, Penny, I changed for a little while. I almost asked you out—even though I didn't think your parents would approve. *I* was the one who discovered Stu Arends was the town's peeping tom."

She gasped, gazing into Sam's eyes. "I always wondered what happened to him. He wouldn't leave me alone."

"Well," Sam growled. "*That* was the main reason why I wanted him gone."

Penny laughed softly.

"And then we discovered Anna Ivers." Sam closed his eyes. "It still haunts me, Penny. It affected Mike Callahan and Jeff Thompson, too, but in different ways. Cal rushed into marriage and Jeff enlisted in the Navy. And I was in a really strange place during my senior year of high school. I didn't even want to get close to anyone, and sex became more of a release. That's probably about the time you saw me here at the beach. Right?"

Reluctantly, Penny nodded.

"I let you go. I didn't think I'd be good for you. But I never forgot you. When I heard you got a scholarship to Wisconsin, where I was going to school, I couldn't help myself. I had to see you again. I found out where you were supposed to be living, and I arranged an *accidental* meeting. But you never showed," he admitted ruefully.

With tears in her eyes, she voiced quietly, "I had to turn down the scholarship to help out with my dad. And since the scholarship was awarded by the state, it would've been rescinded once our family moved away. It about killed me to have to turn that scholarship down, even though by grandfather made sure I eventually got my education."

"Once I graduated from college, I actually attempted to see you one more time."

Somewhat bemused, Penny stared into Sam's gentle brown eyes, filled with exquisite tenderness.

"I came to New York and entered the police academy. But it was too late," he admitted, visibly dejected. "I didn't have the courage to come by Sander's Floral until I graduated from the academy, and I missed your marriage to that *monster* by two lousy weeks, Penny."

Penny was stunned. "Oh, Sam." Her eyes filled with tears.

"Penny. I *love* you," he whispered softly.

"Oh, Sam. I *love* you, too."

Reaching out, and pulling her into his arms, Sam sealed the certainty of their love with warmth and tenderness by covering her lips gently with his.

Resting back against a grassy outcrop, Sam studied the shoreline thoughtfully. "I've been thinking," he whispered. "With Alex here at school, we'll be spending a lot of time on this beach. And we both have memories of this place better left forgotten." He smiled wolfishly. "Let's make this place *ours*." He raised his hand in the air and snapped his fingers.

"*Here?*" Penny squeaked. Jolting upright from the sand, she gazed nervously around the beach.

Sam grinned, waggling his brows. "Out in the water." He held her gaze as he stood up and began pulling off his clothes.

By the time Penny arose, Sam had stripped down to his shorts. "Don't worry. We're pretty isolated out here. No one can see us."

"I figured there had to be a good reason *why* this beach was the local make-out place, back in high school," she responded dryly. Slowly, she began to draw her T-shirt over her head.

"Penny. You've got the *sexiest* underwear," Sam observed, grinning. After making quick work of her lacy white bra, he slipped off her shorts before dropping his own. Unexpectedly, he scooped her up into his arms, before scrambling through the sand and out into the water.

Penny was squealing, and her arms were flailing, when Sam suddenly dropped her.

Sputtering as her head popped up from under the water, Penny grabbed Sam's legs as she stood up, and yanked them out from beneath him.

Wide-eyed and astonished, Sam was laughing heartily when he fell, flopping over with a huge splash. When he emerged, he barked out a long, loud whoop of exuberance, pulling her into his arms and wrapping her legs around his waist.

And then he covered her mouth with his. As he spun her lightly, languidly, through the water, matching sigh for contented sigh and kiss for enduring kiss, Penny responded to Sam's increasing passion eagerly.

Ardently.

Until, finally, he moaned, "I just can't wait." And with that, Sam hastily plunged into her. Urgently thrusting faster and deeper, Sam stepped up his rhythm as Penny began to move with him, keeping perfect pace with each of his frenzied, frantic thrusts.

"Oh, Sam," she finally cried out, thrashing and twisting with the force from a delightful shudder.

Sam moaned her name as a prayer, and when he finally joined her, he was shaking and trembling; his own powerful jolt of ecstatic pleasure leaving him contentedly weak.

Embracing her...cherishing her...and *loving* her, he began softly, "Penny, I..."

Abruptly, the call of a male voice sounded out from the entrance of the beach. *"Sam?"*

"Not again," Sam grumbled.

Penny squeaked, jumping out from Sam's arms.

"We have the worst luck. *Geez. Talk about timing,*" Sam muttered.

Still splashing her way into the shore and behind a line of trees edging the woods, Penny dropped down low under the water.

Crossing his arms, Sam held his ground. "Yeah, Terry?"

Obviously surprised to discover a pile of clothes dropped haphazardly across the sand of the beach, Terry must've finally noticed Sam was out in the water. "Sam. You're naked." Blushing furiously, Terry's face was red as a beet.

"Good observation."

From the shoreline, Penny snorted.

"Uh. I thought we might have a situation—and you might need some help. You know, because of the robberies?"

"We have a situation, alright," Sam responded, dryly.

Penny began giggling.

Raising a brow, Sam smiled patiently.

"Well, uh. I guess you've got everything under control?"

"I'd certainly like to think so."

Penny giggled harder.

"I'd better get outta here before something even *more* stupid comes out of my mouth." And on that note, Terry spun around, strolling briskly along the path leading back to the road.

Both Sam and Penny burst into uproarious laughter.

Approaching Sam determinedly from the shelter of the trees, Penny rushed back into his arms. "I'd say we go back to the cabin and eat some dinner. I'm starved."

"Good idea," Sam agreed, still laughing.

It was nice having time alone with Sam, away from Alex. They were both standing in the kitchen at the cabin, and Penny turned to Sam after they finished washing the dinner dishes. "Danielle and Olivia are watching Alex, so I probably shouldn't stay too much longer."

"You're going back to the house?"

"*With you*. You can't live here at the cabin yet, Sam. Why'd you even *want* to?"

"I didn't," he admitted, appearing sheepish. "I promised you your space. And you were acting kind of distant."

"Diane."

"*Diane?*"

"She was putting all kinds of doubts into my mind. My past experiences with men have left me a little insecure, Sam. But I missed you. I missed you when you went to New Orleans. And Diane said that she was with you after your wife died..."

"I still don't understand what's going on with her, Penny. I think she's fixated on me because she just wants *someone*. I've even had to kick her out of my office," he voiced with obvious frustration.

"Well, Olivia said something, too, about your marriage with Vanessa. About infidelity coming between you two."

"*Her infidelity*, Penny. All those years, *I* was faithful," he muttered fiercely, turning away. "That's how I finally realized I wasn't my father's son."

Gently reaching out, she turned his face back to hers. "Oh, God. I'm sorry for thinking she meant *you*, Sam."

"Ah, Penny." Sam sighed. "I can't really blame you. What else *could* you think, after the way I behaved back in high school? Right now, I can't discuss my marriage with you because of our murder investigation...but I can tell you that Vanessa was a victim, too. I'm looking at my past a lot differently because of what I've discovered."

After locking up the hot tub, Sam made a trip around the cabin, securing windows and doors.

Gathering up their leftovers, Penny met Sam in the driveway.

"Diane can wait for her car until tomorrow," he muttered, glaring at the vehicle. He leaned into the open window of Penny's van.

"Okay. Pack up your stuff. I'll meet you at home." She smiled.

"Home?" he inquired, raising a brow.

"*Our* home," she emphasized. Putting the van into gear, she backed up and turned around, before slowly driving away.

Twenty - nine

*N*ow that most of their secrets were out in the open, Sam and Penny settled into a comfortable routine. With every subtle touch and every tender kiss, their feelings for each other were obvious to pretty much everyone.

Penny was never so relieved to have another person's support when, despite having increased his dosage of thioridizine before arriving in Crystal Rock, Alex began having explosive temper tantrums. Almost one month after the increase, Alex was, again, out of control.

With Sam's booming voice alone, a means of distraction, Alex was slightly easier to manage on the evenings and weekends when Sam exuded his authority. But somehow, Alex still managed to smash his fist into Sam's face.

"Penny. How in the *hell* did you ever handle him alone?" Sam asked, resignedly, covering his eye with a bag of frozen peas.

After a long and volatile temper tantrum, Alex had been exhausted enough to finally drift off to sleep.

Turning away from Sam, Penny stared out unseeing through the kitchen window. "Very difficultly, Sam. I was always stressed. I didn't sleep much. And the bruises..." She sighed, wearily. "If Chad and Greg hadn't been there... He always responds better to a male influence, and the medication's helped a little. He was so *sweet* before the diabetes. But my former pediatrician didn't feel comfortable prescribing larger dosages of thioridizine. You wouldn't believe how difficult it's been to find a doctor who's even willing to take him on. I'm glad you're coming with me and Alex to visit this new doctor."

Dropping the bag of peas, Sam pulled her into his arms reassuringly. "Don't worry. Eventually he'll be in a better place. And I'll be there with you every step of the way. I promise."

Despite Sam's presence, when the doctor began to listen to his heart, Alex, who was obviously outraged, attempted to slug Dr. Donnelly. The doctor immediately doubled Alex's medication. "In a couple of weeks, we'll see how's he's doing. He's on a very low dosage, now. We'll probably have to triple his meds because of his body weight. But we'll have to do it gradually. Increasing his meds too quickly might make his mood swings fluctuate, even more than they do right now. If this doesn't work, I'll find you a doctor who can help you experiment with other medications."

Finally calming Alex down long enough to check out his other vitals, Dr. Donnelly continued, "You seem to have his diabetes regulated. We'll do some blood tests on the *next* visit, since he's so worked up right now."

One week later, Alex *was* better. At least for now, Sam admitted wryly. Although the gradual increases in medication put Alex in a stranger place mentally, Sam was relieved that at least he *behaved.*

"With everything that's been going on, Alex, we haven't had time for your haircut," Penny observed. Laying his dinner down before him, Penny ran her fingers soothingly through his tousled blonde curls.

Ignoring her, Alex eagerly dug into his food.

"This is great, Penny," Sam observed, wolfing down a perfectly seasoned pork chop. Sam had spent the entire week at the office sorting through most of the paperwork he'd retrieved from New Orleans. Unfortunately, he didn't seem to be making any headway assisting the task force. Although he'd discovered several names in Peter

Gerard's files, many of the individuals had already been investigated. Concerned with the lack of progress in the murder investigations, Sam had decided he wanted to study the police and autopsy reports for Vanessa and Peter Gerard. Surprisingly, the members of the task force had granted his request for copies, and the paperwork would arrive sometime next week.

"Thanks. Your mom told me that pork chops were your favorite." Dropping into her seat, Penny grinned wryly. "I wanted to make you something special for being so sweet about Alex giving you that black eye."

"I dropped by the high school today. We've been investigating a few of the local teenagers, because of those robberies around town. Anyway, you wouldn't believe some of the nervous looks I got—particularly from the guys." Sam grinned. "I must look pretty damned scary—maybe it'll help discourage our thieves."

Penny snorted.

Sam decided he'd surprise Penny by taking Alex to the barbershop for a haircut. But this was easier said than done. After sitting in the barber's chair for a total of ten seconds, Alex had one long stripe running over the top of his head, where he was buzzed to the scalp. Apparently terrified by the shrill, squeaking squall of Karl Walter's trusty old shears, Alex had immediately scrambled out from the barber's chair.

Sam sighed. As a reassuring example for Alex, Sam wasn't left with much choice; he'd have to serve as Karl's guinea pig. Closing his eyes as he stared at himself in the mirror, Sam said goodbye to his layered tawny mane.

"Good to have you back, Sam," Karl grumbled. "When was the last time you were even in here? When you were about sixteen?"

Keeping his eyes closed, Sam cleared his throat uneasily. "About that, Karl—I decided, back then, that I liked my hair to be left just a *little* bit longer." *Unlike his father's.* "Jenny Callahan usually cuts it for me now."

Finally opening his eyes, Sam studied his hair resignedly. Well.

When Sam stepped down from the barber's chair, Alex jumped right up. Sitting patiently through his entire haircut, Alex even giggled when Karl was finished.

Alex's reward for behaving was breakfast at the Crystal Rock Tap.

Sam smiled, as they entered through the door. "Hi, ya, Jules."

Greeting them at the door, Jeff Thompson's daughter blinked, when she saw Sam. Grinning, she escorted Sam and Alex to a booth near a window.

"You must be Alex," she observed, handing him a menu.

Alex intently studied the menu and pointed at a picture.

After examining the crowd, Sam said, "We'd better order right away, Jules. Alex isn't too patient in these kinds of circumstances." He laughed, pointing at Alex's selection of bacon and eggs. "That'll be fine, but make it two. Give us a side of waffles, too. And I'll take some coffee."

After Julie left with their order, he pulled Alex discreetly into the restroom and injected his insulin. Sam was proud of himself for picking up on Alex's routine as quickly as he had. And Penny really seemed to appreciate his efforts.

Sam held up a hand when he observed Jeff Thompson seated near the register. Alex was polishing off the last of the waffles, when Jeff appeared at their table. Reaching out, Jeff attempted to shake Alex's hand. "Nice to meet you, Alex."

Limply returning Jeff's handshake, Alex giggled.

Jeff stared at Sam with a grin. "I see you finally got that flattop, Sam."

"I didn't have a whole lot of choice. I couldn't get Alex into the barber's chair without showing him he didn't need to be afraid," Sam mumbled.

Jeff eyed him fondly. "When ya gonna make an honest woman out of Penny, Sam? There's no doubt in my mind that you've got it *bad*."

Sam bolted upright in his seat. Meeting his gaze as Jeff slid into the booth next to Alex, Sam hesitated. "It's too soon. Isn't it?"

"Ah, Sam. It's never too soon when you're in love," Jeff whispered, solemnly.

An hour later, Sam turned into the driveway on Pine Street, and pulled his truck slowly into the garage.

When Sam and Alex entered the kitchen through the breezeway, Penny did a double-take. Her mouth gaped open, until she was finally able to speak. "Oh, Sam. *Your hair.*"

Uncertain, he asked, "You don't like it?" He ran a hand over his head.

"Oh—I didn't say that," she observed, thoughtfully. "It's kind of sexy," she added, waggling her brows. "Although you're probably gonna give me razor burn."

Sam's eyes widened. *What?* Suddenly comprehending the wickedness of her thoughts, he let out a quick bark of laughter. It was hard to believe that Penny was the same woman he'd escorted to the Loughlin's wedding only two months ago.

"Uh, Sam. Don't get me wrong. Going to get Alex a haircut was one of the sweetest things that you could've done. *No one's* ever been so accepting of him, you know..."

"But?"

"But..."

When Penny opened up a case to show him a set of clipping shears, Sam finally understood. Covering his head with his hands, he moaned, "*You* usually cut Alex's hair."

Since Alex was worn out from their earlier excursion, Sam traveled out on his own to the Dragonfly Pointe Inn. Needing some advice, he headed immediately toward the gift shop.

It was a Saturday afternoon, so it was hectic inside. But Dawn appeared to be handling the situation smoothly. Poised with a smile on her face, she was shifting her attention between three different customers, and making helpful suggestions.

"Sam. I was wondering how long it'd be before I saw you again." With that strange observation, Dawn reached down beneath the counter and pulled out a sketchbook. Flipping through the pages, and pointing out several designs, she shoved the notebook into his hands. "I'll take a break in about fifteen more minutes, when my assistant,

Melinda, returns to take over. Why don't you look for an empty bench along the nature walk?"

Sam stood in place for a few more bewildered moments.

Finally walking outside to the nature walk, he seated himself on a wrought iron bench. Flipping through Dawn's designs, his attention was drawn specifically to an exquisitely simple ring. Bordering a square-cut diamond, bands of deep-blue sapphire baguettes were beautifully inset into a stunning engagement ring.

"How'd you know?" Sam asked when Dawn eventually appeared.

"*Geez, Sam.* It's written all over your face. Not to mention the way that you and Penny are always touching and looking at each other. I don't know who's worse—Jake and Danny, or you and Penny."

"Oh, man. We're not *that* bad. *Are we?*"

Nodding decisively, Dawn began laughing when Sam moaned, shaking his head.

A n invitation for his twenty-year college reunion was mixed in with Sam's mail that he received at the police station. Having not communicated with his friend and former football teammate from Wisconsin, Mark Ralston, since his visit in January, he picked up the phone on Monday morning.

"Sam. Good to hear from you," Mark answered, after being transferred by his secretary.

"Hey. I got an invitation for the reunion. Were you and Denise planning on going?"

"We will, if you do."

"I've been seeing someone Mark, and it's pretty serious. I'm thinking that the reunion would be a nice break for us. The only trouble is we've got an autistic son. I don't know if there's anyone here in town that's capable of taking him on for an entire weekend."

"This woman must be special if you're using the word *we* in terms of her kid, Sam. I didn't think you'd ever get serious with anyone again, after our conversation in January."

"She's a girl I knew years ago, Mark. I guess I never really quit thinking about her."

"Well. I'm happy for you, Sam."

"I've got kind of a delicate question for you. Since you and Denise are still close friends with Belinda Myers, I won't have to worry about her stirring up trouble around Penny. Will I? I mean, I hope I didn't leave her expecting anything back in January when we, uh, well..."

At the other end of the line, there was a lengthy silence.

"*Mark?*"

"Sam. You don't *know?*"

"Know what?"

"Belinda's *dead*. She was *murdered*. It happened, probably, about a week after you visited here back in January. I didn't even know that you two—uh—got together. The cops questioned everyone local who had any contact with her the previous couple of weeks before it happened—including me and Denise. The case is still unsolved."

Stunned into silence, Sam felt his blood turn cold. Finally, his voice was emotionless when he asked, "*How* was she killed, Mark?"

"Pretty brutally, Sam. Her throat was slit."

Sam searched his mind apprehensively, suddenly recalling Shane Donnelly's words. *We don't know why they were killed, Sam. This seems personal.*

It couldn't be. Could it? Could these murders have something to do with *him?*

"Mark. I'll give you a call back sometime before the reunion. I've gotta go. But do you happen to remember the name of the detective you spoke with?"

"I think it was Evans, Sam. Be sure to let me know what's going on. Will you? Try to keep in touch."

"Sure thing, Mark. Say *hi* to Denise for me."

"Will do."

After disconnecting from Mark, Sam promptly began punching in numbers. "Crofton, Arkansas, please. I need the number for Geraldine Branyon."

After a moment, a recorded message informed him that the number had been disconnected.

"Oh, God," Sam muttered. "Brad Renfrow."

Quickly, Sam dialed the number for the Crofton Police Department.

"Hi, Sandra," Sam gently interrupted her voice in greeting. "This is Sam Danielson."

"Sam! How are you? How's your mom?"

"She's hanging in there, Sandra. Hey. I'm calling with a few questions. Maybe you can help me—so that I don't have to bother Brad."

"I can sure try. And, besides, Brad's out of the office right now, anyway."

"Remember Gerry? The woman I—uh—dated when I was living there?"

"Sure do."

"Is she doing alright? I mean I just tried to call her and her phone was disconnected."

"She moved away, Sam. She packed up for a new job about a month or two after you left."

"But she was doing okay?"

"Sure, Sam. She even came in to say goodbye before she left.

"Okay. That's all I wanted to know. I appreciate the information, Sandra."

"You're welcome, Sam. Hey. Jim and I just read an interesting article in a magazine about your inn up there. We're thinking about traveling up there for a vacation."

"Well, if you do, you'd better just damn well look me up. There's a chance I might be getting married, Sandra."

"Not to *Gerry?*"

"Oh, no. A girl I knew as a kid. Her name's Penny. Penelope, actually," he admitted, laughing softly.

"That's good to know. I always thought Gerry was a little bit off, Sam."

"She did behave kind of strangely sometimes. Didn't she?" he admitted, thoughtfully.

"I wouldn't mind a road trip with Jim, if we're invited to your wedding. I've got a lot of vacation time coming."

"Sure thing, Sandra. I'm not sure of when or where, but you'll be invited. I promise. Thanks again. You and Jim take care."

"We will, Sam. It's been good talking to you."

After disconnecting with Sandra, Sam promptly called Jake. Quickly detailing his dilemma, he requested Jake's assistance. "It wor-

ries me, Jake. Both Vanessa's and Peter Gerard's murders were personal, Sam. To me. And now with Belinda dead, too...I need a copy of
that autopsy. Before the task force sees it."

"I'll see what I can do, Sam. I can probably pull some strings with
my boss, Art Thomason."

"And one more thing, Jake. Geraldine Branyon—the woman
I was seeing in Crofton. Supposedly, she got a new job and moved
away from town only a month or two after I left. I need to know if
she's okay."

"Alright, Sam. I'll access my federal database before contacting
my private investigator. Tell me everything you know about her."

After several more minutes of discussion, Sam asked for Jake's
advice. "Do you s'pose I should talk to Penny about this? I mean what
if it *is* personal?"

"Let me try to find this woman first, Sam. And wait until after
you study Belinda Myers' autopsy. No use worrying Penny if you don't
have to. This could all just be coincidence."

Sam remained doubtful. "I'll wait until after I compare each of
the autopsies. Can I come back and take a closer look at those videos?
Something keeps bothering me, Jake. I'm thinking there was *something*
important that I missed when I was going over those videos."

"Sure, Sam. Take your time. Our equipment will allow you to
zoom in and transfer images with little distortion. I'll make sure Grace
and Jeff know that you're coming by."

"I'd appreciate that, Jake."

Thirty - one

For the next few days, Sam patiently awaited the arrival of files and autopsies. Per Jake's request, a copy of the details of Belinda Myers' case investigation arrived on Wednesday morning. But, unfortunately, the task force had also been informed of Sam's suspicions. Shane Donnelly would be returning on Friday to go over the details of the investigation with Sam. But Shane also had information and an update regarding the investigation of Gerard International.

Only a few hours after obtaining Belinda's files by special messenger, Sam received the case files for Vanessa and Peter Gerard. Sam should've been relieved discovering the lacerations on all three victims matched up with the same weapon. But, instead, he became more concerned.

Why would someone kill Belinda?

Sam had slept with her. One night.

But several times back in college.

Why would someone kill Vanessa?

Because she and Sam were still married, and Vanessa was insinuating herself back into his life?

Could the killer be a jealous woman?

Someone from his own past?

Then why kill Peter Gerard?

Nothing made sense.

Reading through each report, listing even the most insignificant details, Sam attempted to discover a connection linking his victims to the killer.

Eventually, he began examining the pictures of the tagged physical evidence, studying the list of items that had been labeled at each of the crime scenes. Finding no similarities with the evidence, he finally spread out the contents of each file in rows across the conference table set up in his office.

He turned his gaze on the gruesome pictures detailing each of the crime scenes.

After several long hours of intense examination, Sam was thoroughly frustrated. He wasn't any closer to uncovering answers. He sighed wearily. It was time to go home.

Penny was busy getting dinner ready later that night, while Sam was setting the table.

"I can't believe Alex actually begins school next week."

"I can't believe the school was actually *finished* in time," observed Sam.

"Well, I know you didn't get much of a chance to see anything other than the campgrounds when we were there on your birthday." Penny was obviously recalling their tryst on the beach, because she was blushing becomingly. "Five classrooms are completely ready to go. Even though there're only fifteen students, the board has already hired five teachers. Each teacher will have two assistants or interns."

"A good ratio for Alex, then."

"So far, there's only one other student in Alex's class. And Ms. Downing mentioned that this other boy also has behavior problems. She seems to be really positive about taking on Alex as her student, Sam. There were *sixteen* kids in his class in New York. Plus, Alex will be able to camp out next summer when the cabins are completed."

"Can I go along for his first day of school?"

"Of *course* you can, Sam. I'm hoping that when we finally begin remodeling the mall, you'll be able to help me out, if I can't get away to pick him up from school."

"All you'll have to do is ask. Are you ready to head out to the cabin this weekend, to see the work that's been completed this week?"

"I can't wait. You've actually got Alex's room *done*?"

"Floors, walls, and windows. Not a whole lot more except for his bathroom. I'm hoping we can start on the kitchen next."

"I'm glad that you've finally been able to get out there again, and get more work done."

Sam grinned. "Cal's crew really came through by finishing up my basement here on Pine Street. You know why I haven't been working out at the cabin. Don't you?"

"Mainly, I suppose, because the construction crew has been trying to complete the school for the benefit of *my* son?"

Sam nodded.

"And there's still a lot of work to do at Jake's and Danny's place?"

Sam nodded again.

"And because you're tapped out financially? Maybe because of all the extra work you've had done in *this* house, that you hadn't planned on completing right away?"

Sam became sheepish. So she'd guessed? Rolling his eyes upward, he grimaced.

"Thank you, Sam." Penny's eyes filled with tears. "For doing all of this for me," she whispered, softly.

"Oh, it's for me, too, sweetheart," he murmured, pulling her into his arms. "Definitely for me, too."

Since Shane Donnelly would arrive the next day, once Sam had caught up with his office paperwork the following morning, he drove out to the Dragonfly Pointe Inn. He couldn't put his finger on what was nagging him at the back of his brain, but he needed to study those security videos again.

Paged by Grace Lu, Jeff Ballard met Sam in the lobby. "Sam. Good to see you again. Jake mentioned you'd be by." After a brief handshake, Jeff led Sam into the security office. A couple dozen monitors broadcast images of the exterior property around Dragonfly Pointe, while another couple of dozen pictured key areas of the interior. A long panel of switches, dials, and buttons was tended by another member of Jake's security team.

"Kev—this is Sam Danielson. He's a good friend of Jake's—as well as the police chief here in town. Be sure to answer any of his questions. Sam—this is Kevin Wyatt. He's my assistant and he's gonna demonstrate the equipment we've got set up for you. Sorry, I've gotta go. Jake's got some work for me to do today. I'll come by and check on you later?"

Sam nodded his agreement distractedly, as he began checking out the equipment.

"Nice to meet you, Sam," Kevin said, reaching out and shaking his hand. "We've got two VCR's set up, side by side. This will allow you to transfer tape segments if you need to. Our VCR will also allow you to zoom in and splice. Jake said you have a darkroom. You can use whatever you transfer for better imaging or comparisons."

Sam went right to work. Beginning with the tapes from the wedding, viewing an assortment of images displayed at various angles, Sam spent several hours screening each of the tapes in slow motion. Although he didn't discover what he thought he was looking for in the actual wedding tapes, Sam found his attention drawn to an immaculately dressed, silver-haired gentleman. Instead of mingling with the wedding guests and enjoying the entertainment outdoors, he stood along the sidelines focusing his gaze across the lake.

What had caught Sam's eye was the pair of binoculars hanging around his neck. And something about the man appeared entirely too familiar; even though Sam wasn't able to get a clear shot of his features. Sam transferred the short segment of video to another tape.

Three hours later, he decided he needed a break. "Kevin." Sam motioned at the doorway. "I'm getting some lunch. Can I get you anything?"

"No, thanks, Sam. I'm off duty soon."

As he strolled into the lobby, Sam ran into Jake. "Hey, man," Jake said. I'm glad you're still here. How about lunch? My treat."

Before Sam could answer, Jake shoved him gently through the lobby guiding him along outdoors. Silently circling around the nature walk, they eventually arrived at the lakefront.

"Janet." Jake motioned to a recently abandoned table. "Can we be seated near the waterfall?"

The hostess smiled. "Sure thing, Jake." Rushing to the table, she cleared off the emptied coffee cups.

Jake and Sam took their seats.

"I wanted some privacy." Jake cleared his throat. "She's alive, Sam. That much we know."

"Gerry?"

"Gerry. But something really weird is going on, Sam. We're having some trouble establishing her identity. Sure, we can trace her back to nursing school. But that was pretty late in her life. We can't find any information from before she was twenty-five. I'm almost positive that she's changed her name."

With a smile on her face, a lovely young waitress appeared at their table. "Hey, Mr. Loughlin. What can I get for you today?"

"I'll take a burger and some of those hot fries, Jolene. How about you, Sam?"

"I'll have the same." Sam smiled, handing her the menu. "And black coffee as well, please.

"Coffee for me, too. But I'll take some cream."

"Sure, Mr. Loughlin. Chief." Jolene smiled again and retreated.

"My investigator's asked for one more day. He thinks he's close to coming up with some answers. But, Sam—here's the kicker. After Gerry left Crofton, she moved to Madison."

"*Madison?* But that's where Belinda lived."

"Yeah, Sam." Jake added, grimly, "And Gerry just happened to be residing in Madison when Belinda was killed."

Sam continued his study of the security tapes by moving forward to the day after the wedding. He was beginning to have a nagging suspicion about what he would find. After examining the security tapes that highlighted key areas around the point, in slow motion, Sam began viewing the tapes and focused on the lakefront. Penny and her crew were scurrying across the grounds, picking up stray ribbons and trash, and the crew eventually began moving in closer to the property immediately surrounding the inn.

And then Sam stopped the film, as he activated the transfer VCR. He began forwarding the original tape at its slowest possible speed. Frame by frame, Sam focused in on Penny, as he studied the members of her crew. Most of them strolled casually beside her, while they were awaiting her orders.

Suddenly, his attention was drawn to a stray figure hovering at the edge of the property. Standing near the waterfall dressed in a navy-blue, hooded sweatshirt, a member of the crew appeared to be lingering back deliberately, and staring at Penny.

Maybe stalking her?

Sam anxiously attempted to identify the individual.

But he couldn't make out the face. Zooming in closer with his lens, Sam became frustrated as, blurring out of focus, the face became even more distorted.

Damn.

Becoming discouraged, Sam sighed. *His eyes were killing him.* He'd have to return in the morning.

Later that night, after finally getting Alex off to sleep, Sam and Penny decided to make it an early night as well. Standing in the bathroom, Penny was brushing her teeth while Sam was pulling on his boxers after taking a quick shower.

"So, should we just meet out at the cabin tomorrow night?" Penny asked.

"Sure. It's gonna be a long day of work for me. I'm not sure what time I'll get out there. But Alex might enjoy the hot tub."

"That—and sleeping in his new room in his sleeping bag. I've gotta remember to load up a few of his toys so we can just leave them out there."

"Good idea." Sam considered, thoughtfully. "Should we bring along the VCR?"

"We could always come back and get it."

"At least we don't have to worry about him falling into the water," he observed, dryly.

Penny grinned. "He was definitely scared to death, when we were walking along the pier."

Spending a few hours at the cabin with the workmen the previous week, Sam and Penny had relayed some instructions for the finish work. Alex had been in awe of the deck, pier, and waterfront.

"He's scared of heights, too?"

"Yeah."

"How's he gonna react to that high, open walkway—that runs above the family room in the addition?"

"He'll probably hug the wall and keep away from the railings. It might take him hours to hike up and down the staircase, just so he can get into his bedroom. He'll probably take each step one at a time."

Sam began laughing.

And then he stopped.

When Penny began slipping out from her robe.

Sheer and wispy, the frothy concoction of ivory she wore was low-cut and form-fitting. Sam's mouth went dry as, burning her with his heated stare, his eyes roved hungrily over the enticing curves of her body. With her hair hanging loose and lustrous around her lovely face, Penny's eyes shone bright and brilliant, a sparkling sapphire blue.

Waggling her brows with her hand in the air, she snapped her fingers.

And, determinedly, Sam went running.

"Have I told you how much I love the improvements you've made in this house, Sam?"

Much later, both sated and exhausted, they lay wrapped within each other's arms.

Sam laughed softly. "Not lately."

"As soon as I walked into the door, I felt right at home. I loved all your paint colors and furnishings—even the layout and style of the kitchen. It's almost like you were decorating with me in mind."

Squeezing his arm around her tighter, he whispered in her ear, "I think that I probably was."

Breaking contact, she eased upright in the bed. "What's wrong, Sam? You've been worried about something all week," she added, softly.

Sam asked wryly, "How'd you guess?"

"You've been really distracted when I've been talking to you. And that's not like you."

Drawing in a deep breath, Sam sat up beside her in the bed. He wrapped an arm over her shoulders before confessing, "Jake thought that I should wait to tell you, so you wouldn't be worried. But I feel better when I'm upfront with you—especially after our recent miscommunication."

"I can handle it. Go ahead and tell me what's been going on."

Sam continued hesitantly, "There's a good chance the murders were committed because of *me*, Penny."

Penny blinked. "But *how* could that be?"

"I just discovered that the last woman I slept with, before you, ended up murdered. The lacerations on her throat matched up with both Vanessa's and her father's. She was killed with the same weapon," Sam muttered.

Appearing suddenly apprehensive, Penny moaned, "*Oh, Sam.*"

"And I'm worried about *you*. Terry and Nat have been driving by the house regularly and keeping an eye on you, but still..."

"I'll be careful, Sam. I'll make sure I'm never alone."

"I'm just relieved that I installed a security system—and had all the locks replaced—since I discovered Vanessa was staying here," he mumbled, tiredly.

Penny yawned. "I was wondering why we needed that security system—here, in Crystal Rock, of all places."

They both eased back down into the bed.

"I'd better fill you in a little—about my life before I met you again, too," Sam whispered, spooning her into his body. "It might be important."

"It's up to you, Sam. As far as I'm concerned, our life together began in April, when I met you again. And I trust you."

Relieved by her words, Sam tucked Penny's head in under his chin. He'd been worried sick that his slightly sordid past might've finally caught up with him. Especially if it ended up endangering Penny and Alex. And, subconsciously, he'd been concerned about Penny's reaction when she heard about his lengthy affair with Gerry. "First of all, once I suspected Vanessa was unfaithful, the physical side of our marriage was over with, Penny. When I moved on, to become the police chief in Crofton, after my supposed divorce, I began dating someone—a nurse named Geraldine Branyon." Sam was aware that, as she listened intently, Penny stiffened slightly in his arms. "And I never realized she expected more."

Penny moaned resignedly, "Oh, Sam."

"I hadn't had sex for about five years, Penny, so when I met Gerry..."

"You were lonesome and needed *someone*. I understand. If I hadn't had the experience I had with David, I probably would've found someone else before you. But I'm sure glad it *was* you."

"Likewise," he growled. "But Gerry didn't take it well when I told her I was moving. Jake's had his private eye searching for her—to make sure *she* wasn't a victim of this killer. We just can't understand the motives, though. If it was a woman from my past, what would be the purpose of killing Peter Gerard? At first, we thought his murder had something to do with his business dealings, since he's been associating with some pretty unsavory characters."

"But, no?"

"No. Turns out he was more valuable alive than dead."

Penny asked hesitantly, "And what about this other woman who was killed, Sam?"

"She's an old college girlfriend. She'd just been divorced when I went to Madison to visit my buddy, Mark, back in January. We had a few drinks together at the bar, and one thing led to another. But it was just that once. I was back in Crystal Rock the next day. And there hasn't been anyone since. Not even Diane, who's been throwing herself at me ever since I arrived in town. Even though I unintentionally led Gerry on, I swear that I've changed since my marriage to Vanessa, Penny," he murmured, solemnly.

"*I know, Sam*. And I love you for it." Finally settling back into his arms, she sighed contentedly.

Listening to her breathing turn steady as she tumbled into sleep, Sam's arms remained wrapped around Penny. Unable to shake his apprehension, he'd been remarkably uneasy this entire week. *Why did he feel like all hell was about ready to break loose?*

Thirty - two

fter a sleepless night of tossing and turning, Sam staggered into his office an hour before Shane Donnelly was due to arrive the next morning.

What was it? *What* was he missing? Anxiously, he began studying the crime scene photos again. There was *something* he'd noticed in these photos...but *what*?

By the time Shane Donnelly arrived, now on his third cup of coffee, Sam was feeling a little less weary.

"Well, Sam. I've heard you've stumbled onto something here." Dropping his briefcase to the floor, Shane began studying the crime scene reports, autopsies, and photos Sam had neatly lain out on the conference table. Working his way through the office, he scanned the dry erase board loaded with pertinent details about each of the murders.

Shane raised a brow. "Geraldine Branyon?"

"A woman I had a relationship with back in Crofton. Jake has a private eye researching her whereabouts."

"I don't know about all this, Sam, with you being personally involved."

"Well, *excuse me*, Shane, but it seems that the only thing the task force has done is eliminated the connection of these murders to *your* investigation of Gerard International," Sam muttered, irritably.

Shane sighed. "Yeah, you're right, Sam. Keep at it then. Just give me a day by day report. Will ya? So I can keep my superiors off of my back. I've even noticed their lack of urgency in regard to solving these murders."

Sam nodded, wearily.

Sam and Shane began working through the findings of the task force. Despite the twenty-four hour surveillance of Frank Carlton and his associates, very little had been discovered about their human trafficking operation. Somehow, as individuals, they were remaining detached from their operation.

"But we've got a potential snitch, Sam. One of Frank Carlton's bodyguards is concerned about the safety of his family. He may be willing to work with us if we can keep his family safe."

"I haven't finished searching through all the paperwork, Shane. But I'll begin again next week. Your task force has already been on top of every name I've discovered so far."

"That's what comes with an investigation that's been going on for years, but seems to be going nowhere." He hesitated before he continued, "And I think that's partly because we have a leak within our task force."

Sam's head shot up from the paperwork he was studying. "FBI or NOPD?"

"Either, and, or, both," he replied dryly. "Frank Carlton's been into extortion for years. To tell you the truth, I'm not really sure *who* I can trust.

"I might be able to go through the names of your NOPD members and give you a heads up," Sam added, thoughtfully.

"I'd appreciate that. I'll get you a list. I'm the only one who knows about our potential snitch, Sam, and I'd like to keep it that way. The only reason I'm letting you know about him, by the way, is because he specifically asked for *you* or Jake Loughlin. I reassured him that I was working with you."

"Any idea how he got *my* name?"

"No. But I'll be sure to ask once we strike an agreement." After standing and whipping his Styrofoam coffee cup into the trash, heading for the door, Shane paused. "What's next with the murder investigation, then?"

"I'll return to the inn this afternoon and finish going over those tapes. I'm pretty sure someone's been following me and Penny. But I haven't been able to focus in on the face I discovered on the video."

"Be careful."

Sam nodded distractedly as Shane strode out through the door.

A few minutes later, Sophie slipped into his office carrying a tagged evidence bag in her hand. "Sam. We finally got those candy wrappers back from the lab. You know—the ones you had me send off, last month, when you discovered them near your cabin after seeing that prowler? They found prints. But they weren't in the system."

Sam nearly knocked over his coffee. "Sophie. That's it," he barked, jumping up from his chair. Grabbing the bag from her hand, he pulled her into his arms for a quick embrace.

She cleared her throat. "Are you alright, Sam?"

You might've just helped me solve this case." Pulling out a magnifying glass from his desk and sorting through the photos laid out on the conference table, he focused on enlarging an inconsequential image in Peter Gerard's study.

"Come over here, Soph. *What* do ya see?

Gazing over his shoulder, she gasped. "Candy wrappers. In the ash tray. They look to be the same as the ones you found near your cabin."

Resignedly, Sam muttered, "And I finally remembered that I know someone, Soph—who's fond of the same, exact butterscotch candy that comes packaged in those wrappers."

"Geraldine Branyon, Jake. I just can't believe it. It's gotta be her." Sam sighed. "I'm running through the tapes right now—attempting to locate a clearer visual."

"I'll let you get to it, then. My investigator's in New Orleans, Sam. He's supposed to get back to me by the end of the day. Gerry moved south after leaving Madison."

"New Orleans, huh?" Sam nodded, grimly. "That's what I was afraid of."

Sam desperately attempted to remain patient while running through the visuals on the tapes.

And finally he pulled up a clear shot. Clad in waitressing apparel, Geraldine Branyon was speaking into the receiver of a pay phone in the Dragonfly Pointe Inn lobby.

Sam was shocked by the expression on her face, emblazoned with bitter hatred. Making a mental note of the time and date stamp, Sam attempted to recall his location at the time.

And then it came to him. *He'd been spending the night in the suite. With Penny.*

Who had Gerry been speaking with on the phone? He and Penny must've been preparing to depart for the airport in Eau Claire at the time.

Sam reached for the phone. After her initial consultation with the architects at the mall, Penny had begun working from home because of Alex. Sam had assisted her in setting up an office in the basement.

No answer. Penny and Alex must've headed to the grocery store, preparing for their trip to the cabin.

Sam punched in the numbers for the stationhouse. "Terry?"

"Yeah, Sam?"

"I need a favor. Something's going down with this murder investigation. I need for you to find Penny. There's a chance she could be in danger. Hang out with her and Alex. Will ya? And call me when you find her."

"Sure thing, Sam. I'm out of here now."

"*Thanks*, Terry. I appreciate it," he muttered gruffly.

At that moment, Jake returned to the security office.

"Sam. I've got some news," he said. "Geraldine Branyon was hired on as a combination caregiver and personal assistant for Peter Gerard. Apparently he was having some heart trouble, and he wanted to keep it quiet. She would come to the house to monitor his blood pressure, bring in his meds—stuff like that. The police questioned her and got her prints. They found nothing suspect in her immediate background. And, logically, why suspect her? She could've killed him with an overdose if she wanted him dead. What would be the purpose of slashing his throat instead?"

"And this is her, Jake." Jake peeked over Sam's shoulder. "She was waitressing *here*. Or at least posing as a waitress here."

"*Damn it, Sam!* This is a major breach of our security. What the hell's been going on? I need to discuss this with my security team."

"It's more important to find her, Jake. We can worry about that later." Sam eased back into his chair. "Did you dig up any more information about her background?"

"Apparently her real name *is* Geraldine Branyon. But she has the additional name of Bochner. She was born in..."

"*Madison, Wisconsin.* She has an older half-brother by the name of *Jordan Bochner. Oh, my God, Jake.* I knew Gerry as a *kid.* I used to consider Jordan a friend—until I was forced to turn him in for attempting to rape a coed at Wisconsin over twenty years ago. He claimed I ruined his life. *He always threatened he'd get even.* And the Bochners still have a summer house, here, on Pebble Lake. That's how I met Jordan in the first place. We need to get out there. *Now.*"

Hastily punching in the number for the station, he instructed Sophie to send Nat out to the northeast corner of Pebble Lake. The location of the Bochner property was listed on the district map in the office.

Jake was already racing up to his apartment on the upper floor to retrieve his weapon, while Sam stood up from his seat preparing his own.

Thirty - Three

*W*eapons readied, carefully peering through each of the windows, Jake and Sam crept around the summerhouse searching for signs of activity. With shutters hanging loose and glass punched out from several of the windows, the rundown, sprawling vacation home appeared to have not been improved upon since the reign of Martin Bochner, over twenty years before.

Discovering the back door unlocked, Sam and Jake moved slowly inside with their weapons remaining up and ready. The electricity was working and there were definite signs of occupancy. With the remains of fast food in the ancient, grimy refrigerator and an assortment of emptied cans lining the countertops, the kitchen was a pigsty. Peeking into the living room, Sam realized that much of the filth and destruction inside could probably be attributed to an invasion from birds and squirrels and possibly even raccoons. Could Gerry actually be staying *here*? The place was ready for demolition.

Traveling slowly up the staircase, Jake and Sam discovered that one of the bedrooms appeared to be in use. Several bags of luggage were strewn throughout the room. As he approached a dilapidated loveseat, Sam studied the contents of the bag opened up on top.

Jake raised a questioning brow. "Gloves?"

"Out in the truck. We'd better do this right. Give me a minute."

Sam returned shortly, handing over an additional pair of latex gloves to Jake. Slowly, Sam began sorting through the contents of the purse that was laying inside the bag of luggage. Flipping open a wallet, he studied the identification, and sighed resignedly. "It's her, Jake."

"But where the hell *is* she?"

"That's what worries me. C'mon. Let's go radio in and get some extra help. We'd better search the property."

Radioing in to the station, Sam instructed Sophie to contact Shane Donnelly before notifying the state police.

Sam and Jake circled slowly around the extensive property, eventually arriving at the boathouse. "I think there's an apartment up here, Sam." Observing the brand new deadbolt installed on the door of the upper level, Jake sighed. "We'd better wait for a search warrant."

Sam ran down a steep, long staircase encompassing the rocky shore. "Jake," Sam shouted upward as he opened the door. "The boathouse itself is unlocked." Constructed over the water, the spacious lower level of the boathouse held compartments enough to house six vessels.

Hurrying down the staircase to join him, Jake began studying the equipment lining the inner walls. "I think someone's been living here, Sam. This is all top quality scuba gear. And if I'm not mistaken, a couple of boats have been tied into the dock."

Inspecting two of the exterior doors, Sam recognized the rope and pulley system had been replaced with a modernized alternative. "It's gotta be Jordan," Sam muttered in a monotone. "I need to make sure Penny's okay, Jake. We're supposed to meet at my cabin, but I'd better contact Terry."

Returning quickly to his truck, he radioed back to the station, and spoke with Sophie.

Sounding anxious, she informed him, "Terry called in, Sam. He hasn't been able to locate Penny."

Sam's blood turned cold. "Sophie. Get a hold of Nat. Instead of meeting us at the Bochner property, he and Terry should drive out to my cabin immediately. Tell them to remain on the road till Jake and I arrive, but prepare their weapons. I repeat, they should prepare their weapons."

"*Right away, Sam.* Over and out."

Sam returned to the summerhouse, where Jake was standing outside, ready and waiting. "Do you suppose the phone inside is connected, Jake?"

"Hopefully," Jake muttered, following Sam inside.

Picking up the receiver in the kitchen and hearing a dial tone, Sam breathed in a sigh of relief. Quickly, he dialed the number for the cabin.

"Hello?"

"Penny," he barked. "You could be in danger. Are you guys alone?"

"Yeah, Sam. I thought the construction crew would still be working here, so I arrived a little early."

"Damn it, Penny. I forgot to mention that they were off today." He continued hastily, "its Gerry, Penny. The woman I was seeing in Crofton. She was working with your crew at the inn. We think she's the murderer, Penny. You've gotta get outta there. *Now.*"

"*The phone call.* It must've been *her.* Sam, *I forgot to tell you about the threatening call I got*—the weekend of the wedding—that morning—before we left for the airport."

"*Scoop up Alex and get outta there...*Penny? *Penny...are you there?*" Frantically, Sam batted the receiver up and down on its mounting. "*Damn it, Jake—the phone at the cabin went dead.* Is Jim McClellan still at the Dragonfly?"

"As a matter fact, he is."

"How about calling Danny? Have her get Jim to the cabin by boat. We might need backup on the lake."

After Jake's frenzied call to Danielle, less than five minutes later, Sam and Jake were racing in Sam's truck to the cabin.

Thirty-four

*W*hen the phone went dead, Penny froze with fear. Instinct told her it was too late to depart. She and Alex would have to hide.

Moving out to retrieve Alex from the living room, she halted.

Oh, God. No.

Brown-haired and hazel-eyed, she seemed, at first, to be like any ordinary woman. Slim and attractive, Geraldine Branyon typically would've struck Penny as someone she could trust or befriend.

Think, Penny, think.

Settled next to Alex on the couch, Gerry was distractedly observing him stack up Lego blocks. Playing with the serrated filet knife in her hand, she was patterning long shallow cuts repeatedly along the length of her arm. Switching her attention between Alex and her knife, when the blood began seeping from each freshly made cut, with apparent fascination, Gerry slid her knife hypnotically along to another uncut area of her skin, digging it in slightly deeper.

"I thought I could do it," she muttered numbly, staring at Penny. "I thought I could kill you."

Afraid that she might endanger Alex, Penny made no sudden moves. From her position in the doorway, she pleaded, *"You don't want to kill me. What would happen to my son?"*

"Yes. I've been watching you for a long time. You *are* a good mother," Gerry mumbled dully. "I was a good mother, too. But they took my baby away. She was such a sweet girl. Just like your boy, here. And she needed me. They told me she'd get better—because *they'd* take better care of her than *I* could. They made me put her into one of those places and then *she died.* She needed *me.*"

As if she was in a daze, Gerry arose from the couch, gazing distractedly from Alex to Penny.

Slowly, Penny approached Alex, sinking into the seat that Gerry had just abandoned. Putting an arm over his shoulders, fighting his reluctance, she pulled him into her arms protectively.

Alex giggled.

With a vacant smile, Gerry repeated, "Yes. You *are* a good mother. Your boy loves you. Just like my little girl loved me. No. I can't take you away from him—even though I love Sam."

And still muttering under her breath, Gerry stepped mechanically through the screen door, and began moving out onto the pier.

Frozen in place, while quivering with relief, Penny closed her eyes and gave thanks with a silent prayer. She became distantly aware of the harsh screech of oars being slid and slammed into position. Finally easing up from the couch, Penny ran out onto the porch. Peering down to the boat landing near the water's edge, Penny observed Gerry as, rowing the boat rhythmically, she retreated stealthily along the shoreline.

"*Penny? Penny?* Are you alright? Oh, thank God. *Jake. I can't believe it. They're fine!*" Sam frantically came slamming through the door, gathering Penny into his arms. "What happened? She didn't hurt you?" Quickly patting down her body, once he was reassured that she remained unharmed, he went over to check on Alex.

With their weapons drawn, Jake and Terry came rushing into the room.

"She's in a boat, Sam. She said she couldn't kill me because of Alex," Penny mumbled dazedly. "She said I was a good mother and she just couldn't do it."

Jake and Terry ran through the screen door, so they could search across the lake from atop the pier.

"Oh, God, sweetheart," Sam muttered. Sam was trembling when he closed his eyes, and crushed her again within his arms. "What would I do without *you*?"

Jake stepped back inside. "Danny's arrived with Jim McClellan, but, somehow, Gerry must've slipped by them. It wouldn't be difficult to hide in the thickness of that brush along the water's edge. Just to play it safe, Terry and Nat are guarding the property. Sam—you'd better come along with us to search for Gerry. She's more likely to come with us quietly when we find her."

"Alright, Jake. But get Nat in here to take care of Penny and Alex," he ordered. Sam's eyes gazed pleadingly into hers. "I have to go sweetheart."

"I know, Sam. Be careful. Try not to hurt her. I'm not sure that everything she's doing is of her own volition. She needs help."

"You're right, Penny. But we'll have to talk later." Despite the seriousness of the situation, Sam couldn't help but roll his eyes upward, when he waved goodbye to Alex. With all the excitement, Alex appeared to be having the time of his life, jumping up and down and laughing.

Once Danielle and Nat came rushing through the door, Sam was on his way back out.

Meeting her at the long abandoned dock of Angel's Way, Jordan popped his head up from under the water. "*You incompetent bitch*," he hissed. "You were supposed to *kill* her."

"But she's a good mother, Jordan. Her son *needed* a mother. Look what happened to *our* baby."

"Damn, you're nuts. All my plans are all fucked up because of *you!*" he screamed. "We had a time table. But you keep screwing things up. I still can't believe that you actually killed Gerard."

"But he was gonna hurt *Sam*."

"All you were supposed to do was keep an eye on Sam's *wife*. I told you—I'd let you know *when* it was time to kill her. *You couldn't even do that right.*"

She was just too mentally imbalanced. The plan had been to pin the murder of Vanessa Gerard on Sam Danielson, after the same plan hadn't worked with Sam's college girlfriend. But once Gerry had taken the situation into her own hands *again*, he'd decided to ruin Sam's life by eliminating the woman he appeared to be in love with.

Using Gerry had backfired majorly. He'd have to start over.

But first...

"Let me have a look at that knife, Gerry."

Bracing his hands on the planks, Jordan pulled himself up onto the dock. Still seated in her rowboat, Gerry obligingly held the knife up into the air. Bending over her and wrapping his hand around hers, Jordan abruptly slashed the knife across her throat. A shower of blood sprayed through the air, as the knife dropped down from her hand.

She hadn't even struggled.

As Gerry's eyes stared back at him, glazed and lifeless, Jordan kicked and shoved the boat from the pier, and sent it drifting aimlessly afloat.

Jake and Sam dropped Jim McClellan off at the Bochner pier after their first unsuccessful attempt to locate Gerry. When they finally discovered her rowboat lodged in a shallow hollow along the northern edge of the lake, it was a definite shock to discover Gerry's prone, lifeless body slumped across the seats within.

"Damn," Sam muttered. "I realize she must've been pretty unbalanced, Jake. But I didn't expect *this*. It *was* suicide, wasn't it?"

After a preliminary search of the fishing boat's interior, Jake was wary as he studied her throat. "I'm not so sure, Sam. That slash is pretty long and deep. Although it's possible, I guess, it'd be hard for her to do that to herself."

"*That bastard.* I suppose Jordan's using some of that diving equipment?"

"Most likely. And I wouldn't be surprised if he's already left town."

"That looks to be our murder weapon," Sam murmured, pointing. Half hidden under a seat near the anchor, a shiny fillet knife was covered in blood.

"We'll let the experts handle the comparisons. Since it appears she died in this rowboat, let's tow the boat into the Bochner property. Our reinforcements have probably arrived with a search warrant.

Although I doubt that we'll find Jordan Bochner, at least we can get a call out for the local authorities to detain him."

Sam snorted. "I doubt we'll even be able to *connect* him to any of this, Jake. For all his abhorrent faults, the man was always unbelievably intelligent."

Thirty - five

Looking back, Sam couldn't understand how he'd been totally unaware of the abnormality of the Bochner family. Since he'd only been a child when the family had spent their summers vacationing here in Crystal Rock, he tried not to beat himself up.

According to Jake's hired detective, Geraldine Branyon had a long grim history. Evidently happy and well-adjusted as a child, she'd been a victim of rape at the age of thirteen.

Apparently, she'd been assaulted by her own half-brother, Jordan.

Rather than secure for his daughter the help and support she'd needed, Martin Bochner had stood on the side of his son, Jordan. As far as Martin was concerned, Jordan could do no wrong.

Through his years as an offensive running back playing football at Wisconsin, Sam had remained a casual friend of Jordan's, Wisconsin's starting quarterback. Despite rumors on campus that'd circulated about Jordan's drinking binges and behavior, Sam had never seen evidence until his senior year at college.

When he'd interrupted Jordan attempting to rape a coed at a fraternity party.

Assuming that assaulting the girl, who'd been passed out drunk, was his God-given right, Jordan had actually laughed when Sam had threatened to turn him in. After Sam reported Jordan to the campus police, the college had initiated an investigation.

Martin Bochner had refused to let his son stand accused of attempted rape. Once the female sophomore who'd been attacked had mysteriously withdrawn her charges, Sam's word was the only proof the assault had even occurred.

But half of his fellow teammates had turned on Sam once Jordan had been expelled. Rather bitter at the time, Sam couldn't regret the turn of events. It was the injustice of Jordan's lack of prosecution that'd pushed Sam into entering the police academy.

Although Jordan had been exonerated undeservedly of the crime, at least Martin Bochner had been unable to wield his substantial influence to have him reinstated at Wisconsin.

But why *hadn't* Wisconsin reinstated Jordan? Now Sam's conscience was presenting him with another problem—what *other* indiscretions might've been covered up during Jordan's college career?

Apparently, when Gerry was discovered to be pregnant at thirteen-years old, Martin had attempted to force his daughter into having an abortion. With Gerry's mental state becoming increasingly fragile, Gerry's mother, Madeline, had given in to Gerry's wish to give birth to her baby. Having dealt for years with Martin's obsessive favoritism toward his son, Madeline had finally decided she'd had enough. With Madeline acquiring custody of Gerry, the Bochners eventually divorced.

But Gerry's baby girl had been born with a genetic mutation sometimes inherited by children created from incest. When her health gradually began to deteriorate, the child had been placed in intensive care.

With the death of her child triggering Gerry's long mental breakdown, she'd begun cutting herself. Spending ten years of her life in a mental institution, and losing both of her parents during the interim, Gerry had been released at the age of twenty-five.

According to Jake's detective, after settling in Texas, Gerry had eventually been approached by Jordan. As her only remaining family, she'd apparently still been vulnerable to his influence.

Probably reinventing her identity, Jordan had most likely arranged for Gerry's entry into nursing school and her relocation to Arkansas.

But he probably hadn't planned on Gerry's obsession with Sam once they'd begun dating. Originally, Jordan had intended to frame Sam for the death of Belinda Myers, Sam and Jake concluded. The previous summer, Gerry had been aware of Sam's plans to spend that week in January in Madison with his friends, Mark and Denise Ralston. Jordan or Gerry must've approached Belinda because, as Sam recalled, Belinda had come on to *him* that night at the bar.

But whatever else they'd intended had been disrupted by Sam's early return to Crystal Rock, due to the winter storm forecast for the upper northwest.

And somehow Belinda had ended up dead, anyway.

Had it been because of Gerry's obsession with Sam, or because they hadn't realized Sam had left town? Maybe Jordan had simply wanted any evidence leading back to himself eliminated, if *he'd* been the one to contact Belinda?

But the final, most puzzling question was—*why had Gerry killed Peter Gerard?*

The nearest reason Sam and Jake could figure was, because of her obsession with him, it might've still had something to do with Sam. With her place in the household, she'd most likely been privileged to his private conversations, along with having access to confidential messages or records that'd come across his desk.

Had she been attempting to protect Sam?

They'd probably never know.

What had happened with Vanessa's murder? If Jordan had been trying to set Sam up for her murder, the timing and location had prevented it. Perhaps Jordan had another plan for eliminating Vanessa, intending to put the blame on Sam—but because of her shaky mental state, Gerry had somehow strayed from Jordan's plan?

This was the most likely scenario, Sam and Jake decided.

It *must've* been Jordan who'd been attempting to manipulate Gerry into killing Penny.

The plan that would've annihilated Sam most of all.

With Gerry's tragic death, they'd probably never discover the entire truth.

The FBI had been all too ready to put the blame for the murders on Geraldine Branyon. With no evidence to the contrary, Jordan Bochner had been eliminated as a suspect.

The FBI hastily closed the case.

And Gerry's death had been ruled a probable suicide.

But for Sam and Jake, the case would continue to remain open.

Friday, August 26, 1988

"Alex made it a whole week in school without getting into any trouble. Hurray." When Penny clapped her hands together, Alex giggled, clapping his own.

The banquet room had been reserved for Danielle Loughlin's birthday party, and Sam and Penny, along with Alex, had been invited to celebrate at the Dragonfly Pointe Inn.

Normally not comfortable in a crowded room, Alex was behaving exceptionally well this evening.

Of course he'd spent the entire evening ogling the cake.

And was currently gobbling some down.

"Alex. If you eat it like that, you're not gonna get any in your mouth," Sam observed, laughing.

Crumbs came tumbling from his mouth when Alex continued eating his cake, giggling at the same time.

"That's your limit, kiddo," Sam warned him, when Alex held out his emptied plate.

"Let's get you cleaned up." When Penny stood up from the table, Sam held up a staying hand.

Conveniently strolling up to their table with Jarrod and Rodney Benet in tow, Julie Thompson grabbed Alex by his hand. "Do you mind if I get in a little practice in with Alex, Penny? Has Sam told you that I've decided to go for my degree in Special Education?"

"Your dad actually mentioned something about that to me, Jules—earlier this summer. Where do you plan on going to school?" Penny inquired.

"Right now, for this year, I'm taking my basic courses at Northwest Community College. But I'll have to move on next year if I go into Special Ed. Dad says he wants to be sure that I'm dedicated before he forks out a fortune."

Both Sam and Penny laughed.

"If you're really serious about taking Alex in hand, just stick to the path along the nature walk and near the falls. He's fascinated by the waterfall. With the drop to the lake, I'm sure he'll behave since he's scared of the height," Penny said.

"Wave to your mom and dad, Alex. We'll take you to the bathroom first and get you cleaned up." Waving his hand through the air, Alex skipped alongside Julie and the boys, laughing boisterously.

Suddenly turning back, Julie halted, winking at Sam.

"That's my signal," Sam observed, grinning. "It's time for us to take a walk, Penny. Let's go on down to the beach."

Clearly bemused, Penny reached for his outstretched hand.

Sam led Penny outside before moving along the scenic pathway beyond the parking lot. He kept an arm loosely wrapped over her shoulders as they walked along Beach Road.

Penny had obviously heard the rustling of activity under the dense cover of the nearby pines, because she began searching through the ferns and foliage lining the roadside.

Nodding to the base of a pine, Sam grinned, as he singled out a pair of playful squirrels, twisting and scampering through the branches.

Penny laughed softly.

Finally arriving at the entrance of the beach, they observed a surprising number of vacationers bravely battling the chilly water. Sam determinedly steered Penny along a path that led toward the bay.

The rental cabins demolished during the investigation of the human trafficking ring, the previous fall, had yet to be rebuilt. After discovering numerous underground tunnels at Dragonfly Pointe, the shoreline had been fenced off from tourists. Once the cabins were entirely reconstructed, the bayside property would be accessible in early spring.

Pulling a key from his pocket, Sam unlocked the gate. With all new landscaping in place, this section of the shoreline presented the most picturesque view of the bay.

Sam steered Penny along the path and stopped near a wrought iron bench.

"Oh, Sam. Isn't this bench lovely?" Intricately scrolled with a pattern of dragonflies, the bench was one of a dozen that'd been positioned along the graveled pathway, that followed alongside the shoreline. After running her fingers lightly over the etched design, Penny took a seat on the bench.

Sam smiled. "Jake and Danny sure take this dragonfly stuff to heart. Don't they?"

"They swear that dragonflies bring them good luck."

"Could be. That's why *I'm* here as a matter of fact," Sam added, seating himself beside her. With a thoughtful glance across the bay, he continued, "Danny claims that there's an Indian legend about love lasting forever when you declare your intentions here at Dragonfly Pointe."

Penny blinked. And then, most obviously, recognizing the significance of Sam's words, her eyes began to fill with tears.

Determinedly, Sam cleared his throat. "Penny," he began. "Until I met you again, I'd never really *lived*. After moving from New York to New Orleans, and then even on to Arkansas, I realized that I've just been biding my time. I guess you could kind of say I've been in flight—because I'm pretty sure that I've always been waiting to come home—*to you*."

"Oh, Sam," she whispered, softly. "I was only living half of a life until I met *you* again. And I was content. Or so I thought. I've never been as happy as I am today. And the way you treat my son. I never knew a man could be so loving and caring with a child that wasn't his own." Her face was shiny with tears when she added, "Especially with a kid who has as many problems as Alex does."

"Ah, Penny. But Alex has become *my* son, now, too. And I'd like to adopt him—because he always will be." Reaching into his pocket, and pulling out a box, after gazing into her eyes for a long tender moment, he flipped open the box for Penny. The diamond and sapphire ring Dawn had designed had proved to be even more exquisite than Sam had anticipated.

"*Oh, Sam.* It's *beautiful.*"

Sam slid the ring onto her finger. When Penny began sobbing, Sam pulled her gently into his arms. "Penny. It doesn't have to be right away, if you're not ready yet."

"But, Sam," she whispered. A soft smile lit up her sapphire-blue eyes. "I want it to be *soon*—for the sake of our *baby.*"

Sam's mouth gaped open.

Penny gazed into his eyes and continued to smile.

Sam's mouth finally closed. "But Penny, you said…"

Squeezing his hand reassuringly, she said, "At the time, I think I misunderstood. After my accident and miscarriage, the doctor must've said that I *probably* couldn't get pregnant again. But I am, Sam. I can't believe it, but Dr. Donnelly confirmed it. I *am*!"

With a whoop of joy, Sam jumped up onto his feet from the bench. Hoisting her from the bench, lifting her up from the ground, Sam spun Penny high in the air.

With a startled shriek, Penny burst into laughter.

Finally, after several long moments of heartfelt excitement, Sam and Penny settled back down onto the bench.

"It's not going to be easy, Sam. With Alex, I mean. His behavior problems might make him difficult around the baby. We're probably going to need some extra help eventually."

"I know, Penny. But with our friends and family, we'll manage. Look at how many of our friends are ready to help us with Alex, now, even realizing his behavior could become aggressive at any time."

"We do have the best of friends. Don't we?"

For several minutes more, Sam and Penny gazed contentedly across the tranquil waters of the bay. Fluttering lightly with the movement of the water, hovering languidly over the bay, clusters of dragonflies and damselflies streaked haphazardly through the air.

In flight.

"You know, Sam, when I saw you again, it wasn't just *love* that I was feeling—it was *hope*. I didn't recognize it, because I've never felt it before." With a misty smile, she continued, "Hope that there might be something more in my life than just my job and my son. Hope that I might've finally found someone who understood me— and wouldn't mind sharing my burdens. Hope that I wouldn't always feel so *alone*."

Touched by her words, Sam remained silent, and wrapped his arm more tightly around Penny's shoulders.

Finally, emotionally, Sam cleared his throat, and in a sing song voice, he began, *"Hey, Penny?"*

Penny's eyes were wide when she turned to stare at Sam.

And deliberately raising his hand in the hair, Sam grinned, as he snapped his fingers.

Epilogue

Settling back in his seat, Vincente DeMarcus mechanically flicked on his speakerphone. "I detest this area of the country," the silver-haired man in gray observed, dispassionately.

"You have no choice, Vince. The FBI is searching for you."

"Yes. My greatest weapon is my anonymity. But this Branyon woman has destroyed my plans."

"Well. I got it through a good source that it wasn't just her, Vince. It was someone with a grudge against Danielson. This guy had some kind of screwed up ideas for revenge. He's the half-brother of the Branyon woman—Jordan Bochner."

"Hmm," Vince considered, thoughtfully. "And this man has supposedly disappeared?"

"Yeah. The FBI was ready to dump all the blame on the woman and leave Bochner out of the picture. Makes them look better to have the murders solved."

"Get me all that you have on this Bochner. And find him. I may be able to use him."

"Alright, Vince. We still haven't found that journal. We went through the Danielson place right away, like you asked. We were lucky we got outta there before the FBI showed up."

"I have been reassured by my sources that the FBI team have not yet discovered the journal either. I am almost certain that the woman procured it from her father. She may have had the forethought to secure its safety—since she astutely thought to revise her will. I must consider, carefully, your reports of her movements since departing New Orleans.

"What about our other problem, Vince? *Ryan* Carlton?"

"Ah. His illness insures that time is his enemy. But I am sure that you and I can arrange a more rapid demise, if need be. For now, Mr. Trace, we will leave it to providence."

"Whatever you say, Vince."

About the Author

A member of the Romance Writers of America, Tamara Ferguson is the best-selling, multi-award winning author of the Tales of The Dragonfly Romance Suspense Series. Presently, Tamara's working on *Emergence*, the third book of the multi-award winning Tales of the Dragonfly Series.

Since she remains a full-time caregiver for an autistic son, you can usually find Tammy working at home in central Illinois, where she spends a lot of time not completing her numerous home improvement projects, because she's writing.

Don't Miss Other Books In
The Tales Of The Dragonfly Series
by Tamara Ferguson

In Tandem

Coming Soon

Emergence